EVERYMAN,
I WILL GO WITH THEE,
AND BE THY GUIDE,
IN THY MOST NEED
TO GO BY THY SIDE

NIKOLAI GOGOL

DEAD
SOULS

TRANSLATED FROM THE RUSSIAN BY
RICHARD PEVEAR AND
LARISSA VOLOKHONSKY

WITH AN INTRODUCTION BY
RICHARD PEVEAR

EVERYMAN'S LIBRARY
Alfred A. Knopf New York London Toronto
280

THIS IS A BORZOI BOOK

PUBLISHED BY ALFRED A. KNOPF

English translation copyright © 1996 by Richard Pevear and
Larissa Volokhonsky
Originally published in the United States by Pantheon Books, a division
of Random House, Inc., New York, in 1996 and first published in
Everyman's Library in 2004
This title first included in Everyman's Library, in a different
translation, 1915
Bibliography and Chronology Copyright © 2004 by Everyman's Library
Typography by Peter B. Willberg

US website: www.randomhouse.com/everymans

ISBN: 1-4000-4319-0 (US)
1-85715-280-8 (UK)

A CIP catalogue reference for this book is available from the
British Library

Book design by Barbara de Wilde and Carol Devine Carson

Printed and bound in Germany by GGP Media, Pössneck

DEAD SOULS

CONTENTS

_____

INTRODUCTION

I

Do you like the novel Dead Souls*? I like Tolstoy too but Gogol is necessary along with the light.*

Flannery O'Connor

Gogol designed the title page for the first edition of *Dead Souls* himself. It is an elaborate piece of not-quite-symmetrical baroque scrollwork, surrounded by airy curlicues in which various objects and figures appear. At the top center is a britzka being pulled by a galloping troika and raising a small cloud of dust. Below it to the left is a sketch of a manor house with a gate, then a well with a long sweep pointing upwards, then a tray with a bottle and four glasses the same size as the house and the well sweep. Centered under the britzka is another bottle, and to the right are more bottles (one fallen over), a glass, and a mysterious pointed object, possibly a tower. Further down around the lettering on the page we find a fish on a platter, a wooden bucket, yet another bottle, some dried fish hanging from curlicues; there is a barrel, a plaited bast shoe, a single boot, a small capering figure raising a glass, a pair of boots. A lyre hangs from the ornamentation beside a solemn satyr's mask, balanced by a similar satyr's mask on the other side and what may be more musical instruments. Above the publication date is an oval platter with a big fish on it, surrounded by smaller fish. To the left of the date a balalaika and a guitar, to the right of it a miniature dancing couple. At the very bottom center, amid more scrollwork, is a human face. The curlicues around the words *Dead Souls* turn out, on closer inspection, to be skulls.

The words on the title page are presented in lettering of different styles and very unequal sizes. At the top, in the smallest and plainest letters, we read *Chichikov's Adventures*; then, in very small cursive, the word *or*; then, in larger and bolder letters, *Dead Souls*. In the largest letters of all, in the very center of the page, white against a black background, is

ix

the word *Poema*, the Russian term for a narrarive poem. Below that, in small but elegantly ornate lettering, appears the name of the author: N. Gogol. And finally, on a square plaque under the oval platter with the big fish, comes the date of publication: 1842.

This was Gogol's own introduction to his book. The sketches suggest something of its content and more of its atmosphere: the road, the racing britzka, country estates, a good deal of drinking and eating, music and dancing, and, in the midst of it all, those little skulls, those slightly menacing satyrs, that ambiguous human face looking out at us. These are all the stuff of Gogol's *poema*. But before considering the nature of this paradoxical feast, I want to say something about the words Gogol distinguished so carefully by the size of their lettering and their placement on the page.

Gogol was thirty-three in 1842, when this first edition of the first volume of *Dead Souls* was published. A second edition came out in 1846, but the promised continuation of Chichikov's adventures, the "two big parts to come" mentioned at the end of the first volume, were never finished. Gogol labored over the second part for the last ten years of his life, burned one version in 1845, and another in 1852, a week before his death. What survived among his papers were drafts of the first four chapters, fragmentary themselves, plus part of a later chapter, possibly the last. They were published in 1855, in a volume entitled *The Works of Nikolai Vassilyevich Gogol Found After His Death*. The first volume of *Dead Souls* was, in fact, the last good book Gogol wrote.

N. Gogol, as he modestly styled himself, was in 1842 the brightest name in Russian literature. Vissarion Belinsky, a leading radical and the most influential critic of the time, had hailed him in 1835 as a writer who might finally create a truly Russian literature, independent of foreign models. He saw that promise fulfilled in *Dead Souls*, a new step for Gogol, as he wrote in an article of 1842, "by which he became a Russian national poet in the full sense of the word." But the conservative Slavophils also claimed him as their own, perhaps with more reason. This all sounds lofty and serious, yet the central figure in Gogol's work is laughter. It was laughter that gave such brightness to Gogol's name, that pure laughter which reached its fullest expression in his play *Revizor* (The Inspector, or Government Inspector, or Inspector-general), written in 1835 and first staged on April 19, 1836, at the command and in the presence of the emperor Nikolai I. The play was a tremendous success. Gogol literally set all Russia laughing. The emperor insisted that his ministers see it. "Everyone took it as aimed at himself, I first of all," he is supposed to have said. There are stories of actors laughing as they performed the play, because the audience facing them seemed to be performing it even better themselves. "*Revizor* is the high point of laughter in Gogol's work," Andrei Sinyavsky wrote. "Never either before or after *Revizor* have we laughed like that!" As the "we" implies, such laughter unites people through time as well as across footlights. (Sinyavsky's book *V teni Gogolya* (In Gogol's Shadow) was published in 1975 under the pseudonym of Abram Tertz. It has yet to be translated into English.)

The idea for *Revizor* came from Alexander Pushkin, the greatest of Russian poets, who, as Gogol once observed, also "liked to laugh." Pushkin had been one of the first to recognize Gogol's talent, and published some of his writings, including the famous story *The Nose*, in his magazine *The Contemporary*. Shortly before giving him the idea for *Revizor*, according to Gogol's own testimony, Pushkin gave him the subject of *Dead Souls*, "his own subject, which he wanted to make into a poem." Gogol set to work at once. The first mention of the book in his correspondence is in a letter to Pushkin dated October 7, 1835: "I have begun to write *Dead Souls*. The plot has stretched into a very long novel, and it will, I think, be extremely amusing ... I want to show all Russia – at least from one side – in this novel." In the same letter, he asked Pushkin to give him "some plot ... a purely Russian anecdote," to which Pushkin responded with a story that had actually happened to him two years earlier. While stopping in the town of Nizhni Novgorod in September 1833, he dined once or twice with the governor and his wife. The governor for some reason suspected him of being a *revizor*, an inspector traveling incognito for the emperor, and sent a letter to

Orenburg warning the governor there of Pushkin's coming and informing him of his suspicions. The governor of Orenburg happened to be an old friend of Pushkin's, and he laughingly told him about it. In *Revizor*, Gogol's hero capitalizes on the error throughout the play.

There is no question about the source of the idea for *Revizor*. But for *Dead Souls* Pushkin has a rival much closer to home, and even in Gogol's own family. A distant relation of his, Maria Grigorievna Anisimo-Yanovskaya, left the following reminiscence:

The thought of writing *Dead Souls* was taken by Gogol from my uncle Pivinsky. Pivinsky had a small estate, some thirty peasant souls [that is, adult male serfs], and five children. Life could not be rich, and so the Pivinskys lived by distilling vodka. Many landowners at that time had distilleries, there were no licenses. Suddenly officials started going around gathering information about everyone who had a distillery. The rumor spread that anyone with less than fifty souls had no right to distill vodka. The small landowners fell to thinking; without distilleries they might as well die. But Kharlampy Petrovich Pivinsky slapped himself on the forehead and said: "Aha! Never thought of it before!" He went to Poltava and paid the quitrent for his dead peasants as if they were alive. And since even with the dead ones he was still far short of fifty, he filled his britzka with vodka, went around to his neighbors, exchanged the vodka for their dead souls, wrote them down in his own name, and, having become the owner of fifty souls on paper, went on distilling vodka till his dying day, and so he gave the subject to Gogol, who used to visit Fedunky, Pivinsky's estate, which was about ten miles from Yanovshchina [the Gogol estate]; anyway, the whole Mirgorod district knew about Pivinsky's dead souls.

Maria Grigorievna's information incidentally bears out a passing remark in chapter 8 of *Dead Souls* concerning the ready availability of drink in the provinces of Little Russia (Ukraine). Her account was reprinted in V. Veresaev's book *Gogol v zhizni* (Gogol in life, 1933), which drew high praise ("delightful") from Vladimir Nabokov.

N. Gogol's full name was Nikolai Vassilyevich Gogol-Yanovsky. He was born on April 1, 1809, in Sorochintsy, Mirgorod district, Poltava province, the son of a minor official and amateur playwright whose family had been ennobled in the seventeenth century. He was the eldest of twelve children, of whom six survived. He grew up in Vassilyevka, an estate of some three thousand acres and two hundred peasant souls belonging to his mother. At the age of twelve he went to study in a boarding school in Nezhin, where he spent the next seven years. At school he was called Yanovsky, but even then he had begun to favor his other name. Perhaps he simply liked it because it was unusual. In Russian, *gogol* means "drake." By extension, it also means a dapper fellow, a dandy – inclinations not foreign to our author. With regard to this "totemic" bird, Andrei Sinyavsky cites a legend from northern Russia about the creation of the world:

Upon the primeval ocean-sea there swam two *gogols*: one a white *gogol*, and the other a black *gogol*. And it was so that in these two *gogols* there swam the Lord God Almighty and Satan. By God's command, by the blessing of the Mother of God, Satan breathed up from the bottom of the blue sea a handful of earth . . .

The transformation of the lowest (even infernal) matter into a model of the universe by the action of a mysterious breath or energy has analogies in Gogol's artistic vision and in the style of his prose. Many critics have seen two Gogols in Gogol – unconscious and conscious, artist and moralist, radical and conservative, pagan and Christian – but that is another matter. Believing that he was called to some high mission in service to Russia, Gogol left his native region after graduating from high school (he had been a mediocre student) and went to Petersburg in December 1828, to attempt another sort of transformation. There he suffered one failure as a poet and another as an aspiring actor. And there, in 1830, he published his first story – "St. John's Eve."

Russian prose had attained perfect ease and clarity in the works of Pushkin and Mikhail Lermontov. Gogol admired them greatly, and did not try to match them. He set about creating another sort of medium, not imitative of the natural speech of educated men, not graced with the "prose virtues" of concision and accuracy, but apparently quite the opposite. Sinyavsky comments: "Gogol overcame the language barrier

by resorting not to the speech in which we talk, but rather –
to the inability to speak in an ordinary way, which is prose in
its fullest sense. Without noticing it, he discovered that prose,
like any art, implies a passing into an unfamiliar language,
and in this exotic quality is the equal of poetry." To do this,
he stepped back linguistically into Little Russia, seeking a
stylization towards the lowest levels, from which he could then
leap suddenly into lyrical flight, and so he created the gab of
his first narrator, Rudy Panko, beekeeper, in *Evenings on a Farm
near Dikanka*, a collection of tales published in 1831. With this
lowest matter, this rich linguistic dirt, Gogol transformed
Russian prose. A second collection of *Evenings* appeared in
1832, and in 1835 two more volumes of Ukrainian tales,
collectively entitled *Mirgorod*, as well as *Arabesques*, containing
a series of extraordinary tales about Petersburg. By the autumn
of that year, as we have seen, Gogol was already at work on
Dead Souls. He left Russia in 1836, following the success of
Revizor, and spent most of the next twelve years abroad, mainly
in Rome, returning for seven months in 1839–40, and then at
the end of 1841 with the completed first volume of *Dead Souls*.

In November 1841 the manuscript of Gogol's new work was
submitted to the imperial censors – an ordeal every book
published in Russia had to undergo. This brings us back to
Gogol's title page. Gogol learned about the proceedings from
an acquaintance on the Moscow censorship committee and
described them in a letter to his Petersburg friend Pletnyov
dated January 7, 1842. The acting chairman of the committee,
a certain Golokhvastov, cried out "in the voice of an ancient
Roman" the moment he saw the title: "*Dead Souls!* No, never
will I allow that – the soul is immortal, there can be no such
thing as a dead soul; the author is taking up arms against
immortality!" When it was explained to him that it was not a
question of the human soul, but of deceased serfs not yet
stricken from the tax rolls, the chairman cried: "Even worse!
... That means it is against serfdom." And so it went. Gogol's
one defender on the committee could do nothing. (Not so
the author, who in the second volume of *Dead Souls* gave
Golokhvastov's words about the immortal soul to a smug and
ignorant young clerk.) Gogol then submitted his manuscript

to the censorship committee in Petersburg, where he had hopes of more success. It was eventually passed, but the committee insisted on some thirty small "corrections" and the removal of the interpolated "Tale of Captain Kopeikin" from the tenth chapter. This last Gogol considered one of the best parts, absolutely necessary in the book, and rather than give up his Kopeikin, he rewrote the tale in a way acceptable to the censors (we have translated the original version here). The committee was also uneasy about the title, but accepted the compromise of adding *Chichikov's Adventures* to it. That is how those two words in the plainest and smallest letters appeared at the top of Gogol's design for the title page, though the title was and has always remained *Dead Souls* and nothing else. Thus, nearly intact, the manuscript went to the printer in April 1842. The book was released on May 21. On May 23, Gogol left Moscow for Petersburg, and ten days later he went abroad again, where he stayed for the next six years, moving about a great deal.

We come now to the boldest and most central word in Gogol's design: *Poema.* It is clearly meant to alert readers to the author's own conception of his work, to warn them that what is to come is *not* a novel – that is, an extended prose narrative portraying characters and actions representative of real life, in a plot of more or less complexity, as the manuals have it. In fact, Gogol himself sometimes referred to *Dead Souls* as a novel, for instance in the letter to Pushkin quoted earlier. But that was precisely earlier. As his work progressed, his sense of it grew and changed. Finally, several times in the text itself, and here on its title page, he resolutely asserted its poemity.

Our understanding of what Gogol meant in calling his book a poem is helped considerably by a little manual he wrote himself in the latter part of his life. It is entitled *A Guidebook of Literature for Russian Youth* and contains, among other things, some interesting remarks on the novel as a genre. He describes it as "too static" a form, involving a set of characters introduced at the start and bound to a series of incidents necessarily related to the hero's fate, allowing only for an "overly compressed interaction" among them. If we reverse these strictures, we will have the beginnings of a formal description of *Dead Souls*: a dynamic form, involving characters not necessarily bound up with the hero's fate, who can be introduced (and dropped) at any point, and allowing the author great freedom of movement in time, place, and action. In his guidebook, Gogol introduced his concept of such a form, midway between the novel and the epic, calling it "minor epic." His examples are *Don Quixote* and *Orlando Furioso*. While the epic hero is always an important and conspicuous public figure, the hero of a minor epic can be private and socially insignificant. The author leads him through a series of adventures and changes intended at the same time to present a living picture of the age, a chart of its uses and abuses, and "a full range of remarkable human phenomena." Indeed, Gogol plunges so much *in medias res* that we learn nothing about his hero's life until the last chapter of volume i. Figures and events emerge the way the "dead souls" emerge from Chichikov's chest in the seventh chapter, not part of any plot, but indispensable to the poem. So, too, the theme of Russia ("Rus!") does not derive from situation or character, but is added lyrically by the author, forming part of the poetical ambience of the book, as do the many epic or mock epic similes, the asides, the lyrical flights and apostrophes. To portray "all Russia," Gogol needed this freedom of the road, of movement in several senses, allowing him to include a diversity of images, to multiply views metaphorically, because the road is also the writing itself, the "scrawling" of landscapes along the racing britzka's way. All this is what is promised by the word *poema*.

Many of those who heard Gogol read from the second volume of *Dead Souls* (some listened to as many as seven chapters) praised it in terms similar to those of his friend L. I. Arnoldi, who described such a reading in a memoir of his friendship with the author: " 'Amazing, incomparable!' I cried. 'In these chapters you come even closer to reality than in the first volume; here one senses life everywhere, as it is, without any exaggerarions ...' " Could this be the same Gogol? Had he finally stooped to writing a conventional novel? But, in fact, what we find in the surviving fragments of volume 2 is not life "as it is," but a series of nonpareils – the perfect young lady, the perfect landowner, the perfect wealthy muzhik, the perfect prince, and also, since nonpareils need not be moral ideals, the perfect ruined nobleman, the perfect Germanizer, the perfect do-nothing – all of them verging on the grotesque, but on an unintentional and humorless grotesque. While we can see where Gogol was straining to go, we are aware mostly of the strain. He is still arm in arm with his hero at the end, but, as he says, "This was not the old Chichikov. This was some wreckage of the old Chichikov. The inner state of his soul might be compared with a demolished building, which has been demolished so that from it a new one could be built; but the new one has not been started yet, because the definitive plan has not yet come from the architect and the workers are left in perplexity." Amid the rubble and perplexity of the second volume, the unsinkable squire Petukh, met by chance when Chichikov takes a wrong road, sounds the last great cockcrow of Gogol's genius.

II

They'd plant it right, but what came up you couldn't say: it's not a watermelon, it's not a pumpkin, it's not a cucumber ... devil knows what it is!
N. Gogol, *The Enchanted Spot*

That genius was purely literary. Gogol was a born writer, and his minor epic is a major feast of Russian prose. It caused a sensation when it first appeared, almost all of its characters immediately became proverbial, and its reputation has never suffered an eclipse. The book entered into and became fused with Russian life, owing mainly to its verbal power. The poet Innokenty Annensky, in his essay "The Aesthetics of *Dead Souls* and Its Legacy" (1909), asked: "What would have become of our literature if he *alone for all of us* had not taken up this *burden* and this *torment* and plunged in bottomless physicality our still so timid, now reasonable, now mincing, even if luminously aerial, Pushkinian word?" (Annensky's italics.) The phrase "plunged in bottomless physicality" nicely evokes both the material exuberance of Gogol's style and its artistic procedure.

Such qualities were largely ignored by the first critics of *Dead Souls*, who paid little attention to matters of style. They were most anxious to place Gogol's work within the social polemics of the time, to make him a partisan of one side or the other. Both sides stressed Gogol's "realism" (which we may find surprising), seeing his book as a living portrait of Russia, an embodiment of typical Russian life and of what, following Pushkin, they called "the Russian spirit" or "breath." Gogol represented the first appearance in Russian literature of everyday provincial life in all its details (Belinsky praised in particular the "executed" louse in chapter 8, seeing it as a challenge to literary gentility). Where the critics disagreed was on the character of that life and the nature of its appearance. The Slavophils saw the book as an image of deep Russia, "wooden" Russia, and saw in the figure of the coachman Selifan, for example, a portrait of the "unspoiled" Russian nature. They laughed merrily with Gogol. The radicals saw the book as an attack on landowners and bureaucrats, an unmasking of the social reality hypocritically denied by the ruling classes, and a denunciation of the evils of serf owning. For the Slavophils, *Dead Souls* was the first book fully to embrace Russian reality; for the radicals it represented Gogol's rejection of Russian reality and his (at least implicit) opposition to the established order. You may laugh at these characters in Gogol's book, wrote Belinsky, but you would not laugh at them in real life. The book is only superficially funny; it lays bare the nonsense and triviality of Russian life, implicitly asking how all this could became so important, and in this it is both profound and serious.

Soviet Marxist criticism continued in Belinsky's line, adding its own ideological formulas. Thus *Dead Souls* turned out to be progressive in bringing out the contradictions latent in Russian society of the 1840s – the decay of the old feudal, serf-owning class, and the emergence of its class enemy, the capitalist, in the person of Chichikov (who is also contradictary and in transition). Its characters, representing broad and typical generalities of the time, are determined by their economic behavior – greed, prodigality, acquisitiveness, idleness. Gogol exposes the evils of arbitrary rule, bureaucratic corruption, and petty self-interest, and thus prepares the way for social change. And so on.

Such programmatic readings are themselves contradicted on every page of *Dead Souls*, nowhere more explicitly than when the author, after describing Plyushkin's descent into worthlessness, pettiness, and vileness, suddenly cries out: "Does this resemble the truth? Everything resembles the truth, everything can happen to a man." If "everything resembles the truth," then the laws of this resemblance are of a peculiar sort, and the reality they correspond to is incalculable. That such a will-o'-the-wisp can come so vividly to life is a tribute to the magic of Gogol's prose, with its "plunge into bottomless physicality."

His is in fact an inverted realism: the word creates the world in *Dead Souls*. This process is enacted, parodied, and commented upon all through the poem. One paradigm of it is the apostrophe to the "aptly uttered Russian word" at the end of chapter 5. The word in question is an unprintable epithet, which the author politely omits. It then becomes the subject of a panegyric in Gogol's best lyrical manner, which in its soaring rhetoric makes us forget that the aptly uttered word in question is not only an unprintable epithet, but in fact has not even been uttered. Another paradigm is the simile that ends the second paragraph of chapter 1: "In the corner shop, or, better, in its window, sat a seller of hot punch with a red copper samovar and a face as red as the samovar, so that from a distance one might have thought there were two samovars in the window, if one samovar had not had a pitch-black beard." This replacement of the person by the thing, of narrarive reality by the figure of speech, occurs repearedly in *Dead Souls*. The resulting hybrids – a bearded samovar – are essential Gogolian images. He was, in Annensky's words, "the one poet in the world who, in his ecstatic love of being – not of life, but precisely of being – was able to unite a dusty box of nails and sulphur with the golden streak in the eastern sky, and with whom a transparent and fiery maple leaf shining from its dense darkness did not dare to boast before a striped post by the roadside."

The highest instance of this love of being, revealed in the

creative power of the word, is the moment in chapter 7 when Chichikov sits down in front of his chest, takes from it the lists of deceased peasants he has acquired, and draws up deeds of purchase for them. "Suddenly moved in his spirit," he says: " 'My heavens, there's so many of you crammed in here!' " He reads their names, and from the names alone begins to invent lives for them, resurrecting them one by one. Here, for the only time in the book, the author's voice joins with his hero's, as he takes the relay and continues the inventing himself. Absent presences, and presences made absent (like the five-foot sturgeon Sobakevich polishes off in chapter 8), are the materials of Gogol's poem. He plays on them in a thousand ways, in his intricate manipulation of literary conventions (as when the author profits from the fact that his hero has fallen asleep in order to tell his story), in the lying that goes on throughout the book (along with Chichikov's main business, there is also Nozdryov, who lies from a sort of natural generative force, or the "lady agreeable in all respects," who lies from inner conviction), in such details as the elaborately negated description of Italy superimposed on Russia near the start of chapter 11, or the prosecutor's bushy eyebrows ("all you had, in fact, was bushy eyebrows" – which is literally true). The tremendous paradox of the title – *Dead Souls* – is fraught with all the ambiguities of this inverted realism. "Everything resembles the truth." Such is Gogol's artistic procedure, the plunging into bottomless physicality ... the word. That is, an airy nothing.

The characters Chichikov meets are not real-life landowners, not unspoiled Russian natures or general human types; like the hero himself, they are elemental banalities. In this they are quite unlike the exuberant "souls" he resurrects from his chest. Gogol wrote in a letter of 1843:

I have been much talked about by people who have analyzed some of my aspects but failed to define my essence. Pushkin alone sensed it. He always told me that no other writer before has had this gift of presenting the banality of life so vividly, of being able to describe the banality of the banal man with such force that all the little details that escape notice flash large in everyone's eyes. That is my main quality, which belongs to me alone, and which indeed no other writer possesses.

The word translated as "banality" here is the Russian *poshlost*. For a full comprehension of the meaning of *poshlost* (pronounced "POSHlust"), readers are referred to Vladimir Nabokov's *Nikolai Gogol* (1944), which contains a twelve-page disquisition on the subject. *Poshlost* is a well-rounded, untranslatable whole made up of banality, vulgarity, and sham. It applies not only to obvious trash (verbal or animate), but also to spurious beauty, spurious importance, spurious cleverness. It is an ideal subject for Gogolian treatment, a "gape in mankind," as he calls Plyushkin, an absence he can bring to enormous presence by filling it with verbal matter. Gogol's portrayal of *poshlost* goes far beyond topical satire or a denunciation of social evils. His characters are not time bound; they inhabit an indefinitely expanded time in which they lose the sharply negative features of vice and wickedness and instead became wildly funny. They also have no psychology, "no inner nature." Nabokov thinks they are "bloated dead souls" themselves, and that inside "a *poshlyak* [a male embodiment of *poshlost*] even of Chichikov's colossal dimensions" one can see "the worm, the little shriveled fool that lies huddled up in the depth of the *poshlost*-painted vacuum." But he is not quite right. There is no worm or shriveled fool inside Gogol's characters; they are all external, like landscapes. The process of "growing wild" that has happened to Plyushkin's garden has also happened to Plyushkin himself. At the end of her chapter, Korobochka almost blends back into her barnyard. Everything around Sobakevich says, "I, too, am Sobakevich." Their very lack of inner life gives Gogol's characters a monumental stature, an almost mythical dimension.

But who has ever seen mythical figures of this sort? Looking at them, we may hear ourselves repeating the question Manilov puts to Chichikov: "Here, it may be ... something else is concealed ...?" Yet it is all simply *poshlost*. But the more often Gogol repeats that everything he is describing is "all too familiar" and "the same everywhere," the more exuberant is his verbal invention. He provokes a mutation in the scale of artistic values, as Sinyavsky says, an "ostentation of language" grown out of the commonplace:

As a result, the everyday and the commonplace look somehow extraordinary in Gogol, owing already to the fact that the author, for no apparent reason, has turned his fixed attention on them. Things seem to hide or hold something in themselves, unreal in their real aspect, so wholly familiar that you cannot imagine they are just simply and causelessly standing there without signifying anything, though it is precisely their ordinary being before us and signifying nothing that constitutes their lot and their unsolved mystery.

The unsolved mystery of banality is the lining of the extraordinary behind it. It is Chichikov's chest with its double bottom, in which he stores all sorts of meaningless trash, but from which his "dead souls" also emerge in procession and move across all Russia. It is the renewal and futurity inherent in the road, which Gogol celebrates. It is the sense of promise contained in laughter itself.

Richard Pevear

SELECT BIBLIOGRAPHY

DONALD FANGER, *The Creation of Nikolai Gogol*, Harvard University Press, Cambridge, 1979.

SUSANNE FUSSO, *Designing Disorder: An Anatomy of Disorder in "Dead Souls,"* Stanford University Press, Stanford, 1993.

SUSANNE FUSSO and PRISCILLA MEYER, eds, *Essays on Gogol: Logos and the Russian Word*, Northwestern University Press, Evanston, 1992.

V. V. GIPPIUS, *Gogol*, tr. Robert Maguire, Duke University Press, Durham, 1989.

SIMON KARLINSKY, *The Sexual Labyrinth of Nikolai Gogol*, University of Chicago Press, Chicago, 1992.

ROBERT MAGUIRE, *Exploring Gogol*, Stanford University Press, Stanford, 1994.

VLADIMIR NABOKOV, *Nikolai Gogol*, New Directions, New York, 1944.

RICHARD PEACE, *The Enigma of Gogol*, Cambridge University Press, Cambridge and New York, 1981.

ABRAM TERTZ [Andrei Sinyavsky], *In the Shadow of Gogol*, Collins, London, 1976.

V. V. VINOGRADOV, *Gogol and the Natural School*, tr. Deborah K. Erickson and Ray Parrott, Ardis, Ann Arbor, 1987.

JESSE ZELDIN, *Nikolai Gogol's Quest for Beauty: An Exploration into His Works*, University of Kansas Press, Lawrence, 1978.

CHRONOLOGY

_____

DATE	AUTHOR'S LIFE	LITERARY CONTEXT
1809	Born April 1, in village of Sorochintsy, Mirgorod district, Poltava province, in the Ukraine. Family is of minor aristocracy; father is an amateur playwright.	Goethe: _Elective Affinities._
1812		Birth of Goncharov. Byron: _Childe Harold,_ I–II.
1814		Birth of Lermontov. Scott: _Waverley._
1815		Jane Austen: _Emma._
1816		Constant: _Adolphe._
1818		Mary Shelley: _Frankenstein._
1819		Byron: _Don Juan,_ I–II.
1820		Pushkin: _Ruslan and Lyudmila._
1821–8	Studies at boarding school in the town of Nezhin; poor student but with marked talent as mimic and actor.	1821 Birth of Dostoevsky and Flaubert. De Quincey: _Confessions of an English Opium Eater._ Scott: _Kenilworth._
1824		Griboedov: _Woe from Wit._
1825	Death of father.	
1826		Scott: _Woodstock._
1828	Finishes school. In December, goes to Petersburg to make his career.	Birth of Tolstoy. Mickiewicz: _Conrad Wallenrod._
1829	Writes and publishes a narrative poem, _Hans Küchelgarten_; then buys up the edition and burns it. Makes brief, mysterious visit to Lübeck and Hamburg in northern Germany, returns to Petersburg and enters civil service at the lowest rank.	
1830	Publishes first tale, "St. John's Eve."	Pushkin: _Boris Godunov._ Stendhal: _Le Rouge et le Noir._

1807 Russian defeats at Eylau and Friedland. Alexander I makes peace with Napoleon (Treaty of Tilsit).
Russia annexes Finland from Sweden. French defeat Austrians at Wagram.

Fall and internal exile of Speransky, Alexander's liberal chief minister: replaced by the reactionary Arakcheyev. Russia defeats Turkey, gaining Bessarabia. Napoleon's invasion of Russia and retreat from Moscow. Allied armies take Paris. Napoleon exiled. Congress of Vienna (to 1815).
Napoleon's escape from Elba and defeat at Waterloo. Holy Alliance between Russia, Prussia and Austria to protect European status quo. Russia obtains Poland as part of postwar settlement.

Congress of Aix-la-Chappelle. Allied troops withdrawn from France.

Greek War of Independence.

Death of Alexander I and accession of Nicholas I. Decembrist revolt. Nicholas I founds notorious "Third Section" under Benckendorf to act against subversion and revolution. Russia at war with Persia (to 1828). Russsia at war with Turkey (to 1829).

July revolution in France: accession of Louis Philippe. First metalled road between Moscow and St. Petersburg.

DATE	AUTHOR'S LIFE	LITERARY CONTEXT
1831	In September, publishes first collection of Ukrainian tales, *Evenings on a Farm Near Dikanka*.	Pushkin: *The Tales of Belkin*. Hugo: *Notre-Dame de Paris*.
1831–4	Teaches history in girls' institute and works as private tutor. Meets Alexander Pushkin, Russia's greatest poet, who becomes an enthusiastic admirer of his work.	
1832	Publishes second volume of *Evenings on a Farm Near Dikanka*.	Death of Goethe and Scott.
1833		Pushkin: complete version of *Evgeny Onegin*. Balzac: *Eugénie Grandet*.
1834	Through influential friends, is appointed adjunct professor of world history at St. Petersburg University. Abandons the post a year later.	Belinsky: *Literary Reveries*. Pushkin: "The Queen of Spades". Mickiewicz: *Pan Tadeusz*. Arrest and internal exile of Herzen and his circle.
1835	Publishes *Mirgorod*, his last collection of Ukrainian tales, and *Arabesques*, a collection of articles and tales reflecting the life of Petersburg (including "Nevsky Prospect," "The Diary of a Madman," and the first version of "The Portrait"). Begins work on the novel/poem *Dead Souls*.	Balzac: *Le Père Goriot*.
1836	April sees the triumphant first production of the comedy *Revizor* (*The Inspector General*). Pushkin publishes two of Gogol's stories, "The Carriage" and "The Nose," in the first and third issues of his magazine *The Contemporary*. In June, Gogol leaves Russia for Switzerland, Paris, and Rome. Remains abroad for most of the next twelve years. Works on volume one of *Dead Souls*.	Chaadaev: *Philosophical Letters*. Pushkin founds *The Contemporary*.
1837		Pushkin killed in a duel.

HISTORICAL EVENTS

Failure of Polish uprising against Russia.

Reactionary doctrine of "Official Nationality" – Orthodoxy, autocracy and nationality – proclaimed by Uvavov, minister for education.
Speransky completes codification of Russian law. Treaty of Unkiar-Skelessi between Russia and Turkey. Abolition of slavery throughout British empire.
Full-time inspectors introduced to Russian universities to watch student activities in the classroom.

Death of Francis I of Austria.

Pratasov, Supreme Procurator of the Holy Synod, takes measures to bring the church more thoroughly under government control.

Kieslev begins reorganization of state peasants in Russia. His reforms include shifting of taxation from persons to land. First public Russian railway, from St. Petersburg to Tsarkoe Selo. Accession of Queen Victoria in Great Britain.

DATE	AUTHOR'S LIFE	LITERARY CONTEXT
1838		Dickens: *Oliver Twist*.
1839–40	In Russia from September to May. Returns to Italy.	Stendhal: *La Chartreuse de Parme*. Lermontov: *A Hero of Our Time*.
1841–2	From October to May, back in Russia to see *Dead Souls* through the censorship. Volume one of *Dead Souls* published in May 1842. Gogol leaves Russia, travels for six years, works fitfully on continuation of *Dead Souls*, finishes second version of "The Portrait" and the comedy *The Wedding*.	Lermontov killed in a duel.
1842	Four-volume collected works (minus *Dead Souls*) published; it includes "The Overcoat," Gogol's last and most famous story.	Sue: *Les Mystères de Paris*.
1846		Dostoevsky: *Poor Folk, The Double*. Balzac: *La Cousine Bette*.
1847	Publishes *Selected Passages from Correspondence with Friends*.	Herzen: *Who is to Blame?* Herzen leaves Russia. Goncharov: *An Ordinary Story*.
1848	January to April, pilgrimage to the Holy Land. May, returns to Russia.	Death of Belinsky. Thackeray: *Vanity Fair*.
1848–52	Lives in Moscow, Odessa, Petersburg. Health deteriorates, Visits Optina Pustyn and other monasteries.	Dostoevsky arrested and sent into Siberian exile. Dickens: *David Copperfield*. Turgenev: *A Month in the Country*. Herzen: *From the Other Shore*.
1852	Gravely ill. Burns manuscripts of second part of *Dead Souls*. Dies on May 4.	Turgenev: *A Sportsman's Notebook*. Tolstoy: *Childhood*. Harriet Beecher Stowe: *Uncle Tom's Cabin*.

HISTORICAL EVENTS

1839 Severe fighting in the Caucasus, in which the rebel leader Shamil is largely successful.

Straits Convention (1841) between Turkey and the Great Powers.
1840s and 50s: Slavophil versus Westernizer debate among Russian intellectuals. Westernizers advocate progress by assimilating Western rationalism and civic freedom. Slavophils assert spiritual superiority of Russia to the West and argue that future development should be based upon the traditions of the Orthodox Church and the peasant commune or *mir.*

Year of Revolutions in Europe. Tsar's manifesto calls upon Russians to arouse themselves for "faith, Tsar and country." Russian army occupies Moldavia and Wallachia. Pan-Slav Congress in Prague. *Communist Manifesto* published.
Russian armies join those of the Habsburgs in suppressing Hungarian nationalist rebellion led by Kossuth. Fall of short-lived Roman republic. Re-establishment of absolutism in Prussia and Austria. St. Petersburg–Moscow railway opens.

Louis Napoleon proclaimed Emperor of France.

T R A N S L A T O R S '   N O T E

Russian names are composed of first name, patronymic (from the father's first name), and family name. Formal address requires the use of first name and patronymic. A shortened form of the patronymic is sometimes used in conversation between acquaintances; thus Platon Mikhailovich Platonov, in the second volume of *Dead Souls*, is most often called Platon Mikhalych. Virtually all the names Gogol uses are perfectly plausible in Russian. Some of them, however, also have specific meanings or a more general suggestiveness. (In the following list, accented syllables are given in italics.)

*Chi*chikov, *Pa*vel I*van*ovich: echoic of birds chirping and scissors snipping, it is a flighty, frivolous-sounding name, in apparent contrast to the hero's plumpness and practicality.

Ma*nil*ov (no first name or patronymic): comes from *manit*, "to lure, to beckon." In sound it is moist-lipped, soft, and gooey.

Ko*ro*bochka, Na*stas*ya Pe*trov*na: her family name means "little box."

Nozdr*yov* (no first name or patronymic): comes from *nozdrya*, "nostril," and is suggestive of all sorts of holes and porosities.

Soba*ke*vich, Mikha*il* Sem*yon*ovich: comes from *sobaka*, "dog." Mikhail, Mikhailo, and the diminutives Misha and Mishka are common Russian names for bears.

*Plyu*shkin, Ste*pan* (no patronymic): seems, on the other hand, to have no specific connotations.

Gogol plays with names in several other ways. Sometimes perfectly ordinary names become amusing when put together. So it is with Nozdryov's fellow carousers Potse*lu*ev (from "kiss") and Kuv*shin*nikov (from "jug"), as also with the dishonest clerks in volume 2 – Krasno*nos*ov, Samo*svis*tov, and Kis*lo*yedov (Red-noser, Self-whistler, and Sour-eater). At one point in chapter 8 he mocks Russian formal address by mercilessly listing the names and patronymics of a long series of ladies and gentlemen, ending in complete absurdity with the nonexistent Makla*tura* Alex*an*drovna.

Frequent reference is made in *Dead Souls* to various ranks of the imperial civil service. The following is a list of the fourteen official ranks established by Peter the Great in 1722, from highest to lowest:

1. chancellor
2. actual privy councillor
3. privy councillor
4. actual state councillor
5. state councillor
6. collegiate councillor
7. court councillor
8. collegiate assessor
9. titular councillor
10. collegiate secretary
11. secretary of naval constructions
12. government secretary
13. provincial secretary
14. collegiate registrar

The rank of titular councillor conferred personal nobility, and the rank of actual state councillor made it hereditary. Mention of an official's rank automatically indicates the amount of deference he must be shown, and by whom.

There are two words for "peasant" in Russian: *krestyanin* and *muzhik*. The first is a more neutral and specific term; the second is broader, more common, and may be used scornfully. Gogol uses both words. Since *muzhik* has entered English, we keep it where Gogol has it and use "peasant" where he has *krestyanin*.

Before their emancipation in 1861, Russian peasants were bound to the land and were the property of the landowner. The value of an estate, and thus the "worth" of its owner, was determined by the number of peasant "souls," or adult male serfs, living on it. The peasants worked the master's land and also paid him rent for their own plots, usually in kind. If they knew a trade, they could earn money practicing it and pay quitrent to the master. They remained bound to the land, however, and if they traveled to work, had to have a passport procured for them by their master. Landowners were not required to pay taxes, but their peasants were, and it was up to the landowner to collect them. He was responsible for turning in the tax money for as many souls as had been counted in the latest census. There could be a considerable lapse of time between censuses (the action of *Dead Souls* is set in the period between the seventh official census of 1815 and the eighth, taken in 1833). During that time a number of peasants would die, but the master remained responsible for the tax on them until they were stricken from the rolls at the next census. It was also possible for a landowner to obtain money from the government by mortgaging some or all of the peasants of whom he was the certified owner.

This translation has been made from the Russian text of the Soviet Academy of Sciences edition, volumes 6 and 7 (Leningrad, 1951). We have preferred the earlier (1855) redaction of volume 2 as being both briefer and more complete. We give the unrevised version of "The Tale of Captain Kopeikin" in chapter 10 of volume 1.

DEAD SOULS

VOLUME ONE

CHAPTER ONE

THROUGH THE GATES of the inn in the provincial town of N. drove a rather handsome, smallish spring britzka, of the sort driven around in by bachelors: retired lieutenant colonels, staff captains, landowners possessed of some hundred peasant souls – in short, all those known as gentlemen of the middling sort. In the britzka sat a gentleman, not handsome, but also not bad-looking, neither too fat nor too thin; you could not have said he was old, yet neither was he all that young. His entrance caused no stir whatever in town and was accompanied by nothing special; only two Russian muzhiks standing by the door of the pot-house across from the inn made some remarks, which referred, however, more to the vehicle than to the person sitting in it. "See that?" said the one to the other, "there's a wheel for you! What do you say, would that wheel make it as far as Moscow, if it so happened, or wouldn't it?" "It would," replied the other. "But not as far as Kazan I don't suppose?" "Not as far as Kazan," replied the other. And with that the conversation ended. Then, as the britzka drove up to the inn, it met with a young man in white twill trousers, quite narrow and short, and a tailcoat with presumptions to fashion, under which could be seen a shirtfront fastened with a Tula-made pin shaped like a bronze pistol.[1] The young man turned around, looked at the carriage, held his hand to his peaked cap, which was almost blown off by the wind, and went on his way.

As the carriage drove into the yard, the gentleman was met by a tavern servant, or floorboy, as they are called in Russian taverns, lively and fidgety to such a degree that it was even

5

impossible to tell what sort of face he had. He ran out nimbly, a napkin in his hand, all long himself and in a long half-cotton frock coat with its back almost up to his nape, tossed his hair, and nimbly led the gentleman up along the entire wooden gallery to show him his god-sent chambers. The chambers were of a familiar kind, for the inn was also of a familiar kind, that is, precisely one of those inns in provincial towns where for two roubles a day the traveler is given a comfortable room, with cockroaches peeking like prunes from every corner, and the door to the adjoining quarters always blocked by a chest of drawers, where a neighbor settles, a taciturn and quiet man, yet an extremely curious one, interested in knowing every little detail about the traveler. The external façade of the inn answered to its inside: it was very long, of two stories; the lower had not been stuccoed and was left in dark red little bricks, darkened still more by evil changes of weather, and a bit dirty anyway; the upper was painted with eternal yellow paint; below there were shops selling horse collars, ropes, and pretzels. In the corner shop, or, better, in its window, sat a seller of hot punch with a red copper samovar and a face as red as the samovar, so that from a distance one might have thought there were two samovars in the window, if one samovar had not had a pitch-black beard.

While the visiting gentleman was examining his room, his belongings were brought in: first of all a white leather trunk, somewhat worn, indicating that this was not its first time on the road. The trunk was brought in by the coachman Selifan, a short man in a sheepskin coat, and the lackey Petrushka, a fellow of about thirty in a roomy secondhand frock coat, evidently from his master's back, a somewhat stern fellow by the look of him, with a very large nose and lips. After the trunk, a small mahogany chest inlaid with Karelian birch was brought in, a boot-tree, and a roast chicken wrapped in blue paper. When all this had been brought in, the coachman Selifan went to the stables to potter with the horses, while the lackey Petrushka began to settle himself in a small ante-room, a very dark closet, where he had already managed to drag his overcoat and with it a certain smell of his own, which had also been imparted to the sack of various lackey toiletries brought in after it. In this closet, he fixed a narrow, three-legged bed to the wall and covered it with a small semblance of a mattress, beaten down and flat as a pancake, and perhaps as greasy as a pancake, which he had managed to extort from the innkeeper.

While the servants were settling and pottering, the gentle-man went to the common room. What these common rooms are, every traveler knows very well: the same walls painted with oil paint, darkened above by pipe smoke, and shiny below from the backs of various travelers, and still more of indigenous merchants, for merchants came here on market days in sixes and sevens to drink their well-known two cups of tea; the same besooted ceiling; the same sooty chandelier with its multitude of glass pendants that danced and jingled each time the floor-boy ran across the worn oilcloth deftly balancing a tray on which sat numerous teacups, like birds on the seashore; the same oil paintings all over the wall – in short, the same as everywhere; with the only difference that one painting por-trayed a nymph with such enormous breasts as the reader has probably never seen. Such sports of nature occur, however, in various historical paintings, brought to our Russia no one knows at what time, from where, or by whom, on occasion even by our grand dignitaries, lovers of art, who bought them up in Italy on the advice of the couriers that drove them around. The gentleman took off his peaked cap and unwound from his neck a rainbow-hued woolen scarf, such as married men are provided with by their wives, with their own hands, who furnish them with suitable instructions on how to wrap oneself up, while for bachelors – I cannot say for certain who makes them, God alone knows, I myself have never worn such scarves. Having unwound the scarf, the gentleman ordered dinner to be served. While he was being served various dishes usual in taverns, such as: cabbage soup with puff pastry, preserved over many weeks purposely for travelers, brains and peas, sausages and cabbage, roast poulard, pickles, and eternal sweet puff pastries, always ready to please; while all this was being served, warmed up or simply cold, he made the servant, that is, the floorboy, tell him all sorts of rubbish – about who had kept the tavern before and who kept it now, and did it bring in much income, and was their master a great scoundrel, to which the floorboy gave the customary answer: "Oh, he is, sir. A great crook." As in enlightened Europe, so in enlightened Russia there are now quite a lot of respectable people who cannot have a meal in a tavern without talking with the servant and sometimes even making an amusing joke at his expense. However, the visitor's questions were not all idle; he inquired with extreme precision as to who was the governor of the town, who was the head magistrate, who was the prosecutor – in short, he did not skip a single important official; but with still greater precision, even almost concern, he inquired about all the important landowners: how many peasant souls each one had, how far from town he lived, even what his character was and how often he came to town; he inquired attentively into the condition of the area: whether there were any diseases in their province – epidemics of fever, some deadly agues, smallpox, and the like, and all this so thoroughly and with such precision that it showed more than mere curiosity alone. The gentleman's manners had something solid about them, and he blew his nose with an exceeding loudness. It is not known how he did it, only his nose sounded like a trumpet. This apparently quite innocent virtue, however, gained him great esteem on the part of the tavern servant, who, each time he heard this sound, tossed his hair, drew himself up more respectfully, and, bowing his head from on high, asked: was anything required? After dinner the gentleman took himself a cup of coffee and sat on the sofa, propping his back against a pillow, which in Russian taverns are stuffed not with springy wool, but instead with something extremely like bricks and cobbles. Here he started yawning and asked to be taken to his room, where he lay down and slept for two hours. Having rested, he wrote on a scrap of paper, at the request of the tavern servant, his rank and full name, to be conveyed to the proper quarters, the police. On the paper, mouthing each syllable as he went down the stairs, the floorboy read the following: "Collegiate Councillor Pavel Ivanovich Chichikov, landowner, on private business." While the floorboy was still working through the syllables of the note, Pavel Ivanovich Chichikov himself set out to have a look at the town, with which, it seems, he was satisfied, for he found that the town yielded in nothing to other provincial towns: striking to the eye was the yellow paint on the stone houses, modestly dark was the gray of the wooden ones. The houses were of one, two, and one and a half stories, with those eternal mezzanines so beautiful in the opinion of provincial architects. In some places the houses seemed lost amid the street, wide as a field, and the never-ending wooden fences; in others they clustered together, and here one could note more animation and human commotion. One came across signboards all but washed out by rain, with pretzels and boots, or, in one place, with blue trousers pictured on them and the signature of some Warsaw tailor; then a shop with peaked caps, flat caps, and inscribed: VASSILY FYODOROV, FOREIGNER; in another place a picture of a billiard table with two players in tailcoats of the kind worn in our theater by guests who come on stage in the last act. The players were depicted aiming their cues, their arms somewhat twisted back and their legs askew, having just performed an entrechat in the air. Under all this was written: AND THIS IS THE ESTABLISHMENT. In some places there were tables simply standing in the street, with nuts, soap, and gingerbreads resembling soap; then an eatery with a picture of a fat fish with a fork stuck into it. Most frequently one noted weathered, two-headed state eagles, which have since been replaced by the laconic inscription: PUBLIC HOUSE. The pavement everywhere was of a poorish sort. He also peeked into the town garden, which consisted of skinny trees, badly rooted, propped by supports formed in triangles, very beautifully painted with green oil paint. However, though these little trees were no taller than reeds, it was said of them in the newspapers, as they described some festive decorations, that "our town has been beautified, thanks to the solicitude of the civic ruler, by a garden consisting of shady, wide-branching trees that provide coolness on hot days," and that "it was very moving to see the hearts of the citizens flutter in an abundance of gratitude and pour forth streams of tears as a token of thankfulness to mister governor." Having inquired in detail of a sentry as to the shortest way, in case of need, to the cathedral, the municipal offices, the governor's, he set out to view the river that flowed through the middle of the town, in passing tore off a playbill attached to a post, so as to read it properly when he got home, looked intently at a lady of comely appearance who was walking down the wooden sidewalk, followed by a boy in military livery with a bundle in his hand, and, once more casting his eyes around at it all, as if with the purpose of memorizing well the disposition of the place, went home straight to his room, supported somewhat on the stairs by the tavern servant. After taking tea, he sat down before the table, asked for a candle, took the playbill from his pocket, brought it near the candle, and began to read, squinting his right eye slightly. However, there was little remarkable in the playbill: Mr. Kotzebue's drama[2] was showing, with Rolla played by Mr. Poplyovin, Cora by Miss Zyablova, the rest of the cast being even less remarkable; but he read them all anyway, even got as far as the price for the stalls, and learned that the playbill had been printed on the provincial government press; then he turned it over to the other side: to see if there was anything there, but, finding nothing, he rubbed his eyes, folded it neatly, and put it into his little chest, where he was in the habit of stowing away whatever came along. The day, it seems, was concluded with a helping of cold veal, a bottle of fizzy kvass, and a sound sleep with all pumps pumping, as the saying goes in some parts of the vast Russian state.

The following day was devoted entirely to visits; the new-comer went around visiting all the town dignitaries. He came with his respects to the governor, who, as it turned out, was like Chichikov neither fat nor thin, had an Anna on his neck, and there was even talk of his having been recommended for a star;[3] in any case, he was a jolly good fellow and sometimes even did embroidery on tulle. Next he went to the vice-governor, then to the prosecutor, the head magistrate, the police chief, the tax farmer,[4] the superintendent of the gov-ernment factories . . . alas, it is a bit difficult to remember all the mighty of this world: but suffice it to say that the newcomer displayed an extraordinary activity with regard to visiting: he even went to pay his respects to the inspector of the board of health and the town architect. And for a long time afterwards he sat in his britzka, thinking up someone else he might visit, but there were no more officials to be found in the town. In conversation with these potentates, he managed very artfully to flatter each of them. To the governor he hinted, somehow in passing, that one drove into his province as into paradise, that the roads everywhere were like velvet, and that governments which appointed wise dignitaries were worthy of great praise. To the police chief he said something very flattering about the town sentries; and in conversation with the vice-governor and the head magistrate, who were as yet only state councillors, he twice even made the mistake of saying "Your Excellency," which pleased them very much. The consequence was that the governor extended him an invitation to come that same evening to a party in his home, and the other officials, for their part, also invited him, one to dinner, another for a little game of Boston, another for a cup of tea.

The newcomer, as it seemed, avoided talking much about himself; if he did talk, it was in some sort of commonplaces, with marked modesty, and his conversation on these occasions assumed a somewhat bookish manner: that he was an insignificant worm of this world and not worthy of much concern, that he had gone through many trials in his life, had suffered for the truth in the civil service, had many enemies, who had even made attempts on his life, and that now, wishing to be at peace, he was seeking to choose finally a place to live, and that, having arrived in this town, he considered it his bounden duty to offer his respects to its foremost dignitaries. This was all they learned in the town about this new person, who very shortly did not fail to make his appearance at the governor's party. The preparations for this party took him more than two hours, and here the newcomer displayed an attention to his toilet such as has not even been seen everywhere. After a short after-dinner nap, he ordered himself a washing and spent an extremely long time rubbing his two cheeks with soap, propping them from inside with his tongue; then, taking the towel from the tavern servant's shoulder, he wiped his plump face with it on all sides, starting behind the ears, and first snorting a couple of times right into the tavern servant's face. Then he put on a shirtfront before the mirror, plucked out two hairs that protruded from his nose, and immediately afterwards found himself in a cranberry-colored tailcoat with flecks. Dressed thus, he rolled in his own carriage along the endlessly wide streets, lit by the scant glow of windows now and then flitting by. However, the governor's house was lit up fit for a ball; carriages with lanterns, two gendarmes at the entrance, postillions shouting from afar – in short, everything as it should be. Entering the great hall, Chichikov had to squint his eyes for a moment, because the brilliance of the candles, the lamps, and the ladies' gowns was terrible. Everything was flooded with light. Black tailcoats flitted and darted about separately and in clusters here and there, as flies dart about a gleaming white sugar loaf in the hot summertime of July, while the old housekeeper hacks it up and divides it into glistening fragments before the open window; the children all gather round watching, following curiously the movements of her stiff arms raising the hammer, and the airborne squadrons of flies, lifted by the light air, fly in boldly, like full masters, and, profiting from the old woman's weak sight and the sunshine which troubles her eyes, bestrew the dainty morsels, here scatteredly, there in thick clusters. Satiated by summer's bounty, which anyhow offers dainty dishes at every step, they fly in not at all in order to eat, but only in order to show themselves off, to stroll back and forth on the heap of sugar, to rub their back or front legs together, or to scratch themselves under the wings, or, stretching out both front legs, to rub them over their heads, then turn and fly away, to come back again in new, pestering squadrons. Before Chichikov had time to look around, the governor seized him under the elbow and at once introduced him to his wife. The new-come guest did not let himself down here either: he uttered some compliment most fitting for a middle-aged man of a rank neither too low nor too high. When the dancers paired off, pressing everyone to the wall, he stood with his hands behind his back watching them for about two minutes very attentively. Many of the ladies were dressed well and fashionably, others were dressed in whatever God sends to a provincial town. The men here, as everywhere else, were of two kinds: there were the slim ones, who kept mincing around the ladies; some of these were of a kind difficult to distinguish from Petersburgers, having side-whiskers brushed in as well-considered and tasteful a manner, or else simply decent, quite clean-shaven faces, sitting down as casually beside the ladies, speaking French and making the ladies laugh in the same way as in Petersburg. The other kind of men consisted of the fat ones, or those like Chichikov – that is, not all that fat, and yet not thin either. These, contrariwise, looked askance at the ladies and backed away from them, and only kept glancing around to see whether the governor's servant was setting up a green table for whist. Their faces were plump and round, some even had warts on them, one or two were pockmarked, the hair on their heads was done neither in tufts nor in curls, nor in a "devil-may-care" fashion, as the French say – their hair was either close cropped or slicked down, and the features of their faces were mostly rounded and strong. These were the distinguished officials of the town. Alas! the fat know better than the slim how to handle their affairs in this world. The slim serve mostly on special missions, or else only nominally, and shift about here and there; their existence is somehow too light, airy, and altogether unreliable. Whereas the fat never occupy indirect positions, but always direct ones, and once they sit somewhere, they sit reliably and firmly, so that the position will sooner creak and sag under them than they will fall off of it. External glitter they do not like; their tailcoats are not so smartly cut as the slim men's, but instead God's blessings fill their coffers. In three years the slim man does not have a single soul left that has not been mortgaged; with the fat man all is quiet, then lo and behold – somewhere at the end of town a house appears, bought in his wife's name, then another house at the other end, then a little hamlet nearby, and then an estate with all its appurtenances. Finally, the fat man, having served God and his sovereign, having earned universal respect, leaves the service, moves away, and becomes a landowner, a fine Russian squire, a hospitable man, and he lives and lives well. And, after him, as is the Russian custom, his slim heirs again squander all the paternal goods posthaste. It cannot be concealed that these were almost the sort of reflections that occupied Chichikov as he looked over the company, and the result was that he finally joined the fat ones, where almost all the faces he met were familiar: the prosecutor with extremely black, bushy eyebrows and a slightly winking left eye that seemed to be saying: "Let's go to the other room, brother, I'll tell you a little something there" – a serious and taciturn man, however;

the postmaster, a short man, but a wit and a philosopher; the head magistrate, quite a reasonable and amiable man – all of whom greeted him like an old acquaintance, to which Chichikov responded by bowing slightly to one side, though not without agreeableness. He straightaway made the acquaintance of the most affable and courteous landowner Manilov and the somewhat clumsy-looking Sobakevich, who stepped on his foot first thing, and said: "I beg your pardon." Straightaway a score card for whist was thrust at him, which he accepted with the same polite bow. They sat down at the green table and did not get up again until supper. All conversation ceased entirely, as always happens when people finally give themselves over to a sensible occupation. Though the postmaster was extremely voluble, even he, once he had taken cards in his hands, at the same moment expressed on his face a thoughtful physiognomy, placed his lower lip over the upper one, and maintained that position all through the game. When he played a face card, he would strike the table hard with his hand, saying, if it was a queen, "Go, you old granny!" and if it was a king, "Go, you Tambov muzhik!" And the head magistrate would say, "I'll give it to him in the whiskers! in the whiskers!" Sometimes, as the cards hit the table, such expressions would escape as: "Ah! take it or leave it, make it diamonds, then!" Or simply: "Hearts! Heartaches! Spadilloes!" or "Spadillicups! Spadikins! Spadixies!" or just simply "Spads!" – names with which they had rechristened the suits in their company. As is usual, when the game was over they argued rather loudly. Our new-come guest also argued, but somehow extremely artfully, so that everyone could see he was indeed arguing, yet arguing agreeably. He never said, "You led," but "You were pleased to lead," "I had the honor of beating your deuce," and the like. In order to bring his opponents even more into agreement on something, he each time offered around his enameled silver snuffbox, at the bottom of which they noticed two violets, put there for the scent. The newcomer's attention was occupied particularly by the landowners Manilov and Sobakevich, of whom mention has been made above. He at once inquired about them, straightaway calling the head magistrate and the postmaster a little aside. The few questions he asked showed that the guest was not only inquisitive but also substantial; for he first of all asked how many peasant souls each of them had and what was the condition of their estates, and only then inquired as to their names and patronymics. In a short time he succeeded in charming them completely. The landowner Manilov, a man not at all old, who had eyes as sweet as sugar and narrowed them each time he laughed, was mad about him. He pressed his hand for a very long time and begged him earnestly to do him the honor of coming to his estate, which, according to him, was only ten miles from the town gates. To this, Chichikov, most politely inclining his head and sincerely squeezing his hand, replied that he was not only ready to do so with great willingness, but would even regard it as his most sacred duty. Sobakevich also said somewhat laconically: "And to my place, too" – with a scrape of his foot, shod in a boot of such gigantic size that it would hardly be possible to find a foot corresponding to it, especially nowadays, when in Russia, too, mighty men are beginning to grow scarce.

The next day Chichikov went to dine and spend the evening with the police chief, where they settled down to whist at three o'clock after dinner and played until two o'clock in the morning. There, incidentally, he made the acquaintance of the landowner Nozdryov, a man of about thirty, a rollicksome fellow, who after three or four words began to address him familiarly. He addressed the police chief and the prosecutor in the same way and was on friendly terms with them; yet when they sat down to play for big stakes, the police chief and the prosecutor studied each trick he took with extreme attention and watched almost every card he played. The next day Chichikov spent the evening with the head magistrate, who received his guests in his dressing gown, a slightly greasy one, and some two women among them. Then he attended a soirée at the vice-governor's, a big dinner at the tax farmer's, a small dinner at the prosecutor's, which, however, was as good as a big one; a light lunch after the morning liturgy, given by the town mayor, which was also as good as a dinner. In short, he did not have to stay home for a single hour, and came back to the inn only to sleep. The newcomer was somehow never at a loss and showed himself to be an experienced man of the world. Whatever the conversation, he always knew how to keep up his end: if the talk was of horse breeding, he spoke about horse breeding; if they were speaking of fine dogs, here, too, he made very sensible observations; if the discussion touched upon an investigation conducted by the treasury – he showed that he was not uninformed about legal wiles; if there were some argument about the game of billiards – in the game of billiards, too, he would not go amiss; if they spoke of virtue, on virtue, too, he reasoned very well, tears even came to his eyes; if on the distilling of spirits, then on the distilling of spirits he also knew his stuff; if on customs supervisors and officials, of them, too, he could judge as if he himself had been both an official and a supervisor. Remarkably, he knew how to clothe it all in some sort of decorum, he knew how to bear himself well. He spoke neither loudly nor softly, but absolutely as one ought. In short, however you turned it, he was a very respectable man. The officials were all pleased at the arrival of a new person. The governor opined of him that he was a right-minded man; the prosecutor that he was a sensible man; the colonel of the gendarmes said he was a learned man; the head magistrate that he was a knowledgeable and estimable man; the police chief that he was an estimable and amiable man; the police chief's wife that he was a most amiable and mannerly man. Even Sobakevich himself, who rarely spoke of anyone from the good side, when he returned home rather late from town and, undressing completely, lay down in bed beside his lean-fleshed wife, said to her: "I, my dearest, was at the governor's soirée and dined at the police chief's, and I made the acquaintance of Collegiate Councillor Pavel Ivanovich Chichikov – a most agreeable man!" To which his spouse replied: "Hm!" – and shoved him with her leg.

Such was the opinion, rather flattering for the visitor, that was formed of him in the town, and it persisted until the time when one strange property of the visitor and an undertaking, or *passage*, as they say in the provinces, of which the reader will soon learn, threw almost the whole town into utter perplexity.

CHAPTER TWO

FOR MORE THAN a week already the newly arrived gentleman had been living in the town, driving about to soirées and dinners and thus passing his time, as they say, very pleasantly. At last he decided to transfer his visits outside of town and call on the landowners Manilov and Sobakevich, to whom he had given his word. Perhaps he was impelled to it by some other, more essential reason, some more serious matter, closer to his heart . . . But of all that the reader will learn gradually and in due time, if only he has patience enough to read the proffered tale, a very long one, which is to expand more widely and vastly later on, as it nears the end that crowns the matter. The coachman Selifan was given orders to harness the horses to the familiar britzka early in the morning; Petrushka was ordered to stay home, to keep an eye on the room and the trunk. It will not be superfluous here for the reader to make the acquaintance of these two bondsmen of our hero's. Although, of course, they are not such notable characters, and are what is known as secondary or even tertiary, although the main lines and springs of the poem do not rest on them, and perhaps only occasionally touch and graze them lightly – still, the author is extremely fond of being circumstantial in all things, and in this respect, despite his being a Russian man, he wishes to be as precise as a German. This will not take up much time or space, however, because not much needs to be added to what the reader already knows, to wit, that Petrushka went about in a rather loose brown frock coat from his master's back and had, as is customary for people of his station in life, a large nose and lips. He was more taciturn than talkative in character; he even had a noble impulse for enlightenment, that is, for reading books, the content of which did not trouble him: it made absolutely no difference to him whether it was the adventures of some amorous hero, a simple primer, or a prayer book – he read everything with equal attention; if they slipped him chemistry, he would not refuse that either. He liked not so much what he was reading about as the reading itself, or, better, the process of reading, the fact that letters are eternally forming some word, which sometimes even means the devil knows what. This reading was accomplished mostly in a recumbent position in the anteroom, on a bed and a mattress which, owing to this circumstance, was beaten down and thin as a flapjack. Besides a passion for reading, he had two further customs, which constituted two more of his characteristic traits: to sleep without undressing, just as he was, in the same frock coat; and always to have about him a sort of personal atmosphere of his own peculiar smell, somewhat reminiscent of living quarters, so that it was enough for him merely to set up his bed somewhere, even in a hitherto uninhabited room, and haul his overcoat and chattels there, for it to seem that people had been living there for ten years. Chichikov, being a most ticklish man and even on occasion a finical one, when he drew in air through a fresh nose in the morning, would only wince and toss his head, saying: "Devil knows, brother, you're sweating or something. You ought to go to a bathhouse." To which Petrushka made no reply and straightaway tried to busy himself somehow: either approaching his master's hanging tailcoat with a brush, or simply putting things in order. What he was thinking all the while he stood there silently – perhaps he was saying to himself: "And you're a good one, too, aren't you sick of repeating the same thing forty times?" – God knows, it is hard to tell what a household serf is thinking while his master admonishes him. And so, that is what can be said for a start about Petrushka. The coachman Selifan was a totally different man... But the author is most ashamed to occupy his readers for so long with people of low class, knowing from experience how reluctantly they make acquaintance with the lower estate. Such is the Russian man: strong is his passion for knowing someone at least one rank above himself, and a nodding acquaintance with a count or prince is better to him than any close relations with friends. The author even fears for his hero, who is only a collegiate councillor. Court councillors may well make his acquaintance, but those who are already nearing the rank of general, these, God knows, may even cast at him one of those contemptuous glances a man proudly casts at all that grovels at his feet, or, worse still, pass over him with an inattention deadly for the author. But, however lamentable the one and the other, it is nevertheless necessary for us to return to our hero. And so, having given the necessary orders the evening before, having awakened very early in the morning, having washed, having wiped himself from head to foot with a wet sponge, a thing done only on Sundays – and this day happened to be a Sunday – having shaved in such a way that his cheeks became real satin as regards smoothness and lustre, having put on a cranberry-colored tailcoat with flecks and then an overcoat lined with bearskin, he descended the stairs, supported under his elbow now on one side, now on the other, by the tavern servant, and got into the britzka. With a rumble, the britzka drove through the gates of the inn to the street. A passing priest took off his hat, several urchins in dirty shirts held their hands out, murmuring: "Master, give to the little orphan!" The coachman, noticing that one of them was an avid footboard rider, lashed him with his whip, and the britzka went bouncing off over the cobbles. Not without joy was the striped tollgate beheld in the distance, letting it be known that the pavement, like any other torment, would soon come to an end; and after a few more good hard bumps of his head against the sides, Chichikov was at last racing over soft ground. No sooner had the town dropped back than all sorts of stuff and nonsense, as is usual with us, began scrawling itself along both sides of the road: tussocks, fir trees, low skimpy stands of young pines, charred trunks of old ones, wild heather, and similar gibberish. Strung-out villages happened by, their architecture resembling old stacks of firewood, covered with gray roofs with cutout wooden decorations under them, looking like embroidered towels hanging down. Several muzhiks yawned, as is their custom, sitting on benches before the gates in their sheepskin coats. Women with fat faces and tightly bound bosoms looked out of upper windows; out of the lower ones a calf peeked or a sow stuck her blind snout. Familiar sights, in short. Having driven past the tenth milestone, he recalled that, according to Manilov's words, his estate should be here, but the eleventh mile flew by and the estate was still nowhere to be seen, and had it not been for two muzhiks they met, things would hardly have gone well for them. To the question of how far it was to the village of Zamanilovka, the muzhiks took off their hats and one of them, who was a bit smarter and wore a pointed beard, replied:

"Manilovka, maybe, and not Zamanilovka?"

"Manilovka, then."

"Manilovka! Just keep on another half mile, and there you are, I mean, straight to the right."

"To the right?" the coachman responded.

"To the right," said the muzhik. "That'll be your road to Manilovka; and there's no such place as Zamanilovka. That's her name, I mean, she's called Manilovka, and there's no Zamanilovka at all hereabouts. Right there on the hill you'll see a house, a stone house, two stories, a master's house, I mean, where the master himself lives. That's your Manilovka, and there's never been any such Zamanilovka around here at all."

They drove on in search of Manilovka. Having gone a mile, they came upon a turnoff to a side road, but after going another mile, a mile and a half, maybe two miles, there was still no two-storied stone house in sight. Here Chichikov remembered that if a friend invites you to an estate ten miles away, it means a sure twenty. The village of Manilovka would not entice many by its situation. The master's house stood all alone on a knob, that is, on a rise, open to every wind that might decide to blow; the slope of the hill it stood upon was clad in mowed turf. Over it were strewn, English-fashion, two or three flower beds with bushes of lilac and yellow acacia. Five or six birches in small clumps raised their skimpy, small-leaved tops here and there. Beneath two of them could be seen a gazebo with a flat green cupola, blue wooden columns, and an inscription: THE TEMPLE OF SOLITARY REFLECTION; further down there was a pond covered with green scum, which, however, is no wonder in the English gardens of Russian landowners. At the foot of this rise, and partway up the slope, gray log cottages darkled to right and left, which our hero, for some unknown reason, began that same moment to count, counting up more than two hundred; among them grew not a single tree or anything green; only log looked at you everywhere. The scene was enlivened by two peasant women who, picturesquely gathering their skirts and tucking them up on all sides, waded knee-deep into the pond with two wooden poles, pulling a torn dragnet in which could be seen two entangled crayfish and the gleam of a caught shiner; the women seemed to be engaged in a quarrel and were exchanging abuse over something. Off to one side darkled a pine forest of some boring bluish color. Even the weather itself was most appropriately serviceable: the day was neither bright nor gloomy, but of some light gray color such as occurs only on the old uniforms of garrison soldiers – a peaceful enough army at that, though somewhat unsober on Sundays. Nor was there lacking, to complete the picture, a cock, herald of changing weather, who, though his head had been pecked right to the brain by the beaks of other cocks in the well-known business of philandering, was shouting very loudly and even flapping his wings, ragged as old bast mats. Driving up to the premises,

Chichikov noticed the master himself on the porch, standing in a green shalloon frock coat, his hand held to his forehead like an umbrella, the better to see the approaching carriage. As the britzka drew near the porch, his eyes grew merrier and his smile broadened more and more.

"Pavel Ivanovich!" he cried out at last, as Chichikov climbed out of the britzka. "You've remembered us after all!"

The two friends kissed very warmly, and Manilov led his guest inside. Though the time it will take them to pass through the entryway, the front hall, and the dining room is somewhat shortish, let us try and see if we cannot somehow make use of it to say something about the master of the house. But here the author must confess that this undertaking is a very difficult one. It is much easier to portray large-size characters: just whirl your arm and fling paint on the canvas, dark scorching eyes, beetling brows, a furrow-creased forehead, a cloak, black or fiery scarlet, thrown over one shoulder – and the portrait is done; but now all these gentlemen, who are so many in the world, who resemble each other so much, yet, once you look closer, you see many most elusive peculiarities – these gentlemen are terribly difficult to portray. Here one must strain one's attention greatly, until all the fine, almost invisible features are made to stand out before one, and generally one must further deepen one's gaze, already experienced in the science of elicitation.

God alone perhaps could tell what Manilov's character was. There is a sort of people known by the name of so-so people, neither this nor that, neither Tom of the hill nor Jack of the mill, as the saying goes. It may be that Manilov ought to be put with them. He was a fine man to look at; the features of his face were not lacking in agreeableness, but this agreeableness had, it seemed, too much sugar in it; his ways and manners had about them a certain currying of favor and friendship. He smiled enticingly, was fair-haired, had blue eyes. At the first moment of conversation with him, you cannot help saying: "What an agreeable and kindly man!" The next moment you do not say anything, and the third moment you say: "Devil knows what this is!" – and walk away; or, if you do not walk away, you feel a deadly boredom. You will never get from him any sort of lively or even merely provoking word, such as can be heard from almost anyone, if you touch upon a subject that grips him. Everyone is gripped by something: for one it is borzoi hounds; another fancies himself a great lover of music and wonderfully sensitive to all its profundities; a third is an expert in hearty meals; a fourth in playing a role at least an inch above the one assigned him; a fifth, of more limited desires, sleeps and dreams of taking a stroll with an aide-de-camp, showing off in front of his friends, acquaintances, even non-acquaintances; a sixth is gifted with the sort of hand that feels a supernatural desire to turn down the corner of some ace or deuce of diamonds, while the hand of a seventh is simply itching to establish order somewhere, to get closer to the person of some stationmaster or cabdriver – in short, each has his own, but Manilov had nothing. At home he spoke very little and for the most part reflected and thought, but what he thought about, again, God only knows. One could not say he was occupied with management, he never even went out to the fields, the management somehow took care of itself. When the steward said: "Might be a good thing, master, to do such and such," "Yes, not bad," he would usually reply, smoking his pipe – a habit he had formed while still serving in the army, where he had been considered a most modest, most delicate, and most educated officer. "Yes, indeed, not bad," he would repeat. When a muzhik came to him and, scratching the back of his head, said: "Master, give me leave to go and work, so I can pay my taxes," "Go," he would say, smoking his pipe, and it would never even enter his head that the muzhik was going on a binge. Sometimes, as he gazed from the porch at the yard and pond, he would talk about how good it would be suddenly to make an underground passage from the house, or to build a stone bridge across the pond, and have shops on both sides of it, and shopkeepers sitting in the shops selling all sorts of small goods needed by peasants. At that his eyes would become exceedingly sweet and his face would acquire a most contented expression; however, all these projects ended only in words. In his study there was always some book lying, with a bookmark at the fourteenth page, which he had been reading constantly for the past two years. In his house something was eternally lacking: fine furniture stood in the drawing room, upholstered in stylish silk fabric, which must have been far from inexpensive; but there had not been enough for two of the armchairs, and so these armchairs were left upholstered in simple burlap; however, for several years the host had cautioned his guests each time with the words: "Don't sit on these armchairs, they're not ready yet." In some rooms there was no furniture at all, though it had been said in the first days of their marriage: "Sweetie, we must see to it that furniture is put in this room tomorrow, at least for the time being." In the evening a very stylish candlestick was placed on the table, made of dark bronze with the three Graces of antiquity and a stylish mother-of-pearl shield, while next to it was set some sort of plain copper invalid, lame, hunched over on one side, all covered with tallow, though this was noticed neither by the master, nor by the mistress, nor by the servants. His wife . . . however, they were perfectly satisfied with each other. Though it was already eight years since their wedding, they would still bring each other a little bit of apple, a piece of candy, or a nut, and say in a touchingly tender voice expressive of perfect love: "Open up your little mouth, sweetie, I'll put this tidbit in for you." Needless to say, the little mouth would on these occasions be very gracefully opened. For birthdays, surprises were prepared: some sort of bead-embroidered little toothbrush case. And quite often, as they were sitting on the sofa, suddenly, for perfectly unknown reasons, one would abandon his pipe, and the other her needlework, if she happened to be holding it in her hands at the moment, and they would plant on each other's lips such a long and languid kiss that one could easily have smoked a small cheroot while it lasted. In short, they were what is called happy. Of course, it might be noted that there were many other things besides prolonged kisses and surprises to be done in the house, and many different questions might be asked. Why, for instance, was the cooking in the kitchen done stupidly and witlessly? why was the larder nearly empty? why was the housekeeper a thief? why were the servants so slovenly and drunk? why did the house serfs all sleep so unmercifully and spend the rest of the time carrying on? But these are all low subjects, and Mrs. Manilov had received a good education. And one gets a good education, as we know, in a boarding school. And in boarding schools, as we know, three main subjects constitute the foundation of human virtue: the French language, indispensable for a happy family life; the pianoforte, to afford a husband agreeable moments; and, finally, the managerial part proper: the crocheting of purses and other surprises. However, various improvements and changes in method occur, especially in our time; all this depends largely on the good sense and ability of the boarding school's headmistress. In some boarding schools it even occurs that the pianoforte comes first, then the French language, and only after that the managerial part. And sometime it also occurs that the managerial part, that is, the crocheting of surprises, comes first, then the French language, and only after that the pianoforte. Various methods occur. There will be no harm in making a further observation, that Mrs. Manilov . . . but, I confess, I am very afraid of talking about ladies, and, besides, it is time I returned to our heroes, who have already been standing at the drawing-room door for several minutes, mutually entreating each other to go in first.

"Kindly do not worry so for my sake, I will go in after," Chichikov said.

"No, Pavel Ivanovich, no, you are a guest," Manilov said, motioning him to the door with his hand.

"Do not trouble yourself, please, do not trouble yourself. Go in, please," Chichikov said.

"No, excuse me, I will not allow such an agreeable, well-educated guest to go in after me."

"Why well-educated? . . . Go in, please."

"Ah, no, you go in, please."

"But why?"

"Ah, but, just because!" Manilov said with an agreeable smile.

Finally the two friends went through the door sideways, squeezing each other slightly.

"Allow me to introduce you to my wife," said Manilov. "Sweetie! Pavel Ivanovich!"

Chichikov indeed saw a lady whom he had entirely failed to notice at first, as he was exchanging bows with Manilov in the doorway. She was not bad-looking and was dressed becomingly. Her housecoat of pale-colored silk sat well on her; her small, slender hand hastily dropped something on the table and clutched a cambric handkerchief with embroidered corners. She rose from the sofa on which she was sitting; Chichikov, not without pleasure, went up to kiss her hand. Mrs. Manilov said, even with a slightly French *r*,[5] that they were very glad he had come, and that no day went by without her husband's remembering him.

"Yes," Manilov chimed in, "she indeed kept asking me: 'But why does your friend not come?' 'Wait a bit, sweetie, he will come.' And now at last you've honored us with your visit. It is truly such a delight . . . a May day . . . a heart's feast . . . "

When Chichikov heard that things had already gone as far as a heart's feast, he even became slightly embarrassed, and replied modestly that he had neither a renowned name, nor even any notable rank.

"You have everything," Manilov interrupted with the same agreeable smile, "everything, and even more besides."

"How do you find our town?" Mrs. Manilov chimed in. "Have you spent an agreeable time there?"

"A very good town, a wonderful town," replied Chichikov, "and my time there has been very agreeable: the society is most mannerly."

"And what do you think of our governor?" said Mrs. Manilov.

"A most respectable and amiable man, isn't it true?" Manilov added.

"Absolutely true," said Chichikov, "a most respectable man. And how well he enters into his duty, how he understands it! We can only wish for more such people!"

"And, you know, he has such a way of receiving everyone, of observing delicacy in all he does," Manilov appended with a smile, narrowing his eyes almost completely with pleasure, like a cat that has been tickled lightly behind the ears with a finger.

"A very mannerly and agreeable man," continued Chichikov, "and so artistic! I even never could have imagined it. How well he embroiders various household patterns! He showed me a purse he made: it's a rare lady that can embroider so artfully."

"And the vice-governor, such a dear man, isn't it true?" said Manilov, again narrowing his eyes slightly.

"A very, very worthy man," responded Chichikov.

"And, permit me, how do you find the police chief? A very agreeable man, isn't it true?"

"Exceedingly agreeable, and such an intelligent, such a well-read man! I played whist at his place with the prosecutor and the head magistrate till the last cockcrow – a very, very worthy man."

"And what is your opinion of the police chief's wife?" Mrs. Manilov added. "A most amiable woman, isn't it true?"

"Oh, she is one of the worthiest women I have ever known," replied Chichikov.

Whereupon they did not omit the head magistrate, the postmaster, and in this manner went through almost all the town's officials, all of whom turned out to be most worthy people.

"Do you spend all your time in the country?" Chichikov finally put a question in his turn.

"Mainly in the country," replied Manilov. "Sometimes, however, we go to town, if only so as to meet educated people. One grows wild, you know, if one lives in seclusion all the time."

"True, true," said Chichikov.

"Of course," Manilov continued, "it's another thing if one has a nice neighbor, if one has, for example, the sort of man with whom one can in some way discuss matters of courtesy, of good manners, keep up with some sort of science or other, so as somehow to stir the soul, to lend it, so to speak, a sort of soaring..." Here he wished to express something further, but noticing that he was running off at the mouth, he merely scooped the air with his hand and went on: "Then, of course, the country and its solitude would have a great deal of agree-ableness. But there is decidedly no one... One merely reads the *Son of the Fatherland*⁶ occasionally."

Chichikov agreed with this completely, adding that nothing could be more pleasant than to live in solitude, enjoy the spectacle of nature, and occasionally read some book...

"But, you know," Manilov added, "still, if there is no friend with whom one can share..."

"Oh, that is correct, that is perfectly correct!" Chichikov interrupted. "What are all the treasures of the world then! 'Keep not money, but keep good people's company,' the wise man said."

"And you know, Pavel Ivanovich!" Manilov said, showing on his face an expression not merely sweet but even cloying, like the mixture a shrewd society doctor sweetens unmerci-fully, fancying it will please his patient. "Then one feels a sort of spiritual delight, in some way... As now, for instance, when chance has given me the, one might say, exemplary happiness of talking with you and enjoying your agreeable conversation . . . "

"Good gracious, what agreeable conversation? . . . An insignificant man, nothing more," responded Chichikov.

"Oh! Pavel Ivanovich, allow me to be frank: I would gladly give half of all I possess for a portion of the virtues that are yours! . . . "

"On the contrary, I, for my part, would regard it as the greatest . . . "

There is no knowing what the mutual outpouring of feelings between the two friends would have come to, if an entering servant had not announced that the meal was ready.

"I beg you to join us," said Manilov. "You will excuse us if we do not have such a dinner as on parquet floors and in capitals, we simply have, after the Russian custom, cabbage soup, but from the bottom of our hearts. Join us, I humbly beg you."

Here they spent some more time arguing over who should go in first, and Chichikov finally entered the dining room sideways.

In the dining room there already stood two boys, Manilov's sons, who were of the age when children already sit at the table, but still on raised seats. By them stood their tutor, who bowed politely and with a smile. The hostess sat down to her soup tureen; the guest was seated between the host and the hostess, the servant tied napkins around the children's necks.

"Such dear little children," said Chichikov, having looked at them, "and of what ages?"

"The older one is going on eight, and the younger one turned six just yesterday," said Mrs. Manilov.

"Themistoclus!" said Manilov, addressing the older boy, who was making efforts to free his chin from the napkin the lackey had tied around it.

Chichikov raised an eyebrow slightly on hearing this partly Greek name, to which, for some unknown reason, Manilov gave the ending "-us," but tried at once to bring his face back to its usual state.

"Themistoclus, tell me, what is the best city in France?"

Here the tutor turned all his attention on Themistoclus and seemed to want to jump into his eyes, but calmed himself at last and nodded when Themistoclus said: "Paris."

"And what is our best city?" Manilov asked again.

The tutor again tuned up his attention.

"Petersburg," replied Themistoclus.

"And besides that?"

"Moscow," replied Themistoclus.

"The smarty! The sweetie!" Chichikov said to that. "No, really . . . ," he continued, turning to the Manilovs with a look of some amazement, "such knowledge, at such an age! I must tell you, this child will have great abilities."

"Oh, you still don't know him," responded Manilov, "he has an exceeding amount of wit. The younger one now, Alkides, this one is not so quick, but that one, as soon as he meets something, a bug or a gnat, his eyes suddenly start rolling; he runs after it and investigates it at once. I intend him for the diplomatic line. Themistoclus," he went on, again addressing the boy, "want to be an ambassador?"

"Yes," replied Themistoclus, chewing his bread and wagging his head right and left.

At that moment the lackey who was standing behind him wiped the ambassador's nose, and it was a good thing he did, otherwise a rather sizable extraneous drop would have sunk into the soup. The conversation at table turned to the pleasures of the quiet life, interrupted by the hostess's observations about the town's theater and its actors. The tutor very attentively watched the talkers, and, as soon as he observed that they were about to smile, opened his mouth that same instant and diligently laughed. Most likely he was a grateful man and wanted thus to repay the master for his good treatment. Once, however, his face assumed a severe look and he rapped sternly on the table, aiming his glance at the children sitting across from him. This was appropriate, because Themistoclus had bitten Alkides' ear, and Alkides, screwing up his eyes and opening his mouth, was about to howl in a most pathetic way, but sensing that for that he could easily be deprived of one course, he returned his mouth to its former position and tearfully began gnawing on a lamb bone, which made both his cheeks shiny with grease. The hostess turned to Chichikov very frequently with the words: "You don't eat anything, you've taken very little." To which Chichikov would reply each time: "I humbly thank you, I'm full, agreeable conversation is better than any food."

They had already risen from the table. Manilov was exceedingly pleased and, supporting his guest's back with his arm, was preparing to escort him thus into the drawing room, when the guest suddenly announced with a rather significant air that he intended to discuss with him a certain very necessary matter.

"In that case allow me to invite you to my study," said Manilov, and he led him to a small room with a window looking out on the bluing forest. "Here's my little corner," said Manilov.

"An agreeable little room," said Chichikov, looking it over.

The room was, indeed, not without agreeableness: walls painted a pretty light blue like a sort of gray, four chairs, one armchair, a table, on which lay the book with the bookmark in it, of which we have already had occasion to make mention, several scribbled-on sheets of paper, but mainly there was tobacco. It was in various forms: in paper packets, in the tobacco jar, and, finally, simply poured out in a heap on the table. On both windowsills were also placed little piles of knocked-out pipe ash, arranged not without assiduousness in very handsome rows. It could be observed that this sometimes provided the host with a pastime.

"Allow me to invite you to settle yourself in this armchair," said Manilov. "You'll be more comfortable here."

"I'll sit on a straight chair, if you'll allow me."

"Allow me not to allow you," Manilov said with a smile. "This armchair is reserved for guests: whether you like it or not, you'll have to sit in it."

Chichikov sat down.

"Allow me to treat you to a little pipe."

"No, I don't smoke," Chichikov replied tenderly and as if with an air of regret.

"Why not?" said Manilov, also tenderly and with an air of regret.

"I'm not in the habit, I'm afraid; they say the pipe dries one up."

"Allow me to point out to you that that is a prejudice. I even suppose that to smoke a pipe is much healthier than to take snuff. There was a lieutenant in our regiment, a most wonderful and most educated man, who never let the pipe out of his mouth, not only at table but even, if I may be allowed to say so, in all other places. And here he is now already forty-some years old, and yet, thank God, he's still as healthy as can be."

Chichikov observed that that did indeed happen, and that there were many things in nature which were inexplicable even for a vast mind.

"But first allow me one request...," he uttered in a voice that rang with some strange or almost strange expression, and after that, for no apparent reason, he looked behind him. Manilov, too, for no apparent reason, looked behind him. "How long ago were you so good as to file your census report?"

"Oh, long ago now; or, rather, I don't remember."

"And since that time how many of your peasants have died?"

"I have no way of knowing; that's something I suppose you must ask the steward. Hey, boy! call the steward, he should be here today."

The steward appeared. He was a man approaching forty, who shaved his beard, wore a frock coat, and apparently led a very comfortable life, because his face had about it the look of a certain puffy plumpness, and his little eyes and the yellowish tint of his skin showed that he knew all too well what goose down and feather beds were. One could see at once that he had made his way in life as all estate stewards do: had first been simply a literate boy about the house, then married some housekeeper Agashka, the mistress's favorite, became a house-keeper himself, and then steward. And having become stew-ard, he behaved, naturally, like all stewards: hobnobbed with villagers of the wealthier sort; put additional taxes on the poorer ones; woke up past eight in the morning, waited for the samovar, and drank his tea.

"Listen, my good man! how many of our peasants have died since we filed the census report?"

"Who knows? Quite a lot have died since then," said the steward, and with that he hiccuped, covering his mouth slightly with his hand, as with a little screen.

"Yes, I confess, I thought so myself," Manilov picked up, "precisely, quite a lot have died!" Here he turned to Chichikov and added again: "Exactly, quite a lot."

"How many, for instance?" asked Chichikov.

"Yes, how many?" picked up Manilov.

"Who knows how many? It's not known what number died, nobody counted them."

"Yes, precisely," said Manilov, turning to Chichikov, "I thought so, too, a high mortality; it's quite unknown how many died."

"Count them all up, please," said Chichikov, "and make a detailed list of them all by name."

"Yes, all by name," said Manilov.

The steward said "Yes, sir!" and left.

"And for what reasons do you need this?" Manilov asked after the steward had gone.

This question, it seemed, embarrassed the guest, on whose face there appeared a sort of strained expression, which even made him blush – the strain of expressing something not quite amenable to words. And, indeed, Manilov finally heard such strange and extraordinary things as had never yet been heard by human ears.

"You ask, for what reasons? These are the reasons: I would like to buy peasants . . . ," Chichikov said, faltered, and did not finish his speech.

"But allow me to ask you," said Manilov, "how do you wish to buy them: with land, or simply to have them resettled – that is, without land?"

"No, it's not quite peasants," said Chichikov, "I would like to have dead . . . "

"How's that, sir? Excuse me . . . I'm somewhat hard of hearing, I thought I heard a most strange word . . . "

"I propose to acquire dead ones, who would, however, be counted in the census as living," said Chichikov.

Manilov straightaway dropped his long-stemmed chibouk on the floor, and as his mouth gaped open, so he remained with gaping mouth for the course of several minutes. The two friends, who had been discussing the agreeableness of the life of friendship, remained motionless, their eyes fixed on each other, like those portraits which in the old days used to be hung facing each other on either side of a mirror. Finally Manilov picked up the chibouk and looked into his face from below, trying to see whether there was a smile on his face, whether he was joking; but there was nothing of the sort to be seen; on the contrary, the face seemed even more staid than usual; then he thought his guest might by chance have gone off his head somehow, and in fear he looked intently at him; but the guest's eyes were completely clear, there was in them none of the wild, anguished fire that flickers in the eyes of a madman, everything was decent and in order. However hard Manilov thought about how to behave and what to do, he could think up nothing other than simply to release the remaining smoke from his mouth in a very thin stream.

"And so, I would like to know whether you might turn over to me, cede, or however you deem best, those not alive in reality, but alive with respect to legal form?"

But Manilov was so abashed and confused that he simply stared at him.

"It seems you're hesitant . . . ?" observed Chichikov.

"I? . . . no, it's not that," said Manilov, "but I cannot grasp . . . excuse me . . . I, of course, could not have received such a brilliant education as is perceivable, so to speak, in your every movement; I have no lofty art of expression . . . Here, it may be . . . in this explanation just expressed by you . . . something else is concealed . . . It may be that you were pleased to express it thus for the beauty of the style?"

"No," Chichikov picked up, "no, I mean the subject just as it is, that is, those souls which, indeed, have already died."

Manilov was utterly at a loss. He felt he had to say something, to offer a question, but what question – devil knew. He finished finally by letting out smoke again, only not through his mouth this time, but through the nostrils of his nose.

"And so, if there are no obstacles, with God's help we can proceed to draw up the deed of purchase," said Chichikov.

"What, a deed for dead souls?"

"Ah, no!" said Chichikov. "We will write that they are living, just as it actually stands in the census report. It is my habit never to depart from civil law in anything, though I did suffer for it in the service, but do excuse me: duty is a sacred thing for me, the law – I stand mute before the law."

These last words pleased Manilov, but all the same he by no means caught the drift of the matter itself, and instead of an answer began sucking so hard on his chibouk that it finally started wheezing like a bassoon. It seemed as if he wanted to pull from it an opinion concerning such an unheard-of circumstance; but the pipe wheezed, and that was all.

"It may be that you have some sort of doubts?"

"Oh! good gracious, not a whit. What I say of it is not because I might have some, that is, critical prejudication about you. But allow me to state, won't this undertaking, or, to better express it, so to speak, this negotiation – won't this negotiation be inconsistent with the civil statutes and the further prospects of Russia?"

Here Manilov, having made a certain movement with his head, looked very meaningly into Chichikov's face, showing in all the features of his own face and in his compressed lips such a profound expression as, it may be, has never yet been seen on a human face, except perhaps of some very clever minister, and then in the moment of a most brain-racking affair.

But Chichikov said simply that such an undertaking, or negotiation, was by no means inconsistent with the civil statutes and the further prospects of Russia, and a moment later added that the treasury would even profit by it, for it would receive the legal fees.

"So you suppose . . . "

"I suppose it will be a good thing."

"Ah, if it's good, that's another matter: I have nothing against it," said Manilov, and he calmed down completely.

"Now it remains to agree on the price."

"What price?" Manilov said again and paused. "Do you really think I will take money for souls which, in a certain sense, have ended their existence? If you have indeed been visited by this, so to speak, fantastic desire, then I, for my part, will turn them over to you disinterestedly and take the fees upon myself."

It would be a great reproach to the historian of the events set forth here if he failed to say that, after these words uttered by Manilov, the guest was overcome with delight. Staid and sensible though he was, he almost performed a leap after the manner of a goat, which, as we know, is performed only under the strongest impulses of joy. He turned so sharply in the armchair that the woolen fabric of the cushion burst; Manilov himself looked at him in some bewilderment. Moved by gratitude, he straightaway produced such a heap of thankful words that the other became confused, blushed all over, producing a negative gesture with his head, and finally expressed the opinion that it was a veritable nothing, that he indeed wanted to prove somehow his heart's inclination, the magnetism of the soul, and that the deceased souls were in a way sheer trash.

"By no means trash," said Chichikov, pressing his hand. Here a very profound sigh was emitted. It seemed he was in the mood for outpourings of the heart; not without feeling and expression he finally uttered the following words: "If you only knew what a service you have just rendered, with this ostensible trash, to a man without kith or kin! Yes, really and truly, is there anything I have not suffered? like some bark amidst the savage waves . . . How persecuted, how victimized I have been, what grief I have tasted, and for what? for having observed the truth, for being of pure conscience, for holding my hand out to the helpless widow and the hapless orphan! . . . " At this point he even wiped away an impending tear with his handkerchief.

Manilov was thoroughly touched. The two friends pressed each other's hands for a long time and silently gazed for a long time into each other's eyes, in which welled-up tears could be seen. Manilov simply would not let our hero's hand go and went on pressing it so warmly that the latter could see no way of rescuing it. Finally, having quietly pulled it free, he said it would not be a bad thing to draw up the deed of purchase speedily, and it would be nice if he himself came to town for a visit. Then he took his hat and began bowing out.

"What? you want to leave already?" said Manilov, suddenly coming to himself and almost frightened.

At that moment Mrs. Manilov came into the study.

"Lizanka," said Manilov, with a somewhat pitiful look, "Pavel Ivanovich is leaving us!"

"Because Pavel Ivanovich is tired of us," replied Mrs. Manilov.

"Madame! here," said Chichikov, "here is the place" – and with that he put his hand over his heart – "yes, it is here that the agreeableness of the time spent with you will abide! and believe me, there could be no greater bliss for me than to live with you, if not in the same house, then at least in the nearest vicinity."

"You know, Pavel Ivanovich," said Manilov, who liked this thought very much, "it would indeed be so nice if we were to live somehow together, beneath one roof, or beneath the shade of some elm to philosophize about something, to delve deeper! . . . "

"Oh! that would be a paradisal life!" said Chichikov, sighing. "Good-bye, madam!" he went on, coming up to kiss Mrs. Manilov's hand. "Good-bye, most esteemed friend! Don't forget my request!"

"Oh, rest assured!" replied Manilov. "I am parting with you for no longer than two days."

Everyone went out to the dining room.

"Good-bye, dear little ones!" said Chichikov, seeing Alkides and Themistoclus, who were occupied with some wooden hussar that already lacked an arm and a nose. "Good-bye, my tots. You must excuse me for not bringing you any presents, because, I confess, I didn't even know that you were living in the world, but now I'll be sure to bring something when I come. I'll bring you a sword – want a sword?"

"Yes," replied Themistoclus.

"And you a drum, right? a drum for you?" he went on, bending down to Alkides.

"Dwum," Alkides replied in a whisper, hanging his head.

"Fine, I'll bring you a drum. A real nice drum, it'll go like this: turrr . . . ru . . . tra-ta-ta, ta-ta-ta . . . Good-bye, sweetie, good-bye!" Here he kissed him on the head and turned to

Manilov and his spouse with a little laugh, such as one commonly addresses to parents in letting them know the innocence of their children's wishes.

"Stay, really, Pavel Ivanovich!" Manilov said, when everyone had already come out on the porch. "Look, what clouds!"

"Tiny little clouds," replied Chichikov.

"And do you know the way to Sobakevich's?"

"I wanted to ask you about that."

"Allow me, I'll explain to your coachman right now." Here Manilov, with the same courtesy, explained the matter to the coachman and once even said "sir" to him.

The coachman, hearing that he should skip two turns and take the third, said, "We'll do fine, your honor" – and Chichikov left, accompanied for a long time by the bowing and handkerchief waving of his standing-on-tiptoe hosts.

Manilov stood for a long time on the porch, watching the departing britzka, and when it became quite invisible, he still stood there smoking his pipe. Finally he went inside, sat down on a chair, and gave himself over to reflection, rejoicing in his soul at having given his guest some small pleasure. Then his thoughts imperceptibly turned to other subjects and finally went off God knows where. He was thinking about the well-being of a life of friendship, about how nice it would be to live with a friend on the bank of some river, then a bridge began to be built across this river, then an enormous house with such a high belvedere that one could even see Moscow from it and drink tea there of an evening in the open air while discussing agreeable subjects. Then that he and Chichikov arrived together at some gathering in fine carriages, where they enchanted everyone with the agreeableness of their manners, and that the sovereign, supposedly learning there was such friendship between them, made them generals, and beyond that, finally, God knows what, something he himself could no longer figure out. Chichikov's strange request suddenly interrupted all his reveries. The thought of it somehow especially refused to get digested in his head: whichever way he turned it, he simply could not explain it to himself, and all the while he sat and smoked his pipe, which went on right up to suppertime.

CHAPTER THREE

AND CHICHIKOV IN a contented state of mind was sitting in his britzka, which had long been rolling down the high road. From the previous chapter it will already be clear what constituted the chief subject of his taste and inclinations, and therefore it is no wonder that he was soon immersed in it body and soul. The speculations, estimates, and considerations that wandered over his face were, apparently, very agreeable, for at every moment they left behind them traces of a contented smile. Occupied with them, he paid not the slightest attention to his coachman, who, content with his reception by Manilov's household serfs, was making most sensible observations to the dappled gray outrunner harnessed on the right side. This dappled gray horse was extremely sly and only made a show of pulling, while the bay shaft horse and the chestnut outrunner, who was called Assessor because he had been acquired from some assessor, put their whole hearts into it, so that the satisfaction they derived from it could even be read in their eyes. "Fox away, fox away! I'll still outfox you!" Selifan said, rising a little and lashing the lazybones with his whip. "To learn you your business, you German pantaloon! The bay's a respectable horse, he does his duty, and I'll gladly give him an extra measure, because he's a respectable horse, and Assessor's a good horse, too ... Well, well, why are you twitching your ears? Listen to what you're told, fool! I won't learn you anything bad, you lout! Look at him crawling!" Here he lashed him again with the whip, adding: "Ooh, barbarian! Cursed Bonaparte!" Then he yelled at all of them: "Hup, my gentles!"

and whipped all three of them, not with a view to punishment this time, but to show he was pleased with them. Having given them this pleasure, he again addressed his speech to the dapple-gray: "You think you can hide your behavior. No, you must live by the truth, if you want to be shown respect. At that landowner's now, where we were, they were good people. It's a pleasure for me to talk, if it's with a good man; with a good man I'm always friends, fine companions: whether it's having tea, or a bite to eat – I'm game, if it's with a good man. To a good man everybody shows respect. Our master, now, everybody honors him, because he was in the goverman's service, he's a scollegiate councillor . . . "

Reasoning thus, Selifan wound up finally in the most remote abstractions. If Chichikov had lent an ear to it, he would have learned many details relating to himself personally; but his thoughts were so occupied with his subject that only a loud clap of thunder made him come to himself and look around: the whole sky was completely covered with dark clouds, and the dusty post road was sprinkled with drops of rain. Finally a clap of thunder came louder and nearer, and it suddenly started pouring buckets. At first, assuming an oblique direction, the rain lashed against one side of the kibitka's body, then against the other, then, changing its manner of attack and becoming completely straight, it drummed straight down on the top; splashes finally started flying as far as his face. This induced him to draw the leather curtains with their two round little windows, intended for the viewing of roadside scenes, and order Selifan to drive faster. Selifan, also interrupted in the middle of his speech, realized that he indeed should not dawdle, straightaway pulled some rag of gray flannel from under his seat, thrust his arms into the sleeves, seized the reins in his hands, and yelled to his troika, which had barely been moving its legs, for it felt agreeably relaxed as a result of his instructive speeches. But Selifan simply could not recall whether he had passed two or three turns. Thinking back and recalling the road somewhat, he realized that there had been many turns, all of which he had skipped. Since a Russian man in a critical moment finds what to do without going into further reasonings, he shouted, after turning right at the next crossroads: "Hup, my honored friends!" and started off at a gallop, thinking little of where the road he had taken would lead him.

It looked, however, as if the rain was not going to let up soon. The dust lying in the road was quickly churned to mud, and it became harder every moment for the horses to pull the britzka. Chichikov was already beginning to worry greatly, going so long without sighting Sobakevich's estate. By his reckoning, they should have arrived long ago. He peered out both sides, but it was as dark as the bottom of a well.

"Selifan!" he said finally, poking himself out of the britzka.

"What, master?" answered Selifan.

"Look around, don't you see the village?"

"No, master, it's nowhere to be seen!" After which Selifan, brandishing his whip, struck up, not really a song, but something so long that there was even no end to it. Everything went into it: every inciting and inviting cry to which horses all over Russia, from one end to the other, are treated; adjectives of every sort without further discrimination, whatever came first to his tongue. In this fashion things reached a point where he finally started calling them secretaries.

Meanwhile Chichikov began to notice that the britzka was rocking from side to side and dealing him some very strong jolts; this gave him the feeling that they had turned off the road and were probably dragging themselves over a harrowed field. Selifan seemed to have realized it himself, but he did not say a word.

"How now, you crook, what sort of road are you driving on?" said Chichikov.

"No help for it, master, in a time like this; can't see the whip, it's that dark!" Having said this, he tilted the britzka so much that Chichikov was forced to hold on with both hands. Only here did he notice that Selifan was a bit in his cups.

"Hold it, hold it, you'll tip us over!" he shouted to him.

"No, master, it can't be that I'll tip us over," Selifan said. "It's no good tipping over, I know myself: I'll never tip us over." Then he began to turn the britzka slightly, turned, turned, and finally turned it over completely on its side. Chichikov plopped hand and foot into the mud. Selifan did stop the horses, however, though they would have stopped of themselves, because they were very worn-out. He was completely amazed at such an unforeseen occurrence. Climbing down from the box, he stood in front of the britzka, arms akimbo, all the while his master was floundering in the mud, trying to crawl out of it, and said after some reflection: "Look at that, it tipped over!"

"You're drunk as a cobbler!" said Chichikov.

"No, master, it can't be that I'm drunk! I know it's not a good thing to be drunk. I talked with a friend, because one can have a talk with a good man, there's nothing bad in that; and we had a bite to eat together. There's no offense in a bite to eat; one can have a bite to eat with a good man."

"And what did I tell you when you got drunk the last time? eh? have you forgotten?"

"No, your honor, it can't be that I've forgotten. I know my business. I know it's no good to be drunk. I had a talk with a good man, because . . . "

"I'll give you real whipping, then you'll know how to talk with a good man!"

"As ever your grace pleases," replied the all-agreeable Selifan, "if it's a whipping, it's a whipping; I don't mind about that at all. Why not a whipping, if it's deserved, that's the master's will. Whipping's needed, because a muzhik goes a-frolicking, there's need for order. If it's deserved, give him a whipping: why not give him a whipping?"

The master was completely at a loss how to respond to such reasoning. But at that time it seemed as if fate itself decided to have mercy on him. From far off came the barking of dogs. Overjoyed, Chichikov gave the order to whip up the horses. A Russian driver has good instinct in place of eyes; as a result, he sometimes goes pumping along at full speed, eyes shut, and always gets somewhere or other. Selifan, without seeing a blessed thing, aimed his horses so directly at the estate that he stopped only when the britzka's shafts struck the fence and there was decidedly no way to go further. Chichikov only noticed through the thick sheet of pouring rain something resembling a roof. He sent Selifan in search of the gates, which no doubt would have taken a long time, were it not that in Russia, instead of gatekeepers, there are brave dogs, who announced him so ringingly that he put his fingers in his ears. Light flickered in one little window and its misty stream reached the fence, showing our travelers the gates. Selifan set about knocking, and soon some figure clad in a smock stuck itself out the wicket, and master and servant heard a husky female voice:

"Who's knocking? What's this carrying on?"

"Travelers, dearie, let us stay the night," said Chichikov.

"There's a quick-stepper for you!" said the old woman. "A fine time you picked to come! This isn't an inn: a lady landowner lives here."

"No help for it, dearie: see, we've lost our way. We can't spend the night on the steppe at a time like this."

"Yes, it's a dark time, it's not a good time," added Selifan.

"Quiet, fool," said Chichikov.

"But who are you?" said the old woman.

"A nobleman, dearie."

The word "nobleman" made the old woman reflect a little, it seemed.

"Wait, I'll tell my mistress," she said, and about two minutes later already came back with a lantern in her hand.

The gates were opened. Light flickered in yet another window. The britzka, having driven into the yard, stopped in front of a smallish house, which it was difficult to make out in the darkness. Only half of it was lit by the light coming from the windows; also visible was a puddle in front of the house, which was struck directly by the same light. Rain beat noisily on the wooden roof and poured in burbling streams into the rain barrel. Meanwhile the dogs went off into all possible voices: one, his head thrown back, howled so protractedly and with such diligence as though he were being paid God knows how much for it; another rapped away hurriedly, like a beadle; in their midst, like a postman's bell, rang an irrepressible treble, probably a young puppy's, and all this was crowned by a bass, an old fellow, perhaps, endowed with a stalwart dog's nature, because he was wheezing the way a basso profundo wheezes when the concert is at its peak: the tenors rise on tiptoe in their intense desire to produce a high note, and all that is there strains upwards, heads flung back, while he alone, his unshaven chin thrust into his tie, having hunkered down and lowered himself almost to the ground, from there lets out his note, making the windowpanes shake and rattle. From the dogs' barking alone, composed of such musicians, it might have been supposed that the village was a sizable one; but our drenched and chilled hero had thoughts of nothing but bed. The moment the britzka came to a full stop, he jumped off onto the porch, staggered, and almost fell. Again some woman came out to the porch, a bit younger than the first one, but closely resembling her. She brought him inside. Chichikov took a couple of cursory glances: the room was hung with old striped wallpaper; pictures of some sort of birds; little old-fashioned mirrors between the windows, with dark frames shaped like curled leaves; behind each mirror was stuck either a letter, or an old pack of cards, or a stocking; a wall clock with flowers painted on its face . . . it was beyond him to notice anything more. His eyes felt sticky, as if someone had smeared them with honey. A minute later the mistress came in, an elderly woman in some sort of sleeping bonnet, hastily put on, with a flannel kerchief around her neck, one of those little dearies, small landowners who fret over bad harvests, losses, and keep their heads cocked slightly to one side, and meanwhile little by little are stowing away a bit of cash in bags made of ticking, tucked into different drawers. The roubles all go into one little bag, the half-roubles into another, the quarter-roubles into a third, though to all appearances there is nothing in the chest but underwear, and night jackets, and spools of thread, and an unpicked coat that will later be turned into a dress, if the old one somehow happens to get a hole burnt in it during the frying of holiday pancakes and various fritters, or else wears out by itself. But the dress will not get burnt or wear out by itself; the little old lady is a thrifty one, and the coat is fated to lie for a long time in its unpicked state, and then to be left in her will to the daughter of a cousin twice removed along with various other rubbish.

Chichikov apologized for troubling her by his unexpected arrival.

"Never mind, never mind," said the mistress. "What weather for God to bring you in! Such turmoil and blizzard ... You ought to eat something after your journey, but it's nighttime, no way to prepare anything."

The mistress's words were interrupted by a strange hissing, so that the guest was frightened at first; it sounded as if the whole room had suddenly become filled with snakes; but on glancing up he was reassured, for he realized it was the wall clock making up its mind to strike. The hissing was immediately followed by a wheezing, and finally, straining all its forces, it struck two, with a sound as if someone were banging a cracked pot with a stick, after which the pendulum again began calmly clicking right and left.

Chichikov thanked the mistress, saying that he needed nothing, that she should not trouble about anything, that apart from a bed he asked for nothing, and was only curious to know what parts he had come to and whether it was a long way from there to the landowner Sobakevich's place, to which the old woman said that she had never heard such a name and that there was no such landowner at all.

"Do you know Manilov at least?" said Chichikov.

"And who is this Manilov?"

"A landowner, dearie."

"No, never heard of him, there's no such landowner."

"What is there, then?"

"Bobrov, Svinyin, Kanapatyev, Kharpakin, Trepakin, Pleshakov."

"Are they rich men, or not?"

"No, my dear, none of them is very rich. There's some have twenty souls, some thirty, but such as might have a hundred, no, there's none such."

Chichikov observed that he had wound up in quite a backwater.

"Anyway, is it far to town?"

"Some forty miles, must be. What a pity there's nothing for you to eat! Wouldn't you take some tea, dearie?"

"Thank you, dearie. I need nothing but a bed."

"True, after such a journey one needs rest very badly. Settle yourself right here, dearie, on this sofa. Hey, Fetinya, bring a feather bed, pillows, and a sheet. What weather God has sent us: such thunder – I've had a candle burning in front of the icon all night. Eh, my dear, your back and side are all muddy as a hog's! Where'd you get yourself mucked up like that?"

"Thank God all the same that I only mucked myself up, I should be grateful I've still got all my ribs."

"Saints alive, what a fright! Maybe you should have your back rubbed with something?"

"Thank you, thank you. Don't trouble, but just order your girl to dry and brush my clothes."

"Do you hear, Fetinya!" said the mistress, addressing the woman who had come out to the porch with a candle, and who had now managed to bring a feather bed and plump it up with her hands, loosing a flood of feathers all over the room. "Take his coat and underwear and dry them first in front of the fire, as you used to do for the late master, and then brush them and give them a good beating."

"Yes, ma'am," Fetinya said, as she covered the feather bed and arranged the pillows.

"Well, there's your bed made up for you," said the mistress. "Good-bye, dearie, I wish you a good night. Is there anything else you need? Perhaps, my dear, you're used to having your heels scratched before bed? My late husband could never fall asleep without it."

But the guest also declined the heel scratching. The mistress went out, and he straightaway hastened to undress, giving Fetinya all the trappings he took off himself, over and under, and Fetinya, having for her part wished him good night as well, carried off this wet armor. Left alone, he gazed not without pleasure at his bed, which reached almost to the ceiling. One could see that Fetinya was an expert at plumping up feather beds. When, having brought over a chair, he climbed onto the bed, it sank under him almost down to the floor, and the feathers he displaced from under himself flew into every corner of the room. Putting out the candle, he covered himself with the cotton quilt and, curling up under it, fell asleep that same moment. He woke up rather late the next morning. The sun was shining through the window straight into his eyes, and the flies which yesterday had been quietly asleep on the walls and ceiling now all addressed themselves to him: one sat on his lip, another on his ear, a third kept making attempts to settle right on his eye, while one that had been so imprudent as to alight close to the nostril of his nose, he drew into the nose itself while he slept, which made him sneeze violently – a circumstance that was the cause of his waking up. Glancing around the room, he now noticed that the pictures were not all of birds: among them hung a portrait of Kutuzov and an oil painting of some old man with a red-cuffed uniform such as was worn in the time of Pavel Petrovich.[7] The clock again let out a hiss and struck ten; a woman's face peeked in the door and instantly hid itself, for Chichikov, wishing to sleep better, had thrown off absolutely everything. The face that had peeked in seemed somehow slightly familiar to him. He began recalling to himself: who might it be? – and finally remembered that it was the mistress. He put on his shirt; his clothes, already dried and brushed, lay next to him. Having dressed, he went up to the mirror and sneezed again so loudly that a turkey cock, who was just then approaching the window – the window being very near the ground – started babbling something to him suddenly and quite rapidly in his strange language, probably "God bless you," at which Chichikov called him fool. Going to the window, he began to examine the views that spread before him: the window opened almost onto the poultry yard; at least the narrow pen that lay before him was all filled with fowl and every sort of domestic creature. There were turkeys and hens without number; among them a rooster paced with measured steps, shaking his comb and tilting his head to one side as if listening to something; a sow and her family also turned up right there; right there, rooting in a heap of garbage, she incidentally ate a chick and, without noticing it, went on gobbling up watermelon rinds in good order. This small pen or poultry yard was enclosed by a wooden fence, beyond which stretched a vast kitchen garden with cabbages, onions, potatoes, beets, and other household vegetables. Strewn here and there over the kitchen garden were apple and other fruit trees, covered with nets to protect them from magpies and sparrows, the latter of which rushed in whole slanting clouds from one place to another. Several scarecrows had been set up for the same purpose, on long poles with splayed arms; one of them was wearing the mistress's own bonnet. Beyond the kitchen garden came the peasants' cottages, which, though built in a scattered way and not confined to regular streets, nevertheless showed, to Chichikov's observation, the prosperity of their inhabitants, for they were kept up: decrepit roof planks had everywhere been replaced by new ones; the gates were nowhere askew, and in those of the peasants' covered sheds that faced him he noticed here an almost new spare cart, and there even two. "It's no little bit of an estate she's got here," he said and resolved straightaway to get into conversation and become better acquainted with the mistress. He peeked through the crack in the door from which she had just stuck her head, and, seeing her sitting at the tea table, went in to her with a cheerful and benign look.

"Good morning, dearie. Did you sleep well?" said the mistress, rising from her place. She was better dressed than yesterday – in a dark dress, and not in a sleeping bonnet now, though there was still something wrapped around her neck.

"Quite well, quite well," said Chichikov, seating himself in an armchair. "And you, dearie?"

"Poorly, my dear."

"How so?"

"Insomnia. My lower back aches, and there's a gnawing pain in my leg, here, just above this little bone."

"It will pass, it will pass, dearie. Pay it no mind."

"God grant it passes. I did apply lard to it, and also wet it with turpentine. Will you have a sip of something with your tea? There's fruit liqueur in the flask."

"Not bad, dearie, let's have a sip of fruit liqueur."

The reader, I suppose, will already have noticed that Chichikov, despite his benign air, nevertheless spoke with greater liberty than with Manilov, and did not stand on any ceremony. It must be said that if we in Russia are still behind foreigners in some other things, we have far outstripped them in the art of address. Countless are all the nuances and subtleties of our address. No Frenchman or German will ever puzzle out and comprehend all its peculiarities and distinctions; he will speak in almost the same voice and language with a millionaire and with a mere tobacconist, though, of course, in his soul he will grovel duly before the first. Not so with us: there are such sages among us as will speak quite differently to a landowner with two hundred souls than to one with three hundred, and to one with three hundred, again, not as he will speak to one with five hundred, and to one with five hundred, again, not as to one with eight hundred – in short, you can go right up to a million, there will always be nuances. Suppose, for instance, that there exists an office, not here, but in some far-off kingdom, and in that office suppose there exists the head of the office. I ask you to look at him as he sits among his subordinates – one cannot even utter a word from fear! – pride and nobility, and what else does his face not express? Just take a brush and paint him: a Prometheus, decidedly a Prometheus! His gaze is like an eagle's, his step is smooth, measured. And this same eagle, as soon as he leaves his room and approaches his own superior's office, scurries, papers under his arm, just like a partridge, so help me. In society or at a party, if everyone is of low rank, Prometheus simply remains Prometheus, but if there is someone a bit above him, Prometheus will undergo such a metamorphosis as even Ovid could not invent: a fly, less than a fly, he self-annihilates into a grain of sand! "No, this is not Ivan Petrovich," you say, looking at him. "Ivan Petrovich is taller, and this is a short and skinny little fellow; Ivan Petrovich talks in a loud voice, a basso, and never laughs, while this one, devil knows, he peeps like a bird and can't stop laughing." You step closer, you see – it really is Ivan Petrovich! "Ah-ha-ha," you think to yourself... But, anyhow, let us return to our cast of characters. Chichikov, as we have already seen, decided to do without ceremony altogether, and therefore, taking a cup of tea in his hand and pouring some liqueur into it, he held forth thus:

"You've got a nice little estate here, dearie. How many souls are there?"

"Nigh onto eighty souls, my dear," the mistress said, "but the trouble is the weather's been bad, and there was such a poor harvest last year, God help us."

"Still, the muzhiks have a hearty look, the cottages are sturdy. But allow me to know your last name. I'm so absent-minded . . . arrived in the night . . . "

"Korobochka, widow of a collegiate secretary."

"I humbly thank you. And your first name and patronymic?"

"Nastasya Petrovna."

"Nastasya Petrovna? A nice name, Nastasya Petrovna. My aunt, my mother's sister, is Nastasya Petrovna."

"And what's your name?" the lady landowner asked. "I expect you're a tax assessor?"

"No, dearie," Chichikov replied, smiling, "don't expect I'm a tax assessor, I'm just going around on my own little business."

"Ah, so you're a buyer! Really, my dear, what a pity I sold my honey to the merchants so cheaply, and here you would surely have bought it from me."

"No, your honey I wouldn't have bought."

"Something else, then? Hemp maybe? But I haven't got much hemp now either: only half a bale."

"No, dearie, mine are a different kind of goods: tell me, have any of your peasants died?"

"Oh, dearie, eighteen men!" the old woman said, sighing. "Died, and all such fine folk, all good workers. Some were born after that, it's true, but what's the use of them: all such runts; and the tax assessor comes – pay taxes on each soul, he says. Folk are dead, and you pay on them like the living. Last week my blacksmith burnt up on me, such a skillful one, and he knew locksmithing, too."

"So you had a fire, dearie?"

"God spared us such a calamity, a fire would have been all that much worse; he got burnt up on his own, my dear. It somehow caught fire inside him, he drank too much, just this little blue flame came out of him,

55

and he smoldered, smoldered, and turned black as coal, and he was such a very skillful blacksmith! And now I can't even go out for a drive: there's no one to shoe the horses."

"It's all as God wills, dearie!" said Chichikov, sighing, "there's no saying anything against the wisdom of God... Why not let me have them, Nastasya Petrovna?"

"Whom, dearie?"

"But, all that have died."

"But how can I let you have them?"

"But, just like that. Or maybe sell them. I'll give you money for them."

"But how? I really don't quite see. You're not going to dig them out of the ground, are you?"

Chichikov saw that the old woman had overshot the mark and that it was necessary to explain what it was all about. In a few words he made clear to her that the transfer or purchase would only be on paper, and the souls would be registered as if they were living.

"But what do you need them for?" the old woman said, goggling her eyes at him.

"That's my business."

"But they really are dead."

"But who ever said they were alive? That's why it's a loss for you, because they're dead: you pay for them, but now I'll rid you of the trouble and the payments. Understand? And not only rid you of them, but give you fifteen roubles to boot. Well, is it clear now?"

"I really don't know," the mistress said with deliberation. "I never yet sold any dead ones."

"I should think not! It would be quite a wonder if you'd sold them to anyone. Or do you think they really are good for anything?"

"No, I don't think so. What good could they be, they're no good at all. The only thing that troubles me is that they're already dead."

"Well, the woman seems a bit thick-headed," Chichikov thought to himself.

"Listen, dearie, you just give it some good thought: here you are being ruined, paying taxes for them as if they were alive . . . "

"Oh, my dear, don't even mention it!" the lady land-owner picked up. "Just two weeks ago I paid more than a hundred and fifty roubles. And had to grease the assessor's palm at that."

"Well, you see, dearie. And now consider only this, that you won't have to grease the assessor's palm any longer, be-cause now I will pay for them; I, and not you; I will take all the obligations upon myself. I'll even have the deed drawn up at my own expense, do you understand that?"

The old woman fell to thinking. She saw that the business indeed seemed profitable, yet it was much too novel and unprecedented; and therefore she began to fear very much that this buyer might somehow hoodwink her; he had come from God knows where, and in the night, too.

"So, then, dearie, shall we shake hands on it?" said Chichikov.

"Really, my dear, it has never happened to me before to sell deceased ones. I did let two living ones go, two wenches, for a hundred roubles each, to our priest, the year before last, and he was ever so grateful, they turned out to be such good workers: they weave napkins."

"Well, this is nothing to do with the living – God be with them. I'm asking for dead ones."

"Really, I'm afraid this first time, I may somehow suffer a loss. Maybe you're deceiving me, my dear, and they're . . . somehow worth more."

"Listen, dearie . . . eh, what a one! How much could they be worth? Consider: it's dust. Do you understand? It's just dust. Take any last worthless thing, even some simple rag, for instance, still a rag has its value: it can at least be sold to a paper mill – but for this there's no need at all. No, you tell me yourself, what is it needed for?"

"That's true enough. It's not needed for anything at all; but there's just this one thing stops me, that they're already dead."

"Bah, what a blockhead!" Chichikov said to himself, beginning to lose patience now. "Go, try getting along with her! I'm all in a sweat, the damned hag!" Here he took his handkerchief from his pocket and began mopping the sweat which in fact stood out on his brow. However, Chichikov need not have been angry: a man can be greatly respectable, even statesmanly, and in reality turn out to be a perfect Korobochka. Once he gets a thing stuck in his head, there's no overcoming him; present him with as many arguments as you like, all clear as day – everything bounces off him, like a rubber ball bouncing off a wall. Having mopped his sweat, Chichikov decided to see whether she could be guided onto the path from another side.

"Either you don't wish to understand my words, dearie," he said, "or you're saying it on purpose, just to say something . . . I'm offering you money: fifteen roubles in banknotes. Do you understand that? It's money. You won't find it lying in the street. Confess now, how much did you sell your honey for?"

"Thirty kopecks a pound."

"That's a bit of a sin on your soul, dearie. You didn't sell it for thirty kopecks."

"By God, I did, too."

"Well, you see? Still, that was honey. You collected it for maybe a year, with care, with effort, with trouble; you had to go, smoke the bees, feed them in the cellar all winter; but the thing with the dead souls is not of this world. Here you made no effort on your side, it was God's will that they depart this life, to the detriment of your household. There you get twelve roubles for your labor, your effort, and here you take them for nothing, for free, and not twelve but fifteen, and not in silver but all in blue banknotes." – After such strong assurances,

Chichikov had scarcely any doubt that the old woman would finally give in.

"Really," the lady landowner replied, "I'm so inexperienced, what with being a widow and all! I'd better take a little time, maybe merchants will come by, I'll check on the prices."

"For shame, for shame, dearie! simply for shame! Think what you are saying! Who is going to buy them? What use could they possibly be to anyone?"

"Maybe they'd somehow come in handy around the house on occasion . . . ," the old woman objected and, not finishing what she was saying, opened her mouth and looked at him almost in fear, wishing to know what he would say to that.

"Dead people around the house! Eh, that's going a bit far! Maybe just to frighten sparrows in your kitchen garden at night or something?"

"Saints preserve us! What horrors you come out with!" the old woman said, crossing herself.

"Where else would you like to stick them? No, anyhow, the bones and graves – all that stays with you, the transfer is only on paper. So, what do you say? How about it? Answer me at least."

The old woman again fell to thinking.

"What are you thinking about, Nastasya Petrovna?"

"Really, I still can't settle on what to do; I'd better sell you the hemp."

"What's all this hemp? For pity's sake, I ask you about something totally different, and you shove your hemp at me! Hemp's hemp, the next time I come, I'll take the hemp as well. So, how about it, Nastasya Petrovna?"

"By God, it's such queer goods, quite unprecedented!"

Here Chichikov went completely beyond the bounds of all patience, banged his chair on the floor in aggravation, and wished the devil on her.

Of the devil the lady landowner was extraordinarily frightened.

"Oh, don't remind me of that one, God help him!" she cried out, turning all pale. "Just two days ago I spent the whole night dreaming about the cursed one. I had a notion to tell my fortune with cards that night after prayers, and God sent him on me as a punishment. Such a nasty one; horns longer than a bull's."

"I'm amazed you don't dream of them by the dozen. It was only Christian loving-kindness that moved me: I saw a poor widow wasting away, suffering want . . . no, go perish and drop dead, you and all your estate! . . ."

"Ah, what oaths you're hanging on me!" the old woman said, looking at him in fear.

"But there's no way to talk with you! Really, you're like some – not to use a bad word – some cur lying in the manger: he doesn't eat himself, and won't let others eat. I thought I might buy up various farm products from you, because I also do government contracting . . ." Here he was fibbing, though by the way and with no further reflection, but with unexpected success. The government contracting produced a strong effect on Nastasya Petrovna, at least she uttered now, in an almost pleading voice:

"But why all this hot anger? If I'd known before that you were such an angry one, I wouldn't have contradicted you at all."

"What's there to be angry about! The whole affair isn't worth a tinker's dam – as if I'd get angry over it!"

"Well, as you please, I'm prepared to let you have them for fifteen in banknotes! Only mind you, my dear, about those contracts: if you happen to buy up rye flour, or buckwheat flour, or grain, or butchered cattle, please don't leave me out."

"No, dearie, I won't leave you out," he said, all the while wiping off the sweat that was streaming down his face. He inquired whether she had some attorney or acquaintance in town whom she could authorize to draw up the deed and do all that was necessary.

"Of course, our priest, Father Kiril, has a son who serves in the treasury," said Korobochka.

Chichikov asked her to write a warrant for him, and, to save her needless trouble, even volunteered to write it himself.

"It would be nice," Korobochka meanwhile thought to herself, "if he'd start buying my flour and meat for the government. I must coax him: there's still some batter left from yesterday, I'll go and tell Fetinya to make some pancakes; it would also be nice to do up a short-crust pie with eggs, my cook does them so well, and it takes no time at all." The mistress went to carry out her thought concerning the doing-up of a pie, and probably to expand it with other productions of domestic bakery and cookery; and Chichikov went to the drawing room where he had spent the night, to get the necessary papers from his chest. In the drawing room everything had long since been tidied up, the sumptuous feather bed had been taken out, and a set table stood in front of the sofa. Having placed the chest on it, he rested briefly, for he felt he was all in a sweat, as if in a river: everything he had on, from his shirt down to his stockings, everything was wet. "She really wore me out, the damned hag!" he said, after resting a little, and he unlocked the chest. The author is sure that there are such curious readers as would even like to know the plan and internal arrangement of the chest. Very well, why not satisfy them! Here, then, is the internal arrangement: right in the middle a soap box, next to the soap box six or seven narrow partitions for razors; then square nooks for a sandbox and an ink bottle, with a hollowed-out little boat for pens, sealing wax, and everything of a longer sort; then various compartments with or without lids for things that were shorter, filled with calling cards, funeral announcements, theater tickets, and the like, stored away as mementos. The whole upper box with all its little partitions was removable, and under it was a space occupied by stacks of writing paper; then came a secret little drawer for money, which slid out inconspicuously from the side of the chest. It was always so quickly pulled open and pushed shut in the same instant by its owner that it was impossible to tell for certain how much money was in it. Chichikov got down to business at once and, having sharpened his pen, began to write. At that moment the mistress came in.

"A nice box you've got there, my dear," she said, sitting herself down next to him. "I expect you bought it in Moscow?"

"Yes, Moscow," Chichikov replied, continuing to write.

"I knew it: always good workmanship there. Two years ago my sister brought some warm children's boots from there: such sturdy goods, they're still wearing them. Oh, look at all the stamped paper you've got here!" she went on, peeking into his chest. And there was indeed no small amount of stamped paper there. "You ought to give me one sheet at least! I'm so short of it; if a petition happens to need filing in court, there's nothing to write it on."

Chichikov explained to her that this was the wrong kind of paper, that it was for drawing up deeds, not for petitions. However, to quiet her down he gave her some sheets worth a rouble. Having written the letter, he gave it to her to sign and asked for a little list of the muzhiks. It turned out that the lady landowner did not keep any records or lists, but knew almost everyone by heart; he straightaway had her dictate them to him. Some of the peasants amazed him a bit with their last names, and still more with their nicknames, so that each time, on hearing one, he would pause first and only then begin to write. He was especially struck by a certain Pyotr Saveliev Disrespect-Trough, so that he could not help saying: "My, that's a long one!" Another had "Cow's Brick" hitched to his name, still another turned out to be simply: Wheel, Ivan. As he finished writing, he drew in air slightly through his nose and sensed the enticing smell of something hot in butter.

"I humbly invite you to have a bite to eat," said the mistress.

Chichikov turned around and saw the table already laden with mushrooms, pirozhki, savory dumplings, cheesecakes, pancakes thick and thin, open pies with all kinds of fillings: onion filling, poppy seed filling, cottage cheese filling, smelt filling, and who knows what else.

"Short-crust pie with eggs!" said the mistress.

Chichikov moved closer to the short-crust pie with eggs and, having straightaway eaten slightly more than half of it, praised it. And in fact the pie was tasty in itself, but after all the fussing and tricks with the old woman it seemed tastier still.

"And some pancakes?" said the mistress.

In response to which, Chichikov rolled three pancakes up together, dipped them in melted butter, sent them into his mouth, and wiped his fingers with a napkin. After repeating this three times or so, he asked the mistress to order his britzka harnessed. Nastasya Petrovna straightaway sent Fetinya, at the same time ordering her to bring more hot pancakes.

"Your pancakes, dearie, are very tasty," said Chichikov, going for the hot ones just brought in.

"Yes, my cook makes them well," said the mistress, "but the trouble is that the harvest was bad, and the flour turned out so uncommendable . . . But, my dear, why are you in such a rush?" she said, seeing that Chichikov had taken his peaked cap in his hand, "the britzka hasn't been harnessed yet."

"They'll harness it, dearie, they'll harness it. We harness fast."

"So, now, please don't forget about the contracts."

"I won't forget, I won't forget," Chichikov said as he went out to the front hall.

"And do you buy lard?" the mistress said, following after him.

"Why shouldn't I? I'll buy it, only later."

"Around Christmastide I'll have lard."

"We'll buy it, we'll buy it, we'll buy everything, we'll buy the lard, too."

"Maybe you'll need bird feathers. I'll have bird feathers by St. Philip's fast."[8]

"Very good, very good," said Chichikov.

"There, you see, my dear, your britzka still isn't ready," the mistress said, when they came out to the porch.

"It will be, it will be. Only tell me how to get to the main road."

"How shall I do that?" said the mistress. "It's hard to explain, there's a lot of turns; unless I give you a young girl to take you there. I expect you've got room on the box where she could sit."

"Sure thing."

"Why don't I give you a girl then; she knows the way – only watch out! don't carry her off, one of mine already got carried off by some merchants."

Chichikov promised her that he would not carry the girl off, and Korobochka, reassured, started inspecting everything that was in her yard; she fixed her eyes on the housekeeper, who was carrying a wooden stoup full of honey from the larder, on a muzhik who appeared in the gateway, and gradually settled herself back wholly into her life of management. But why occupy ourselves for so long with Korobochka? Mrs. Korobochka, Mrs. Manilov, the life of management, or of non-management – pass them by! Otherwise – marvelous is the world's makeup – the merry will turn melancholy in a trice, if you stand a long time before it, and then God knows what may enter your head. Perhaps you will even start thinking: come now, does Korobochka indeed stand so low on the endless ladder of human perfection? Is there indeed so great an abyss separating her from her sister, inaccessibly fenced off behind the walls of her aristocratic house with its fragrant cast-iron stairways, shining brass, mahogany and carpets, who yawns over an unfinished book while waiting for a witty society visit, which will give her a field on which to display her sparkling intelligence and pronounce thoughts learned by rote, thoughts which, following the law of fashion, occupy the town for a whole week, thoughts not of what is going on in her house or on her estates, confused and disorderly thanks to her ignorance of management, but of what political upheaval is brewing in France, of what direction fashionable Catholicism has taken. But pass by, pass by! why talk of that? But why, then, in the midst of unthinking, merry, carefree moments does another wondrous stream rush by of itself: the laughter has not yet had time to leave your face completely, yet you are already different among the same people and your face is already lit by a different light . . .

"Ah, here's the britzka, here's the britzka!" Chichikov cried out, seeing his britzka drive up at last. "You dolt, what have you been pottering with so long? It must be your yesterday's vapors haven't aired out yet."

To this Selifan made no reply.

"Good-bye, dearie! And, say, where's your girl?"

"Hey, Pelageya!" the lady landowner said to a girl of about eleven who was standing by the porch, in a dress of homespun blue linen and with bare legs which from a distance might have been taken for boots, so caked they were with fresh mud. "Show the master the road."

Selifan helped the girl climb up on the box, who, placing one foot on the master's step, first dirtied it with mud, and only then clambered to the top and settled herself beside him. After her, Chichikov himself placed his foot on the step and, tilting the britzka on the right side, because he was a bit of a load, finally settled himself, saying:

"Ah! that's good now! Bye-bye, dearie!"

The horses started off.

Selifan was stern all the way and at the same time very attentive to his business, which always happened with him either after he had been found at fault in something, or after he had been drunk. The horses were surprisingly well-groomed. The collar of one of them, hitherto always torn, so that the oakum kept coming out from under the leather, had been skilfully stitched up. He kept silent all the way, only cracking his whip, and not addressing any edifying speeches to his horses, though the dapple-gray would, of course, have liked to hear something admonitory, because at such times the reins lay somehow lazily in the loquacious driver's hands, and the whip wandered over their backs only for the sake of form. But this time from the sullen lips there came only monotonously unpleasant exclamations: "Come on, come on, mooncalf! wake up! wake up!" and nothing more. Even the bay and Assessor were displeased, not once hearing either "my gentles" or "honored friends." The dapple-gray felt most disagreeable strokes on his broad and full parts. "Just look how he's got himself going!" he thought, twitching his ears slightly. "Don't worry, he knows where to hit! He won't whip right on the back, he goes and chooses a tenderer spot: catches the ears, or flicks you under the belly."

"To the right, is it?" With this dry question Selifan turned to the girl sitting next to him, and pointed with his whip to a rain-blackened road between bright green, freshened fields.

"No, no, I'll show you," the girl replied.

"Where, then?" said Selifan, when they came nearer.

"There's where," replied the girl, pointing with her hand.

"Eh, you!" said Selifan. "But that is to the right: she doesn't know right from left!"

Although the day was very fine, the earth had turned so much to mud that the wheels of the britzka, picking it up, soon became covered with it as with thick felt, which made the carriage considerably heavier; besides, the soil was clayey and extraordinarily tenacious. The one and the other were the reason why they could not get off the back roads before noon. Without the girl it would have been hard to do even that, because the roads went crawling in all directions like caught crayfish dumped out of a sack, and Selifan would have rambled about through no fault of his own.

Soon the girl pointed her hand at a building blackening in the distance, saying:

"There's the high road."

"And the building?" asked Selifan.

"A tavern," said the girl.

"Well, now we can get along by ourselves," said Selifan, "so home you go."

He stopped and helped her get down, saying through his teeth: "Ugh, you blacklegs!"

Chichikov gave her a copper, and she trudged off home-wards, pleased enough that she had gotten to ride on the box.

CHAPTER FOUR

DRIVING UP TO the tavern, Chichikov ordered a stop for two reasons. On the one hand, so that the horses could rest, and on the other hand, so that he could have a little snack and fortify himself. The author must admit that he is quite envious of the appetite and stomach of this sort of people. To him those gentlemen of the grand sort mean decidedly nothing, who live in Petersburg or Moscow, spend their time pondering what they would like to eat the next day and what dinner to devise for the day after, and who will not partake of that dinner without first sending a pill into their mouths; who swallow oysters, sea spiders, and other marvels, and then set off for Karlsbad or the Caucasus.[9] No, those gentlemen have never aroused envy in him. But gentlemen of the middling sort, those who order ham at one station, suckling pig at another, a hunk of sturgeon or some baked sausage with onions at a third, and then sit down to table as if nothing had happened, whenever you like, and a sterlet soup with burbot and soft roe hisses and gurgles between their teeth, accompanied by a tart or pie with catfish tails, so that even a vicarious appetite is piqued – now, these gentlemen indeed enjoy an enviable gift from heaven! More than one gentleman of the grand sort would instantly sacrifice half of his peasant souls and half of his estates, mortgaged and unmort-gaged, with all improvements on a foreign or Russian footing, only so as to have a stomach such as a gentleman of the middling sort has; but the trouble is that no amount of money, no estates with or without improvements, can buy such a stomach as the gentleman of the middling sort happens to have.

The weathered wooden tavern received Chichikov under its narrow, hospitable porch roof on turned wooden posts, resembling old church candlestands. The tavern was rather like a Russian peasant cottage, on a somewhat bigger scale. Carved lacy cornices of fresh wood around the windows and under the eaves stood out in sharp and vivid patches against its dark walls; pots of flowers were painted on the shutters.

Having gone up the narrow wooden steps into the wide front hall, he met a door creaking open and a fat old woman in motley chintzes, who said: "This way, please!" Inside he found all the old friends that everyone finds in little wooden taverns, such as have been built in no small number along the roadsides – namely: a hoary samovar, smoothly scrubbed pinewood walls, a triangular corner cupboard with teapots and cups, gilded porcelain Easter eggs hanging on blue and red ribbons in front of icons, a recently littered cat, a mirror that reflected four eyes instead of two and some sort of pancake instead of a face; finally, bunches of aromatic herbs and cloves stuck around the icons, dried up to such a degree that whoever tried to smell them only sneezed and nothing more.

"Do you have suckling pig?" With this question Chichikov turned to the woman standing there.

"We do."

"With horseradish and sour cream?"

"With horseradish and sour cream."

"Bring it here."

The old woman went poking about and brought a plate, a napkin so starched that it stuck out like dry bark, then a knife, thin-bladed as a penknife, with a yellowed bone handle, a fork with two prongs, and a saltcellar that simply would not stand upright on the table.

Our hero, as usual, entered into conversation with her at once and inquired whether she kept the tavern herself, or was there a proprietor, and how much income it brought, and whether their sons lived with them, and was the eldest son a bachelor or a married man, and what sort of wife he had taken, with a big dowry or not, and was the father-in-law pleased, and was he not angry that he had received too few presents at the wedding – in short, he skipped nothing. It goes without saying that he was curious to find out what landowners there were in the vicinity, and found out that there were all sorts of land-owners: Blokhin, Pochitaev, Mylnoy, Cheprakov the colonel, Sobakevich. "Ah! You know Sobakevich?" he asked, and straightaway heard that the old woman knew not only Soba-kevich, but also Manilov, and that Manilov was a bit more refeened than Sobakevich: he orders a chicken boiled at once, and also asks for veal; if there is lamb's liver, he also asks for lamb's liver, and just tries a little of everything, while Sobake-vich asks for some one thing, but then eats all of it, and will even demand seconds for the same price.

As he was talking in this way, and dining on suckling pig, of which only one last piece now remained, there came a rattle of wheels from a carriage driving up. Peeking out the window, he saw a light britzka, harnessed to a troika of fine horses, standing in front of the tavern. Two men were getting out of it. One was tall and fair-haired, the other a little shorter and dark-haired. The fair-haired one was wearing a navy blue Hungar-ian jacket, the dark-haired one simply a striped quilted smock. In the distance another wretched carriage was dragging along, empty, drawn by a four-in-hand of shaggy horses with torn collars and rope harness. The fair-haired one went up the steps at once, while the dark-haired one stayed behind and felt around for something in the britzka, talking all the while with a servant and at the same time waving to the carriage coming after them. His voice seemed to Chichikov as if it were slightly familiar. While he was studying him, the fair-haired one had already managed to feel his way to the door and open it. He was a tall man with a lean, or what is known as wasted, face, and a red little mustache. From his tanned face one could deduce that he knew what smoke was – if not of the battlefield, then at least of tobacco. He bowed politely to Chichikov, to which the latter responded in kind. In the course of a few minutes they would probably have struck up a conversation and come to know each other well, because a start had already been made, and almost at one and the same time they had expressed their satisfaction that the dust of the road had been completely laid by yesterday's rain and the driving was now both cool and agreeable, when his dark-haired comrade entered, flinging his peaked cap from his head onto the table, and dashingly ruffling his thick black hair. Of average height and rather well-built, he was a dashing fellow with full, ruddy cheeks, teeth white as snow, and whiskers black as pitch. He was fresh as milk and roses; health, it seemed, was simply bursting from his face.

"Aha!" he cried out suddenly, spreading both arms at the sight of Chichikov. "What brings you here?"

Chichikov recognized Nozdryov, the very one with whom he had dined at the prosecutor's and who within a few minutes had got on such an intimate footing with him that he had even begun to address him familiarly, though, incidentally, he had given no occasion for it on his side.

"Where have you been?" Nozdryov said, going on without waiting for an answer: "And I, brother, am coming from the fair. Congratulate me, I blew my whole wad! Would you believe it, never in my life have I blown so much. I even drove here with hired horses! Here, look out the window on purpose!" Whereupon he bent Chichikov's head down himself so that he almost bumped it against the window frame. "See, what trash! They barely dragged themselves here, curse them; I had to climb into his britzka." As he said this, Nozdryov pointed his finger at his comrade. "And you're not acquainted yet? My in-law, Mizhuev! We've been talking about you all morning. 'Well, just watch,' I said, 'we're going to run into Chichikov.' Well, brother, if only you knew how much I blew! Would you believe it, I didn't just dump my four trotters – everything went. There's neither chain nor watch left on me . . . " Chichikov glanced and saw that there was indeed neither chain nor watch left on him. It even seemed to him that his side-whiskers on one side were smaller and not as thick as on the other. "If only I had just twenty roubles in my pocket," Nozdryov went on, "precisely no more than twenty, I'd get everything back, I mean, on top of getting everything back, as I'm an honest man, I'd put thirty thousand in my wallet straight off."

"You were saying the same thing then, however," the fair-haired one responded, "but when I gave you fifty roubles, you lost it at once."

"I wouldn't have lost it! By God, I wouldn't have lost it! If I hadn't done a stupid thing myself, I really wouldn't have lost it. If I hadn't bluffed on that cursed seven after the paroli, I could have broken the bank."

"You didn't break it, however," said the fair-haired one.

"I didn't because I bluffed at the wrong time. And you think your major is a good player?"

"Good or not, however, he beat you."

"Eh, who cares!" said Nozdryov. "I could beat him, too, that way! No, let him try doubling, then I'll see, then I'll see what kind of player he is! But still, brother Chichikov, how we caroused those first days! True, the fair was an excellent one. The merchants themselves said there had never been such a gathering. Everything we brought from my estate was sold at the most profitable price. Eh, brother, how we caroused! Even now, when I remember . . . devil take it! I mean, what a pity you weren't there. Imagine, a dragoon regiment was stationed two miles from town. Would you believe it, the officers, all there were of them, forty men just of officers alone, came to town; and, brother, how we started drinking . . . Staff Captain Potseluev . . . what a nice one he is! a mustache, brother, like this! Bordeaux he calls simply brewdeaux. 'Bring us some of that brewdeaux, brother!' he says. Lieutenant

Kuvshinnikov... Ah, brother, what a sweetheart! Him, now, him we can call a carouser by all the rules. We were always together. What wine Ponomaryov brought out for us! You should know that he's a crook and one oughtn't to buy anything in his shop: he mixes all sorts of trash with his wine – sandalwood, burnt cork, he even rubs red elderberry into it, the scoundrel; but to make up for that, if he does go and fetch some bottle from his far-off little room, the special room, he calls it – well, brother, then you're simply in the empyrean. We had such a champagne – what's the governor's next to that? mere kvass. Imagine, not clicquot, but some sort of clicquot-matradura, meaning double clicquot.[10] And he also brought out one little bottle of a French wine called 'bonbon.' Bouquet? – rosebuds and whatever else you like. Oh, did we carouse!... After us some prince arrived, sent to a shop for champagne, there wasn't a bottle left in the whole town, the officers drank it all. Would you believe it, I alone, in the course of one dinner, drank seventeen bottles of champagne!"

"No, you couldn't drink seventeen bottles," observed the fair-haired one.

"As I'm an honest man, I say I did," replied Nozdryov.

"You can say whatever you like, but I'm telling you that you couldn't drink even ten."

"Well, let's make a bet on it!"

"Why bet on it?"

"Well, then stake that gun you bought in town."

"I don't want to."

"Well, go on, chance it!"

"I don't want to chance it."

"Right, you'd be without a gun, just as you're without a hat. Eh, brother Chichikov, I mean, how sorry I was that you weren't there. I know you'd never part from Lieutenant Kuvshinnikov. How well you'd get along together! A far cry from the prosecutor and all the provincial skinflints in our town, who tremble over every kopeck. That one, brother, will sit down to quinze, or faro, or anything you like. Eh, Chichikov, would it have cost you so much to come? Really, aren't you a little pig after that, you cattle breeder! Kiss me, dear heart, on my life I do love you! Mizhuev, look how fate has brought us together: what is he to me or I to him? He came from God knows where, and I also live here . . . And there were so many carriages, brother, and all that *en gros*. I spun the wheel of fortune: won two jars of pomade, a porcelain cup, and a guitar; then I staked again, spun it, and lost, confound it, six roubles on top of that. And what a philanderer Kuvshinnikov is, if you only knew! He and I went to nearly all the balls. There was one girl there so decked out, all ruche and truche and devil knows what not . . . I just thought to myself: 'Devil take it!' But Kuvshinnikov, I mean, he's such a rascal, he sat himself down next to her and started getting at her with all these compliments in the French language . . . Would you believe it, he didn't pass by the simple wenches either. That's what he calls 'going strawberry-ing.' And the abundance of wonderful fish and *balyks*![11] I brought one with me; it's a good thing I thought of buying it while I still had money. Where are you going now?"

"Oh, to see a certain little fellow."

"Well, forget your little fellow! let's go to my place!"

"No, I can't, it's to close a deal."

"Well, so it's a deal now! What else will you think up! Ah, you Opodealdoc Ivanovich!"[12]

"A deal, yes, and quite an important one at that."

"I bet you're lying! Well, so tell me, who are you going to see?"

"Well, it's Sobakevich."

Here Nozdryov guffawed with that ringing laughter into which only a fresh, healthy man can dissolve, showing all his teeth, white as sugar, to the last one; his cheeks quiver and shake, and his neighbor, two doors away, in the third room, jumps up from his sleep, goggling his eyes, and saying: "Eh, how he carries on!"

"What's so funny?" said Chichikov, somewhat displeased by this laughter.

But Nozdryov went on guffawing at the top of his lungs, all the while saying:

"Oh, spare me, really, I'll split my sides!"

"There's nothing funny: I gave him my word," said Chichikov.

"But you'll be sorry you were ever born when you get there, he's a real jew-eater! I know your character, you'll be cruelly disconcerted if you hope to find a little game of faro there and a good bottle of some bonbon. Listen, brother: to the devil with Sobakevich, let's go to my place! I'll treat you to such a *balyk*! Ponomaryov, that rascal, was bowing and scraping so: 'For you alone,' he said. 'Go look around the whole fair, you won't find another like it.' A terrible rogue, though. I told him so to his face: 'You and our tax farmer,' I said, 'are top-notch crooks!' He laughed, the rascal, stroking his beard. Kuvshinnikov and I had lunch in his shop every day. Ah, brother, I forgot to tell you: I know you won't leave me alone now, but I won't let you have it even for ten thousand, I'm telling you beforehand. Hey, Porfiry!" Going to the window, he shouted to his man, who was holding a knife in one hand and in the other a crust of bread and a piece of *balyk*, which he had luckily cut off in passing as he was getting something from the britzka. "Hey, Porfiry," Nozdryov shouted, "go and fetch the puppy! What a puppy!" he went on, turning to Chichikov. "A stolen one, the owner wouldn't have parted with it even for my own head. I offered him the chestnut mare, remember, the one I took in trade from Khvostyrev . . . " Chichikov, however, had never in his born days seen either the chestnut mare or Khvostyrev.

"Master! wouldn't you like a snack?" the old woman said, coming up to him just then.

"Nothing. Eh, brother, how we caroused! As a matter of fact, bring me a glass of vodka. What kind have you got?"

"Aniseed," replied the old woman.

"Make it aniseed, then," said Nozdryov.

"Bring me a glass, too," said the fair-haired one.

"In the theater one actress sang so well, the scamp, just like a canary! Kuvshinnikov is sitting next to me. 'Hey, brother,' he says, 'how about a little strawberrying!' Of booths alone I think there must have been fifty. Fenardi[13] spun around like a windmill for four hours." Here he received a glass from the hands of the old woman, who gave him a low bow for it. "Ah, bring him here!" he shouted, seeing Porfiry come in with the puppy. Porfiry was dressed just like his master, in a sort of striped smock of quilted cotton, but somewhat greasier.

"Bring him, put him here on the floor!"

Porfiry placed the puppy on the floor, who, splaying his four paws, sniffed the ground.

"There's the puppy!" said Nozdryov, taking him by the back and lifting him up with his hand. The puppy let out a rather pitiful howl.

"You, however, did not do as I told you," said Nozdryov, addressing Porfiry and carefully examining the puppy's belly, "you didn't even think of combing him out?"

"No, I did comb him out."

"Why are there fleas, then?"

"I'm not able to say. Possibly they crawled over somehow from the britzka."

"Lies, lies, you never even dreamed of combing him; I think, fool, that you even added some of your own. Look here, Chichikov, look, what ears, go ahead and feel them."

"But why, I can see as it is: a good breed!" replied Chichikov.

"No, go ahead, feel his ears on purpose!"

Chichikov, to please him, felt the ears, adding:

"Yes, he'll make a fine dog."

"And the nose, did you feel how cold it is? Hold your hand to it."

Not wishing to offend him, Chichikov also held his hand to the nose, saying:

"Keen scent."

"A genuine bulldog," Nozdryov went on. "I confess, I've long wanted to get my paws on a bulldog. Here, Porfiry, take him!"

Porfiry took the puppy under the belly and carried him out to the britzka.

"Listen, Chichikov, you absolutely must come to my place now, it's just three miles away, we'll be there in a wink, and then, if you please, you can also go to Sobakevich."

"Well, why not?" Chichikov thought to himself. "I may in fact go to Nozdryov's. He's no worse than the rest, a man like any other, and what's more he just gambled his money away. He's game for anything, as one can see, which means one may get something out of him gratis."

"All right, let's go," he said, "but, mind you, no delays, my time is precious."

"Well, dear heart, that's more like it! That's really nice, wait, I'm going to kiss you for that." Here Chichikov and Nozdryov kissed each other. "Fine, then: we'll drive off, the three of us!"

"No, thank you very much, you'd better leave me out," said the fair-haired one, "I must get home."

"Trifles, trifles, brother, I won't let you go."

"Really, my wife will be angry; and now, look, you can switch over to his britzka."

"Tut, tut, tut! Don't even think of it."

The fair-haired man was one of those people in whose character there is at first sight a certain obstinacy. Before you can open your mouth, they are already prepared to argue and, it seems, will never agree to anything that is clearly contrary to their way of thinking, will never call a stupid thing smart, and in particular will never agree to dance to another man's tune; but it always ends up that there is a certain softness in their character, that they will agree precisely to what they had rejected, will call a stupid thing smart, and will then go off dancing their best to another man's tune – in short, starts out well, ends in hell.

"Nonsense!" said Nozdryov in response to some representation from the fair-haired one, put the cap on the man's head, and – the fair-haired one followed after them.

"You didn't pay for the vodka, master...," said the old woman.

"Oh, all right, all right, dearie. Listen, in-law! pay her, if you please. I haven't got a kopeck in my pocket."

"How much?" said the in-law.

"Just twenty kopecks, dearie," said the old woman.

"Lies, lies. Give her half that, it's more than enough for her."

"It's a bit short, master," said the old woman, though she took the money gratefully and hastened to run and open the door for them. She suffered no loss, since she had asked four times the price of the vodka.

The travelers took their seats. Chichikov's britzka drove alongside the britzka in which Nozdryov and his in-law were sitting, and therefore the three of them could freely converse with each other on the road. After them, constantly lagging behind, followed Nozdryov's wretched carriage, drawn by the scrawny hired hacks. In it sat Porfiry with the puppy.

As the conversation that the wayfarers conducted with each other is of no great interest for the reader, we shall do better if we tell something about Nozdryov himself, who will perhaps have occasion to play by no means the last role in our poem.

The person of Nozdryov, surely, is already somewhat familiar to the reader. Everyone has met not a few such people. They are known as rollicksome fellows, have the reputation of boon companions already in childhood and at school, and for all that they sometimes get quite painfully beaten. In their faces one always sees something open, direct, daring. They strike up an acquaintance quickly, and before you can turn around they are already on personal terms with you. They embark on friendship, as it seems, forever; but it almost always happens that the new friend will pick a fight with them that same evening at a friendly party. They are always big talkers, revelers, daredevils, conspicuous folk. Nozdryov at thirty-five was exactly the same as he had been at eighteen and twenty: a great carouser. His marriage had not changed him a bit, especially as his wife soon departed for the next world, leaving him two youngsters whom he decidedly did not need. The children, however, were looked after by a pretty nanny. He could never sit for longer than a day at home. For several dozen miles around, his sharp nose could scent where there was a fair with all sorts of gatherings and balls; in the twinkling of an eye he was already there, arguing, causing a commotion at the green table, for, like all his kind, he had a passion for a little game of cards. He played his little game of cards, as we saw in the first chapter, not quite sinlessly and cleanly, knowing many different manipulations and other subtleties, and therefore the game very often ended with a game of another sort: either he would get booted about, or else a manipulation would be performed on his thick and very fine side-whiskers, so that he sometimes came home with side-whiskers only on one side, and rather thin ones at that. Yet his healthy and full cheeks were so well fashioned and contained in themselves so much generative force that his whiskers would soon grow again even better than before. And – what was strangest of all, what can happen only in Russia – not long afterwards he would again meet the friends who had thrashed him, and they would meet as if nothing had happened, and it was, as they say, fine with him, and fine with them.

Nozdryov was in a certain respect a storied man. Not one gathering he attended went by without some story. Some sort of story inevitably occurred: either he was taken under the arm and removed from the hall by gendarmes, or his own friends were obliged to throw him out. And if that did not happen, then something else did, of a sort that never happened to others: either he would get so potted at the buffet that he could do nothing but laugh, or he would pour out such a wicked pack of lies that he would finally become ashamed himself. And he lied absolutely without any need: he would suddenly tell about a horse he had of some blue or pink color, or similar nonsense, so that his listeners would all finally walk away, saying: "Well, brother, it seems you've started talking through your hat." There exist people who have something of a passion for doing dirt to their neighbor, sometimes without any reason. One, for example, even a man of a certain rank, with a noble appearance, with a star on his breast, will press your hands, will get to talking with you about profound subjects that invite reflection, and then, lo and behold, right there, before your very eyes, he does you dirt. And he does you dirt like a mere collegiate registrar, not at all like a man with a star on his breast who talks about subjects that invite reflection, so that you just stand there marveling, shrugging your shoulders, and nothing more. Nozdryov, too, had this strange passion. The closer you got with him, the sooner he would muck things up for you: spread some cock-and-bull story, than which it would be hard to invent a stupider, thwart a wedding or a business deal, and yet by no means consider himself your enemy; on the contrary, if chance should bring him together with you again, he would again treat you in a friendly way, and even say: "What a scoundrel you are, you never come to see me." Nozdryov was in many respects a many-sided man, that is, a Jack-of-all-trades. In the same moment he would offer to go with you wherever you please, even to the ends of the earth, join in any undertaking you like, trade whatever there was for whatever you like. A gun, a dog, a horse – everything was up for trade, but not at all with a view to gain: it came simply from some irrepressible briskness and friskiness of character. If he was lucky enough to come across a simpleton at a fair and beat him at cards, he would buy up a heap of all that had first caught his eye in the shops: yokes, scented candles, kerchiefs for the nanny, a colt, raisins, a silver washbasin, Holland linen, cake flour, tobacco, pistols, herring, paintings, a grindstone, crockery, boots, faïence dishes – for all the money he had. However, it rarely happened that these things got brought home; almost the same day it would all be gambled away to another, luckier player, sometimes even with the addition of his own pipe, tobacco pouch and mouthpiece included, or another time with his entire four-in-hand, everything included: coach and coachman – so that the master himself had to set out in a short frock coat or a striped smock to look for some friend and use his carriage. Such was Nozdryov! People may call him a trite character, they may say that Nozdryov is no more. Alas! mistaken will they be who say so. It will be long before Nozdryov passes from this world. He is among us everywhere, and is perhaps only wearing a different caftan; but people are light-mindedly unperceptive, and a man in a different caftan seems to them a different man.

Meanwhile, the three carriages had already driven up to the porch of Nozdryov's house. No preparations had been made in the house for receiving them. In the middle of the dining room stood wooden trestles, and two muzhiks were standing on them, whitewashing the walls, intoning some endless song; the floor was all spattered with whitewash. Nozdryov straightaway ordered the muzhiks and trestles out and ran to the other room to give commands. The guests heard him ordering dinner from the cook; realizing this, Chichikov, who was already beginning to feel slightly hungry, understood that they would not sit down to table before five o'clock. Nozdryov, returning to his guests, took them around to look at everything there was to be seen on his estate, and in a little over two hours had shown them decidedly everything, so that there was nothing else left to show. First of all they went to look at the stables, where they saw two mares, one a dapple-gray, the other a light chestnut, then a bay stallion, a homely sight, but for whom Nozdryov swore by God he had paid ten thousand.

"You didn't pay ten thousand for him," the in-law observed. "He's not worth even one."

"By God, I paid ten thousand," said Nozdryov.

"You can swear by God all you want," the in-law replied.

"Well, if you want, we can bet on it!" said Nozdryov.

The in-law did not want to bet.

Then Nozdryov showed them the empty stalls where there had also been good horses once. In the same stable they saw a billy goat, which, according to an old belief, it was considered necessary to keep with horses, and who seemed to be getting along well with them, strolling under their bellies as if he was right at home. Then Nozdryov took them to see a wolf cub that he kept tied up. "There's the wolf cub!" he said. "I feed him raw meat on purpose. I want to make an utter beast of him!" They went to look at the pond, in which, according to Nozdryov's words, there lived fish so big that it was hard for two men to pull one out, which the relative, however, did not fail to doubt. "I'm going to show you, Chichikov," said Nozdryov, "a most excellent pair of dogs: the strength of their hunkers simply fills one with amazement, their snouts are like needles!" – and he led them to a very prettily constructed little house, surrounded by a big yard fenced on all sides. Having entered the yard, they saw there all sorts of dogs, long-haired and short-haired, of every possible color and coat: tawny, black and tan, tan-spotted, tawny-spotted, red-spotted, black-eared, gray-eared . . . There were all sorts of names, all sorts of imperatives: Shoot, Scold, Flutter, Fire, Fop, Boast, Roast, Coast, Arrow, Swallow, Prize, Patroness. Nozdryov was amid them just like a father amid his family; they all shot up their tails, which dog fanciers call sweeps, flew straight to meet the guests, and began to greet them. A good ten of them put their paws on Nozdryov's shoulders. Scold displayed the same friendliness towards Chichikov and, getting up on his hind legs, licked him right on the lips with his tongue, so that Chichikov straightaway spat. They looked at the dogs that filled one with amazement with the strength of their hunkers – fine dogs they were. Then they went to look at a Crimean bitch that was now blind and, according to Nozdryov, would soon die, but some two years ago had been a very fine bitch; they looked at the bitch as well – the bitch was, indeed, blind. Then they went to look at a water mill with a missing flutterer, in which the upper millstone is set and turns rapidly on a spindle – "flutters," in the wonderful expression of the Russian muzhik.

"And soon we'll be coming to the smithy!" said Nozdryov.

Going on a bit further, they indeed saw a smithy; and they looked at the smithy as well.

"In this field here," said Nozdryov, pointing his finger at the field, "it's so thick with hares you can't see the ground; I myself caught one by the hind legs with my bare hands."

"No, you couldn't catch a hare with your bare hands!" observed the in-law.

"But I did catch one, I caught one on purpose!" replied Nozdryov. "Now," he went on, turning to Chichikov, "I'll take you for a look at the boundary where my land ends."

Nozdryov led his guests across the field, which in many places consisted of tussocks. The guests had to make their way between fallow land and ploughed fields. Chichikov was beginning to get tired. In many places water squeezed out from under their feet, so low-lying the place was. At first they were careful and stepped cautiously, but then, seeing that it served no purpose, they plodded straight on without choosing between greater and lesser mud. Having gone a considerable distance, they indeed saw a boundary, which consisted of a wooden post and a narrow ditch.

"There's the boundary!" said Nozdryov. "Everything you see on this side of it is all mine, and even on that side, all that forest bluing over there, and all that's beyond the forest, is all mine."

"And since when is that forest yours?" asked the in-law. "Did you buy it recently? It never used to be yours."

"Yes, I bought it recently," replied Nozdryov.

"When did you manage to buy it so quickly?"

"Well, so I bought it two days ago, and paid a lot for it, too, devil take it."

"But you were at the fair then."

"Eh, you Sophron!¹⁴ Can't a man be at a fair and buy land at the same time? So, I was at the fair, and my steward here bought it without me!"

"Well, the steward maybe!" said the in-law, but here, too, he was doubtful and shook his head.

The guests returned over the same nasty route to the house. Nozdryov led them to his study, in which, however, there was no trace to be seen of what is usually found in studies, that is, books or papers; there hung only sabers and two guns – one worth three hundred and the other eight hundred roubles. The in-law, having examined them, merely shook his head. Then they were shown some Turkish daggers, on one of which there had been mistakenly engraved: *Savely Sibiryakov, Cutler*. After that, a barrel organ appeared before the guests. Nozdryov straightaway ground something out for them. The barrel organ played not unpleasantly, but something seemed to have happened inside it, for the mazurka ended with the song "Malbrough Went Off to War,"¹⁵ and "Malbrough Went Off to War" was unexpectedly concluded by some long-familiar waltz. Nozdryov had long stopped grinding, but there was one very perky reed in the organ that simply refused to quiet down, and for some time afterwards went on tooting all by itself. Then pipes appeared – of wood, clay, meerschaum, broken-in and un-broken-in, covered with chamois and not covered, a chibouk with an amber mouthpiece recently won at cards, a tobacco pouch embroidered by some countess who had fallen head over heels in love with him somewhere at a posting station, whose hands, according to him, were most subdiminally superflu – a phrase that for him probably meant the peak of perfection. After a snack of *balyk*, they sat down to eat at around five o'clock. Dinner, obviously, did not constitute the main thing in Nozdryov's life; the dishes did not play a big role: some were burnt, some were totally underdone. It was obvious that the cook was guided more by some sort of inspiration and put in the first thing he laid his hands on: if pepper was standing there, he poured in pepper; if there happened to be cabbage, he stuck in cabbage; he threw in milk, ham, peas – in short, slapdash, as long as it was hot, and some sort of taste was bound to result. Instead, Nozdryov applied himself to the wines: the soup had not yet been served, and he had already poured his guests a big glass of port, and another of ho-sauterne,[16] because in provincial and district capitals plain sauterne is not to be found. Then Nozdryov called for a bottle of madeira, than which no field marshal ever tasted better. The madeira, indeed, even burned the mouth, for the merchants, knowing the taste of landowners who like fine madeira, doctored it unmercifully with rum, and sometimes even poured aqua regia into it, in hopes that the Russian stomach could endure anything. Then Nozdryov called for some special bottle which, according to him, was burgognon and champagnon in one. He poured very zealously into both glasses, to his right and to his left, for his in-law and for Chichikov. Chichikov noticed, however, somehow by the way, that he did not pour much for himself. This put him on his guard, and as soon as Nozdryov got somehow distracted, talking or pouring for his in-law, he would at once empty his glass onto his plate. After a short while, a rowanberry liqueur was brought to the table, which, according to Nozdryov, tasted altogether like cream, but which, amazingly, gave off a potent smell of moonshine. They then drank some sort of cordial, which had a name that was even difficult to remember, and which the host himself next time called by some different name. Dinner had long been over, and the wines had all been tried, but the guests were still sitting at the table. Chichikov by no means wanted to begin talking with Nozdryov about the main subject in the in-law's presence. After all, the in-law was a third party, and the subject called for private and friendly conversation. However, the in-law could hardly be a dangerous man, because he seemed to have gotten fairly loaded, and kept nodding as he sat in his chair. Noticing himself that he was in rather unreliable condition, he finally started asking to go home, but in such a lazy and languid voice as though he were, as the Russian saying goes, pulling a collar on a horse with a pair of pliers.

"Tut, tut! I won't let you!" said Nozdryov.

"No, don't offend me, my friend, I really must go," the in-law said, "you'll offend me very much."

"Trifles, trifles! We'll put up a little bank this very minute."

"No, you put it up by yourself, brother, I can't, my wife will be very upset, really, I must tell her about the fair. I must, brother, really, I must give her that pleasure. No, don't keep me."

"Well, that wife of yours can go to . . . ! You've indeed got big doings to do together!"

"No, brother! She's so respectable and faithful! She does me such services . . . believe me, it brings tears to my eyes. No, don't keep me; as an honest man, I must go. I assure you of it with a clean conscience."

"Let him go, what's the good of him!" Chichikov said softly to Nozdryov.

"Right you are!" said Nozdryov. "Damn me, how I hate these slobberers!" and he added aloud: "Well, devil take you, go and sit by your wife's skirts, you foozle!"

"No, brother, don't call me a foozle," the in-law replied. "I owe her my life. She's so kind, really, so sweet, she shows me such tenderness . . . it moves me to tears; she'll ask what I saw at the fair, I must tell her everything, really, she's so sweet."

"Well, go then, tell her your nonsense! Here's your cap."

"No, brother, you shouldn't talk like that about her, one might say you're offending me myself, she's so sweet."

"Well, then quickly take yourself to her."

"Yes, brother, I'm going, forgive me, I can't stay. I'd love to, but I can't."

The in-law went on repeating his apologies for a good while, not noticing that he had long been sitting in his britzka, had long since gone out the gates, and had long had nothing before him but empty fields. It must be supposed that his wife did not hear many details about the fair.

"What trash!" Nozdryov said, standing before the window and watching the departing carriage. "Look at him dragging along! The outrunner's not a bad horse, I've been wanting to hook him for a long time. But it's impossible to deal with the man. A foozle, simply a foozle."

Thereupon they went to the other room. Porfiry brought candles, and Chichikov noticed that a pack of cards had appeared in his host's hands as if from nowhere.

"And now, brother," Nozdryov said, squeezing the sides of the pack with his fingers and bending it slightly, so that the wrapper cracked and popped off. "So, just to while away the time, I'll put up a bank of three hundred roubles!"

But Chichikov pretended he had not heard what it was about, and said, as if suddenly recollecting:

"Ah! so that I don't forget: I have a request to make of you."

"What is it?"

"First give me your word that you'll do it."

"But what's the request?"

"No, first give me your word!"

"All right."

"Word of honor?"

"Word of honor."

"The request is this: you have, I expect, many dead peasants who have not yet been crossed off the census list?"

"Well, what if I have?"

"Transfer them to me, to my name."

"What for?"

"Well, I just need it."

"But what for?"

"Well, I just need it . . . it's my business – in short, I need it."

"Well, you're surely up to something. Confess, what is it?"

"But what could I be up to? With such trifles there's nothing to be up to."

"But what do you need them for?"

"Oh, what a curious one! You want to finger each bit of trash, and sniff it besides."

"But why don't you want to tell me?"

"But what's the good of your knowing? Well, just like that, I've got this fancy."

"So, then: as long as you don't tell me, I won't do it!"

"Well, there, you see, that's dishonest on your part; you gave your word, and now you're backing out."

"Well, that's as you please, I won't do it until you tell me what for."

"What can I possibly tell him?" thought Chichikov, and after a moment's reflection he announced that he needed the dead souls to acquire weight in society, that he was not an owner of big estates, so that in the meantime there would be at least some wretched little souls.

"Lies, lies!" said Nozdryov, not letting him finish. "Lies, brother!"

Chichikov himself noticed that his invention was not very clever, and the pretext was rather weak.

"Well, then I'll tell you more directly," he said, correcting himself, "only please don't let on to anyone. I have a mind to get married; but you must know that the father and mother of the bride are most ambitious people. It's such a mishap, really: I'm sorry I got into it, they absolutely insist that the bridegroom own not less than three hundred souls, and since I'm lacking almost as many as a hundred and fifty souls ..."

"No, lies! lies!" Nozdryov cried again.

"No, this time," said Chichikov, "I did not lie even that much," and with his thumb he indicated the tiniest part of his little finger.

"I'll bet my head you're lying!"

"Now, that is an insult! What indeed do you take me for! Why am I so sure to be lying?"

"As if you didn't know: you're a great crook, allow me to tell you that in all friendliness. If I were your superior, I'd hang you from the nearest tree."

Chichikov was offended by this remark. Any expression the least bit crude or offensive to propriety was disagreeable to him. He even did not like on any occasion to allow himself to be treated with familiarity, excepting only when the person was of very high rank. And therefore he was now thoroughly insulted.

"By God, I'd hang you," Nozdryov repeated, "I tell it to you openly, not to insult you, but simply as a friend."

"There are limits to everything," Chichikov said with dignity. "If you wish to flaunt such talk, go to the barracks," and then he appended: "If you don't want to give them, sell them."

"Sell them! Don't I know you're a scoundrel and are not going to give me much for them?"

"Eh, and you're a good one, too! Look at you! What, are they made of diamonds or something?"

"Well, there it is. I knew you all along."

"For pity's sake, brother, what Jewish instincts you have! You ought simply to give them to me."

"Well, listen, to prove to you that I'm not some kind of niggard, I won't ask anything for them. Buy the stallion from me, and I'll throw them in to boot."

"For pity's sake, what do I need a stallion for?" said Chichikov, amazed indeed at such an offer.

"You ask what for? But I paid ten thousand for him, and I'm giving him to you for four."

"But what do I need with a stallion? I don't keep a stud."

"But listen, you don't understand: I'll take only three thousand from you now, and you can pay me the remaining thousand later."

"But I don't need a stallion, God bless him!"

"Well, then buy the chestnut mare."

"No need for a mare either."

"For the mare and the gray horse, the one I showed you, I'll ask only two thousand from you."

"But I don't need any horses."

"You can sell them, you'll get three times more for them at the nearest fair."

"Then you'd better sell them yourself, if you're so sure you'll make three times more."

"I know I'll make more, but I want you to profit, too."

Chichikov thanked him for his benevolence and declined outright both the gray horse and the chestnut mare.

"Well, then buy some dogs. I'll sell you such a pair, they just give you chills all over! Broad-chested, mustached, coat standing up like bristles. The barrel shape of the ribs is inconceivable to the mind, the paw is all one ball, never touches the ground!"

"But what do I need dogs for? I'm not a hunter."

"But I want you to have dogs. Listen, if you don't want dogs, then buy my barrel organ, it's a wonderful barrel organ; as I'm an honest man, I got it for fifteen hundred myself: I'm giving it to you for nine."

"But what do I need a barrel organ for? Am I some kind of German, to go dragging myself over the roads begging for money?"

"But this is not the sort of barrel organ Germans go around with. This is a real organ; look on purpose: it's all mahogany. Come, I'll show it to you again!" Here Nozdryov, seizing Chichikov by the hand, started pulling him into the other room, and no matter how he dug his heels into the floor and assured him that he already knew this barrel organ, he still had to listen again to precisely how Malbrough went off to war. "If you don't want to stake money, listen, here's what: I'll give you the barrel organ and all the dead souls I have, and you give me your britzka and three hundred roubles on top of it."

"Well, what next! And how am I going to get around?"

"I'll give you another britzka. Let's go to the shed, I'll show it to you! Just repaint it, and it'll be a wonder of a britzka."

"Eh, what a restless demon's got into him!" Chichikov thought to himself, and resolved to be rid at whatever cost of every sort of britzka, barrel organ, and all possible dogs, despite any inconceivable-to-the-mind barrel shape of ribs or ball-likeness of paws.

"But it's britzka, barrel organ, and dead souls all together."

"I don't want to," Chichikov said yet again.

"Why don't you want to?"

"Because I just don't want to, that's all."

"Eh, really, what a man you are! I can see there's no getting along with you like good friends and comrades – what a man, really! . . . It's clear at once that you're a two-faced person!"

"But what am I, a fool, or what? Consider for yourself: why should I acquire something I decidedly do not need?"

"Well, spare me your talk, please. I know you very well now. Such scum, really! Well, listen, want to have a little go at faro? I'll stake all my dead ones, and the barrel organ, too."

"Well, venturing into faro means subjecting oneself to uncertainty," Chichikov said and at the same time glanced out of the corner of his eye at the cards in the man's hands. Both decks seemed very much like false ones to him, and the back design itself looked highly suspicious.

"Why uncertainty?" said Nozdryov. "None whatsoever! If only luck is on your side, you can win a devil of a lot! Look at that! What luck!" he said, starting to slap down cards so as to egg him on. "What luck! what luck! there: it keeps hitting!

There's that damned nine I blew everything on! I felt it was going to sell me out, but then I shut my eyes and thought to myself: 'Devil take you, sell me out and be damned!' "

As Nozdryov was saying this, Porfiry brought in a bottle. But Chichikov refused decidedly either to play or to drink.

"Why don't you want to play?" said Nozdryov.

"Well, because I'm not disposed to. And, truth to tell, I'm not at all an avid gambler."

"Why not?"

Chichikov shrugged his shoulders and added:

"Because I'm not."

"Trash is what you are!"

"No help for it. God made me this way."

"Simply a foozle. I used to think you were at least a somewhat decent man, but you have no notion of manners. It's impossible to talk with you like someone close…no straightforwardness, no sincerity! a perfect Sobakevich, a real scoundrel!"

"But what are you abusing me for? Am I to blame for not gambling? Sell me just the souls, if you're the sort of man who trembles over such nonsense."

"The hairy devil is what you'll get! I was going to, I was just going to make you a gift of them, but now you won't get them! Not even for three kingdoms would I give them to you. You're a cheat, you vile chimney sweep! From now on I don't want to have anything to do with you. Porfiry, go and tell the stable boy not to give any oats to his horses, let them eat only hay."

This last conclusion Chichikov had not expected at all.

"You'd better simply not show your face to me!" said Nozdryov.

In spite of this falling out, however, guest and host had supper together, though this time no wines with fanciful names stood on the table. There was just one bottle sticking up, containing some sort of Cyprian wine which was what is known as sourness in all respects. After supper, Nozdryov, leading Chichikov to a side room where a bed had been prepared for him, said:

"There's your bed! I don't even want to wish you good night!"

Chichikov remained after Nozdryov's departure in a most unpleasant state of mind. He was inwardly vexed with himself, scolded himself for having come to him and lost time for nothing. But he scolded himself even more for having talked with him about business, for having acted imprudently, like a child, like a fool: for the business was not at all the sort to be entrusted to Nozdryov...Nozdryov was trash, Nozdryov could tell a pack of lies, add on, spread the devil knows what, gossip might come of it – not good, not good. "I'm simply a fool," he kept saying to himself. That night he slept very badly. Some small, most lively insects kept biting him unbearably painfully, so that he raked at the wounded spot with all five fingers, repeating: "Ah, the devil take you along with Nozdryov!" He woke up early in the morning. The first thing he did after putting on his dressing gown and boots was go across the yard to the stables and order Selifan to harness the britzka at once. Coming back across the yard, he met with Nozdryov, who was also in his dressing gown, a pipe clenched in his teeth.

Nozdryov greeted him amiably and asked how he had slept.

"So-so," Chichikov replied rather dryly.

"And I, brother," said Nozdryov, "kept dreaming about such vileness all night, it's disgusting to speak of it, and after yesterday it feels as if a squadron spent the night in my mouth. Just fancy: I dreamed I got a whipping, by gosh! and imagine who from? You'll never guess: Staff Captain Potseluev and Kuvshinnikov."

"Yes," Chichikov thought to himself, "it would be nice if you got a thrashing in reality."

"By God! and a most painful one! I woke up: devil take it, something's itching for a fact – must be these cursed fleas. Well,

93

you go and get dressed now, I'll come to you at once. I've only got to yell at that scoundrel of a steward."

Chichikov went to his room to dress and wash. When he came out to the dining room after that, a tea service and a bottle of rum were already standing on the table. The room bore traces of yesterday's dinner and supper; it seemed not to have been touched by a broom. The floor was strewn with bread crumbs, and tobacco ashes could even be seen on the tablecloth. The host himself, who was not slow to come in, had nothing under his dressing gown except a bare chest on which some sort of beard was growing. Holding a chibouk in his hand and sipping from a cup, he was a fine subject for a painter with a terrible dislike of sleek and curled gentlemen who look like barbers' signboards, or those with shaved necks.

"Well, what do you think?" Nozdryov said, after a short silence. "You don't want to play for the souls?"

"I've already told you, brother, I don't gamble; as for buying – I will if you like."

"I don't want to sell, it wouldn't be friendly. I'm not going to skim from the devil knows what. But faro – that's another thing. Just once through the deck!"

"I already told you no."

"And you don't want to trade?"

"I don't."

"Well, listen, let's play checkers – if you win, they're all yours. I do have a lot that ought to be crossed off the lists. Hey, Porfiry, bring us the checkerboard."

"Wasted effort, I won't play."

"But this isn't faro; there can't be any luck or bluffing here: it's all art; I'm even warning you that I can't play at all, unless you give me some kind of handicap."

"Why not sit down and play checkers with him!" Chichikov thought. "I used to be not so bad at checkers, and it will be hard for him to pull any tricks here."

"If you like, so be it, I'll play checkers."

"The souls against a hundred roubles."

"Why so much? Fifty's enough."

"No, what kind of stake is fifty? Better let me throw in some puppy of a middling sort or a gold seal for a watch for the same money."

"Well, if you like!" said Chichikov.

"How much of a handicap are you giving me?" said Nozdryov.

"Why on earth? Nothing, of course."

"At least let me have the first two moves."

"I will not, I'm a poor player myself."

"We know what a poor player you are!" said Nozdryov, advancing a piece.

"I haven't touched checkers in a long time!" said Chichikov, also moving a piece.

"We know what a poor player you are!" said Nozdryov, moving a piece, and at the same time moving another piece with the cuff of his sleeve.

"I haven't touched checkers in a long... Hey, hey, what's this, brother? Put that one back!" said Chichikov.

"Which one?"

"That piece there," said Chichikov, and just then he saw almost under his very nose another piece that seemed to be sneaking towards being kinged; where it had come from God only knew. "No," said Chichikov, getting up from the table, "it's absolutely impossible to play with you! You can't move like that, three pieces at a time!"

"What do you mean three? It was a mistake. One got moved by accident, I'll move it back if you like."

"And the other one came from where?"

"Which other one?"

"This one that's sneaking towards being kinged?"

"Come now, as if you don't remember!"

"No, brother, I counted all the moves and remember everything; you stuck it in there just now. It belongs here!"

"What, where does it belong?" Nozdryov said, flushing. "Ah, yes, brother, I see you're an inventor!"

"No, brother, it seems you are the inventor, only not a very successful one."

"What do you take me for?" said Nozdryov. "Would I go and cheat?"

"I don't take you for anything, I'll just never play with you from now on."

"No, you can't refuse," Nozdryov said, getting excited, "the game's begun!"

"I have the right to refuse, because you're not playing as befits an honest man."

"No, you're lying, you can't say that!"

"No, brother, it's you who are lying!"

"I wasn't cheating, and you can't refuse, you have to finish the game!"

"That you will not make me do," Chichikov said coolly, and going over to the board, he mixed up the pieces.

Nozdryov flushed and came up to Chichikov so close that he retreated a couple of steps.

"I'll make you play! Never mind that you've mixed up the pieces, I remember all the moves. We'll put them back the way they were."

"No, brother, the matter's ended, I won't play with you."

"So you don't want to play?"

"You can see for yourself that it's impossible to play with you."

"No, tell me straight out that you don't want to play," Nozdryov said, stepping still closer.

"I don't!" said Chichikov, bringing both hands closer to his face anyhow, just in case, for things were indeed getting heated.

This precaution was quite appropriate, because Nozdryov swung his arm . . . and it might very well have happened that one of our hero's pleasant and plump cheeks was covered in indelible dishonor; but, successfully warding off the blow, he seized Nozdryov by his two eager arms and held him fast.

"Porfiry, Pavlushka!" Nozdryov shouted in rage, trying to tear himself free.

Hearing these words, Chichikov, not wishing to have household serfs witness this tempting scene, and at the same time feeling that it was useless to hold Nozdryov, let go of his arms. At the same time, in came Porfiry and with him Pavlushka, a stalwart fellow, to deal with whom would have been altogether unprofitable.

"So you don't want to finish the game?" Nozdryov said. "Answer me straight out!"

"It is impossible to finish the game," Chichikov said and peeked out the window. He saw his britzka standing all ready, and Selifan seemed to be waiting for a sign to drive up to the porch, but it was impossible to get out of the room: in the doorway stood two stalwart bonded fools.

"So you don't want to finish the game?" Nozdryov repeated, his face burning as if it were on fire.

"If you played as befits an honest man. But now I can't."

"Ah! so you can't, scoundrel! You saw the game was going against you, so now you can't! Beat him!" he shouted frenziedly, turning to Porfiry and Pavlushka, and himself seizing hold of his cherrywood chibouk. Chichikov turned pale as a sheet. He wanted to say something, but felt that his lips were moving soundlessly.

"Beat him!" shouted Nozdryov, charging forward with his cherrywood chibouk, all hot and sweaty, as if he were assaulting an impregnable fortress. "Beat him!" he shouted in the same voice in which some desperate lieutenant, during a major assault, shouts "Forward, boys!" to his detachment, his extravagant valor already of such renown that a special order has been issued to hold him by the arms when things get hot. But the lieutenant has already caught the feeling of martial fervor, his head is all in a whirl; Suvorov[17] hovers before his eyes, he pushes on towards a great deed. "Forward, boys!" he shouts, charging, not thinking of how he is damaging the already worked-out plan for the general assault, of the millions of gun barrels thrust through the embrasures of the fortress walls, impregnable, soaring beyond the clouds, of how his powerless detachment will be blown into the air like swans-down, or of the fatal bullet already whistling and about to slam shut his clamorous gullet. But if Nozdryov himself represented the desperate, lost, fortress-assaulting lieutenant, the fortress he was attacking in no way resembled an impregnable one. On the contrary, the fortress was so afraid that its heart sank right into its shoes. Already the chair with which he had thought to defend himself had been torn from his hands by the serfs, already, with eyes shut, more dead than alive, he was preparing to get a taste of his host's Circassian chibouk, and God knows what was going to happen to him; but it pleased the fates to spare the ribs, the shoulders, and all the polite parts of our hero. Unexpectedly, there suddenly came a clinking, as if from the clouds, a jingling sound of bells, there was a rattle of wheels as a cart flew up to the porch, and even into the room itself came the heavy snorting and heavy breathing from the overheated horses of the stopped troika. Everyone involuntarily glanced at the window: someone, with a mustache, in a half-military frock coat, was getting out of the cart. After making inquiries in the front hall, he entered at the very moment when Chichi-kov, having not yet managed to collect himself after his fear, was in the most pitiful position a mortal had ever been in.

"May I know which of you here is Mr. Nozdryov?" said the stranger, looking in some perplexity at Nozdryov, who was standing with the chibouk in his hand, and at Chichikov, who was barely beginning to recover from his unprofitable position.

"May I first know to whom I have the honor of speaking?" said Nozdryov, going up closer to him.

"The district captain of police."

"And what would you like?"

"I have come to announce to you the notification which has been communicated to me that you are under arrest until the decision of your case is concluded."

"Nonsense, what case?" said Nozdryov.

"You have been implicated in an episode on the occasion of the inflicting of a personal offense upon the landowner Maximov with birch rods in a drunken state."

"You're lying! I've never laid eyes on any landowner Maximov!"

"My dear sir! Allow me to report to you that I am an officer. You may say that to your servant, but not to me!"

Here Chichikov, without waiting for Nozdryov's response to that, quickly took hat in hand, and behind the police captain's back, slipped out to the porch, got into his britzka, and told Selifan to whip up the horses to full speed.

CHAPTER FIVE

OUR HERO, HOWEVER, had turned quite properly chicken. Though the britzka was racing along like wildfire, and Nozdryov's estate had long since rushed from sight, covered by fields, slopes, and hummocks, he still kept looking back in fear, as if he expected at any moment to be swooped upon by the pursuit. He had difficulty catching his breath, and when he tried putting his hand to his heart, he felt it fluttering like a quail in a cage. "Eh, what a hot time he gave me! just look at him!" Here all sorts of unholy and strong wishes were vowed upon Nozdryov; occasionally even in not very nice words. No help for it! A Russian man, and in a temper besides! Moreover, it was by no means a laughing matter. "Say what you like," he said to himself, "if the police captain hadn't shown up, I might not have been granted another look at God's world! I'd have vanished like a bubble on water, without a trace, leaving no posterity, providing my future children with neither fortune nor an honest name!" Our hero was very much concerned with his posterity.

"What a bad master!" Selifan was thinking to himself. "I've never yet seen such a master. I mean, spit on him for that! Better not give a man food to eat, but a horse must be fed, because a horse likes oats. It's his victuals: what provender is to us, for instance, oats is to him, it's his victuals."

The horses' notions of Nozdryov also seemed to be unadvantageous: not only the bay and Assessor, but even the dapple-gray was out of spirits. Though it always fell to his lot to get the worst oats, and Selifan never poured them into his trough without first saying: "Eh, you scoundrel!" – still they were oats and not mere hay, he chewed them with pleasure and often shoved his long muzzle into his comrades' troughs to have a taste of what they got for vittles, especially when Selifan was not in the stable, but now just hay – that was not nice; everyone was displeased.

But soon all the displeased were interrupted amid their outpourings in a sudden and quite unexpected way. Everyone, not excluding the coachman himself, recollected and re-covered themselves only when a coach and six came galloping down on them and they heard, almost over their heads, the cries of the ladies sitting in the coach, the curses and threats of the other coachman: "Ah, you knave, didn't I shout out to you: keep right, gawker! Are you drunk, or what?" Selifan felt himself at fault, but since a Russian man does not like to admit before another that he is to blame, he at once uttered, assuming a dignified air: "And what are you a-galloping like that for? Pawned your eyes in a pot-house?" After which he started backing the britzka up, so as to free it from the other's harness, but nothing doing, it all got into a tangle. The dapple-gray sniffed curiously at his new friends, who ended up on either side of him. Meanwhile, the ladies sitting in the coach looked at it all with an expression of fear on their faces. One was an old lady, the other a young girl, a sixteen-year-old, with golden hair quite artfully and prettily smoothed back on her small head. Her lovely face was rounded like a fresh egg, and resem-bled one when, white with a sort of transparent whiteness, fresh, only just laid, it is held up by the housekeeper's dark-skinned hand to be checked in the light and the rays of the shining sun pass through it; her thin little ears were also trans-parent, aglow with the warm light coming through them. That, and the fright on her parted, motionless lips, and the tears in her eyes – it was all so pretty in her that our hero gazed at her for several minutes, paying no attention to the tumult that was going on among the horses and coachmen. "Back off, will you, you Nizhni-Novgorod gawk!" the other coach-man was shouting. Selifan pulled at the reins, the other coachman did the same, the horses backed up a little, then lurched into each other again, having stepped over the traces. In these circumstances, the dapple-gray took such a liking to his new acquaintance that he did not want at all to leave the rut to which the unforeseen fates had brought him, and, resting his muzzle on the neck of his new friend, seemed to be whispering right into his ear, probably some terrible nonsense, because the other horse was ceaselessly twitching his ears.

This commotion managed, however, to attract the muzhiks of a village which, fortunately, was not far away. Since such a spectacle is a real godsend for a muzhik, the same as newspapers or his club for a German, a whole multitude of them soon accumulated around the carriages, and there were only old women and small children left in the village. The traces were undone; a few prods in the dapple-gray's muzzle made him back up; in short, they were separated and drawn apart. But whether from the vexation they felt at being parted from their friends, or from sheer cussedness, however much the coach-man whipped them, the other horses would not move and stood as if rooted to the spot. The muzhiks' sympathy increased to an unbelievable degree. They vied with each other in offering advice: "Go, Andryushka, take the outrunner, the one on the right, and Uncle Mityai will get up on the shaft horse! Get up there, Uncle Mityai!" Long and lean Uncle Mityai, with his red beard, climbed onto the shaft horse and came to resemble a village belfry, or, better, the crane used to draw water from a well. The coachman lashed the horses, but nothing doing, Uncle Mityai was no help. "Wait, wait!" the muzhiks shouted. "You, Uncle Mityai, get on the outrunner, and let Uncle Minyai get on the shaft horse!" Uncle Minyai, a broad-shouldered muzhik with a beard as black as coal and a belly resembling the giant samovar in which hot punch is brewed for a whole chilled marketplace, eagerly got on the shaft horse, who sagged almost to the ground under him. "Now it'll work!" shouted the muzhiks. "Heat him up; heat him up! wallop him with the whip, that one, the sorrel, why's he wriggling there like a daddy longlegs!" But seeing that it was not going to work and that no heating up helped, Uncle Mityai and Uncle Minyai together got on the shaft horse, and Andryushka was put on the outrunner. Finally the coachman lost patience and chased away both Uncle Mityai and Uncle Minyai, and it was a good thing he did, because the horses were steaming as if they had just ripped through a whole stage without stopping for breath. He gave them a minute's rest, after which they went off by themselves. While all this was happening, Chichikov was looking very attentively at the unknown young girl. He made several attempts to converse with her, but somehow it did not come about. And meanwhile the ladies drove off, the pretty head with its fine features and the slender waist disappeared, like something resembling a vision, and what remained was again the road, the britzka, the troika of horses familiar to the reader, Selifan, Chichikov, the flatness and emptiness of the surrounding fields. Wherever in life it may be, whether amongst its tough, coarsely poor, and untidily moldering mean ranks, or its monotonously cold and boringly tidy upper classes, a man will at least once meet with a phenomenon which is unlike anything he has happened to see before, which for once at least awakens in him a feeling unlike those he is fated to feel all his life. Wherever, across whatever sorrows our life is woven of, a resplendent joy will gaily race by, just as a splendid carriage with golden harness, picture-book horses, and a shining brilliance of glass sometimes suddenly and unexpectedly goes speeding by some poor, forsaken hamlet that has never seen anything but a country cart, and for a long time the muzhiks stand gaping open-mouthed, not putting their hats back on, though the wondrous carriage has long since sped away and vanished from sight. So, too, did the blond girl suddenly, in a completely unexpected manner, appear in our story and also disappear. If, instead of Chichikov, some twenty-year-old youth had happened to be standing there, a hussar, or a student, or simply one starting out on his path in life – then, God! what would not have awakened, stirred, spoken up in him! For a long time he would have stood insensibly on the same spot, gazing senselessly into the distance, having forgotten the road, and all the reprimands that lay ahead of him, and the scoldings for the delay, having forgotten himself, and the office, and the world, and all there is in the world.

But our hero was already middle-aged and of a circumspectly cool character. He, too, waxed thoughtful and started thinking, but his reflections were more positive, not so unaccountable, and even in part quite substantial. "A nice wench!" he said, opening his snuffbox and taking a pinch. "But what is it, chiefly, that's so good in her? What's good in her is that, as one can see, she has just come out of some boarding school or institute, there's nothing about her that is female, as they say, which is precisely what is most disagreeable in them. She's like a child now, everything is simple in her, she says what she likes, she laughs when she wants to. Anything can be made of her, she may become a wonder, or she may turn out trash, and trash is what she'll turn out. Just let the mamas and aunties start working on her now. In a year they'll have her so filled with all sorts of female stuff that her own father won't recognize her. Out of nowhere will come conceit and pomposity, she'll start turning around on memorized instructions, she'll start racking her brains thinking up with whom, and how, and for what length of time she should speak, how to look at whom, she'll be afraid every moment of saying more than is necessary, she'll finally get confused, and in the end she'll finally start lying all her life, and the result will be devil knows what!" Here he fell silent for a short time, then added: "And it would be curious to know who her people are, what and who her father is, is he a rich landowner of respectable character or simply a well-meaning man with capital acquired in the service? For if, say, to this girl there were added some two-hundred-thousand-rouble dowry, she would make a very, very tasty little morsel. That might constitute happiness, so to speak, for a decent man." The tidy little two hundred thousand began to picture itself so attractively in his head that he inwardly became vexed with himself for not having found out who the travelers were from the postillion or the coachman, while the bustle around the carriages was going on. Soon, however, the appearance of Sobakevich's estate distracted his thoughts and made them turn to their perennial subject.

The estate seemed rather big to him; two forests, of birch and of pine, like two wings, one darker and one lighter, stood to right and left of it; in the middle could be seen a wooden house with a mezzanine, a red roof, and dark gray or, better, natural sides − a house like those built here for military settlements and German colonists.[18] It was obvious that during its construction the architect had been in constant conflict with the owner's taste. The architect was a pedant and wanted symmetry, the owner wanted convenience and, evidently as a result of that, boarded up all the corresponding windows on one side and in their place poked through one small one, probably needed for a dark storeroom. The pediment was also not at all in the center of the house, however much the architect had struggled, because the owner had ordered a column on one side thrown out, so that instead of four columns, as in the original design, there were only three. The yard was surrounded by a strong and exceedingly stout wooden lattice. The landowner seemed greatly concerned with solidity. For the stable, sheds, and kitchens stout and hefty logs had been used, meant to stand for centuries. The village cottages of the muzhiks were also a marvel of construction: the sides were not adzed, there were no carved patterns or fancywork, but everything was snugly and properly fitted together. Even the well was housed in such strong oak as is used only for gristmills and ships. In short, all that he looked upon was sturdy, shakeless, in some strong and clumsy order. As he drove up to the porch, he saw two faces peek almost simultaneously out the window: a woman's, in a bonnet, narrow, long, like a cucumber; and a man's, round, broad, like those Moldavian gourds called crooknecks, from which balalaikas are made in Russia, light two-stringed balalaikas, the jewel and delight of a snappy twenty-year-old lad, a winker and a fop, winking and whistling at the white-bosomed, white-necked lasses who have gathered to listen to his soft-stringed strumming. Having peeked out, the two faces hid at the same moment. A lackey in a gray jacket with a light blue standing collar came to the porch and led Chichikov into the front hall, where the host himself had already come. Seeing the visitor, he abruptly said: "Please!" and led him to the inner rooms.

When Chichikov glanced sidelong at Sobakevich, it seemed to him this time that he looked exactly like a medium-sized bear. To complete the resemblance, the tailcoat he was wearing was of a perfect bear color; his sleeves were long, his trousers were long, his feet shambled this way and that, constantly stepping on other people's toes. His face was of a roasted, hot color, such as one sees on copper coins. It is well-known that there are many faces in the world over the finishing of which nature did not take much trouble, did not employ any fine tools such as files, gimlets, and so on, but simply hacked them out with round strokes: one chop – a nose appears; another chop – lips appear; eyes are scooped out with a big drill; and she lets it go into the world rough-hewn, saying: "Alive!" Of such strong and marvelous fashioning was the visage of Sobakevich: he held it rather more down than up, did not swivel his neck at all, and, on account of this non-swiveling, rarely looked at the person he was speaking to, but always either at the corner of the stove or at the door.

Chichikov gave him one more sidelong glance as they were going through the dining room: a bear! a veritable bear! If there were any need for such strange approximation, he was even named Mikhailo Semyonovich.[19] Knowing his habit of stepping on people's toes, he himself stepped very carefully and let him go ahead. The host seemed sensible of this failing himself, and at once asked him: "Have I inconvenienced you?" But Chichikov thanked him, saying that so far he had suffered no inconvenience.

Going into the drawing room, Sobakevich pointed to an armchair, saying "Please!" again. As he sat down, Chichikov glanced at the walls and the pictures hanging on them. They were all fine fellows in the pictures, all Greek generals, engraved at full length: Mavrocordato in red pantaloons and officer's jacket, with spectacles on his nose, Miaoulis, Canaris. These heroes all had such fat haunches and unheard-of mustaches as sent shivers through one's whole body. Among these sturdy Greeks, who knows how or why, Bagration had lodged himself, skinny, thin, with little banners and cannons underneath, in the narrowest of frames. Then again there followed the Greek heroine Bobelina, whose leg alone seemed bigger than the entire body of one of those fops who fill our present-day drawing rooms.[20] The host, being a healthy and sturdy man himself, seemed to want his room, too, to be adorned with sturdy and healthy people. Near Bobelina, just by the window, hung a cage from which peered a thrush of a dark color with white speckles, also very much resembling Sobakevich. Host and guest had managed to be silent for no more than two minutes when the drawing-room door opened and the hostess came in, a rather tall lady in a bonnet with ribbons dyed in homemade colors. She came in decorously, holding her head erect, like a palm tree.

"This is my Feodulia Ivanovna!" said Sobakevich.

Chichikov went up to kiss Feodulia Ivanovna's hand, which she almost shoved into his lips, affording him the occasion to observe that her hands had been washed in pickling brine.

"Sweetie," Sobakevich went on, "allow me to introduce Pavel Ivanovich Chichikov! I had the honor of meeting him at the governor's and at the postmaster's."

Feodulia Ivanovna invited him to sit down, also saying "Please!" and making a motion with her head, as actresses do when playing queens. Then she seated herself on the sofa, covered herself with her merino shawl, and thereafter moved neither eye nor eyebrow.

Chichikov again raised his eyes and again saw Canaris with his fat haunches and interminable mustaches, Bobelina, and the thrush in the cage.

For the space of nearly a whole five minutes, they all preserved their silence; the only sound was the tapping of the thrush's beak against the wood of the wooden cage, on the bottom of which he was fishing for grains of wheat. Chichikov glanced around the room once more: everything that was in it, everything, was solid, clumsy in the highest degree, and bore some strange resemblance to the master of the house himself; in the corner of the drawing room stood a big-bellied walnut bureau on four most preposterous legs, a veritable bear. The table, the chairs, the armchairs – all was of the most heavy and uncomfortable quality – in short, every object, every chair seemed to be saying: "I, too, am Sobakevich!" or "I, too, am very like Sobakevich!"

"We were remembering you at the head magistrate's, at Ivan Grigorievich's," Chichikov said finally, seeing that no one was disposed to begin the conversation, "last Thursday. We had a very pleasant time there."

"Yes, I wasn't at the magistrate's then," replied Sobakevich.

"A wonderful man!"

"Who is?" said Sobakevich, staring at the corner of the stove.

"The magistrate."

"Well, maybe it seemed so to you: he's a mason, but otherwise as big a fool as the world has yet produced."

Chichikov was a bit taken aback by this rather sharp definition, but then recovered himself and went on:

"Of course, no man is without weaknesses, but the governor, on the other hand, is such an excellent man!"

"The governor is an excellent man?"

"Yes, isn't it true?"

"The foremost bandit in the world!"

"What, the governor a bandit?" said Chichikov, totally unable to understand how the governor could come to be a bandit. "I confess, I would never have thought it," he went on. "But allow me, nevertheless, to observe: his actions are not like that at all, on the contrary, there is even a good deal of softness in him." Here he held up as evidence even the purses embroidered by his own hands, and spoke with praise of the gentle expression of his face.

"And he has the face of a bandit!" said Sobakevich. "Just give him a knife and set him out on the highway – he'll stick it in you, he'll do it for a kopeck! He and the vice-governor – they're Gog and Magog!"[21]

"No, he's not on good terms with them," Chichikov thought to himself. "I'll try talking with him about the police chief: it seems he's a friend of his."

"Anyhow, as for me," he said, "I confess, I like the police chief most of all. He has a direct, open sort of character; there's something simple-hearted in his face."

"A crook!" Sobakevich said very coolly. "He'll sell you, deceive you, and then sit down to dinner with you! I know them all: they're all crooks, the whole town is the same: a crook mounted on a crook and driving him with a crook. Judases, all of them. There's only one decent man there: the prosecutor – and to tell the truth, he, too, is a swine."

After such laudatory, if somewhat brief, biographies, Chichikov saw that there was no point in mentioning any other officials, and remembered that Sobakevich did not like to speak well of anyone.

"Now then, sweetie, let's go and have dinner," Sobakevich's spouse said to him.

"Please!" said Sobakevich.

Whereupon, going up to the table where the hors d'oeuvres were, guest and host fittingly drank a glass of vodka each, and snacked as the whole of Russia snacks in towns and villages – that is, on various pickled things and other savory blessings – and they all flowed into the dining room; at their head, like a gliding goose, swept the hostess. The small table was set for four. The fourth place was very quickly claimed, it is hard to say positively by whom, a lady or a young maid, a relation, a housekeeper, or simply a woman living in the house: something without a bonnet, about thirty years old, in a motley shawl. There are persons who exist in the world not as objects, but as alien specks or spots on objects. They sit in the same place, hold their head in the identical manner, one is ready to take them for furniture and thinks that in all their born days no word has ever passed those lips; but somewhere in the servants' quarters or the pantry it turns out simply – oh-ho-ho!

"The cabbage soup is very good today, my sweet!" said Sobakevich, having slurped up some soup and heaped on his plate an enormous piece of *nyanya*, a well-known dish served with cabbage soup, consisting of a sheep's stomach stuffed with buckwheat groats, brains, and trotters. "Such *nyanya* you'll never get in town," he went on, addressing Chichikov, "they'll serve you the devil knows what there!"

"The governor, however, keeps a rather good table," said Chichikov.

"But do you know what it's all made from? You wouldn't eat it if you found out."

"I don't know how it's prepared, I can't judge about that, but the pork cutlets and poached fish were excellent."

"It seemed so to you. I know what they buy at the market. That rascal of a cook, who learned from a Frenchman, buys a cat, skins it, and serves it instead of hare."

"Pah! what an unpleasant thing to say," said Sobakevich's spouse.

"But, sweetie, that's what they do, it's not my fault, that's what they all do. Whatever they've got that's unusable, that our Akulka throws, if I may say so, into the pig bucket, they put into the soup! into the soup! right plop into it!"

"What things you're always telling about at the table!" Sobakevich's spouse objected again.

"But, my sweet," said Sobakevich, "it's not as if I were doing it myself, but I'll tell you right to your face, I will not eat any vileness. No frog, even if it's pasted all over with sugar, will ever go near my mouth, and no oyster either: I know what oysters are like. Take this lamb," he went on, addressing Chichikov, "this is a rack of lamb with buckwheat groats! It's not that fricassee they make in squires' kitchens out of lamb that's been lying around the marketplace for four days! It was German and French doctors who invented it all, I'd have the whole lot of them hung for it! They invented the diet, the hunger treatment! With their thin-boned German nature, they fancy they can take on the Russian stomach, too! No, it's all wrong, all these inventions, it's all . . . " Here Sobakevich even shook his head angrily. "They say: enlightenment, enlightenment, and this enlightenment – poof! I'd use another word, only it wouldn't be proper at the table. With me it's not like that. With me, if it's pork – let's have the whole pig on the table, if it's lamb – drag in the whole sheep, if goose – the whole goose! Better that I eat just two courses, but eat my fill, as my soul demands." Sobakevich confirmed this in action: he dumped half of the rack of lamb onto his own plate, ate it all up, gnawed it, and sucked it out to the last little bone.

"Yes," thought Chichikov, "there's no flies on this one."

"With me it's not like that," Sobakevich said, wiping his hands on a napkin, "with me it's not like with some Plyushkin: he owns eight hundred souls, yet he lives and eats worse than my shepherd!"

"Who is this Plyushkin?" asked Chichikov.

"A crook," replied Sobakevich. "Such a niggard, it's hard to imagine. Jailbirds in prison live better than he does: he's starved all his people to death..."

"Indeed!" Chichikov picked up with interest. "And you say his people are actually dying in large numbers?"

"Dropping like flies."

"Like flies, really! And may I ask how far away he lives?"

"Three miles."

"Three miles!" exclaimed Chichikov, and he even felt a slight throb in his heart. "But if one were driving out your gate, would it be to the right or the left?"

"I wouldn't advise you even to know the way to that dog's!" said Sobakevich. "It's more excusable to go and visit some indecent place than him."

"No, I wasn't asking for any reason, but just because I'm interested in learning about all sorts of places," Chichikov replied to that.

After the rack of lamb came cheesecakes, each much bigger than a plate, then a turkey the size of a calf, chock-full of all sorts of good things: eggs, rice, livers, and whatnot else, all of which settled in one lump in the stomach. With that dinner ended; but when they got up from the table, Chichikov felt himself a good ton heavier. They went to the drawing room, where a saucer of preserves was already waiting – not pear, not plum, not any other berry – which, however, neither guest nor host touched. The hostess stepped out in order to put more in other saucers. Taking advantage of her absence, Chichikov addressed Sobakevich, who was lying in an armchair, only letting out little groans after such a hearty dinner and producing some unintelligible sounds with his mouth, crossing and covering it with his hand every moment.[22] Chichikov addressed him in the following words:

"I would like to talk with you about a little business."

"Here's more preserves," said the hostess, returning with a saucer, "black radish, cooked in honey."

"We'll get to it later!" said Sobakevich. "You go to your room now, Pavel Ivanovich and I are going to take our coats off and rest a bit."

The hostess at once expressed a readiness to send for feather beds and pillows, but the host said: "Never mind, we'll rest in the armchairs," and the hostess left.

Sobakevich inclined his head slightly, preparing to hear what the little business was about.

Chichikov began somehow very remotely, touched generally on the entire Russian state, and spoke in great praise of its vastness, saying that even the most ancient Roman monarchy was not so big, and foreigners are rightly astonished . . . Sobakevich went on listening, his head bent. And that according to the existing regulations of this state, unequaled in glory, the souls listed in the census, once their life's path has ended, are nevertheless counted equally with the living until the new census is taken, so as not to burden the institutions with a quantity of petty and useless documents and increase the complexity of the already quite complex state machinery . . . Sobakevich went on listening, his head bent – and that, nevertheless, for all the justice of this measure, it was often somewhat burdensome for many owners, obliging them to pay taxes as if for the living object, and that he, feeling a personal respect for him, would even be ready to take this truly heavy responsibility partly upon himself. With regard to the main object, Chichikov expressed himself very cautiously: he never referred to the souls as dead, but only as nonexistent.

Sobakevich went on listening in the same way, his head bowed, and nothing in the least resembling expression showed on his face. It seemed there was no soul in this body at all, or if there was, it was not at all where it ought to be, but, as with the deathless Koshchey,[23] was somewhere beyond the mountains, and covered with such a thick shell that whatever stirred at the bottom of it produced decidedly no movement on the surface.

"And so . . . ?" said Chichikov, waiting not without some anxiety for an answer.

"You want dead souls?" Sobakevich asked quite simply, without the least surprise, as if they were talking about grain.

"Yes," replied Chichikov, and again he softened the expression, adding, "nonexistent ones."

"They could be found, why not . . . ," said Sobakevich.

"And if so, then you, undoubtedly . . . would be pleased to get rid of them?"

"If you like, I'm ready to sell," said Sobakevich, now raising his head slightly, as he realized that the buyer must certainly see some profit in it.

"Devil take it," Chichikov thought to himself, "this one's already selling before I've made a peep!" and said aloud:

"And, for instance, about the price? . . . though, anyhow, it's such an object . . . that a price is even a strange thing to . . . "

"Well, so as not to ask too much from you, let's make it a hundred apiece!" said Sobakevich.

"A hundred!" cried Chichikov, opening his mouth and looking him straight in the eye, not knowing whether he himself had not heard right or Sobakevich's tongue, being of a heavy nature, had turned the wrong way and blurted out one word instead of another.

"Why, is that too costly for you?" Sobakevich said, and then added: "And what, incidentally, would your price be?"

"My price? Surely we've made a mistake somehow, or not understood each other, or have forgotten what the object in question is. I suppose, for my part, laying my hand on my heart, that eighty kopecks per soul would be the fairest price."

"Eh, that's overdoing it – a mere eighty kopecks!"

"Well, in my judgment, to my mind, it can't be more."

"But I'm not selling bast shoes."

"However, you must agree, they're not people either."

"So you think you'll find someone fool enough to take a few kopecks for a registered soul?"

"I beg your pardon, but why do you call them registered, when the souls themselves have been dead for a long time, and all that's left is a sensually imperceptible sound. However, not to get into further conversation along this line, I'll give you a rouble and a half, if you please, but more I cannot do."

"It's a shame for you even to mention such a sum! Come on, bargain, tell me the real price!"

"I cannot, Mikhail Semyonovich, trust my conscience, I cannot: what's impossible is impossible," Chichikov said, yet he did add another fifty kopecks.

"How can you be so stingy?" said Sobakevich. "Really, it's not so costly! Some crook would cheat you, sell you trash, not souls; but mine are all hale as nuts, all picked men: if not craftsmen, then some other kind of sturdy muzhiks. Just look: there's Mikheev the cartwright, for example! Never made any other kind of carriage than the spring kind. And not like your typical Moscow workmanship, good for an hour – really solid, and he does the upholstery and lacquering himself!"

Chichikov opened his mouth to observe that Mikheev had, however, long since departed this life; but Sobakevich had entered, as they say, into his full speaking strength, wherever on earth he got this clip and gift of words:

"And Cork Stepan, the carpenter? I'll bet my life you won't find such a muzhik anywhere. What tremendous strength! If he'd served in the guards, God knows what they'd have given him, he was seven feet tall!"

Chichikov was again about to observe that Cork, too, had departed this life; but Sobakevich obviously could not contain himself: speech poured out in such torrents that one could only listen:

"Milushkin, the bricklayer! Could put a stove into any house you like. Maxim Telyatnikov, the cobbler: one prick of the awl and your boots are done, and boots they are, too, thank you very much, and never a drop of liquor in him. And Yeremey Sorokoplyokhin! This muzhik alone is worth all the others, he went trading in Moscow, brought five hundred roubles in quitrent alone. That's the kind of folk they are! A far cry from what some sort of Plyushkin would sell you."

"I beg your pardon," Chichikov said finally, amazed by such an abundant flood of speeches, which also seemed to have no end, "but why do you enumerate all their qualities, they're not good for anything now, these are all dead folk. A dead body's a good fence prop, as the proverb says."

"Yes, of course, they're dead," Sobakevich said, as if catching himself and remembering that they were indeed already dead, and then added: "Though one can also say: what about those people who are now listed as living? What sort of people are they? Flies, not people."

"Still, they do exist, while these are a dream."

"Oh, no, not a dream! I'll tell you what sort Mikheev was, one of those people you don't find anymore: such a huge machine, he wouldn't fit into this room; no, it's not a dream! And there was such tremendous strength in his tremendous shoulders as no horse ever had; I'd like to know where else you'll find such a dream!"

These last words he spoke addressing the portraits of Bagration and Colocotronis[24] hanging on the wall, as commonly happens when people are conversing and one of them suddenly, for some unknown reason, addresses not the one whom his words concern, but some third who chances to come in, even a total stranger, from whom he knows he will hear neither a reply, nor an opinion, nor a confirmation, but at whom he will nevertheless direct his gaze, as if calling on him to act as intermediary; and the stranger, slightly confused for the first moment, does not know whether to answer him on the matter, of which he has heard nothing, or to stand there for a moment, maintaining the proper decorum, and only then walk away.

"No, more than two roubles I cannot give," said Chichikov.

"If you please, so that you won't claim I'm asking too much and don't want to do you a favor, if you please – seventy-five roubles per soul, only in banknotes, really, only for the sake of our acquaintance!"

"What indeed is with him," Chichikov thought to himself, "does he take me for a fool, or what?" and then added aloud:

"I find it strange, really: it seems some theater performance or comedy is going on between us, otherwise I can't explain it to myself . . . You seem to be quite an intelligent man, you possess educated knowledge. The object is simply pooh-pooh. What is it worth? Who needs it?"

"Well, you're buying it, that means you need it."

Here Chichikov bit his lip and could find no reply. He tried to begin talking about some family and domestic circum-stances, but Sobakevich responded simply:

"I have no need to know what your relations are; I don't interfere in family affairs, that's your business. You're in need of souls, I'm selling them to you, and you'll regret it if you don't buy them."

"Two roubles," said Chichikov.

"Eh, really, the parrot calls everyone Poll, as the proverb says; you're stuck on this two and don't want to get off it. Give me your real price!"

"Well, devil take him," Chichikov thought to himself, "I'll add fifty kopecks, the dog, to buy nuts with!"

"If you please, I'll add fifty kopecks."

"Well, if you please, I'll also give you my final word: fifty roubles! It's my loss, really, you won't get such fine folk so cheaply anywhere else!"

"What a pinchfist!" Chichikov said to himself, and then continued aloud in some vexation:

"What indeed is this...as if it were all quite a serious matter; I can get them for nothing elsewhere. Anyone would be eager to unload them on me, just to get rid of them the sooner. Only a fool would keep them and pay taxes on them!"

"But, you know, this kind of purchase – I say it between the two of us, in friendship – is not always permissible, and if I or someone else were to tell, such a person would not enjoy any confidence with regard to contracts or on entering into any sort of profitable obligations."

"So that's what he's aiming at, the scoundrel!" thought Chichikov, and he straightaway uttered with a most cool air:

"As you wish, I'm not buying out of any sort of need, as you think, but just like that, following the bent of my own thoughts. If you don't want two and a half – good-bye!"

"He won't be thrown off, the tough one!" thought Sobakevich.

"Well, God help you, give me thirty and take them!"

"No, I can see you don't want to sell, good-bye!"

"Excuse me, excuse me," said Sobakevich, not letting go of his hands and stepping on his foot, for our hero had forgotten his caution, in punishment for which he had to hiss and jump about on one foot.

"I beg your pardon! I seem to have inconvenienced you. Do sit down here! Please!" Whereupon he seated him in an armchair even with a certain dexterity, like a bear that has had some training and knows how to turn somersaults and perform various tricks in response to questions like: "Show us, Misha, how peasant women take a steam bath" or "Misha, how do little children steal peas?"

"Really, I'm wasting my time, I must hurry."

"Stay for one little minute, I'm going to tell you something right now that you'll find very pleasant." Here Sobakevich sat down closer to Chichikov and said softly in his ear, as if it were a secret: "Want a quarter?"

"You mean twenty-five roubles? No, no, no, not even a quarter of a quarter, I won't add a single kopeck."

Sobakevich fell silent. Chichikov also fell silent. The silence lasted about two minutes. From the wall, Bagration with his aquiline nose looked extremely attentively upon this purchasing.

"So what's your final price?" Sobakevich said at last.

"Two-fifty."

"Really, for you a human soul is the same as a stewed turnip. Give me three roubles at least!"

"I can't."

"Well, there's nothing to do with you, if you please! It's a loss, but I have this beastly character: I can't help gratifying my neighbor. And I expect we'll have to draw up a deed of purchase, so that everything will be in order."

"Certainly."

"Well, that means going to town."

Thus the deal was concluded. They both decided to be in town the next day and take care of the deed of purchase. Chichikov asked for a little list of the peasants. Sobakevich agreed willingly, straightaway went to his bureau, and began writing them all down with his own hand, not only by name but with mention of their laudable qualities.

And Chichikov, having nothing to do, occupied himself, while standing behind him, with an examination of his entire vast frame. As he gazed at his back, broad as a squat Vyatka horse's, and his legs, which resembled iron hitching posts set along the sidewalk, he could not help exclaiming inwardly: "Eh, God really endowed you well! Just as they say, crudely cut but stoutly stitched! . . . Were you born such a bear, or did you get bearified by the backwoods life, sowing grain, dealing with muzhiks, and turn through all that into what's known as a pinchfist? But no, I think you'd be just the same even if you'd been raised according to fashion, got your start and lived in Petersburg, and not in this backwoods. The whole difference is that now you tuck away half a rack of lamb with groats, followed by a cheesecake as big as a plate, and then you'd eat some sort of cutlets with truffles. Yes, and now you have muzhiks under your rule: you get along with them and, of course, wouldn't mistreat them, because they're yours and it would be the worse for you; and then you'd have officials, whom you could knock about roughly, realizing that they're not your serfs, or else you could rob the treasury! No, if a man's a pinchfist, he'll never open his hand! And if you get him to open one or two fingers, it will come out still worse. If he slightly grazes the tips of some science, he'll let it be known later, when he occupies some prominent post, to all those who actually do know some science. What's more, he may later say: 'Why don't I just show myself!' And he'll think up such a wise decree that lots of people will find themselves in a pickle ... Eh, if all these pinchfists ... "

"The list's ready," said Sobakevich, turning around.

"Ready? Let me have it, please!" He ran down it with his eyes and marveled at its accuracy and precision: not only were trade, name, age, and family situation thoroughly indicated, but there were even special marginal notes concerning behavior, sobriety – in short, it was lovely to look at.

"And now a little down payment, please!" said Sobakevich.

"Why a little down payment? You'll get all the money at once, in town."

"You know, that's how it's always done," objected Sobakevich.

"I don't know how I can give it to you, I didn't bring any money with me. Wait, here's ten roubles."

"What's ten roubles! Give me fifty at least!"

Chichikov started telling him no, he could not do that; but Sobakevich said so affirmatively that he did have money, that he brought out another banknote, saying:

"Oh, well, here's another fifteen for you, twenty-five in all. Only give me a receipt, please."

"But why do you need a receipt?"

"You know, it's always better with a receipt. If perchance something should happen."

"All right, give me the money then."

"Why the money? It's right here in my hand! As soon as you've written the receipt, you can take it that same moment."

"Excuse me, but how am I to write the receipt? I have to see the money first."

Chichikov let the paper notes go from his hand to Sobakevich, who, approaching the table, covered them with the fingers of his left hand, and with the other wrote on a scrap of paper that a down payment of twenty-five roubles in government banknotes for the bought souls had been received in full. Having written the receipt, he once again examined the banknotes.

"The paper's a bit old!" he said, studying one of them in the light, "and slightly torn – well, but among friends that's nothing to look at."

"A pinchfist, a real pinchfist!" Chichikov thought to himself, "and a knave to boot!"

"You don't want any of the female sex?"

"No, thank you."

"I wouldn't ask much. One little rouble apiece, for the sake of acquaintance."

"No, I have no need of the female sex."

"Well, if you have no need, there's nothing to talk about. Taste knows no rules: one man loves the parson, another the parsoness, as the proverb says."

"I also wanted to ask you to keep this deal between us," Chichikov said as he was taking his leave.

"But that goes without saying. No point mixing a third person up in it; what takes place between close friends in all sincerity ought to be kept to their mutual friendship. Goodbye! Thank you for coming; I beg you not to forget us in the future: if you happen to have a free moment, come for dinner and spend some time. Maybe we'll chance to be of service to each other again."

"Oh, sure thing!" Chichikov thought to himself, getting into his britzka. "Hustled me out of two-fifty for a dead soul, the devil's pinchfist!"

He was displeased with Sobakevich's behavior. After all, one way or another he was still an acquaintance, they had met at the governor's and at the police chief's, but he had acted like a complete stranger, had taken money for trash! As the britzka drove out of the yard, he looked back and saw that Sobakevich was still standing on the porch and seemed to be watching, as if he wished to know where the guest would go.

"The scoundrel, he's still standing there!" he said through his teeth, and told Selifan to turn towards the peasants' cottages and drive off in such a way that the carriage could not be seen from the master's yard. He wished to go and see Plyushkin, whose people, in Sobakevich's words, were dying like flies, but he did not wish Sobakevich to know of it. When the britzka was already at the end of the village, he beckoned to the first muzhik they met, who, having chanced upon a really stout beam somewhere on the road, was dragging it on his shoulder, like an indefatigable ant, back to his cottage.

"Hey, graybeard! how can I get from here to Plyushkin's, so as not to go past the master's house?"

The muzhik seemed to have difficulty with the question.

"What, you don't know?"

"No, your honor, I don't."

"Eh, you! And with all your gray hairs, you don't know the niggard Plyushkin, the one who feeds his people so badly?"

"Ah! the patchy one, the patchy one!" the muzhik cried.

He added a noun to the word "patchy," a very felicitous one, but not usable in polite conversation, and therefore we shall omit it. However, one could tell that the expression was very apt, because, although the muzhik had long disappeared from view and they had driven a good way on, Chichikov still sat chuckling in the britzka. Strongly do the Russian folk express themselves! and if they bestow a little word on someone, it will go with him and his posterity for generations, and he will drag it with him into the service, and into retirement, and to Petersburg, and to the ends of the earth. And no matter how clever you are in ennobling your nickname later, even getting little scriveners to derive it for hire from ancient princely stock, nothing will help: the nickname will caw itself away at the top of its crow's voice and tell clearly where the bird has flown from.[25] Aptly uttered is as good as written, an axe cannot destroy it. And oh, how apt is everything that comes from deep Russia, where there are no German, or Finnish, or any other tribes, but all is native natural-born, lively and pert Russian wit, which does not fish for a word in its pockets, does not brood on it like a hen on her chicks, but pastes it on at once, like a passport, for eternal wear, and there is no point in adding later what sort of nose or lips you have – in one line you are portrayed from head to foot!

As a numberless multitude of churches and monasteries with their cupolas, domes, and crosses is scattered over holy, pious Russia, so a numberless multitude of tribes, generations, peoples also throngs, ripples, and rushes over the face of the earth. And each of these peoples, bearing within itself the pledge of its strength, filled with the creative capacity of the soul, with its own marked peculiarity and other gifts of God, is in an original fashion distinguished by its own word, which, whatever subject it may express, reflects in that expression a portion of its character. A knowledge of hearts and a wise comprehension of life resound in the word of the Briton; like a nimble fop the short-lived word of the Frenchman flashes and scatters; whimsically does the German contrive his lean, intelligent word, not accessible to all; but there is no word so sweeping, so pert, so bursting from beneath the very heart, so ebullient and vibrant with life, as an aptly spoken Russian word.

CHAPTER SIX

ONCE, LONG AGO, in the days of my youth, in the days of my flashed-by never-to-return childhood, I used to rejoice when I approached an unknown place for the first time: no matter whether it was a little village, a wretched provincial town, a settlement, a hamlet – much that was curious in it revealed itself to a child's curious eyes. Every building, everything that bore on itself the stamp of some noticeable peculiarity – everything arrested and amazed me. A stone government building of familiar architecture with half its windows false, sticking up all by itself amid a trimmed log pile of common one-storied tradesmen's houses, or a regular round cupola, all clad in white sheet metal, soaring high above a snowy, white-washed new church, or a marketplace, or a provincial fop who turned up in the middle of town – nothing escaped my fresh, keen attention, and, poking my nose out of my traveling cart, I gazed at the never-before-seen cut of some frock coat, and at the wooden boxes of nails, of sulphur yellowing from afar, of raisins and soap, flashing by in the doorway of a grocer's shop together with jars of stale Moscow candy, gazed also at an infantry officer walking off to one side, brought from God knows what district capital into provincial boredom, and at a merchant in a tight-waisted coat flashing by in a racing droshky, and mentally I would be carried off with them into their poor lives. Should a provincial official pass by, it was enough to set me thinking: where is he going, to spend the evening with some crony of his, or straight to his own home, to linger for half an hour or so on the porch, until dusk gathers fully, and then sit down to an early supper with his mama, his wife, his wife's sister, and the whole family, and what will be talked about among them, while a serf girl in a coin necklace or a lad in a thick jacket comes in after the soup bringing a tallow candle in a long-lived homemade candlestick. Approaching the estate of some landowner, I looked with curiosity at the tall, narrow wooden belfry or the broad, dark old wooden church. From far off through the green of the trees, the red roof and white chimneys of the landowner's house flashed enticingly to me, and I waited impatiently for the gardens screening it to part on both sides and show the whole of the house with its – then, alas! – by no means trite appearance; and from it I tried to guess what the landowner himself was, whether he was fat, and whether he had sons or as many as six daughters with ringing girlish laughter, games, and the youngest sister invariably a beauty, and whether they had dark eyes, and whether he himself was a jolly man, or sullen as the last days of September, looking at the calendar and boring the young folk with talk of rye and wheat.

Now it is with indifference that I approach any unknown estate, and with indifference that I gaze at its trite appearance; my chilled glance finds no refuge, I do not laugh, and that which in earlier days would have awakened a lively movement in my face, laughter and unceasing talk, now flits by, and my motionless lips preserve an impassive silence. Oh, my youth! Oh, my freshness!

While Chichikov thought and chuckled inwardly over the nickname the muzhiks had bestowed upon Plyushkin, he failed to notice that he had driven into the middle of a vast settlement with a multitude of cottages and lanes. Soon, however, it was brought to his notice by a quite decent jolt, produced by the log pavement, to which town cobblestones are nothing in comparison. These logs, like piano keys, kept rising up and down, and the unwary traveler would acquire a bump on his head, or a bruise on his brow, or might chance to give a painful bite with his own teeth to the tip of his own tongue. He noticed a sort of special dilapidation in all the village buildings: the logs of the cottages were dark and old; many of the roofs were riddled like sieves; some had just a ridge pole on top and rafters like ribs on the sides. It seemed as if the owners themselves had torn off the shingles and laths, con- sidering – correctly, of course – that one does not roof cottages in the rain, and in fair weather there is no dripping anyway, so why sit around women's skirts inside, when there is free space enough in the pot-house and on the high road – in short, anywhere you like. The windows of the cottages had no glass, some were stopped up with a rag or a jacket; the little roofed balconies with railings, which for unknown reasons are built onto some Russian cottages, were lopsided and blackened, not even picturesquely. Behind the cottages in many places stretched rows of huge stacks of wheat, which had evidently been standing there for a long time; in color they resembled old, poorly baked brick, trash of all kinds was growing on top of them, and bushes even clung to their sides. The wheat evidently belonged to the master. From behind the wheat stacks and dilapidated roofs there soared and flashed in the clear air, now right, now left, according to the turns the britzka made, two village churches, one next to the other: an abandoned wooden one, and a stone one, its yellowed walls all stains and cracks. Parts of the master's house came into view and finally the whole of it appeared in a gap where the chain of cottages broke off and in their place was left a vacant lot, formerly a kitchen garden or cabbage patch, surrounded by a low, in places broken, fence. Long, immeasurably long, the strange castle looked like some decrepit invalid. In places it had one story, in places two; on the dark roof, which did not everywhere reliably shield its old age, two belvederes had been stuck, facing each other, both of them shaky now, de- prived of the paint that had once covered them. The walls of the house showed bare lath in places and had evidently suffered much from all sorts of bad weather, rains, gales, and autumnal changes. Of the windows, only two were open, the rest being either shuttered or even boarded up. These two windows, for their part, were also weak-sighted; one of them had a dark triangle of blue sugar paper glued to it.

A vast, old garden stretching behind the house, extending beyond the village and then disappearing in the fields, overgrown and overrun, alone seemed to refresh this vast estate and alone was fully picturesque in its scenic devastation. In green clouds and irregular, leaf-fluttering cupolas against the sky's horizon lay the joined tops of the freely branching trees. The colossal white trunk of a birch, deprived of its crown, broken off in a tempest or thunderstorm, rose out of this green thickness and rounded in the air like a regular, gleaming marble column; the sharp, slanting break that topped it instead of a capital showed dark against its snowy whiteness, like a hat or a black bird. Wild hops, smothering the elder, mountain ash, and hazel bushes underneath and then running over the top of the whole thicket, finally raced upwards, twining around half the length of the broken birch. Having reached the middle, it hung down from there and began to catch at the tops of other trees or else dangled in air, tying its thin, grasping hooks into rings, swayed lightly by the air. In places the green thickets, lit by the sun, parted and revealed an unlit gap between them, yawning like a dark maw; it was all shrouded in shadow, and in its dark depths there barely flashed a running, narrow path, a collapsed railing, a rickety gazebo, the hollowed, decrepit trunk of a willow, a hoary hawthorn sticking out from behind the willow in a dense stubble of tangled and intertwined leaves and branches, withered in that terrible occlusion, and, finally, a young maple bough, stretching from the side its green pawlike leaves, one of them suddenly transformed by the sun, which got under it God knows how, into something transparent and fiery, shining wondrously in that dense darkness. To one side, at the very edge of the garden, several tall aspens, grown beyond the level of the rest, lifted up huge crows' nests on their fluttering tops. From some of them, broken but not quite sundered branches hung down with their withered leaves. In short, it was all just right, as neither nature nor art can contrive, but as only occurs when they join together, when, after the heaped-up, often senseless, labors of men, nature makes a finishing pass with her chisel, lightening the heavy masses, removing the crude-feeling regularity and indigent gaps through which the bare, undisguised plan peeps out, and imparts a wondrous warmth to all that was created in coldly measured cleanness and neatness.

Having made one or two turns, our hero finally found himself right in front of the house, which now seemed more mournful still. Green mold covered the already decayed wood of the fence and gate. A crowd of buildings – servants' quarters, barns, cellars, all visibly decaying – filled the courtyard; near them, to right and left, gates could be seen leading to other yards. Everything bespoke the vast scale on which estate life had once gone on here, and everything now looked dismal. Nothing to enliven the picture could be noticed: no doors opening, no people coming out from anywhere, no lively household hustle and bustle! Only the main gates were open, and that because a muzhik had driven in with a loaded cart covered with bast matting, appearing as if by design to enliven this desolate place; at other times the gates, too, were tightly locked, for a giant padlock was hanging in the iron staple. By one of the buildings Chichikov soon noticed some figure, who had begun squabbling with the muzhik on the cart. For a long time he could not make out the figure's sex, male or female. It was dressed in something completely indefinite, much like a woman's housecoat, with a cap on its head such as household serf wenches wear in the country, only the voice seemed to him rather too husky for a woman. "Ai, a female!" he thought to himself, and added at once: "Ah, no!" Finally he said, "A female, of course!" – having looked more intently. The figure for her part was also staring intently at him. It seemed that a visitor was a remarkable thing for her, because she scrutinized not only him, but also Selifan and the horses, from tail to muzzle. By the keys hanging from her belt, and by the fact that she was scolding the muzhik in rather abusive terms, Chichikov concluded that this must be the housekeeper.

"Listen, dearie," he said, getting out of the britzka, "about the master..."

"Not home," the housekeeper interrupted, without waiting for the end of the question, and then, after a minute, she added: "What do you want?"

"It's business."

"Go in!" said the housekeeper, turning away and showing him her back, dusted with flour, with a big rip lower down.

He stepped into the dark, wide front hall, from which cold air blew as from a cellar. From the hall he got into a room, also dark, faintly illumined by light coming through a wide crack under a door. Opening this door, he at last found himself in the light and was struck by the disorder that confronted him. It looked as if they were washing the floors in the house, and all the furniture had for the time being been piled up here. On one table there even stood a broken chair, and next to it a clock with a stopped pendulum to which a spider had already attached its web. Near it, leaning its side against the wall, stood a cupboard with old silver, decanters, and Chinese porcelain. On the bureau, inlaid with mother-of-pearl mosaic, which in places had fallen out and left only yellow grooves filled with glue, lay a various multitude of things: a stack of papers written all over in a small hand, covered by a marble paperweight, gone green, with a little egg on top of it, some ancient book in a leather binding with red edges, a completely dried-up lemon no bigger than a hazelnut, the broken-off arm of an armchair, a glass with some sort of liquid and three flies in it, covered by a letter, a little piece of sealing wax, a little piece of rag picked up somewhere, two ink-stained pens, dried up as if with consumption, a toothpick, turned completely yellow, with which the master had probably picked his teeth even before the invasion of Moscow by the French.[26]

On the walls, hung quite close together and haphazardly, were a number of pictures: a long, yellowed engraving of some battle, with enormous drums, shouting soldiers in three-cornered hats, and drowning horses, without glass, in a mahogany frame with thin bronze strips and bronze rounds at the corners. Next to it, half the wall was taken up by an enormous, blackened oil painting portraying flowers, fruit, a sliced watermelon, a boar's head, and a duck hanging upside down. From the middle of the ceiling hung a chandelier in a hempen sack, which the dust made to resemble a silk cocoon with a worm sitting inside it. On the floor in the corner of the room was heaped a pile of whatever was more crude and unworthy of lying on the tables. Precisely what was in this pile it was hard to tell, for there was such an abundance of dust on it that the hands of anyone who touched it resembled gloves; most conspicuously, there stuck out from it a broken-off piece of a wooden shovel and an old boot sole. One would never have known that the room was inhabited by a living being, were its presence not announced by an old, worn nightcap lying on the table. While he was examining all these strange adornments, a side door opened and in came the same housekeeper he had met in the yard. But here he perceived that the housekeeper was a man, rather than a woman; a woman, in any case, does not shave, while this one, on the contrary, did shave, though apparently not very often, because his whole chin along with the lower part of his cheeks resembled a currycomb made of iron wire, used in stables for grooming horses. Chichikov, giving his face an inquisitive expression, waited impatiently for what the housekeeper wanted to say to him. The housekeeper, for his part, also waited for what Chichikov wanted to say to him. Finally the latter, astonished at such strange perplexity, decided to ask:

"About the master? Is he in, or what?"

"The master's here," said the housekeeper.

"But where?" Chichikov reiterated.

"What, my dear, are you blind or something?" said the housekeeper. "Egad! But I am the master!"

Here our hero involuntarily stepped back and looked at him intently. He had chanced to meet many different kinds of people, even kinds such as the reader and I may never get to meet; but such a one he had never met before. His face presented nothing unusual; it was about the same as in many lean old men, only his chin protruded very far forward, so that he had to cover it with a handkerchief all the time to keep from spitting on it; his small eyes were not yet dim and darted from under his high arched eyebrows like mice when, poking their sharp little snouts from their dark holes, pricking up their ears and twitching their whiskers, they spy out whether there is a cat or a mischievous boy in hiding, and sniff the very air suspiciously. Far more remarkable was his outfit: no means or efforts would avail to discover what his robe was concocted of: the sleeves and front were so greasy and shiny that they looked like the tarred leather used for making boots; behind, instead of two skirts, four hung down, with tufts of cotton wool emerging from them. Around his neck, too, something un-identifiable was tied: a stocking, a garter, a bellyband, anything but a cravat. In short, if Chichikov had met him, attired thus, somewhere at a church door, he probably would have given him a copper. For to our hero's credit it must be said that he had a compassionate heart and could never refrain from giving a poor man a copper. But before him stood no beggar, before him stood a landowner. This landowner had more than a thousand souls, and it would have been hard to find another who had so much wheat in grain, flour, or simply in stacks, whose storerooms, barns, and granaries were crammed with so much linen, felt, sheepskin dressed and raw, dried fish, and all sorts of vegetables and foodstuff. Had anyone peeked into his workshop, where all kinds of wood and never-used wares were stored up in reserve – he would have thought he had landed somehow on woodworkers' row in Moscow, where spry beldames set out daily, with their scullery maids in tow, to make their household purchases, and where there gleam mountains of wooden articles – nailed, turned, joined, and plaited: barrels, halved barrels, tubs, tar buckets, flagons with and without spouts, stoups, baskets, hampers in which village women keep their skeins of flax and other junk, panniers of thin bent aspen, corbeils of plaited birchbark, and much else that is put to service in rich and poor Rus.[27] What need, one might ask, did Plyushkin have for such a mass of these artifacts? Never in all his life could they have been used even on two such estates as his – but to him it still seemed too little. Not satisfied with it, he walked about the streets of his village every day, looked under the little bridges and stiles, and whatever he came across – an old shoe sole, a woman's rag, an iron nail, a potsherd – he carried off and added to the pile that Chichikov had noticed in the corner of the room. "The fisherman's off in pursuit again!" the muzhiks would say, when they saw him going for his booty. And, indeed, after him there was no need to sweep the streets: if a passing officer happened to lose a spur, the spur would immediately be dispatched to the famous pile; if a woman started mooning by the well and forgot her bucket, he would carry off the bucket. However, if a muzhik noticed and caught him in the act, he would not argue and would surrender the purloined thing; but if it did make it to the pile, it was all over: he would swear to God that he had bought the thing at such and such a time from such and such a person, or inherited it from his grandfather. In his room he picked up whatever he saw on the floor – a bit of sealing wax, a scrap of paper, a feather – and put it all on the bureau or the windowsill.

And yet once upon a time he had been simply a thrifty manager! was married and had a family, and a neighbor would come to dine with him, to listen and learn from him the ways of management and wise parsimony. Everything flowed briskly and was accomplished at a regular pace: the gristmills and fulling mills turned, the felting, wood-turning, and spinning machines worked; into everything everywhere the manager's keen glance penetrated, and, like an industrious spider, ran busily yet efficiently to all ends of his managerial spiderweb. His features reflected no very strong emotions, but one could see intelligence in his eyes; his speech was pervaded by experience and knowledge of the world, and it was pleasant for a guest to listen to him; the affable and talkative mistress of the house was famous for her hospitality; two comely daughters came to meet the guest, both blond and fresh as roses; the son ran out, a frolicsome lad, and kissed everyone, paying little heed to whether the guest was glad of it or not. All the windows were open in the house, the garret was occupied by the French tutor, who shaved splendidly and was a great shot: he always brought home grouse or duck for dinner, but on occasion only sparrow eggs, which he ordered served as an omelette for himself, since no one else in the house would eat them. In the garret there also lived a young lady compatriot of his, who taught the two girls. The master himself used to come to table in a frock coat, somewhat worn but neat, the elbows in good order: not a patch anywhere. But the good mistress died; part of the keys, and of the petty cares along with them, passed to him. Plyushkin grew more restless and, like all widowers, more suspicious and stingy. He could not rely altogether on his eldest daughter, Alexandra Stepanovna, and right he was, because Alexandra Stepanovna soon eloped with a staff captain of God knows what cavalry regiment and married him hastily somewhere in a village church, knowing that her father disliked officers, from the strange prejudice that the military are all supposed to be gamblers and spendthrifts. The father sent her a curse for the road, but did not bother pursuing her. The house became still emptier. In the master of the house, stinginess displayed itself still more noticeably, furthered in its development by its faithful friend, the gray flickering in his coarse hair; the French tutor was dismissed, because the time came for the son to enter the civil service; *madame* was chased out, because she was found not guiltless in Alexandra Stepanovna's elopement; the son, having been sent to the provincial capital to learn in a government office what, in his father's view, real service was, enlisted in a regiment instead and wrote to his father only after he enlisted, asking for money to equip himself; for which, quite naturally, he got what among common folk is known as a fig. Finally the last daughter, who had stayed at home with him, died, and the old man found himself the sole guardian, keeper, and master of his riches. Solitary life gave ample nourishment to his avarice, which, as is known, has a wolf's appetite and grows more insatiable the more it devours; human feelings, never very deep in him anyway, became shallower every moment, and each day something more was lost in this worn-out ruin. There came a moment, as if on purpose to confirm his opinion of the military, when his son happened to lose heavily at cards; he sent him a paternal curse from the bottom of his heart, and was never again interested in knowing whether his son existed in the world or not. Each year more windows in his house were closed up, until finally only two were left, one of which, as the reader already knows, had paper glued over it; each year more and more of the main parts of management were lost sight of, and his petty glance turned to the little scraps and feathers he collected in his room; he grew more unyielding with the buyers who came to take the products of his estate; the buyers bargained, bargained, and finally dropped him altogether, saying he was a devil, not a man; the hay and wheat rotted, the stooks and ricks turned to pure dung, good for planting cabbages in; the flour in the cellars became stone and had to be hacked up; the felt, linen, and homespun materials were even frightening to touch: they turned to dust. He himself had forgotten by then how much he had of what, and only remembered where in the cupboard he kept a little decanter with the remainder of some liqueur, on which he himself had made a mark, so that no one could steal a drink from it, or where a feather or a bit of sealing wax lay. But meanwhile the revenues of the estate were collected as before: the muzhik had to bring the same amount of quitrent, every woman was taxed the same amount of nuts, or as many lengths of linen if she was a weaver – all this was dumped in the storerooms, and it all turned to rot and gape, and he himself finally turned into a sort of gape in mankind. Alexandra Stepanovna once came a couple of times with her little son, trying to see if she could get anything; apparently camp life with the staff captain was not as attractive as it had seemed before the wedding. Plyushkin forgave her, however, and even gave his little grandson a button that was lying on the table to play with, but money he gave none. The next time Alexandra Stepanovna came with two little ones and brought him a *kulich*[28] for tea and a new robe, because her papa's robe was such that it was not only embarrassing but even shameful to behold. Plyushkin was nice to both grandchildren and, placing one of them on his right knee and the other on his left, rocked them in exactly the same way as if they had been riding a horse; he accepted the *kulich* and the robe, but gave his daughter decidedly nothing; and with that Alexandra Stepanovna left.

And so, this was the sort of landowner who stood before Chichikov! It must be said that one rarely comes upon such a phenomenon in Russia, where everything prefers rather to expand than to shrink, and it is all the more striking when, right there in the neighborhood, there happens to be a landowner who carouses to the full breadth of Russian dash and largesse – who, as they say, burns up his whole life. A newcomer passing by will stop in amazement at the sight of his dwelling, wondering what sovereign prince has suddenly appeared among small, obscure landowners: there is the look of a palace about his white stone mansions with their numberless multitude of chimneys, belvederes, weather vanes, surrounded by a flock of cottages and all sorts of lodgings for long-term guests. Is there anything he lacks? Theatricals, balls; all night the garden shines, adorned with lights and lampions, resounding with the thunder of music. Half the province is decked out and gaily strolling under the trees, and in this forcible illumination no one sees it as wild and menacing when a branch leaps out theatrically from the thick of the trees, lit by the false light, robbed of its bright green; and, through all that, the night sky up above appears darker and sterner and twenty times more menacing; and the stern treetops, their leaves trembling in the far-off heights, sink deeper into the impenetrable darkness, indignant at this tinsel glitter illuminating their roots below.

For several minutes already Plyushkin had been standing there, not saying a word, yet Chichikov was still unable to begin talking, distracted as much by the look of the master himself as by all that was in his room. For a long time he was unable to think up any words to explain the reason for his visit. He was just about to express himself in some such spirit as, having heard of his virtue and the rare qualities of his soul, he felt it his duty personally to pay a tribute of respect, but he checked himself, feeling it was too much. Casting one more sidelong glance at all that was in the room, he felt that the words "virtue" and "rare qualities of soul" could successfully be replaced by the words "economy" and "order"; and therefore, transforming the speech in this manner, he said that, having heard of his economy and rare skill in running his estate, he felt it his duty to make his acquaintance and offer his respects personally. Of course, it would have been possible to produce another, better reason, but nothing else came into his head just then.

To this Plyushkin muttered something through his lips – for there were no teeth – precisely what is not known, but the meaning was probably this: "Ah, devil take you and your respects!" But since hospitality is so much the thing with us that even a niggard cannot transgress its laws, he added at once, somewhat more distinctly: "Pray be seated!"

"It's quite a while since I've seen visitors," he said, "and, I confess to say, I see little benefit in it. There's a most indecent custom of going and visiting each other, while the work of the estate is neglected... plus giving hay to their horses! I had my dinner long ago, and my kitchen is low, very shabby, and the chimney's all falling to pieces: heat it up and you'll start a fire."

"So that's how it is!" Chichikov thought to himself. "A good thing I snatched a cheesecake and a slice of lamb at Sobakevich's."

"And, such a nasty story, there's not a wisp of hay on the whole estate!" Plyushkin went on. "And how, indeed, can one save any? – wretched little piece of land, lazy muzhiks, don't like to work at all, dream only of the pot-house... I'm afraid I'll find myself a beggar in my old age."

"I was told, however," Chichikov observed modestly, "that you have more than a thousand souls."

"Who told you so? You ought, my dear, to have spit in the eye of the one who said it! He's a joker, obviously, and wanted to poke fun at you. A thousand souls, they say, but you just try counting them and there'll be nothing to count! In the last three years the cursed fever has killed off a healthy lot of muzhiks on me."

"You don't say! So a lot were killed off?" Chichikov exclaimed with sympathy.

"Yes, a lot got carted away."

"How many, if I may inquire?"

"About eighty."

"No!"

"I wouldn't lie, my dear."

"And, if I may ask: these souls have been counted up, I assume, since the day you submitted the last census report?"

"Would to God it were so," said Plyushkin, "but the pox of it is that since then it may have gone as high as a hundred and twenty."

"Really? A whole hundred and twenty?" Chichikov exclaimed and even opened his mouth slightly in amazement.

"I'm too old to lie, my dear: I'm in my sixties!" said Plyushkin. He seemed offended by such an almost joyful exclamation. Chichikov noticed that such indifference to another's misfortune was indeed improper, and therefore he straightaway sighed and offered his condolence.

"But condolence can't be put in the pocket," said Plyushkin. "There's this captain in the neighborhood, devil knows where he came from, says he's my relative – 'Uncle! Uncle!' and kisses my hand – and once he starts his condoling, hold your ears, he sets up such a howl. He's all red in the face: keeps a deathly grip on the home brew, I expect. Must have blown all his cash serving as an officer, or else some theater actress lured it out of him, so now he's here condoling!"

Chichikov tried to explain that his condolence was not at all of the same sort as the captain's, and he was ready to prove it, not with empty words, but with deeds, and, not putting the matter off any longer, without beating around the bush, he straightaway expressed his readiness to take upon himself the duty of paying taxes on all the peasants who had died through such unfortunate occasions. The offer, it seemed, utterly astounded Plyushkin. He stared pop-eyed at him for a long time, and finally asked:

"You, my dear, were never in military service?"

"No," Chichikov replied rather slyly, "I was in the civil service."

"In the civil service?" Plyushkin repeated, and he began munching his lips as if he were eating something. "But how can it be? Won't you yourself come out the loser?"

"For your pleasure I am even ready to come out the loser."

"Ah, my dear! ah, my benefactor!" Plyushkin cried, not noticing in his joy that snuff was peeking quite unpicturesquely from his nose, after the manner of thick coffee, and the skirts of his robe had opened revealing garments none too fit for inspection. "What a boon for an old man! Ah, my Lord! Ah, saints alive! . . . " Further Plyushkin could not even speak. But before a minute passed, this joy, which had appeared so instantaneously on his wooden face, just as instantaneously left, as if it had never been, and his face again assumed a worried expression. He even wiped it with a handkerchief, which he then bunched into a ball and began dragging over his upper lip.

"So then, with your permission, not wishing to anger you, are you undertaking to pay the tax on them each year? and will you give the money to me or to the treasury?"

"Here's what we'll do: we'll make out a deed of purchase, as if they were alive and as if you were selling them to me."

"Yes, a deed of purchase . . . ," Plyushkin said, lapsed into thought, and began chewing with his lips again. "This deed of purchase, you see – it all costs money. The clerks are such a shameless lot! Before, you used to get off with fifty coppers and a sack of flour, but now you must send them a whole cartload of grain, and a red banknote[29] on top of it – such cupidity! I don't know how it is the priests don't pay attention to it; they should read some sort of lesson: say what you like, no one can stand against the word of God."

"But you'd stand, I imagine!" Chichikov thought to himself, and straightaway said that, out of respect for him, he was even ready to take upon himself the costs of the deed.

Hearing that he would even take the costs of the deed upon himself, Plyushkin concluded that the visitor must be completely stupid and was only pretending he had been in the civil service, but had really been an officer and dangled after actresses. For all that, however, he was unable to conceal his joy and wished all kinds of boons not only upon him, but even upon his children, without asking whether he had any or not.

Going to the window, he rapped on it with his fingers and shouted: "Hey, Proshka!" A minute later someone could be heard running into the front hall in a flurry, pottering about there and thumping with his boots for a long time, then the door finally opened and in came Proshka, a boy of about thirteen, in such big boots that he almost walked out of them as he stepped. Why Proshka had such big boots can be learned at once: Plyushkin had for all his domestics, however many there were in the house, only one pair of boots, which had always to be kept in the front hall. Anyone summoned to the squire's quarters would usually do a barefoot dance across the whole yard, but, on coming into the front hall, would put on the boots and in that manner enter the room. On leaving the room, he would put the boots back in the front hall and set off again on his own soles. Someone looking out the window in the fall, especially when there begins to be a little frost in the mornings, would see all the domestics making such leaps as the most nimble dancer in the theater is scarcely able to bring off.

"Just look, my dear, what a mug!" Plyushkin said to Chichikov, pointing his finger at Proshka's face. "Stupid as a log, but try putting something down and he'll steal it in a trice! Well, what have you come for, fool, can you tell me that?" Here he produced a small silence, to which Proshka also responded with silence. "Prepare the samovar, do you hear, and take this key and give it to Mavra so she can go to the pantry: there's a rusk of the *kulich* Alexandra Stepanovna brought on the shelf there, to be served with tea! . . . Wait, where are you going? A tomfool! egad, what a tomfool! Have you got a devil itching in your feet, or what? . . . You listen first: the rusk, I expect, has gone bad on the outside, so have her scrape it with a knife, but don't throw the crumbs out, take them to the henhouse. And look out, brother, don't go into the pantry yourself, or you'll get you know what! with a birch broom, to make it taste better! You've got a nice appetite now, so that'll improve it for you! Just try going into the pantry with me watching out the window all the while. They can't be trusted in anything," he went on, turning to Chichikov, once Proshka had cleared out together with his boots. Then he began glancing suspiciously at Chichikov as well. The traits of such extraordinary magnanimity began to seem incredible to him, and he thought to himself: "Devil knows about him, maybe he's just a braggart, like all those spendthrifts: he'll lie and lie, just to talk and have some tea, and then he'll up and leave!" Hence, as a precaution and at the same time wishing to test him a little, he said it would not be a bad idea to sign the deed as soon as possible, because there's no trusting in man: today he's alive, but tomorrow God knows.

Chichikov expressed a readiness to sign it that very minute and asked only for a list of all the peasants.

This reassured Plyushkin. One could see that he was think-ing about doing something, and, in fact, taking his keys, he approached the cupboard and, opening the little door, rum-maged for a long time among the glasses and cups and finally said:

"I can't seem to find it, but I did have a splendid little liqueur, unless they drank it! Such thievish folk! Ah, could this be it?" Chichikov saw in his hands a little decanter, all covered with dust as with a fuzzy jacket. "My late wife made it," Plyushkin went on, "the crook of a housekeeper neglected it completely and didn't even put a stopper in it, the slut! Bugs and other trash got into it, but I removed all the bits, and now it's nice and clean; I'll pour you a glass."

But Chichikov tried to decline this nice little liqueur, saying that he already drank and ate.

"Already drank and ate!" said Plyushkin. "Yes, of course, a man of good society is recognizable anywhere: he doesn't eat but is full; but just take one of these little thieves, the more you feed him . . . There's this captain turns up: 'Uncle,' he says, 'give me something to eat!' And I'm as much his uncle as he's my carbuncle. Must have nothing to eat at home, so he hangs around here! Ah, yes, you want a little list of all those parasites? Look here, just as if I'd known, I wrote them all down on a separate piece of paper, so as to cross them off at the next census report."

Plyushkin put on his spectacles and began rummaging among his papers. Untying various bundles, he treated his visitor to so much dust that he sneezed. At last he pulled out a sheet that was written all over. Peasant names covered it as thickly as gnats. Every sort was there: Paramonov, Pimenov, Panteleimonov, even a certain Grigory Go-never-get peeked out – a hundred and twenty-something in all. Chichikov smiled to see such numerousness. Tucking it away in his pocket, he observed to Plyushkin that he would have to go to town to sign the deed.

"To town? But how? . . . how can I leave the house? All my folk are either thieves or crooks: they'll strip the place bare in a day, there'll be nothing left to hang a caftan on."

"Don't you have some acquaintance then?"

"Have I some acquaintance? My acquaintances all either died off or got unacquainted. Ah, my dear! but I do have one, I do!" he cried. "I know the head magistrate himself, he used to come here in the old days, of course I know him! we supped from the same trough, we used to climb fences together! of course we're acquainted! As if we're not acquainted! So mightn't I just write to him?"

"But, of course, write to him."

"Really, as if we're not acquainted! We were friends at school."

And some warm ray suddenly passed over his wooden face, expressing not a feeling, but some pale reflection of a feeling, a phenomenon similar to the sudden appearance of a drowning man on the surface, drawing a joyful shout from the crowd on the bank. But in vain do the rejoicing brothers and sisters throw a rope from the bank and wait for another glimpse of the back or the struggle-weary arms – that appearance was the last. Everything is desolate, and the stilled surface of the unresponding element is all the more terrible and deserted after that. So, too, Plyushkin's face, after the momentary passage of that feeling, became all the more unfeeling and trite.

"There was a piece of clean writing paper lying on the table," he said, "I don't know where on earth it's gone: my people are such a worthless lot!" Here he began peering under the table, and over the table, feeling everywhere, and finally shouted: "Mavra! hey, Mavra!"

At his call a woman appeared with a plate in her hands, on which lay a rusk, already familiar to the reader. Between them the following conversation took place:

"You robber, what did you do with that paper?"

"By God, master, I never saw any, save that little scrap you were pleased to cover the wine glass with."

"Ah, but I can see by your eyes that you filched it."

"And why would I filch it? I've got no use for it; I don't know how to write."

"Lies, you took it to the beadle's boy: he knows how to scribble, so you took it to him."

"Why, the beadle's boy can get paper for himself if he wants. Much he needs your scrap!"

"But just you wait: at the Last Judgment the devils will make it hot for you with the iron tongs! You'll see how hot!"

"And why make it hot, since I never laid a finger on your writing paper? Sooner some other female weakness, but no one has yet reproached me for thievery."

"Ah, but the devils will make it hot for you! They'll say: 'Ah, but take that, you crook, for deceiving your master!' and they'll get you with the hot ones."

"And I'll say: 'It's not fair! by God, it's not fair, I didn't take it . . .' Why, look, it's lying there on the table. You're always nattering at me for nothing."

Plyushkin indeed saw the writing paper, paused for a moment, munched his lips, and said:

"So, why get yourself worked up like that? Bristling all over! Say just one word to her, and she comes back with a dozen! Go fetch some fire to seal the letter. Wait, you're going to grab a tallow candle, tallow's a melting affair: it'll burn up and – gone, nothing but loss, you'd better bring me a spill!"

Mavra left, and Plyushkin, sitting down in an armchair and taking pen in hand, spent a long time turning the piece of paper in all directions, considering whether it was possible to save part of it, but finally became convinced that it was not possible; he dipped the pen into an ink pot with some moldy liquid and a multitude of flies at the bottom of it and began to write, producing letters that resembled musical notes, constantly restraining the zip of his hand, which went galloping all across the paper, stingily cramming in line upon line and thinking, not without regret, that there was still going to be a lot of blank space in between.

To such worthlessness, pettiness, vileness a man can descend! So changed he can become! Does this resemble the truth? Everything resembles the truth, everything can happen to a man. The now ardent youth would jump back in horror if he were shown his own portrait in old age. So take with you on your way, as you pass from youth's tender years into stern, hardening manhood, take with you every humane impulse, do not leave them by the wayside, you will not pick them up later! Terrible, dreadful old age looms ahead, and nothing does it give back again! The grave is more merciful, on the grave it will be written: "Here lies a man!" – but nothing can be read in the cold, unfeeling features of inhuman old age.

"And don't you know some friend of yours," Plyushkin said, folding the letter, "who might be in need of runaway souls?"

"You have runaways, too?" Chichikov asked quickly, coming to his senses.

"The point is that I have. My son-in-law made inquiries: he says the tracks are cold, but he's a military man: an expert in jingling his spurs, but as for dealing with the courts . . . "

"And how many might there be?"

"Oh, they'd also add up to about seventy."

"No!"

"By God, it's so! Every year someone runs away on me. These folk are mighty gluttons, got into the habit of stuffing themselves from idleness, and I myself have nothing to eat...So I'd take whatever I was given for them. You can advise your friend: if only a dozen get found, he's already making good money. A registered soul is worth about five hundred roubles."

"No, we won't let any friend get a whiff of this," Chichikov said to himself, and then explained that there was no way to find such a friend, that the cost of the procedure alone would be more than it was worth, for one had better cut off the tails of one's caftan and run as far as one can from the courts; but that if he was actually in such straits, then, being moved by compassion, he was ready to give...but it was such a trifle that it did not deserve mention.

"And how much would you give?" Plyushkin asked, turning Jew: his hands trembled like quicksilver.

"I'd give twenty-five kopecks per soul."

"And how would you buy them, for cash?"

"Yes, ready money."

"Only, my dear, for the sake of my beggarliness, you might give me forty kopecks."

"Most honorable sir!" said Chichikov, "not only forty kopecks, I would pay you five hundred roubles! With pleasure I would pay it, because I see – an honorable, kindly old man is suffering on account of his own good-heartedness."

"Ah, by God, it's so! by God, it's true!" said Plyushkin, hanging his head down and shaking it ruefully. "All from good-heartedness."

"So, you see, I suddenly grasped your character. And so, why shouldn't I give you five hundred roubles per soul, but...I haven't got a fortune; five kopecks, if you please,

I'm ready to add, so that each soul would, in that case, cost thirty kopecks."

"Well, my dear, as you will, just tack on two kopecks."

"Two little kopecks I will tack on, if you please. How many of them do you have? I believe you were saying seventy?"

"No. It comes to seventy-eight in all."

"Seventy-eight, seventy-eight, at thirty kopecks per soul, that would make . . . " Here our hero thought for one second, not more, and said suddenly: " . . . that would make twenty-four roubles, ninety-six kopecks!" – he was good at arithmetic. Straightaway he made Plyushkin write a receipt and handed him the money, which he received in both hands and carried to his bureau as carefully as if he were carrying some liquid, fearing every moment to spill it. Coming to his bureau, he looked through it once more and then placed it, also with extreme care, in one of the drawers, where it was probably doomed to lie buried until such time as Father Carp and Father Polycarp, the two priests of his village, came to bury him himself, to the indescribable delight of his son-in-law and daughter, and perhaps also of the captain who had enrolled himself among his relatives. Having put the money away, Plyushkin sat down in his armchair, at which point, it seemed, he was unable to find any further matter for conversation.

"What, you're already preparing to go?" he said, noticing a slight movement which Chichikov had made only so as to take his handkerchief from his pocket.

This question reminded him that in fact he had no reason to linger longer.

"Yes, it's time!" he said, picking up his hat.

"And a spot of tea?"

"No, better save the spot of tea for another time."

"Well, there, and I've sent for the samovar. I confess to say, I'm not an avid tea drinker: it's expensive, and the price of sugar has risen unmercifully. Proshka! never mind the samovar! Take the rusk to Mavra, do you hear: let her put it back in the same place – or, no, give it to me, I'd better take it myself. Good-bye, my dear, God bless you, and do give my letter to the magistrate. Yes! let him read it, he's my old acquaintance. Why, of course, we supped from the same trough!"

Whereupon this strange phenomenon, this wizened little old man, saw him off the premises, after which he ordered the gates locked at once, then made the round of the storerooms, to check whether the guards, who stood at every corner, banging with wooden spades on empty barrels instead of iron rails, were all in their places; after that, he peeked into the kitchen, where, on the pretext of testing whether people were being properly fed, he downed a goodly quantity of cabbage soup with groats and, having scolded every last one of them for thievery and bad behavior, returned to his room. Left alone, he even had the thought of somehow rewarding his guest for such indeed unexampled magnanimity. "I'll give him the pocket watch," he thought to himself. "It's a good silver watch, not some sort of pinchbeck or brass one; it's slightly broken, but he can have it repaired; he's still a young man, he needs a pocket watch so his fiancée will like him! Or, no," he added, after some reflection, "I'd better leave it to him after my death, in my will, so that he remembers me."

But our hero, even without the watch, was in the merriest spirits. Such an unexpected acquisition was a real gift. Indeed, whatever you say, not just dead souls alone, but runaways as well, and over two hundred persons in all! Of course, while still approaching Plyushkin's estate, he had had a presentiment of some pickings, but he had never expected anything so profitable. For the whole way he was extraordinarily merry, kept whistling, played on his lips, putting his fist to his mouth as if he were blowing a trumpet, and finally broke into some sort of song, extraordinary to such a degree that Selifan himself listened, listened, and then, shaking his head slightly, said: "Just look how the master's singing!" It was thick dusk by the time they drove up to the town. Shadow and light were thoroughly mingled, and objects themselves also seemed to mingle. The particolored tollgate took on some indefinite hue; the mustache of the soldier standing sentry seemed to be on his forehead, way above his eyes, and his nose was as if not there at all. A rumbling and jolting made it known that the britzka had come to the pavement. The streetlamps were not yet burning, only here and there the windows of the houses were beginning to light up, and in nooks and crooks there occurred scenes and conversations inseparable from that time of day in all towns where there are many soldiers, coachmen, workers, and beings of a special kind, in the form of ladies in red shawls and shoes without stockings, who flit about like bats at the street-corners. Chichikov paid them no notice, and even did not notice the many slim clerks with canes, who were probably returning home after taking a stroll out of town. From time to time there reached his ears certain, apparently feminine, exclamations: "Lies, you drunkard! I never allowed him no such rudeness!" or "Don't fight, you boor, go to the police, I'll prove it to you there!..." In short, words which suddenly pour like boiling pitch over some dreamy twenty-year-old youth, when he is returning from the theater, carrying in his head a street in Spain, night, the wondrous image of a woman with a guitar and curls. Is there anything, any dream, not in his head? He is in heaven and has come calling on Schiller[30] – and suddenly over him there resound, like thunder, the fatal words, and he sees that he is back on earth, and even on Haymarket Square, and even near a pot-house, and workaday life again goes strutting before him.

Finally, after a decent bounce, the britzka sank, as if into a hole, into the gates of the inn, and Chichikov was met by Petrushka, who held the skirts of his frock coat with one hand, for he did not like them to come open, and with the other began helping him to get out of the britzka. The floorboy also ran out with a candle in his hand and a napkin on his shoulder. Whether Petrushka was glad of his master's arrival is not known; in any case, he exchanged winks with Selifan, and his ordinarily stern exterior this time seemed to brighten a little.

"You've been off on a long one, sir," said the floorboy, lighting the stairway.

"Yes," said Chichikov, as he went up the stairs. "And how's with you?"

"Well, thank God," the floorboy replied, bowing. "Yesterday some army lieutenant came and took number sixteen."

"A lieutenant?"

"Some unknown kind, from Ryazan, bay horses."

"Very good, very good, keep up the good behavior," Chichikov said and went into his room. Passing through the anteroom, he wrinkled his nose and said to Petrushka: "You might at least have opened the windows!"

"But I did open them," Petrushka said, lying. Incidentally, the master knew he was lying, but he had no wish to object. After the trip he had made, he felt great fatigue. Having asked for a very light supper, consisting only of suckling pig, he straightaway got undressed and, slipping under the blanket, fell asleep soundly, deeply, fell asleep in the wondrous way that they alone sleep who are so fortunate as to know nothing of hemorrhoids, or fleas, or overly powerful mental abilities.

CHAPTER SEVEN

HAPPY THE WAYFARER who, after a long, boring journey with its cold, slush, dirt, sleepy stationmasters, clanking bells, repairs, altercations, coachmen, blacksmiths, and all sorts of scoundrels of the road, sees at last the familiar roof with its lights rushing to meet him, and before him stand familiar rooms, the joyful shout of his people running to meet him, the noise and scampering of children, and soothing soft speech, interrupted by burning kisses with the power to wipe out all that is mournful from the memory. Happy the family man who has such a corner, but woe to the bachelor!

Happy the writer who, passing by characters that are boring, disgusting, shocking in their mournful reality, approaches characters that manifest the lofty dignity of man, who from the great pool of daily whirling images has chosen only the rare exceptions, who has never once betrayed the exalted tuning of his lyre, nor descended from his height to his poor, insignificant brethren, and, without touching the ground, has given the whole of himself to his elevated images so far removed from it. Twice enviable is his beautiful lot: he is among them as in his own family; and meanwhile his fame spreads loud and far. With entrancing smoke he has clouded people's eyes; he has flattered them wondrously, concealing what is mournful in life, showing them a beautiful man. Everything rushes after him, applauding, and flies off following his triumphal chariot. Great world poet they name him, soaring high above all other geniuses in the world, as the eagle soars above other high fliers. At the mere mention of his name, young ardent hearts are filled with trembling, responsive tears shine in all eyes... No one equals him in power – he is God! But such is not the lot, and other is the destiny of the writer who has dared to call forth all that is before our eyes every moment and which our indifferent eyes do not see – all the terrible, stupendous mire of trivia in which our life is entangled, the whole depth of cold, fragmented, everyday characters that swarm over our often bitter and boring earthly path, and with the firm strength of his implacable chisel dares to present them roundly and vividly before the eyes of all people! It is not for him to win people's applause, not for him to behold the grateful tears and unanimous rapture of the souls he has stirred; no sixteen-year-old girl will come flying to meet him with her head in a whirl and heroic enthusiasm; it is not for him to forget himself in the sweet enchantment of sounds he himself has evoked; it is not for him, finally, to escape contemporary judgment, hypocritically callous contemporary judgment, which will call insignificant and mean the creations he has fostered, will allot him a contemptible corner in the ranks of writers who insult mankind, will ascribe to him the qualities of the heroes he has portrayed, will deny him heart, and soul, and the divine flame of talent. For contemporary judgment does not recognize that equally wondrous are the glasses that observe the sun and those that look at the movements of inconspicuous insects; for contemporary judgment does not recognize that much depth of soul is needed to light up the picture drawn from contemptible life and elevate it into a pearl of creation; for contemporary judgment does not recognize that lofty ecstatic laughter is worthy to stand beside the lofty lyrical impulse, and that a whole abyss separates it from the antics of the street-fair clown! This contemporary judgment does not recognize; and will turn it all into a reproach and abuse of the unrecognized writer; with no sharing, no response, no sympathy, like a familyless wayfarer, he will be left alone in the middle of the road. Grim is his path, and bitterly will he feel his solitude.

And for a long time still I am destined by a wondrous power to walk hand in hand with my strange heroes, to view the whole of hugely rushing life, to view it through laughter visible to the world and tears invisible and unknown to it! And still far off is the time when, in a different key, a fearsome tempest of inspiration will rise from a head wreathed in sacred awe and radiance, and in confused trepidation will be heard the majestic thunder of a different speech . . .

Onward! onward! away with the wrinkle that furrows the brow and the stern gloom of the face! At once and suddenly let us plunge into life with all its noiseless clatter and little bells and see what Chichikov is doing.

Chichikov woke up, stretched his arms and legs, and felt he had had a good sleep. After lying on his back for a minute or two, he snapped his fingers and remembered with a beaming face that he now owned nearly four hundred souls. He straightaway jumped out of bed, not even looking at his face, which he sincerely loved and in which, it seemed, he found the chin most attractive of all, for he quite often boasted of it to one or another of his friends, especially if it was while shaving. "Just look," he would usually say, stroking it with his hand, "what a chin I've got: quite round!" But this time he did not glance either at his chin or at his face, but directly, just as he was, put on his morocco boots with multicolor appliqué, an object of brisk trade in Torzhok thanks to the lounge-robe inclinations of the Russian nature, and, Scottish-fashion, in nothing but a short shirt, forgetting his staid and decorous middle age, performed two leaps across the room, smacking himself quite adroitly with his heel. Then at that same moment he got down to business: facing the chest, he rubbed his hands with the same pleasure as the incorruptible circuit court, having come for an inquest, does when approaching the hors d'oeuvres, and instantly took the papers out of it. He wanted to finish everything quickly, without letting it simmer. He decided to draw up the deeds himself, writing them out and copying them, so as to pay nothing to scriveners. He knew the formal order perfectly. Briskly he set forth in big letters: "The year one thousand eight hundred and such-and-such," then in smaller letters following that: "The landowner so-and-so," and everything else necessary. In two hours it was all done. Afterwards, as he looked at these papers, at these muzhiks who, indeed, had been muzhiks once, had worked, ploughed, drunk, driven, deceived their masters, or perhaps had simply been good muzhiks, some strange feeling, incomprehensible to himself, took hold of him. It was as if each list had some peculiar character, and as if through it the muzhiks themselves acquired a character of their own. The muzhiks who had belonged to Korobochka almost all had additions and nick-names. Plyushkin's list was distinguished by brevity of style: often only the initial letters of names and patronymics were put down, and then two dots. Sobakevich's register was striking in its extraordinary fullness and thoroughness; not one of the muzhik's qualities was omitted: "good cabinetmaker" was said of one; "knows what he's about, and never touches the liquor" was added to another. It was also thoroughly noted who the father and mother were and how they had behaved themselves; only for a certain Fedotov it was written: "father unknown, was born of the serf girl Capitolina, but is of good character and not a thief." All these details gave off a peculiar air of freshness: it seemed the muzhiks had been alive only yesterday. Looking at their names for a long time, he was moved in his spirit and, sighing, said: "My heavens, there's so many of you crammed in here! What did you do in your lives, dear hearts, how did you get by?" And his eyes involuntarily paused on one family name: it was our acquaintance, Pyotr Saveliev Disrespect-Trough, who had once belonged to the landowner Korobochka. Again he could not keep from saying: "Eh, what a long one, stretched over a whole line! Were you a craftsman, or simply a peasant, and what sort of death took you? In a pot-house, was it, or did some clumsy train of carts drive over you while you were asleep in the middle of the road? Cork Stepan, carpenter, of exemplary sobriety. Ah! here he is, Stepan Cork, that mighty man, fit to serve in the guards! I expect you walked over all the provinces, an axe tucked into your belt, boots slung over your shoulders, eating a half-kopeck's worth of bread and a kopeck's worth of dried fish, and I expect each time you brought home up to a hundred silver roubles in your pouch, or maybe had a thousand-rouble banknote sewn into your hempen britches or stuck in your boot. Where were you when you got taken? Did you hoist yourself for greater gain up under the church cupola, or maybe drag yourself all the way to the cross, slip from the crossbeam, and fall flop to the ground, and only some Uncle Mikhei standing there, after scratching the back of his head, observed: 'Eh, Vanya, you sure came a cropper!' – and, tying the rope on, went up himself to replace you? Maxim Telyatnikov, cobbler. Hah, a cobbler! 'Drunk as a cobbler!' the saying goes. I know, I know you, my sweet fellow; I'll tell your whole story if you like: you were apprenticed to a German, who fed you all together, beat you on the back with a belt for sloppiness, and wouldn't let you out for any rascality, and you were a wonder, not a cobbler, and the German couldn't praise you enough when he was talking with his wife or a comrade. And when your apprenticeship was up, you said: 'And now I'll open shop, and not do like some German, pulling himself out of a kopeck, but get rich all at once.' And so, having offered your master a handsome quitrent, you started a little shop, got yourself a pile of orders, and set to work. Procured some rotten leather dirt-cheap somewhere, and in fact made double your money on each boot, but in two weeks your boots all popped apart, and you were abused in the meanest way. And so your little shop fell into neglect, and you took to drinking and lying about in the streets, saying all the while: 'No, it's a bad world! There's no life for a Russian man, the Germans keep getting in the way.' What sort of muzhik is this? Elizaveta Sparrow. Pah, drat it all – a female! How did she get in there? That scoundrel Sobakevich has hoodwinked me here, too!" Chichikov was right: it was, in fact, a female. How she got there no one knows, but she was so artfully written that from a distance she could be taken for a muzhik, and her name even had a masculine ending, that is, not Elizaveta, but Elizavet. However, he did not pay her any respect, and straightaway crossed her out. "Grigory Go-never-get! What sort of man were you? Did you set up as a hauler and, having got yourself a troika and a bast-covered wagon, renounce your house, your native den, forever and go dragging yourself with merchants to the fairs? Did you give up the ghost on the road, or did your own companions do you in over some fat and red-cheeked soldier's wife, or did some forest tramp take a liking to your leather-palmed mittens and your troika of squat but brawny horses, or maybe you yourself, lying on your plank bed, kept thinking and thinking, and for no reason at all steered for a pot-house, and then straight into a hole in the ice, and so made your exit. Eh, Russian folk! they don't like dying a natural death! And how about you, my sweet ones!" he went on, shifting his eyes to the paper on which Plyushkin's runaway souls were listed. "Though you're still alive, what's the use of you! you're as good as dead, and where are your quick feet taking you now? Was it so bad for you at Plyushkin's, or are you simply roaming the forests of your own will, fleecing passersby? Are you locked up in prisons, or are you with other masters, tilling the soil? Yeremei Karyakin, Vitaly Dillydally, his son Anton Dillydally – these are good runners, you can even tell by their nicknames. Popov, a house serf, must be a literate one: you didn't take up the knife, I expect, but went around stealing in a noble fashion. But here you are now, caught by the police captain without a passport. You stand cheerfully at the confrontation. 'Whose are you?' the police captain says, using this sure opportunity to put in some strong epithet for you. 'Landowner so-and-so's,' you reply pertly. 'What are you doing here?' the police captain says.

'I'm free on quitrent,' you reply without a hitch. 'Where's your passport?' 'With my landlord, the tradesman Pimenov.' 'Summon Pimenov! Are you Pimenov?' 'I'm Pimenov.' 'Did he give you his passport?' 'No, he never gave me any passport.' 'Why are you lying?' the police captain says, with the addition of some strong epithet. 'Exactly right,' you reply pertly, 'I didn't give it to him, because I came home late, so I gave it to Antip Prokhorov, the bell ringer, for safekeeping.' 'Summon the bell ringer! Did he give you his passport?' 'No, I never got any passport from him.' 'So you're lying again!' says the police captain, clinching his speech with some strong epithet. 'So where is your passport?' 'I had it,' you say briskly, 'but it seems I must somehow have dropped it in the road.' 'And how is it,' says the police captain, again tacking on some strong epithet for you, 'that you filched a soldier's greatcoat? And a priest's chest with copper money in it?' 'No, sir,' you say, without budging, 'I've never yet found myself in any thievish dealings.' 'And why, then, was the soldier's greatcoat found with you?' 'I can't say: someone else must have brought it.' 'Ah, you knave, you!' says the police captain, shaking his head, arms akimbo. 'Put the clogs on him and take him to prison.' 'As you like! It's my pleasure!' you reply. And so, taking a snuffbox from your pocket, you amiably treat the pair of invalids who are putting the clogs on you, asking them how long they've been retired and what war they were in. And so there you are now living in prison, while your case is being processed in court. And the court writes that you are to be transferred from Tsarevokokshaisk to the prison in such-and-such town, and the court there writes that you are to be transferred to some Vesyegonsk, and so you keep moving from prison to prison, saying, as you look over your new abode: 'No, the Vesyegonsk prison is a bit better, there's at least room enough to play knucklebones, and the company's bigger!' Abakum Fyrov! What about you, brother? Where, in which parts, are you hanging about? Did you get blown as far as the

Volga, and join the boatmen there, having come to love the life of freedom?..." Here Chichikov paused and pondered a little. Over what was he pondering? Was he pondering over Abakum Fyrov's lot, or was he pondering just like that, as any Russian falls to pondering, whatever his age, rank, or fortune, when he begins to reflect on the revels of a broad life? And, indeed, where is Fyrov now? He is carousing noisily and merrily on the grain wharf, after striking a bargain with the merchants. Flowers and ribbons on their hats, the whole gang of boatmen are making merry, taking leave of their lovers and wives, tall, well-built, in necklaces and ribbons; round dances, songs, the whole square is seething, and meanwhile the steve-dores, with shouts, curses, and heave-ho's, hoist as much as three hundred pounds on their backs with a hook, noisily pour peas and wheat into the deep holds, pile up bags of oats and groats, and farther off, all over the square, one can see sacks piled up like cannonballs in pyramids, and the whole grain arsenal stands enormous, until it has all been loaded into the deep Sura boats, and the endless flotilla rushes off in file together with the spring ice! There will be work enough for you, boatmen! And in unison, just as you reveled and rioted before, you will start to toil and sweat, hauling the line to one song as endless as Russia.

"Oh-oh! twelve o'clock!" Chichikov said at last, glancing at his watch. "What am I doing dawdling like this? It wouldn't matter if I was getting something done, but first I started pouring out drivel for no reason at all, and then I fell to pondering. Eh, what a fool I am, really!" Having said this, he changed his Scottish costume for a European one, drew the belt buckle tight over his plump belly, sprinkled himself with eau de cologne, took a warm cap in his hand and the papers under his arm, and set out for the government offices to execute his deeds. He was hurrying not because he was afraid of being late – he was not afraid of being late, for the head magistrate was a man of his acquaintance, and could lengthen or shorten his office hours at will, like the ancient Zeus of Homer, who prolonged days or sent quicker nights when he wanted to stop the combat of heroes dear to him or give them the means to finish their fight – but he felt in himself a desire to bring the business to a close as soon as possible; until then everything seemed uneasy and uncomfortable to him; it kept occurring to him that, after all, the souls were not quite real, and that in such cases one must hasten to get the burden off one's shoulders. No sooner had he gone out, reflecting upon all this and at the same time dragging onto his shoulders a bear covered with brown flannel, when just at the corner of the lane he ran into a gentleman also in a bear covered with brown flannel and a warm cap with ear flaps. The gentleman uttered a cry: it was Manilov. They straightaway locked each other in an embrace and stood that way in the street for about five minutes. The kisses were so hard on both sides that both men had an ache in their front teeth for almost the whole day. Manilov's eyes disappeared completely from joy, leaving only the nose and lips on his face. For about a quarter of an hour he held Chichikov's hand in both of his hands and made it terribly warm. In the most refined and pleasant turns of phrase he told how he had flown to embrace Pavel Ivanovich; the speech was concluded with a compliment such as is perhaps fitting only for a girl one is taking to a dance. Chichikov opened his mouth, still not knowing how to thank him, when suddenly Manilov took from under his fur coat a piece of paper rolled into a tube and tied with a pink ribbon, and deftly held it out with two fingers.

"What's this?"

"My little muzhiks."

"Ah!" He unrolled it straightaway, ran his eyes over it, and marveled at the neatness and beauty of the handwriting. "So nicely written," he said, "no need even to copy it. And a border around it! Who made such an artful border?"

"Oh, you mustn't ask," said Manilov.

"You?"

"My wife."

"Ah, my God! I really am ashamed to have caused so much trouble."

"When it's for Pavel Ivanovich, there's no such thing as trouble."

Chichikov bowed in gratitude. On learning that he was going to court to execute the deed, Manilov expressed a readiness to accompany him. The friends linked arms and set off together. At every little rise, bump, or step, Manilov supported Chichikov and almost lifted him up by the arm, adding with a pleasant smile that he would by no means allow Pavel Ivanovich to hurt his little feet. Chichikov was abashed, not knowing how to thank him, for he was aware that he was a bit on the heavy side. With mutual services they finally reached the square where the offices were located: a big three-story stone house, all white as chalk, probably to represent the purity of soul of the functions located within; the other structures on the square did not answer to the hugeness of the stone building. These were: a sentry box, where a soldier with a gun stood, two or three cabstands, and, finally, long fences with well-known fence inscriptions and drawings scrawled on them in charcoal or chalk; there was nothing else to be found on this solitary, or, as we say, beautiful square. From the windows of the second and third stories the incorruptible heads of the priests of Themis peeked out and ducked back at the same moment: probably a superior had come into the room just then. The friends did not so much walk as run up the stairs, because Chichikov, trying to elude the supporting arm from Manilov's side, kept quickening his pace, while Manilov, on his side, rushed ahead, trying to keep Chichikov from tiring himself, with the result that they were both quite breathless as they entered the dark corridor. Neither in the corridors nor in the rooms were their eyes struck by cleanliness. Back then people did not bother about it, and what was dirty simply stayed dirty, not assuming an attractive appearance. Themis received her guests as she was, in négligée and dressing gown. The chancellery rooms through which our heroes passed ought to be described, but the author feels a great timidity before all official places. Even happening to pass through them when they were splendid and ennobled of aspect, with polished floors and tables, he has tried to run as quickly as possible, humbly lowering his eyes and casting them on the ground, with the result that he is totally ignorant of how everything there prospers and flourishes. Our heroes saw lots of paper, rough drafts and fair copies, bent heads, broad napes, tailcoats, frock coats of a provincial cut, and even simply some light gray jacket, which stood out quite sharply, its head twisted to one side and almost lying on the paper as it traced, deftly and boldly, some protocol on an appropriation of land or the perquisition of an estate taken over by some peaceful landowner, who was quietly living out his life under lawsuit and had acquired children and grandchildren for himself under its protection, and they heard scraps of short phrases, uttered in a hoarse voice: "Hey, Fedosei Fedoseevich, lend me that little case no. 368!" "You always walk off somewhere with the cork to the office ink bottle!" Sometimes a more majestic voice, undoubtedly that of one of the superiors, resounded commandingly: "Here, copy this! or we'll take your boots away and you'll sit here for six days without food." The noise of pens was great and resembled that of several carts loaded with brushwood moving through a forest two feet deep in dry leaves.

Chichikov and Manilov went up to the first desk, where sat two clerks still young in years, and asked:

"May we inquire where deeds are dealt with here?"

"And what is it you want?" said both clerks, turning around.

"And what I want is to make an application."

"And what is it you've bought?"

"I would first like to know where the deeds desk is, here or somewhere else."

"But first tell us what you've bought and for what price, and then we'll tell you where, otherwise there's no knowing."

Chichikov saw at once that the clerks were simply curious, like all young clerks, and wanted to give more weight and significance to themselves and their occupation.

"Listen, my gentle sirs," he said, "I know very well that all deeds, whatever the price, are dealt with in one place, and therefore I ask you to point out the desk to us, and if you don't know what goes on in your own office, we'll ask others."

The clerks made no reply to this, one of them merely jabbed with his finger towards a corner of the room, where some old man sat at a desk, marking up some papers. Chichikov and Manilov moved between the desks straight to him. The old man was working very attentively.

"May I inquire," Chichikov said with a bow, "if it is here that deeds are dealt with?"

The old man raised his eyes and uttered with deliberation:

"Deeds are not dealt with here."

"And where, then?"

"In the deeds section."

"And where is the deeds section?"

"That's at Ivan Antonovich's."

"And where is Ivan Antonovich's?"

The old man jabbed his finger towards another corner of the room. Chichikov and Manilov set out for Ivan Antonovich's. Ivan Antonovich had already cast one eye back and given them a sidelong look, but at once immersed himself more attentively in his writing.

"May I inquire," Chichikov said with a bow, "if this is the deeds section?"

Ivan Antonovich seemed not to hear and buried himself completely in paper, making no reply. One could see at once that he was already a man of reasonable age, not some young babbler and whippersnapper. Ivan Antonovich seemed already well past forty; his hair was black, thick; the whole middle of his face projected forward and went mostly into nose – in short, it was the type of face commonly known as a jug mug.

"May I inquire if this is the deeds section?" said Chichikov.

"It is," Ivan Antonovich said, swung his jug mug, and again applied himself to his writing.

"And my business is this: I've bought peasants from various owners in this district, to be resettled; I have the deed, it remains to execute it."

"And are the sellers present?"

"Some are here, and I have warrants from the others."

"And have you brought the application?"

"I have brought the application. I'd like . . . I must hurry . . . so mightn't we, for instance, finish the business today?"

"Today! hm, today's impossible," said Ivan Antonovich. "Inquiries must be made, to see that there are no interdictions."

"By the way, to do with speeding the business up, Ivan Grigorievich, the head magistrate, is a great friend of mine . . . "

"Yes, but Ivan Grigorievich is not the only one; others exist," Ivan Antonovich said sternly.

Chichikov understood the little hitch Ivan Antonovich had just thrown in, and said:

"The others won't come out losers, I've been in the service myself, I know the business . . . "

"Go to Ivan Grigorievich," said Ivan Antonovich in a voice slightly more benign, "let him give orders in the proper places, we'll hold our end up."

Chichikov, taking a banknote from his pocket, placed it in front of Ivan Antonovich, who utterly failed to notice it and covered it at once with a book. Chichikov was about to point it out to him, but Ivan Antonovich, with a motion of his head, gave a sign that there was no need to point it out.

"This one here will take you to the front office," said Ivan Antonovich, nodding his head, and one of the votaries, right there beside them, who had been sacrificing to Themis so zealously that he had gone through both coatsleeves at the elbow and the lining had long been sticking out, for which in due time he had been made a collegiate registrar, offered his services to our friends, as Virgil once offered his services to Dante, and led them to the front office, where there stood nothing but a wide armchair and in it, at a desk, behind a zertsalo[31] and two thick books, alone as the sun, sat the magistrate. In this place the new Virgil felt such awe that he simply did not dare to set foot in it, but turned away, showing his back, threadbare as a bast mat, with a chicken feather stuck to it somewhere. Entering the chamber of the front office, they saw that the magistrate was not alone, Sobakevich was sitting with him, completely hidden by the zertsalo. The visitors' arrival produced exclamations, the governmental armchair was noisily pushed back. Sobakevich, too, rose from his chair, and he and his long sleeves became visible from all sides. The magistrate took Chichikov into his embrace, and the office resounded with kisses; they inquired after each other's health; it turned out that they both had some slight lower-back pain, which was straightaway ascribed to the sedentary life. The magistrate seemed already to have been informed of the purchase by Sobakevich, because he set about offering congratulations, which embarrassed our hero somewhat at first, especially when he saw that Sobakevich and Manilov, both sellers with whom deals had been struck in private, were now standing face to face. However, he thanked the magistrate and, turning at once to Sobakevich, asked:

"And how is your health?"

"No complaints, thank God," said Sobakevich.

And, indeed, he had nothing to complain of: iron would catch cold and start coughing sooner than this wondrously fashioned landowner.

"Yes, you've always been known for your health," said the magistrate, "and your late father was also a sturdy man."

"Yes, he used to go alone after bear," replied Sobakevich.

"It seems to me, however," said the magistrate, "that you'd also bring down your bear, if you chose to go against one."

"No, I wouldn't," replied Sobakevich, "the old man was sturdier than I am," and, sighing, he went on: "No, people aren't what they used to be; look at my life, what kind of a life is it? just sort of something . . . "

"It's a fine life, isn't it?" said the magistrate.

"No good, no good," said Sobakevich, shaking his head. "Consider for yourself, Ivan Grigorievich: I'm in my forties, and never once have I been sick; never even a sore throat, never even a pimple or a boil breaking out . . . No, it doesn't bode well! Some day I'll have to pay for it." Here Sobakevich sank into melancholy.

"Eh, you," Chichikov and the magistrate thought simultaneously, "what a thing to bemoan!"

"I've got a little letter for you," Chichikov said, taking Plyushkin's letter from his pocket.

"From whom?" the magistrate said and, opening it, exclaimed: "Ah! from Plyushkin. So he's still vegetating in this world. What a fate! Once he was an intelligent, wealthy man, and now . . . "

"A sonofabitch," said Sobakevich, "a crook, starved all his people to death."

"If you please, if you please," said the magistrate, "I'm ready to act as his attorney. When do you want to execute the deed, now or later?"

"Now," said Chichikov. "I will even ask you to do it, if possible, today, because I would like to leave town tomorrow. I've brought the deed and the application."

"That's all very well, only, like it or not, we won't let you go so soon. The deeds will be executed today, but all the same you must stay on with us a bit. Here, I'll give the order at once," he said, and opened the door to the chancellery, all filled with clerks, who could be likened to industrious bees scattered over a honeycomb, if a honeycomb may be likened to chancellery work. "Is Ivan Antonovich here?"

"Here," responded a voice from inside.

"Send him in."

Ivan Antonovich, the jug mug, already known to our readers, appeared in the front office and bowed reverently.

"Here, Ivan Antonovich, take these deeds of his . . . "

"And don't forget, Ivan Grigorievich," Sobakevich picked up, "there must be witnesses, at least two on each side. Send for the prosecutor right now, he's an idle man and must be sitting at home, everything's done for him by the attorney Zolotukha, the world's foremost muckworm. The inspector of the board of health is also an idle man and must be at home, unless he went somewhere to play cards, and there's a lot more around – Trukhachevsky, Begushkin, all of them a useless burden on the earth!"

"Precisely, precisely!" said the magistrate, and he at once dispatched a clerk to fetch them all.

"And I will ask you," said Chichikov, "to send for the attorney of a lady landowner with whom I also concluded a deal, the son of the archpriest Father Kiril; he works with you here."

"Well, so, we'll send for him, too!" said the magistrate. "It will all get done, and you are to give nothing to any of the clerks, that I beg of you. My friends should not pay." Having said this, he straightaway gave some order to Ivan Antonovich, which he evidently did not like. The deeds seemed to make a good impression on the magistrate, especially when he saw that the purchases added up to almost a hundred thousand roubles. For several minutes he gazed into Chichikov's eyes with an expression of great contentment, and finally said:

"So that's how! That's the way, Pavel Ivanovich! That's how you've acquired!"

"Acquired," replied Chichikov.

"A good thing, truly, a good thing."

"Yes, I myself can see that I could not have undertaken any better thing. However it may be, a man's goal is never defined until he finally sets a firm foot on solid ground, and not on some freethinking chimera of youth." Here he quite appropriately denounced all young people, and rightly so, for liberalism. Yet, remarkably, there was still some lack of firmness in his words, as if he were saying to himself at the same time: "Eh, brother, you're lying, and mightily, too!" He did not even glance at Sobakevich and Manilov, for fear of encountering something on their faces. But he need not have feared: Sobakevich's face did not stir, and Manilov, enchanted by the phrase, just kept shaking his head approvingly, immersed in that state in which a music lover finds himself when the soprano has outdone the fiddle itself and squeaked on such a high note as is even too much for the throat of a bird.

"But why don't you tell Ivan Grigorievich," Sobakevich responded, "precisely what you've acquired; and you, Ivan Grigorievich, why don't you ask what acquisitions he has made? Such folk they are! Pure gold! I even sold him the cartwright Mikheev."

"No, you mean you sold him Mikheev?" said the magistrate. "I know the cartwright Mikheev: a fine craftsman; he rebuilt my droshky. Only, excuse me, but how . . . Didn't you tell me he died . . . "

"Who died? Mikheev?" said Sobakevich, not in the least embarrassed. "It's his brother who died, but he's as alive as can be and healthier than ever. The other day he put together such a britzka as they can't make even in Moscow. He ought, in all truth, be working just for the sovereign alone."

"Yes, Mikheev's a fine craftsman," said the magistrate, "and I even wonder that you could part with him."

"As if Mikheev's the only one! There's Cork Stepan, the carpenter, Milushkin, the bricklayer, Telyatnikov Maxim, the cobbler – they all went, I sold them all!" And when the magistrate asked why they had all gone, seeing they were craftsmen and people necessary for the household, Sobakevich replied with a wave of the hand: "Ah! just like that! I've turned foolish: come on, I said, let's sell them – and so I sold them like a fool!" Whereupon he hung his head as if he regretted having done so, and added: "A gray-haired man, and I still haven't grown wise."

"But, excuse me, Pavel Ivanovich," said the magistrate, "how is it you're buying peasants without land? Or is it for resettlement?"

"For resettlement."

"Well, resettlement is something else. And to what parts?"

"What parts . . . to Kherson province."

"Oh, there's excellent land there!" said the magistrate, and he spoke in great praise of the size of the grass in that region. "And is there sufficient land?"

"Sufficient, as much as necessary for the peasants I've bought."

"A river or a pond?"

"A river. However, there's also a pond." Having said this, Chichikov glanced inadvertently at Sobakevich, and though Sobakevich was as immobile as ever, it seemed to him as if there were written on his face: "Oh, are you lying! there's nary a river there, nor a pond, nor any land at all!"

While the conversation continued, the witnesses gradually began to appear: the blinking prosecutor, already known to the reader, the inspector of the board of health, Trukhachevsky, Begushkin, and others who, in Sobakevich's words, were a useless burden on the earth. Many of them were completely unknown to Chichikov: the lacking and the extras were recruited on the spot from among the office clerks. Not only was the archpriest Father Kiril's son brought, but even the archpriest himself. Each of the witnesses put himself down, with all his dignities and ranks, one in backhand script, one slanting forward, one simply all but upside down, putting himself in such letters as had never even been seen before in the Russian alphabet. The familiar Ivan Antonovich managed quite deftly: the deeds were recorded, marked, entered in the register and wherever else necessary, with a charge of half a percent plus the notice in the *Gazette*, and so Chichikov had to pay the smallest sum. The magistrate even ordered that he be charged only half the tax money, while the other half, in some unknown fashion, was transferred to the account of some other petitioner.

"And so," said the magistrate, when everything was done, "it only remains now to wet this tidy little purchase."

"I'm ready," said Chichikov. "It's for you to name the time. It would be a sin on my part if I didn't uncork two or three bottles of fizz for such a pleasant company."

"No, you're mistaking me: we'll provide the fizz ourselves," said the magistrate, "it's our obligation, our duty. You're our guest: we must treat you. Do you know what, gentlemen? For the time being this is what we'll do: we'll all go, just as we are, to the police chief's. He's our wonder-worker, he has only to wink as he passes a fish market or a cellar, and you know what a snack we'll have! And also, for the occasion, a little game of whist!"

To such a suggestion no one could object. The witnesses felt hungry at the mere mention of the fish market; they all straightaway picked up their hats and caps, and the session was ended. As they passed through the chancellery, Ivan Antonovich, the jug mug, with a courteous bow, said softly to Chichikov:

"You bought up a hundred thousand worth of peasants and gave me just one twenty-fiver for my labors."

"But what sort of peasants?" Chichikov answered him, also in a whisper. "The most empty and paltry folk, not worth even half that."

Ivan Antonovich understood that the visitor was of firm character and would not give more.

"And how much per soul did you pay Plyushkin?" Sobakevich whispered in his other ear.

"And why did you stick in that Sparrow?" Chichikov said in reply to that.

"What Sparrow?" said Sobakevich.

"That female, Elizaveta Sparrow, and what's more you took the *a* off the end."

"No, I never stuck in any Sparrow," said Sobakevich, and he went over to the other guests.

The guests finally arrived in a crowd at the police chief's house. The police chief was indeed a wonder-worker: having only just heard what was going on, he sent that same moment for a policeman, a perky fellow in patent leather jackboots, and seemed to whisper just two words in his ear, adding only: "Understand!" – and there, in the other room, while the guests were hard at their whist, there appeared on the table beluga, sturgeon, salmon, pressed caviar, freshly salted caviar, herring, red sturgeon, cheeses, smoked tongues and *balyks* – all from the fish market side. Then there appeared additions from the host's side, products of his own kitchen: a fish-head pie into which went the cheeks and cartilage of a three-hundred-pound sturgeon, another pie with mushrooms, fritters, dumplings, honey-stewed fruit. The police chief was in a certain way the father and benefactor of the town. Among the townspeople he was completely as in his own family, and stopped in at shops and on merchants' row as if visiting his own larder. Generally, he was, as they say, suited to his post, and understood his job to perfection. It was even hard to decide whether he had been created for the post or the post for him. The business was handled so intelligently that he received double the income of all his predecessors, and at the same time earned the love of the whole town. The merchants were the first to love him, precisely because he was not haughty; in fact, he stood god-father to their children, was chummy with them, and though he occasionally fleeced them badly, he did it somehow extremely deftly: he would pat the man on the shoulder, and laugh, and stand him to tea, and promise to come for a game of checkers, asking about everything: how's he doing, this and that. If he learned that a young one was a bit sick, he would suggest some medicine – in short, a fine fellow! He drove around in his droshky, keeping order, and at the same time dropping a word to one man or another: "Say, Mikheych, we ought to finish that card game some day." "Yes, Alexei Ivanovich," the man would reply, doffing his hat, "so we ought." "Well, Ilya Paramonych, stop by and have a look at my trotter: he'll outrun yours, brother; harness up your racing droshky, and we'll give it a try." The merchant, who was crazy about his own trotter, smiled at that with especial eagerness, as they say, and, stroking his beard, said: "Let's give it a try, Alexei Ivanovich!" At which point even the shop clerks usually took off their hats and glanced with pleasure at each other, as if wishing to say: "Alexei Ivanovich is a good man!" In short, he managed to win universal popularity, and the merchants' opinion of Alexei Ivanovich was that "though he does take, on the other hand he never gives you up."

Noticing that the hors d'oeuvres were ready, the police chief suggested that his guests finish their whist after lunch, and everyone went into the other room, the smell wafting from which had long ago begun pleasantly to tickle the nostrils of the guests, and into which Sobakevich had long been peeking through the door, aiming from afar at the sturgeon that lay to one side on a big platter. The guests, having drunk a glass of vodka of the dark olive color that occurs only in those transparent Siberian stones from which seals are carved in Russia, accosted the table from all sides with forks and began to reveal, as they say, each his own character and inclinations, applying themselves one to the caviar, another to the salmon, another to the cheese. Sobakevich, letting all these trifles go unnoticed, stationed himself by the sturgeon, and while the others were drinking, talking, and eating, he, in a little over a quarter of an hour, went right through it, so that when the police chief remembered about it, and with the words: "And what, gentlemen, do you think of this work of nature?" approached it, fork in hand, along with the others, he saw that the only thing left of this work of nature was the tail; and Sobakevich scrooched down as if it was not him, and, coming to a plate some distance away, poked his fork into some little dried fish. After polishing off the sturgeon, Sobakevich sat in an armchair and no longer ate or drank, but only squinted and blinked his eyes. The police chief, it seemed, did not like to stint on wine; the toasts were innumerable. The first toast was drunk, as our readers might guess for themselves, to the health of the new Kherson landowner, then to the prosperity of his peasants and their happy resettlement, then to the health of his future wife, a beauty, which drew a pleasant smile from our hero's lips. They accosted him on all sides and began begging him insistently to stay in town for at least two weeks:

"No, Pavel Ivanovich! say what you will, in and out just makes the cottage cold! No, you must spend some time with us! We'll get you married: isn't that right, Ivan Grigorievich, we'll get him married?"

"Married, married!" the magistrate picked up. "Even if you resist hand and foot, we'll get you married! No, my dear, you landed here, so don't complain. We don't like joking."

"Come now, why should I resist hand and foot," said Chichikov, grinning, "marriage isn't the sort of thing, that is, as long as there's a bride."

"There'll be a bride, how could there not be, there'll be everything, everything you want! . . . "

"Well, if there'll be . . . "

"Bravo, he's staying!" they all shouted. "Viva, hurrah, Pavel Ivanovich! hurrah!" And they all came up with glasses in their hands to clink with him.

Chichikov clinked with everyone. "No, no, again!" said the more enthusiastic ones, and clinked again all around; then they came at him to clink a third time, and so they all clinked a third time. In a short while everyone was feeling extraordinarily merry. The magistrate, who was the nicest of men when he got merry, embraced Chichikov several times, uttering in heartfelt effusion: "My dear soul! my sweetie pie!" and, snapping his fingers, even went around him in a little dance, singing the well-known song: "Ah, you blankety-blank Komarinsky muzhik."[32] After the champagne a Hungarian wine was broached, which raised their spirits still more and made the company all the merrier. Whist was decidedly forgotten; they argued, shouted, discussed everything – politics, even military affairs – expounded free thoughts for which, at another time, they would have whipped their own children. Resolved on the spot a host of the most difficult questions. Chichikov had never felt himself in so merry a mood, already imagined himself a real Kherson landowner, talked of various improvements – the three-field system, the happiness and bliss of twin souls – and began reciting to Sobakevich Werther's letter in verse to Charlotte,[33] at which the man only blinked from his armchair, for after the sturgeon he felt a great urge to sleep. Chichikov himself realized that he was beginning to get much too loose, asked about a carriage, and availed himself of the prosecutor's droshky. The prosecutor's coachman, as it turned out on the way, was an experienced fellow, because he drove with one hand only, while holding up the master behind him with the other. Thus, on the prosecutor's droshky, he reached his inn, where for a long time still he had all sorts of nonsense on the tip of his tongue: a fair-haired bride, blushing and with a dimple on her right cheek, Kherson estates, capital. Selifan was even given some managerial orders: to gather all the newly resettled muzhiks, so as to make an individual roll call of them all personally. Selifan listened silently for quite a while and then walked out of the room, saying to Petrushka: "Go undress the master!" Petrushka started taking his boots off and together with them almost pulled the master onto the floor. But the boots were finally taken off, the master got undressed properly, and after tossing for some time on his bed, which creaked unmercifully, fell asleep a confirmed Kherson landowner. And Petrushka meanwhile brought out to the corridor the trousers and the cranberry-colored tailcoat with flecks, spread them on a wooden clothes rack, and set about beating them with a whip and brush, filling the whole corridor with dust. As he was about to take them down, he glanced over the gallery railing and saw Selifan coming back from the stable. Their eyes met, and they intuitively understood each other: the master has hit the sack, so why not peek in somewhere or other. That same moment, after taking the tailcoat and trousers to the room, Petrushka came downstairs, and the two went off together, saying nothing to each other about the goal of their trip and gabbing on the way about totally unrelated matters. They did not stroll far: to be precise, they simply crossed to the other side of the street, to the house that stood facing the inn, and entered a low, sooty glass door that led almost to the basement, where various sorts were already sitting at wooden tables: some who shaved their beards, and some who did not, some in sheepskin coats, and some simply in shirts, and a few even in frieze greatcoats. What Petrushka and Selifan did there, God only knows, but they came out an hour later holding each other by the arm, keeping a perfect silence, according each other great attention, with mutual warnings against various corners. Arm in arm, not letting go of each other, they spent a whole quarter of an hour going up the stairs, finally managed it and got up. Petrushka paused for a moment before his low bed, pondering the most suitable way of lying down, and then lay down perfectly athwart it, so that his feet rested on the floor. Selifan lay himself down on the same bed, placing his head on Petrushka's stomach, forgetting that he ought not to be sleeping there at all, but perhaps somewhere in the servants' quarters, if not in the stable with the horses. They both fell asleep that same moment and set up a snoring of unheard-of density, to which the master responded from the other room with a thin nasal whistle. Soon after them everything quieted down, and the inn was enveloped in deep sleep; only in one little window was there still light, where lived some lieutenant, come from Ryazan, a great lover of boots by the look of it, because he had already ordered four pairs made and was ceaselessly trying on a fifth. Several times he had gone over to his bed with the intention of flinging them off and lying down, but he simply could not: the boots were indeed well made, and for a long time still he kept raising his foot and examining the smart and admirable turn of the heel.

CHAPTER EIGHT

CHICHIKOV'S PURCHASES BECAME a subject of conversation. Gossip went around town, opinions, discussions of whether it was profitable to buy peasants for resettlement. In the debate, many distinguished themselves by their perfect knowledge of the subject. "Of course," said some, "it's so, there's no arguing against it: the land in the southern provinces is good and fertile; but what will Chichikov's peasants do without water? There's no river at all." "That would still be nothing, that there's no water, that would be nothing, Stepan Dmitrievich, but resettlement is an unreliable thing. We all know the muzhik: on new land, and he has to start farming it, and he's got nothing, neither cottage nor yard – he'll run away sure as two times two, walk his chalks and leave no trace behind." "No, Alexei Ivanovich, excuse me, excuse me, I don't agree with what you're saying, that Chichikov's muzhiks will run away. The Russian man is apt for anything and can get used to any climate. Send him all the way to Kamchatka, give him just a pair of warm mittens, and he'll clap his hands, pick up his axe, and off he goes building himself a new cottage." "But, Ivan Grigorievich, you've lost sight of an important thing: you haven't asked yet what sort of muzhiks Chichikov's are. You've forgotten that a landowner will never sell a good man; I'm ready to bet my head that Chichikov's muzhiks are thieves and drunkards to the last degree, idle loafers and of riotous behavior." "Yes, yes, I agree with that, it's true, no one's going to sell good people, and Chichikov's muzhiks are drunkards, but you must take into consideration that it is here that we find the moral, here the moral lies: they are scoundrels now, but resettled on new land they may suddenly become excellent subjects. There have been not a few examples of it, simply in the world, and from history as well." "Never, never," the superintendent of the government factories said, "believe me, that can never be. For Chichikov's peasants will now have two powerful enemies. The first enemy is the proximity of the provinces of Little Russia, where, as everyone knows, drink is sold freely. I assure you: in two weeks they'll be liquored up and thoroughly pie-eyed. The other enemy is the habit of the vagabond life itself, acquired of necessity during their relocation. They would have to be eternally before Chichikov's eyes, and he would have to keep them on a short tether, come down hard on them for every trifle, and, relying on no one save himself in person, give them a clout or a cuff when it's called for." "Why should Chichikov bother cuffing them himself? He can find a steward." "Oh, yes, go find a steward: they're all crooks." "They're crooks because the masters don't concern themselves with things." "That's true," many picked up. "If the master himself knew at least something about management, and was discerning of people, he would always have a good steward." But the superintendent said one could not find a good steward for less than five thousand. But the magistrate said it was possible to find one for as little as three thousand. But the superintendent said: "Where are you going to find him, unless it's up your own nose?" But the magistrate said: "No, not up my nose, but right in our district – namely: Pyotr Petrovich Samoilov: there's the kind of steward needed for Chichikov's muzhiks!" Many entered earnestly into Chichikov's predicament, and the difficulty of relocating such an enormous number of peasants awed them exceedingly; there was great fear that a riot might even break out among such restless folk as Chichikov's peasants. To this the police chief observed that there was no need to fear a riot, that the power of the district captain of police was there to avert it, that the captain of police had no need to go himself, but in his place could merely send his peaked cap, and this peaked cap alone would drive the peasants all the way to their place of settlement. Many offered opinions as to how to eradicate the riotous spirit that possessed Chichikov's peasants. These opinions were of various sorts: there were some that smacked excessively of military cruelty and severity, almost to superfluousness; there were also such, however, as breathed of mildness. The postmaster observed that Chichikov was faced with a sacred duty, that he could become something like a father among his peasants, as he put it, even introducing beneficent enlightenment, and he took the occasion to refer with much praise to the Lancastrian school of mutual education.[34]

Thus went the talk and discussion in town, and many, moved by sympathy, even conveyed some of this advice to Chichikov personally, even offered a convoy to escort the peasants to their place of settlement. Chichikov thanked them for the advice, saying that in the event he would not fail to make use of it, but he decidedly rejected the convoy, saying it was totally unnecessary, that the peasants he had bought were of superbly placid character, felt benevolently disposed towards resettlement themselves, and that a riot among them was in any event impossible.

All this gossip and discussion produced, however, as favorable a result as Chichikov could possibly have looked for. Namely, the rumor spread that he was no more nor less than a millionaire. The inhabitants of the town, as we have already seen in the first chapter, had taken a hearty liking to Chichikov even without that, but now, after such rumors, their liking became heartier still. Truth to tell, however, they were all kindly folk, got along well among themselves, treated each other with perfect friendliness, and their conversations bore the stamp of some especial simple-heartedness and familiarity: "My gentle friend Ilya Ilych," "Listen, brother Antipator Zakharievich!" "You're lying like a rug, Ivan Grigorievich,

dear heart." To the postmaster, whose name was Ivan Andreevich, they always added: "Sprechen sie Deych, Ivan
Andreych?"[35] – in short, everything was on a quite familial
footing. Many were not without cultivation: the head magistrate knew by heart Zhukovsky's *Lyudmila*,[36] which was then a
not-yet-faded novelty, and masterfully recited many passages,
especially "The forest sleeps, the valley slumbers" and the word
"hark!" so that one actually seemed to see the valley slumbering; for greater similitude he even shut his eyes at that moment.
The postmaster delved more into philosophy and read quite
diligently, even at night, in Young's *Night Thoughts* and *The
Key to Nature's Mysteries* by Eckartshausen,[37] from which
he copied out quite lengthy excerpts, though of what sort no
one ever knew; anyhow, he was a wit, had a florid style, and
liked, as he put it, to rig out his speech. And rig it out he did,
with a host of various particles, such as: "my good sir, some
such one, you know, you understand, can you imagine, rela-
tively so to speak, in a certain fashion," and others, which
he poured out by the bagful; he also rigged out his speech
rather successfully with winking, or squinting one eye, all of
which lent quite a caustic expression to his many satirical
allusions. Others, too, were more or less enlightened people:
one read Karamzin, another the *Moscow Gazette*,[38] another
even read nothing at all. One was what is known as a sad
sack, the sort of person who has to be roused with a kick to
do anything; another was simply a slug-a-bed, lying on his
back age in and age out, as they say, whom it was even useless
to rouse: he would not get up in any case. As for seemliness, we
know already that they were all reliable people, there were no
consumptives among them. They were all the kind to whom
wives, in those tender conversations which take place in private, gave such appellations as: chubsy, tubsy, tumsy, blackie,
kiki, zhuzhu, and so on. But generally they were kindly folk,
full of hospitality, and the man who sat down to table with
them or spent an evening at whist was already an intimate, all

the more so Chichikov, with his enchanting qualities and ways, who did indeed know the great secret of being liked. They grew so fond of him that he saw no way of tearing himself free of the town; all he heard was: "Come, a little week, you can spend one more little week with us, Pavel Ivanovich!" – in short, he was, as they say, made much of. But incomparably more remarkable was the impression (altogether an object of amazement!) that Chichikov made on the ladies. To begin to explain it, one would have to say a lot about the ladies themselves, about their society, to describe in vivid colors, so to speak, their qualities of soul; but for the author that is very difficult. On the one hand, he is prevented by his boundless respect for the wives of the dignitaries, and on the other hand . . . on the other hand – it is simply difficult. The ladies of the town of N. were . . . no, it is in no way possible for me: I really feel timid. The most remarkable thing about the ladies of the town of N. was . . . It is even strange, I cannot lift the pen at all, as if there were some kind of lead inside it. So be it: evidently it must be left to one whose colors are more vivid and who has more of them on his palette to speak of their characters, and we will just say a word or two of their appearance and of what is more superficial. The ladies of the town of N. were what is called presentable, and in this respect they may boldly be held up as an example to all others. As for knowing how to behave themselves, keeping tone, observing etiquette, a host of proprieties of the subtlest sort, and above all following fashion down to the least detail, in this they surpassed even the ladies of Petersburg and Moscow. They dressed with great taste, went for drives around town in carriages, as the latest fashion dictated, with lackey and gold-braided livery swaying behind. The visiting card, even if written on a deuce of clubs or ace of diamonds, was a very sacred thing. On account of it two ladies, great friends and even relatives, quarreled altogether, precisely because one of them once neglected a return visit. And how hard their husbands and relatives tried to reconcile them afterwards, but no, it turned out that while anything in the world might be done, only one thing could not be done: to reconcile two ladies who had quarreled over a neglected visit. And so these ladies remained mutually ill-disposed, in the expression of town society. With regard to occupying the foremost positions, a lot of rather big scenes also took place, which sometimes inspired the husbands to perfectly chivalrous, magnanimous notions of intercession. Duels, of course, did not take place between them, because they were all civil servants, but instead they tried to do each other dirt wherever possible, which, as everyone knows, can sometimes be worse than any duel. In morals the ladies of the town of N. were strict, filled with noble indignation against all vice and any temptation, and they punished any weaknesses without any mercy. And if there did occur among them something of what is known as *this-or-that*, it occurred in secret, so that there was no sign of its having occurred; full dignity was preserved, and the husband himself was so prepared that even if he saw *this-or-that* or heard about it, he would respond briefly with a proverb: "It's always fair weather when friends get together." It must also be said that the ladies of the town of N. were distinguished, like many Petersburg ladies, by an extraordinary prudence and propriety in their words and expressions. Never would they say: "I blew my nose," "I sweated," "I spat," but rather: "I relieved my nose" or "I resorted to my handkerchief." It was in no case possible to say: "This glass or this plate stinks." And it was even impossible to say anything that hinted at it, but instead they would say: "This glass is being naughty," or something of the sort. To ennoble the Russian language still more, almost half of its words were banished from conversation altogether, and therefore it was quite often necessary to have recourse to the French language, although there, in French, it was a different matter: there such words were allowed as were much coarser than those aforementioned. And so, that is what can be told about the ladies of the town of N., speaking superficially. But if one were to look more deeply, then, of course, many other things would be discovered; but it is quite dangerous to look more deeply into ladies' hearts. And so, confining ourselves to the superficial, we shall continue. Up to now the ladies had all somehow talked little about Chichikov, doing him full justice, however, as to the agreeableness of his social comportment; but since the rumors spread about his millions, other qualities were found. However, the ladies were not self-seeking in the least; the word "millionaire" was to blame for it all – not the millionaire himself, but precisely the word alone; for the sound of this word alone, aside from any bag of money, contains something that affects people who are scoundrels, and people who are neither this nor that, and people who are good – in short, it affects everyone. The millionaire has this advantage, that he is able to observe meanness, a perfectly disinterested, pure meanness, not based on any calculations: many know very well that they will not get anything from him and have no right to get anything, but they want to be sure at least to run ahead for him, at least to laugh, at least to doff their hats, at least to wangle themselves an invitation to dinner where they know the millionaire has been invited. It cannot be said that this tender inclination to meanness was felt by the ladies; nevertheless, in many drawing rooms there was talk of Chichikov being, not outstandingly handsome, of course, but still such as a man ought to be, that if he were any fuller or fatter, it would be not so good. Along with that, something was said which was even rather insulting with regard to the slim man: that he was nothing more than a sort of toothpick, and not a man. A great variety of additions occurred in the ladies' attire. There was crowding in the shopping district, almost a crush; a fête even formed itself from all the carriages driving through. The merchants were amazed to see several lengths of cloth they had brought back from the fair and could not get rid of because the price seemed too high, suddenly come into demand and get snatched up. During the Sunday liturgy one lady was observed to have such a rouleau at the hem of her dress that it spread half the width of the church, so that a police officer who was there gave orders for the folk to move farther back, that is, nearer to the porch, to keep her ladyship's toilette from being somehow crumpled. Even Chichikov himself could not fail partly to notice such extraordinary attention. Once, on returning home, he found a letter on his table; of whence and by whom it had been brought, nothing could be learned; the tavern servant replied that it had been brought with an order not to say whom it was from. The letter began very resolutely, namely thus: "No, I must write to you!" Then came talk about there being a mysterious affinity between souls; this truth was clinched by some dots, taking up almost half a line; then there followed some thoughts, quite remarkable in their correctness, so that we regard it as almost necessary to write them down: "What is our life? A vale wherein grief dwells. What is this world? A crowd of people who do not feel." At that the writer mentioned that she was wetting with tears these lines of a tender mother who, for twenty-five years now, had not existed in this world; Chichikov was invited to the desert, to leave forever the town where people, behind stifling walls, make no use of the air; the ending of the letter even rang with decided despair and concluded with these verses:

> Two turtle doves will show
> My cold remains to thee,
> With languid cooing so
> As to say that in tears died she.

There was no meter in the last line, but that, however, was nothing: the letter was written in the spirit of the times. There was no signature either: no name, no family name, not even the month and day. It was only added in a postscriptum that his own heart should guess the lady who wrote it, and that, at the governor's ball, which was to take place the next day, the original would be present in person.

This greatly intrigued him. The anonymity had so much that was alluring and arousing of curiosity in it, that he read it over again and then a third time, and finally said: "It would be curious, however, to know who the writer might be!" In short, it looked as if the matter was turning serious; for more than an hour he kept thinking about it, and at last, spreading his arms and inclining his head, he said: "The letter is very, very fancily written!" After which, it goes without saying, the letter was folded and put away in the chest, in the vicinity of some playbill and a wedding invitation preserved for seven years in the same position and the same place. A short time later he was in fact brought an invitation to the governor's ball – quite a usual thing in provincial capitals: where the governor is, there will also be a ball, otherwise there would be no love or respect on the part of the nobility.

All unrelated things were instantly ended and suspended, and everything was focused on preparing for the ball: for there were, in fact, many stimulating and provoking causes. And perhaps not since the very creation of the world has so much time been spent on toilet. A whole hour was devoted merely to studying his face in the mirror. Attempts were made to impart to it a multitude of different expressions: now dignified and grave, now deferential but with a certain smile, now simply deferential without the smile; several bows were delivered to the mirror, accompanied by vague sounds somewhat resembling French ones, though Chichikov knew no French at all. He even gave himself a multitude of pleasant surprises, winked with his eyebrow and lips, and even did something with his tongue; in short, one does all sorts of things when one is left alone, feels oneself a fine fellow besides, and is also certain that no one is peeking through a crack. In the end he patted himself lightly on the chin, saying: "Ah, you sweet mug, you!" and began to dress. The most contented disposition accompanied him all the while he was dressing: putting on his suspenders or tying his tie, he bowed and scraped with special adroitness and, though he never danced, performed an entrechat. This entrechat produced a small, innocuous consequence: the chest of drawers shook, and a brush fell off the table.

His appearance at the ball produced an extraordinary effect. All that were there turned to meet him, one with cards in his hand, another saying, at the most interesting point in the conversation: " . . . and the lower circuit court's answer to that was . . . ," but whatever the circuit court's answer was, it was brushed aside as the man hastened to greet our hero. "Pavel Ivanovich! Ah, my God, Pavel Ivanovich! My gentle Pavel Ivanovich! My most esteemed Pavel Ivanovich! Pavel Ivanovich, my dear soul! So here's where you are, Pavel Ivanovich! Here he is, our Pavel Ivanovich! Allow me to hug you, Pavel Ivanovich! Let him come here till I give him a good kiss, my dearest Pavel Ivanovich!" Chichikov felt himself simultaneously in several embraces. Before he had quite managed to scramble out of the magistrate's embrace, he found himself in the police chief's embrace; the police chief handed him on to the inspector of the board of health; the inspector of the board of health to the tax farmer, the tax farmer to the architect . . . The governor, who at that moment was standing by the ladies holding a candy-kiss motto in one hand and a lapdog in the other, dropped both dog and motto to the floor on seeing him – only the pup let out a squeal; in short, he spread joy and extraordinary merriment. There was not a face that did not express pleasure, or at least a reflection of the general pleasure. The same thing takes place on the faces of officials when a superior arrives to inspect the work entrusted to their management: once the initial fear has passed, they see that there is much that pleases him, and he himself finally deigns to make a joke – that is, to utter a few words with an agreeable smile. Twice as hard do the closely surrounding officials laugh in response to that; with all their hearts others laugh who, incidentally, had not heard very well what the man said, and finally some policeman standing way off by the door, by the very exit, who from the day he was born has never laughed in his whole life, and who a moment before was shaking his fist at the people, even he, by the immutable laws of reflection, puts some sort of smile on his face, though this smile is more like the look of someone about to sneeze after a pinch of strong snuff. Our hero responded to each and all, and felt himself somehow extraordinarily adroit: bowed right and left, somewhat to one side as usual, but with perfect ease, so that he enchanted everyone. The ladies surrounded him at once in a sparkling garland and brought with them whole clouds of varied fragrances; one breathed roses, another gave off a whiff of spring and violets, a third was perfumed throughout with mignonette; Chichikov just kept lifting his nose and sniffing. Their attire evinced no end of taste: the muslins, satins, cambrics were of such pale fashionable shades as could not even be matched with any names (taste had reached such a degree of fineness). Ribbon bows and bouquets of flowers fluttered here and there over the dresses in a most picturesque disorder, though this disorder had been much labored over by some orderly head. Light headdresses held on only at the ears and seemed to be saying: "Hey, I'm flying away, only it's a pity I can't take this beauty with me!" Waists were tight-fitting and formed in a way most firm and pleasing to the eye (it should be noted that generally the ladies of the town of N. were all a bit plump, but they laced themselves up so artfully and were of such pleasing comportment that the fatness simply could not be noticed). Everything about them had been designed and foreseen with extraordinary circumspection; neck and shoulders were revealed precisely as far as necessary, and no further; each one bared her possessions to the point to which she felt convinced in herself that they could be the ruin of a man; the rest was all secreted away with extraordinary taste: either some light little ribbon tie, or a scarf lighter than the pastry known by the name of "kiss,"[39] ethereally embraced her neck, or else there peeked out around her shoulders, from under the dress, those little serrated trimmings of light cambric known by the name of "modesties." These "modesties," in front or behind, concealed that which could no longer be the ruin of a man, and yet made one suspect that ruin itself lay precisely there. Long gloves were worn not up to the sleeves, but deliberately leaving bare the arousing parts of the arms above the elbow, which in many ladies breathed an enviable plumpness: some kid gloves even burst in their striving to move further up – in short, everything seemed to have written on it: No, this is no province, this is a capital, this is Paris itself! Only in places would some bonnet stick out such as had never been seen on earth, or even almost some sort of peacock feather, contrary to all fashion, following its own taste. But there's no avoiding it, such is the property of a provincial town: it is simply bound to trip up somewhere. Chichikov was thinking, as he stood before them: "Which of them, however, was the writer of that letter?" and he tried to stick his nose out; but right against his nose brushed a whole row of elbows, cuffs, sleeves, ends of ribbons, fragrant chemisettes, and dresses. Everything was galloping headlong: the postmaster's wife, the captain of police, a lady with a blue feather, a lady with a white feather, the Georgian prince Chipkhaikhilidzev, an official from Petersburg, an official from Moscow, the Frenchman Coucou, Perkhunovsky, Berebendovsky – everything rose up and rushed on . . .

"There the province goes scrawling!" Chichikov said, backing up, and as soon as the ladies took their seats, he again began spying out whether it was possible by the expression of the face and eyes to tell which one was the writer; but it was not possible to tell either by the expression of the face, or by the expression of the eyes, which one was the writer. One could see everywhere something so faintly disclosed, so elusively subtle, ooh! so subtle! . . . "No," Chichikov said to himself, "women are such a subject . . . " (here he even waved his hand) "there's simply no point in talking! Go on, try telling or conveying all that flits across their faces, all those little curves and allusions – you simply won't convey a thing. Their eyes alone are such an endless country, a man gets into it – and that's the last you hear of him! You won't pull him out of there with hooks or anything. Try, for instance, just telling about the lustre of them: moist, velvety, sugary. God knows what not else! – hard, and soft, and even altogether blissful, or, as some say, in languor, or else without languor, but worse than in languor – it just grips your heart and passes over your whole soul as if with a fiddle bow. No, there's simply no way to find a word: the cockety half of mankind, and nothing else!"

Beg pardon! It seems a little word picked up in the street just flew out of our hero's mouth. No help for it! Such is the writer's position in Russia! Anyway, if a word from the street has got into a book, it is not the writer's fault, the fault is with the readers, high-society readers most of all: they are the first not to use a single decent Russian word, but French, German, and English they gladly dispense in greater quantity than one might wish, and dispense even preserving all possible pronunciations: French through the nose and with a burr, English they pronounce in the manner of a bird, and even assume a bird's physiognomy, and they will even laugh at anyone who cannot assume a bird's physiognomy; and they will only not dispense anything Russian, unless perhaps out of patriotism they build themselves a Russian-style cottage as a country house. Such are readers of the higher ranks, and along with them all those who count themselves among the higher ranks! And yet what exactingness! They absolutely insist that everything be written in the most strict, purified, and noble of tongues – in short, they want the Russian tongue suddenly to descend from the clouds on its own, all properly finished, and settle right on their tongue, leaving them nothing to do but gape their mouths open and stick it out. Of course, the female half of mankind is a puzzle; but our worthy readers, it must be confessed, are sometimes even more of a puzzle.

And Chichikov meanwhile was getting thoroughly perplexed deciding which of the ladies was the writer of the letter. Trying to aim an attentive glance at them, he saw that on the ladies' part there was also the expression of a certain something that sent down both hope and sweet torment at once into the heart of a poor mortal, so that he finally said: "No, it's simply impossible to guess!" That, however, in no way diminished the merry mood he was in. With ease and adroitness he exchanged pleasant words with some of the ladies, approaching one or another of them with small, rapid steps, or, as they say, mincingly, as foppish little old men, called "mousey colts," usually do, scampering around the ladies quite nimbly on their high heels. After mincing through some rather adroit turns to the right and left, he made a little scrape with his foot, in the form of a short tail or comma. The ladies were very pleased and not only discovered a heap of agreeable and courteous things in him, but even began to find a majestic expression in his face, something even Mars-like and military, which, as everyone knows, women like very much. They were even beginning to quarrel a bit over him: noticing that he usually stood by the door, some hastened to vie with each other in occupying the chair nearest the door, and when one had the good fortune of being the first to do so, it almost caused a very unpleasant episode, and to many who wished to do the same, such impudence seemed all too repugnant.

Chichikov was so taken up by his conversations with the ladies – or, better, the ladies so took him up and whirled him around with their conversations, adding a heap of the most fanciful and subtle allegories, which all had to be penetrated, even making sweat stand out on his brow – that he forgot to fulfill his duty to propriety and go up to the hostess first of all. He remembered it only when he heard the voice of the governor's wife herself, who had been standing before him for several minutes. She said in a somewhat tender and coy voice, accompanied by a pleasant shaking of the head: "Ah, Pavel Ivanovich, so that's how you are!..." I cannot convey the lady's words exactly, something was said full of great courtesy, in the spirit in which ladies and gentlemen express themselves in the novellas of our society writers, who love to describe drawing rooms and boast of their knowledge of high tone, in the spirit of: "Can it be that your heart is so possessed that there is no longer any room, not even the tiniest corner, for those whom you have mercilessly forgotten?" Our hero turned to the governor's wife that same instant and was ready to deliver his reply, probably in no way inferior to those delivered in fashionable novels by the Zvonskys, the Linskys, the Lidins, the Gremins, and various other adroit military men, when, chancing to raise his eyes, he stopped suddenly, as if stunned by a blow.

Before him stood not only the governor's wife: on her arm she had a young girl of sixteen, a fresh blonde with fine and trim features, a sharp chin, a charmingly rounded face, the sort an artist would choose as a model for a Madonna, a sort rarely occurring in Russia, where everything likes to be on a vast scale, whatever there is – mountains and forests and steppes, and faces and lips and feet; the same blonde he had met on the road, leaving Nozdryov's, when, owing to the stupidity either of the coachmen or of the horses, their carriages had so strangely collided, entangling their harnesses, and Uncle Mityai and Uncle Minyai had set about disentangling the affair. Chichikov was so abashed that he was unable to utter a single sensible word and mumbled devil knows what, something no Gremin or Zvonsky or Lidin would ever have said.

"You don't know my daughter yet?" said the governor's wife. "A boarding-school girl, just graduated."

He replied that he had already had the happiness of accidentally making her acquaintance; tried to add something more, but the something did not come off at all. The governor's wife, after saying two or three words, finally walked away with her daughter to other guests at the other end of the ballroom, while Chichikov still stood motionless on the same spot, like a man who merrily goes out for a stroll, his eyes disposed to look at everything, and suddenly stops motionless, recalling that he has forgotten something, and there can be nothing stupider than such a man then: instantly the carefree expression leaves his face; he strains to remember what he has forgotten – was it his handkerchief? but his handkerchief is in his pocket; was it money? but his money is also in his pocket; he seems to have everything, and yet some unknown spirit whispers in his ear that he has forgotten something. And so he now looks vaguely and perplexedly at the crowd moving before him, at the carriages flying along, at the shakos and guns of the regiment passing by, at the signboards – and sees nothing clearly. So, too, did Chichikov suddenly become a stranger to everything going on around him. During this time the ladies' fragrant lips poured at him a multitude of hints and questions, thoroughly pervaded by subtlety and courtesy. "Is it permitted us poor earth-dwellers to be so bold as to ask what you are dreaming about?" "Where are those happy places in which your thought is fluttering?" "May we know the name of her who has plunged you into this sweet vale of reverie?" But he responded to it all with decided inattention, and the pleasant phrases vanished into thin air. He was even so impolite as to walk away from them soon, over to the other side, wishing to spy out where the governor's wife had gone with her daughter. But the ladies seemed unwilling to give him up so soon; each of them resolved inwardly to employ all possible means, so dangerous for our hearts, and bring her best into play. It should be noted that some ladies – I say some, which is not the same as all – have a little weakness: if they notice that they have something particularly good – brow, or lips, or arms – they right away think that their best feature will be the first to catch everyone's eye, and that they will all suddenly start saying with one voice: "Look, look, what a fine Greek nose she has!" or "What a well-formed, lovely brow!" And she who has handsome shoulders is certain beforehand that all the young men will be utterly enraptured and will not cease repeating as she passes by: "Ah, how wonderful those shoulders are!" and will not even glance at her face, hair, nose, brow, or, if they do, only as at something beside the point. So certain ladies think. Each lady inwardly vowed to herself to be as charming as possible while dancing and show in all its splendor the excellence of that which was most excellent in her. The postmaster's wife, as she waltzed, held her head to one side with such languor that it indeed gave one the feeling of something unearthly. One very amiable lady – who had by no means come with the intention of dancing, owing to the occurrence, as she herself put it, of a slight *incommodité*, in the form of a little bump on her right foot, as a result of which she even had to wear velveteen booties – was nevertheless unable to help herself and took several turns in her velveteen booties, precisely so that the postmaster's wife should not indeed take too much into her head.

But all this in no way produced the intended effect on Chichikov. He was not even looking at the turns produced by the ladies, but was constantly getting on tiptoe to seek over the heads where the engaging blonde might have gotten to; he also crouched down, looking between shoulders and backs, and finally succeeded in his search and spotted her sitting with her mother, above whom some sort of oriental turban with a feather swayed majestically. It seemed as if he wanted to take them by storm; whether it was a spring mood affecting him, or someone was pushing him from behind, in any case he was decidedly pressing forward despite all; the tax farmer got such a shove from him that he staggered and barely managed to keep himself on one leg, otherwise he certainly would have brought down a whole row along with him; the postmaster also stepped back and looked at him with amazement, mingled with rather subtle irony, but he did not look at them; all he saw was the blond girl in the distance, putting on a long glove and undoubtedly burning with desire to start flying over the parquet. And there, to one side, four couples were already jigging away at the mazurka; heels were smashing the floor, and one army staff captain was working body and soul, and arms, and legs, pulling off such steps as no one had ever pulled off before even in a dream. Chichikov slipped past the mazurka almost right on their heels, and made straight for the place where the governor's wife sat with her daughter. However, he approached them very timidly, did not mince his steps so perkily and foppishly, even became somewhat confused, and in all his movements showed a certain awkwardness.

It is impossible to say for certain whether the feeling of love had indeed awakened in our hero – it is even doubtful that gentlemen of his sort, that is, not really fat and yet not really thin, are capable of love; but for all that there was something strange here, something of a sort he could not explain to himself: it seemed to him, as he himself confessed later, that the whole ball with all its talk and noise had for a few moments moved as if to somewhere far away; fiddles and trumpets were hacking out somewhere beyond the mountains and everything was screened by a mist, resembling a carelessly daubed field in a painting. And on this hazy, haphazardly sketched field nothing stood out in a clear and finished way except the fine features of the engaging blonde: her ovally rounding little face, her slender, slender waist, such as boarding-school girls have for the first few months after graduation, her white, almost plain dress, lightly and nicely enveloping everywhere her young, shapely limbs, which were somehow purely outlined. All of her seemed to resemble some sort of toy, cleanly carved from ivory; she alone stood out white, transparent and bright against the dull and opaque crowd.

Evidently it can happen in this world; evidently the Chichikovs, too, for a few moments of their lives, can turn into poets; but the word "poet" would be too much here. In any case, he felt himself altogether something of a young man, all but a hussar. Seeing an empty chair beside them, he at once occupied it. The conversation faltered at first, but then things got going, and he even began to gather strength, but . . . here, to our profound regret, it must be observed that men of dignity who occupy important posts are somehow a bit heavy in their conversation with ladies; the experts here are gentlemen lieutenants or at least those of no higher rank than captain. How they do it, God only knows: the man seems to be saying nothing very clever, yet the girl keeps rocking with laughter in her chair; while a state councillor will talk about God knows what: he will speak of Russia being a very vast country, or deliver a compliment certainly not conceived without wit, but smacking terribly of books; and if he does say something funny, he himself will laugh incomparably more than she who is listening to him. This observation is made here so that the reader may see why the blond girl began to yawn while our hero talked. Our hero, however, did not notice it at all, telling a multitude of pleasant things, which he had already had the chance to utter on similar occasions in various places: namely, in Simbirsk province, at Sophron Ivanovich Bespechny's, where his daughter Adelaida Sophronovna then happened to be, with her three sisters-in-law – Marya Gavrilovna, Alexandra Gavrilovna, and Adelheida Gavrilovna; at Fyodor Fyodorovich Perekroev's in Ryazan province; at Frol Vassilievich Pobedonosny's in Penza province, and at his brother Pyotr Vassilievich's, where were his sister-in-law Katerina Mikhailovna and her second cousins Rosa Fyodorovna and Emilia Fyodorovna; in Vyatka province at Pyotr Varsonofievich's, where Pelageya Yegorovna, his daughter-in-law's sister, was with her niece Sofya Rostislavovna and two half sisters, Sofya Alexandrovna and Maklatura Alexandrovna.

The ladies were all thoroughly displeased with Chichikov's behavior. One of them purposely walked past him to make him notice it, and even brushed against the blond girl rather carelessly with the thick rouleau of her dress, and managed the scarf that fluttered about her shoulders so that its end waved right in her face; and at the same time, from behind him, along with the scent of violets, a rather pointed and caustic remark wafted from one lady's lips. But either he actually did not hear, or he pretended not to hear, though that was not good, because the opinion of the ladies must be appreciated: he repented of it, but only afterwards, and therefore too late.

Indignation, justified in all respects, showed on many faces. However great Chichikov's weight in society might be, though he were a millionaire and with an expression of majesty, even of something Mars-like and military, in his face, still there are things that ladies will not forgive anyone, whoever he may be, and then he can simply be written off. There are cases when a woman, however weak and powerless of character in comparison with a man, suddenly becomes harder, not only than a man, but than anything else in the world. The scorn displayed almost inadvertently by Chichikov even restored the harmony among the ladies, which had been on the brink of ruin since the occasion of the capturing of the chair. Certain dry and ordinary words that he chanced to utter were found to contain pointed allusions. To crown the disaster, one of the young men made up some satirical verses about the dancers, which, as we know, almost no provincial ball can do without. These verses were straightaway ascribed to Chichikov. The indignation was mounting, and ladies in different corners began to speak of him in a most unfavorable way; while the poor boarding-school graduate was totally annihilated and her sentence was already sealed.

And meanwhile a most unpleasant surprise was being prepared for our hero: while the girl yawned, and he went on telling her little stories of some sort that had happened at various times, even touching on the Greek philosopher Diogenes, Nozdryov emerged from the end room. Whether he had torn himself away from the buffet or from the small green sitting room, where a game a bit stiffer than ordinary whist was under way, whether it was of his own free will or he had been pushed out, in any case he appeared gay, joyful, grasping the arm of the prosecutor, whom he had probably been dragging about for some time, because the poor prosecutor was turning his bushy eyebrows in all directions, as if seeking some way to get out of this friendly arm-in-arm excursion. Indeed, it was insufferable. Nozdryov, having sipped up some swagger in two cups of tea, not without rum, of course, was lying unmercifully. Spotting him from afar, Chichikov resolved even upon sacrifice, that is, upon abandoning his enviable place and withdrawing at all possible speed: for him their meeting boded no good. But, as ill luck would have it, at that same moment the governor turned up, expressing extraordinary joy at having found Pavel Ivanovich, and stopped him, asking him to arbitrate in his dispute with two ladies over whether woman's love is lasting or not; and meanwhile Nozdryov had already seen him and was walking straight to meet him.

"Ah, the Kherson landowner, the Kherson landowner!" he shouted, approaching and dissolving in laughter, which caused his cheeks, fresh and ruddy as a rose in spring, to shake. "So, have you bought up a lot of dead ones? You don't even know, Your Excellency," he went on bawling, addressing the governor, "he deals in dead souls! By God! Listen, Chichikov! you really – I'm telling you out of friendship, all of us here are your friends, yes, and His Excellency here, too – I'd hang you, by God, I'd hang you!"

Chichikov simply did not know where he was.

"Would you believe it, Your Excellency," Nozdryov went on, "when he said 'Sell me dead souls,' I nearly split with laughter. I come here, and they tell me he's bought up three million worth of peasants for resettlement – resettlement, hah! he was trying to buy dead ones from me. Listen, Chichikov, you're a brute, by God, a brute, and His Excellency here, too, isn't that right, prosecutor?"

But the prosecutor, and Chichikov, and the governor himself were so nonplussed that they were utterly at a loss what to reply, and meanwhile Nozdryov, without paying the least attention, kept pouring out his half-sober speech:

"And you, brother, you, you ... I won't leave your side till I find out why you were buying dead souls. Listen, Chichikov, you really ought to be ashamed, you know you have no better friend than me. And His Excellency here, too, isn't that right, prosecutor? You wouldn't believe, Your Excellency, how attached we are to one another, that is, if you simply said – I'm standing here, see, and you say: 'Nozdryov, tell me in all conscience, who is dearer to you, your own father or Chichikov?' I'd say: 'Chichikov,' by God ... Allow me, dear heart, to plant one *baiser*[40] on you. You will allow me to kiss him, Your Excellency. So, Chichikov, don't resist now, allow me to print one bitsy *baiser* on your snow-white cheek!"

Nozdryov was pushed away with his *baisers*, so hard that he almost went sprawling on the floor: everyone left him and no longer listened to him; but all the same his words about the buying of dead souls had been uttered at the top of his voice and accompanied by such loud laughter that they had attracted the attention even of those in the farthest corners of the room. This news seemed so strange that everyone stopped with some sort of wooden, foolishly quizzical expression. Chichikov noticed that many of the ladies winked at each other with a sort of spiteful, caustic grin, and certain faces bore an expression of something so ambiguous that it further increased his confusion. That Nozdryov was an inveterate liar everyone knew, and there was no wonder at all in hearing decided balderdash from him; but mortal man – truly, it is hard to understand how your mortal man is made: however banal the news may be, as long as it is news, he will not fail to pass it on to some other mortal, even if it is precisely with the purpose of saying:

"See what a lie they're spreading!" and the other mortal will gladly incline his ear, though afterwards he himself will say: "Yes, that is a perfectly banal lie, not worthy of any attention!" and thereupon he will set out at once to look for a third mortal, so that, having told him, they can both exclaim with noble indignation: "What a banal lie!" And it will not fail to make the rounds of the whole town, and all mortals, however many there are, will have their fill of talking and will then admit that it is unworthy of attention and not worth talking about.

This apparently absurd occurrence noticeably upset our hero. However stupid a fool's words may be, they are sometimes enough to confound an intelligent man. He began to feel uneasy, ungainly – exactly as if he had suddenly stepped with a beautifully polished shoe into a dirty, stinking puddle; in short, not good, not good at all! He tried not to think about it, tried to get diverted, distracted, sat down to whist, but it all went like a crooked wheel: twice he played into his opponents' strong suit, and, forgetting that one does not double trump, he swung his arm and, like a fool, took his own trick. The magistrate simply could not understand how Pavel Ivanovich, who had such a good and, one might say, subtle understanding of the game, could make such mistakes and even put under the axe his king of spades, in which, to use his own words, he trusted as in God. Of course, the postmaster and the magistrate, and even the police chief himself, kept poking fun at our hero, as is customary, suggesting that he might be in love, and don't we know that Pavel Ivanovich's heart has been smitten, and don't we know who shot the dart; but all this was no comfort, however much he tried to smile and laugh it off. At supper, too, he was quite unable to be expansive, though the company at table was pleasant and Nozdryov had long ago been taken out; for even the ladies themselves finally noticed that his behavior was becoming much too scandalous. In the midst of the cotillion, he got down on the floor and started grabbing the dancers by their skirt hems, which was really beyond everything, as the ladies put it. The supper was very gay, all the faces flitting before the three-stemmed candlesticks, flowers, sweets, and bottles radiated the most unconstrained pleasure. Officers, ladies, tailcoats – everything became courteous, even to the point of cloying. Men jumped up from their chairs and ran to take dishes from the servants in order to offer them, with extraordinary adroitness, to the ladies. One colonel offered a dish of sauce to a lady on the tip of his bare sword. The men of respectable age, among whom Chichikov sat, were arguing loudly, following their sensible words with fish or beef dipped unmercifully in mustard, and arguing about subjects he had even always been interested in; but he was like a man worn-out or broken by a long journey, whose mind is closed to everything and who is unable to enter into anything. He did not even wait until supper was over, and went home incomparably earlier than was his custom.

There, in that little room so familiar to the reader, with the door blocked up by a chest of drawers, and cockroaches occasionally peeking from the corners, the state of his mind and spirit was uncomfortable, as uncomfortable as the armchair in which he sat. His heart felt unpleasant, troubled; some burdensome emptiness lingered in it. "Devil take all of you who thought up these balls!" he said in vexation. "What are the fools so glad about? There are crop failures, high prices in the provinces, and here they are with their balls! A fine thing: decked out in their female rags! So what if she's wrapped herself in a thousand roubles' worth! And it's at the expense of peasant quitrent or, worse still, at the expense of our own good conscience. Everyone knows why you take bribes and bend the truth: so as to pay for your wife's shawl or hoopskirt or whatever they're called, confound them. And what for? So that some strumpet Sidorovna won't say the postmaster's wife's dress was better, and so – bang, there goes a thousand roubles. They shout: 'A ball, a ball, a gay time!' – a ball is just trash, not in the Russian spirit, not in the Russian nature; devil knows what it is: an adult, a man of age, suddenly pops out all in black, plucked and tightly fitted like a little imp, and goes mincing away with his feet. Some man, dancing with his partner, can be discussing important business with someone else, while at the same time twirling his legs right and left like a little goat . . . It's all apery, all apery! The Frenchman at forty is the same child he was at fifteen, so let's all do likewise! No, really . . . after each ball it's as if you'd committed some sin; you don't even want to remember it. The head is simply empty, as after talking with a man of society; he talks about all sorts of things, touches lightly on everything, says everything he's pulled out of books, brightly, prettily, but there's no trace of any of it in his head, and you see then that even talking with a simple merchant who knows only his business, but knows it firmly and practically, is better than all these baubles. So, what can possibly be squeezed out of this ball? So, what if some writer, say, decided to describe the whole scene as it is? So, then in the book it would come out just as witless as in nature. What is it – moral? immoral? It's simply devil-knows-what! You'd spit and close the book." So unfavorable was Chichikov's opinion of balls in general; but it seems another reason for indignation was mixed in here. He was mainly vexed not at the ball, but at the fact that he had happened to trip up, that he had suddenly appeared before everyone looking like God knows what, that he had played some strange, ambiguous role. Of course, looking at it with the eye of a reasonable man, he saw that it was all absurd, that a stupid word meant nothing, particularly now, when the main business had already been properly done. But man is strange: he was greatly upset by the ill disposition of those very people whom he did not respect and with regard to whom he had spoken so sharply, denouncing their vanity and finery. This was the more vexatious to him since, on sorting out the matter clearly, he saw that he himself was partly the cause of it. He did not, however, get angry with himself, and in that, of course, he was right. We all have a little weakness for sparing ourselves somewhat, and prefer to try and find some neighbor on whom to vent our vexation, a servant, for instance, or a subordinate official who turns up at that moment, or a wife, or, finally, a chair, which gets flung devil knows where, straight at the door, so that the armrest and back come flying off: that will teach it what wrath is. So Chichikov, too, soon found a neighbor who could drag onto his own back everything his vexation might suggest to him. This neighbor was Nozdryov, and, needless to say, he got it from all sides and ends, as only some crook of a village elder or coachman gets it from some traveled, experienced captain, or even general, who on top of many expressions that have become classical, adds many unknown ones, the invention of which belongs properly to himself. The whole of Nozdryov's genealogy was examined and many members of his family in the line of ascent suffered greatly.

But all the while he was sitting in his hard armchair, troubled by thoughts and sleeplessness, zealously giving what for to Nozdryov and all his kin, and the tallow candle glimmered before him, its wick long covered by a black cap of snuff, threatening to go out at any moment, and blind, dark night looked in his window, ready to turn blue with approaching dawn, and somewhere far away far-off roosters whistled to each other, and in a completely sleeping town, perhaps, a frieze greatcoat plodded along somewhere, a wretch of unknown class and rank, who knows (alas!) one path only, all too well beaten by the devil-may-care Russian people – during this time, at the other end of town, an event was taking place which was about to increase the unpleasantness of our hero's situation. Namely, through the remote streets and alleys of the town there came clattering a rather strange vehicle, causing bewilderment with regard to its name. It resembled neither a tarantass, nor a barouche, nor a britzka, but more closely resembled a round, fat-cheeked watermelon on wheels. The cheeks of this watermelon – the doors, that is – bearing traces of yellow paint, closed very poorly on account of the poor condition of the handles and latches, which were tied anyhow with string. The watermelon was filled with cotton pillows shaped like pouches, bolsters, and simple pillows, and it was stuffed with sacks of bread, *kalatchi*,[41] cheesecakes, filled dumplings, and doughnuts. A chicken pie and a mince pie even peeked from the top. The footboard was occupied by a person of lackey origin, in a jacket of homespun ticking, with an unshaved beard shot with gray – a person known by the name of "lad." The noise and screeching of iron clamps and rusty bolts awakened a sentinel on the other side of town, who, raising his halberd, shouted, half awake, with all his might: "Who goes there?" – but seeing no one going there, and hearing only a distant clatter, he caught some beast on his collar and, going up to the streetlamp, executed it then and there on his nail. After which, setting his halberd aside, he fell asleep again according to the rules of his knightly order. The horses kept falling on their knees, because they were not shod and, besides, evidently had little familiarity with the comforts of town cobblestones. The rattletrap made several turns from one street to another and finally turned onto a dark lane by the small parish church of St. Nicholas on Nedotychki[42] and stopped by the gates of the archpriest's wife's house. A wench climbed out of the britzka in a quilted jacket, with a kerchief on her head, and banged on the gate with both fists as good as a man (the lad in the homespun jacket was later pulled down by his feet, for he was sleeping like the dead). The dogs barked and the gates, having gaped open, finally swallowed, though with great difficulty, this clumsy traveling contraption. The vehicle drove into a small yard cluttered with firewood, chicken coops, and all sorts of sheds; out of the vehicle climbed a lady: this lady was a landowner, the widow of a collegiate secretary, Korobochka. Soon after our hero's departure, the old woman had become so worried with regard to the possible occurrence of deceit on his side that, after three sleepless nights in a row, she had resolved to go to town, even though the horses were not shod, and there find out for certain what was the going price for dead souls, and whether she had, God forbid, gone amiss, having perhaps sold them dirt cheap. What consequences this arrival produced, the reader may learn from a certain conversation that took place between a certain two ladies. This conversation...but better let this conversation take place in the next chapter.

CHAPTER NINE

IN THE MORNING, even earlier than the hour fixed for visits in the town of N., there came fluttering out the doors of an orange wooden house with a mezzanine and light blue columns a lady in a stylish checked cloak, accompanied by a lackey in a greatcoat with several collars and gold braid on his round, glossy hat. The lady, with extraordinary haste, fluttered straight up the folding steps into the carriage standing at the front door. The lackey straightaway slammed the door on the lady, flung up the steps behind her, and, catching hold of the straps at the back of the carriage, shouted "Drive!" to the coachman. The lady was bearing some just-heard news and felt an irresistible urge to communicate it quickly. Every other moment she peeked out the window and saw to her unspeakable vexation that there was still halfway to go. Every house seemed longer than usual to her; the white stone almshouse with its narrow windows dragged on unbearably, so that she finally could not bear it and said: "Cursed building, there's just no end to it!" The coachman had already twice been given the order: "Faster, faster, Andryushka! You're taking insufferably long today!" At last the goal was attained. The carriage stopped in front of another one-storied wooden house, of a dark gray color, with little white bas-reliefs over the windows, and just in front of the windows a high wooden lattice and a narrow front garden, the slim trees of which were all white behind the lattice from the ever-abiding dust of the town. In the windows flashed flowerpots, a parrot swinging in his cage, clutching the ring with his beak, and two little dogs asleep in the sun.

In this house lived the bosom friend of the arriving lady. The author is in the greatest perplexity how to name the two ladies in such a way that people do not get angry with him again, as they used to in olden times. To refer to them by fictitious names is dangerous. Whatever name one comes up with, there is sure to be found in some corner of our state, given its greatness, someone who bears that name and who is sure to get mortally angry and start saying that the author came secretly with the purpose of ferreting out everything about who he was, what kind of woolly coat he went around in, and what Agrafena Ivanovna he came calling on, and upon what food he liked to dine. To refer to them by their ranks, God forbid, is even more dangerous. Our ranks and estates are so irritated these days that they take personally whatever appears in printed books: such, evidently, is the mood in the air. It is enough simply to say that there is a stupid man in a certain town, and it already becomes personal; suddenly a gentleman of respectable appearance pops up and shouts: "But I, too, am a man, which means that I, too, am stupid" – in short, he instantly grasps the situation. And therefore, to avoid all this, we shall refer to the lady who received the visit as she was referred to almost unanimously in the town of N. – namely, as a lady agreeable in all respects. She acquired this appellation legitimately, for she indeed spared nothing in making herself amiable to the utmost degree, but oh, of course, what nimble alacrity of female character lurked behind this amiableness! and oh, what a pin sometimes pricked through every agreeable word of hers! and God alone knew what seethed in that heart against any woman who might somewhere, somehow creep to the forefront. But all this was clothed in the subtlest worldliness, such as exists only in a provincial capital. Every movement she produced was tasteful, she even loved poetry, she even knew how to hold her head in a dreamy way on occasion – and everyone concurred that she was indeed a lady agreeable in all respects. Now the other lady, that is, the arriving one, was not possessed of so versatile a character, and therefore we shall refer to her as the simply agreeable lady. The arrival of the visitor woke the little dogs that were sleeping in the sun: the shaggy Adèle, ceaselessly entangled in her own fur, and Potpourri on his skinny legs. The one and the other, barking, carried the rings of their tails to the front hall, where the visitor was being freed from her cloak and emerged in a dress of fashionable pattern and color and with long tails around the neck; jasmine wafted through the whole room. The moment the lady agreeable in all respects learned of the arrival of the simply agreeable lady, she rushed to the front hall. The ladies seized each other's hands, kissed each other, and uttered little cries, as boarding-school girls do when they meet soon after graduation, before their mamas have had time to explain to them that one has a father who is poorer and of lower rank than the other. The kiss was performed noisily, so that the dogs started barking again, for which they received a flick of a shawl, and the two ladies went to the drawing room, a light blue one, naturally, with a sofa, an oval table, and even a little screen covered with ivy; after them, growling, ran shaggy Adèle and tall Potpourri on his skinny legs. "Here, here, in this little corner!" the hostess said as she sat her visitor down in a corner of the sofa. "That's right! that's right! here's a pillow for you!" So saying, she stuffed a pillow behind her back, on which a knight was embroidered in worsted the way things are always embroidered on canvas: the nose came out as a ladder, and the lips as a rectangle. "I'm so glad it's you ... I heard someone drive up and asked myself who it could be so early. Parasha said, 'The vice-governor's wife,' and I said, 'So that fool is coming to bore me again,' and I was just about to say I wasn't home ... "

The visitor was about to get down to business and tell her news. But the exclamation that the lady agreeable in all respects let out at that moment suddenly gave a different direction to the conversation.

"What a gay little print!" the lady agreeable in all respects exclaimed, looking at the dress of the simply agreeable lady.

"Yes, very gay. Praskovya Fyodorovna, however, finds that it would be nicer if the checks were a bit smaller and the speckles were not brown but light blue. Her sister was sent a fabric – it's simply charming beyond words; imagine to yourself: narrow little stripes, as narrow as human imagination can possibly conceive, a light blue background, and between the stripes it's all spots and sprigs, spots and sprigs, spots and sprigs... Incomparable, in short! One can say decidedly that nothing comparable has ever existed in the world."

"It's gaudy, my dear."

"Ah, no, not gaudy."

"Ah, gaudy!"

It must be noted that the lady agreeable in all respects was something of a materialist, inclined to negation and doubt, and she rejected quite a lot in life.

Here the simply agreeable lady explained that it was by no means gaudy, and cried out:

"Besides, I congratulate you: flounces are no longer being worn."

"Not worn?"

"It's little festoons now."

"Ah, that's not pretty – little festoons!"

"Little festoons, little festoons all over: a pelerine of little festoons, sleeves with little festoons, epaulettes of little festoons, little festoons below, little festoons everywhere."

"It's not pretty, Sofya Ivanovna, if it's little festoons all over."

"It's sweet, Anna Grigorievna, unbelievably sweet. It's made with double seams: wide armholes and above... But here, here is something amazing for you, now you're going to say... Well, be amazed: imagine, the bodices are even longer now, vee-shaped in front, and the front busk goes beyond all bounds; the skirt is gathered around as it used to be with the old-fashioned farthingale, and they even pad it out a little behind with cotton batting, so as to make for a perfect belle-femme."

"Now that's just – I declare!" said the lady agreeable in all respects, making a movement of her head expressive of dignity.

"Precisely, it is indeed – I declare!" replied the simply agreeable lady.

"As you like, but I wouldn't follow that for anything."

"Neither would I . . . Really, when you imagine what fashion comes to sometimes . . . it's beyond everything! I begged my sister to give me the pattern just for fun; my Melanya's started sewing."

"So you have the pattern?" the lady agreeable in all respects cried out, not without a noticeable tremor of excitement.

"Of course, my sister brought it."

"Give it to me, dear heart, by all that's holy."

"Ah, I've already promised it to Praskovya Fyodorovna. Perhaps after her."

"Who's going to wear it after Praskovya Fyodorovna? It would be all too strange on your part to prefer others to your own."

"But she's also my aunt twice removed."

"God knows what kind of aunt she is to you: it's on your husband's side . . . No, Sofya Ivanovna, I don't even want to listen, since you intend to hand me such an insult . . . Obviously, I'm already boring to you, obviously you wish to stop all acquaintance with me."

Poor Sofya Ivanovna absolutely did not know what to do. She herself felt that she had put herself between a rock and a hard place. So much for her boasting! She was ready to prick her stupid tongue all over with needles for it.

"Well, and how's our charmer?" the lady agreeable in all respects said meanwhile.

"Ah, my God! why am I sitting in front of you like this? Aren't I a good one! Do you know, Anna Grigorievna, what I've come to you with?" Here the visitor's breath was taken away; words, like hawks, were ready to rush in pursuit of each other, and one had to be as inhuman as her bosom friend to venture to stop her.

"No matter how you go praising and exalting him," she said, with greater animation than usual, "I will say straight out, and say it to his face, that he is a worthless man, worthless, worthless, worthless."

"But just listen to what I'm going to reveal to you . . . "

"Word is going around that he's good-looking, but he's not good-looking at all, not at all, and his nose . . . a most disagreeable nose."

"But let me tell you, just let me tell you . . . darling Anna Grigorievna, let me tell you! It's a whole story, do you under-stand, a story, sconapel istwar,"[43] the visitor said with an expres-sion almost of despair and in an utterly imploring voice. It will do no harm to mention that the conversation of the two ladies was interspersed with a great many foreign words and some-times entire long phrases in French. But filled though the author is with reverence for the saving benefits that the French lan-guage brings to Russia, filled though he is with reverence for the praiseworthy custom of our high society which expresses itself in it at all hours of the day – out of a deep feeling of love for the fatherland, of course – for all that he simply cannot bring himself to introduce any phrase from any foreign language whatsoever into this Russian poem of his. And so let us continue in Russian.

"What is the story?"

"Ah, Anna Grigorievna, dear heart, if you could only imagine the position I was in, just fancy: this morning the archpriest's wife comes to me – the wife of the archpriest, Father Kiril – and what do you think: our humble fellow, our visitor here, is quite a one, eh?"

"What, you don't mean he was making sheep's eyes at the archpriest's wife?"

"Ah, Anna Grigorievna, if it was only sheep it would be nothing; but just listen to what the archpriest's wife said:

the lady landowner Korobochka comes to her, she says, all frightened and pale as death, and tells her, and how she tells her, just listen, it's a perfect novel: suddenly, in the dead of night, when the whole house is asleep, there comes a knocking at the gate, the most terrible knocking you could possibly imagine, and a shout: 'Open up, open up, or we'll break down the gate!' How do you like that? What do you think of our charmer after that?"

"And this Korobochka is what, young and good-looking?"

"Not a whit, an old crone."

"Ah, how charming! So he's taken up with an old crone. Talk about our ladies' taste after that! They found who to fall in love with!"

"But no, Anna Grigorievna, it's not at all what you're thinking. Just imagine to yourself how he comes in, armed from head to foot like Rinaldo Rinaldini,[44] and demands: 'Sell me all your souls that have died.' And Korobochka answers very reasonably, saying: 'I can't sell them, because they're dead.' 'No,' he says, 'they're not dead, it's my business to know whether they're dead or not, and they're not dead,' he shouts, 'they're not, they're not!' In short, he caused a terrible scandal: the whole village came running, babies were crying, everything was shouting, no one understood anyone else – well, simply orerr, orerr, orerr! . . . But you cannot imagine to yourself, Anna Grigorievna, how alarmed I was when I heard it all. 'Dearest mistress,' Mashka says to me, 'look in the mirror: you're pale.' 'Who cares about the mirror,' I say, 'I must go and tell Anna Grigorievna.' That same moment I order the carriage readied: the coachman Andryushka asks me where to go, and I cannot even say anything, I just gaze into his eyes like a fool – I think he thought I was mad. Ah, Anna Grigorievna, if you could only imagine how alarmed I was!"

"It is strange, though," said the lady agreeable in all respects. "What might they mean, these dead souls? I confess, I understand precisely nothing of it. It's the second time I've heard about these dead souls; but my husband still says Noz-dryov's lying. No, there must be something to it."

"But do imagine, Anna Grigorievna, the position I was in when I heard it. 'And now,' says Korobochka, 'I don't know what I'm to do. He made me sign some false paper,' she says, 'threw down fifteen roubles in banknotes. I'm an inexperi-enced, helpless widow,' she says, 'I know nothing...' Such goings-on! But if only you could imagine at least slightly to yourself how totally alarmed I was."

"But, as you will, only it's not dead souls here, there's something else hidden in it."

"I confess, I think so, too," the simply agreeable lady said, not without surprise, and straightaway felt a strong desire to learn what it was that might be hidden in it. She even said in measured tones: "And what do you think is hidden in it?"

"Well, what do you think?"

"What do I think?... I confess, I'm completely at a loss."

"But, all the same, I'd like to know your thoughts concerning it."

But the agreeable lady found nothing to say. She knew only how to be alarmed, but as for arriving at some sort of clever conjecture, she was not equal to the task, and therefore, more than any other woman, she was in need of tender friendship and advice.

"Well, listen then, here's what it is with these dead souls," said the lady agreeable in all respects, and at these words the visitor became all attention: her little ears pricked up of them-selves, she rose slightly, almost not sitting or holding on to the sofa, and though she was somewhat on the heavy side, she suddenly became slenderer, like a light bit of fluff about to fly into the air with a breath of wind.

Thus a Russian squire, a dog-lover and hunter, approaching the woods from which a hare, startled by the beaters, is just about to leap, turns, all of him, together with his horse and raised crop, for one frozen moment into powder that is just about to be ignited. He is all fastened on the murky air with his eyes, and he will catch the beast, he will finish it off, ineluctably, no matter how the whole rebellious, snowy steppe rises up against him, sending silver stars into his mouth, his mustache, his eyes, his eyebrows, and his beaver hat.

"The dead souls...," pronounced the lady agreeable in all respects.

"What, what?" the visitor picked up, all excitement.

"The dead souls!..."

"Ah, speak, for God's sake!"

"That was simply invented as a cover, and here's the real thing: he wants to carry off the governor's daughter."

This conclusion was, indeed, quite unanticipated and in all respects extraordinary. The agreeable lady, on hearing it, simply froze on the spot, turned pale, pale as death, and, indeed, became seriously alarmed.

"Ah, my God!" she cried out, clasping her hands, "that is something I would never have thought."

"And, I confess, as soon as you opened your mouth, I grasped what it was," replied the lady agreeable in all respects.

"But what is boarding-school education after that, Anna Grigorievna! There's innocence for you!"

"What innocence! I've heard her say such things as, I confess, I would never have the courage to utter."

"You know, Anna Grigorievna, it's simply heartrending to see where immorality has finally come to."

"And men lose their minds over her. As for me, I confess, I find nothing in her... She's insufferably affected."

"Ah, Anna Grigorievna, dear heart, she's a statue, and if only she at least had some expression in her face."

"Ah, how affected! Ah, how affected! God, how affected! Who taught her I do not know, but I have never yet seen a woman in whom there was so much mincing."

"Darling! she's a statue, and pale as death."

"Ah, don't tell me, Sofya Ivanovna: she's sinfully rouged."

"Ah, how can you, Anna Grigorievna: she's chalk, chalk, the purest chalk!"

"My dear, I sat next to her: rouge finger-thick, and it comes off in pieces, like plaster. The mother taught her, she's a coquette herself, and the daughter will outdo her mama."

"No, excuse me, I'll take any oath you like, I'm ready to be deprived this instant of my children, my husband, all my property, if she wears the least drop, the least particle, the least shadow of any sort of rouge!"

"Ah, what are you saying, Sofya Ivanovna!" said the lady agreeable in all respects, clasping her hands.

"Ah, you really are the one, Anna Grigorievna! . . . I look at you in amazement!" the agreeable lady said, also clasping her hands.

Let it not seem strange to the reader that the two ladies could not agree between them on what they had seen at almost the same time. There are, indeed, many things in the world that have this quality: when one lady looks at them, they come out perfectly white, and when another lady looks, they come out red, red as a cranberry.

"Now, here's another proof for you that she's pale," the simply agreeable lady went on. "I remember, as if it were today, sitting next to Manilov and saying to him: 'Look how pale she is!' Really, our men must be altogether witless to admire her. And our charmer . . . Ah, how disgusting I found him! You cannot imagine, Anna Grigorievna, to what extent I found him disgusting."

"But, all the same, certain ladies turned up who were not indifferent to him."

"Me, Anna Grigorievna? Now, that you can never say, never, never!"

"But I'm not talking about you, as if there were no one else but you."

"Never, never, Anna Grigorievna! Allow me to point out to you that I know myself very well; but perhaps on the part of certain other ladies who play the role of untouchables."

"I beg your pardon, Sofya Ivanovna! Allow me to inform you that such scandaleusities have never yet occurred with me. Perhaps with someone else, but not with me, do allow me to point that out to you."

"Why are you so offended? There were other ladies present, there were even such as would be the first to grab the chair by the door in order to sit closer to him."

Well, now, after such words uttered by the agreeable lady, a storm had inevitably to ensue, but, to the greatest amazement, the two ladies suddenly quieted down, and absolutely nothing ensued. The lady agreeable in all respects recalled that the pattern for the fashionable dress was not yet in her hands, and the simply agreeable lady realized that she had not yet succeeded in ferreting out any details with regard to the discovery made by her bosom friend, and therefore peace very quickly ensued. Incidentally, it cannot be said that either lady had in her nature any need to inflict disagreeableness, and generally there was nothing wicked in their characters, but just like that, imperceptibly, a little wish to needle each other was born of itself in the course of conversation; one of them would simply thrust a lively little phrase at the other now and then, for the sake of a little pleasure: there, that's for you! take that and eat it! All sorts of needs exist in the hearts of both the male and the female sex.

"The one thing I can't understand, however," said the simply agreeable lady, "is how Chichikov, being a passing traveler, could resolve on such a bold venture. It can't be that there are no accomplices."

"And do you think there aren't any?"

"And who do you suppose could be helping him?"

"Well, let's say Nozdryov."

"Nozdryov, really?"

"And why not? He's capable of it. You know he wanted to sell his own father, or, better still, lose him at cards."

"Ah, my God, such interesting news I learn from you! I'd never have supposed Nozdryov could also be mixed up in this story!"

"And I always supposed so."

"When you think, really, the sorts of things that happen in the world! Now, could one have thought, when Chichikov had just come to our town, remember, that he would produce such a strange demarch in the world? Ah, Anna Grigorievna, if only you knew how alarmed I was! If it weren't for your good will and friendship . . . indeed, it was the brink of ruin . . . where, then? My Mashka saw I was pale as death. 'Darling mistress,' she says to me, 'you are pale as death.' 'Mashka,' I say, 'I can't be bothered with that.' What a thing to happen! So Nozdryov is in it, too, if you please!"

The agreeable lady wanted very much to ferret out further details concerning the abduction, such as the hour and so on, but that was wanting too much. The lady agreeable in all respects responded with outright ignorance. She was incapable of lying: to suppose something or other – that was a different matter, but then only in case the supposition was based on inner conviction; if she did feel an inner conviction, then she was capable of standing up for herself, and if some whiz of a lawyer, famous for his gift of refuting other people's arguments, went and tried to compete with her – he would see what inner conviction means.

That both ladies finally became decidedly convinced of what they had first supposed only as a supposition is in no way extraordinary. Our sort – intelligent folk, as we call ourselves – act in almost the same way, and our learned reasoning serves as proof of it. At first the scholar sidles up to it with extraordinary lowliness; he begins timidly, with moderation, starting from the most humble inquiry: "Can it be from there? Was it not from that corner that such and such a country took its name?" or "Does this document not belong to some other, later time?" or "Should we not take this people as in fact meaning that people?" He immediately quotes one or another ancient writer, and as soon as he sees some hint, or something he takes for a hint, he sets off at a trot and plucks up his courage; he converses with ancient writers on familiar terms, he asks them questions and even answers for them himself, forgetting entirely that he started with a timid supposition; it already seems to him that he can see it, that it is clear – and the reasoning concludes with the words: "This is how it was, this is the people that must be meant, this is the point of view to take on the subject!" Then, proclaimed publicly, from the podium, the newly discovered truth goes traveling all over the world, gathering followers and admirers.

At that moment, just as the ladies so successfully and cleverly resolved this tangled state of affairs, the prosecutor entered the drawing room with his eternally motionless physiognomy, bushy eyebrows, and blinking eye. The ladies began vying with each other in informing him of all the events, told him about the purchase of the dead souls, the intention to carry off the governor's daughter, and got him completely bewildered, so that no matter how long he went on standing on one and the same spot, batting his left eye, flicking his beard with a handkerchief to brush off the snuff, he could understand decidedly nothing. With that the two ladies left him and set out each in her own direction to rouse the town. They managed to accomplish this enterprise in a little over half an hour. The town was decidedly aroused; all was in ferment, though no one could understand anything. The ladies managed to blow so much smoke in everyone's eyes that for a while everyone, the officials especially, remained dumbfounded. Their position for the first moment was like that of a sleeping schoolboy whose comrades, getting up earlier, have put a hussar in his nose – that is, a rolled-up paper filled with snuff. Unwittingly inhaling all the snuff with all the zeal of a still-sleeping man, he awakes, jumps up, stares like a fool, goggle-eyed, in all directions, unable to understand where he is or what has happened, and only then notices the indirect ray of sun shining on the wall, the laughter of his comrades hiding in the corners, and the dawning day looking in the window, the awakened forest sounding with the voices of thousands of birds, the light shining on the river, disappearing now and then in its gleaming curlicues amid the slender rushes, all strewn with naked children calling others to come for a swim, and only then finally feels the hussar sitting in his nose. This was precisely the position of the inhabitants and officials of the town for the first moment. Each of them stood like a sheep, goggling his eyes. The dead souls, the governor's daughter, and Chichikov got confused and mixed up in their heads extraordinarily strangely; and only later, after the first befuddlement, did they begin to distinguish them, as it were, and separate them from one another, did they begin to demand an accounting and to be angry that the matter refused to explain itself. What was this riddle, indeed, what was this riddle of the dead souls? There was no logic whatsoever in dead souls. Why buy dead souls? Where would such a fool be found? What worn-out money would one pay for them? To what end, to what business, could these dead souls be tacked? And why was the governor's daughter mixed up in it? If he wanted to carry her off, why buy dead souls for that? And if he was buying dead souls, why carry off the governor's daughter? Did he want to make her a gift of these dead souls, or what? What was this nonsense, really, that had been spread around town? What was this tendency, that before you could turn around there was already a story let out? And if only there were any sense ... They did spread it, however, so there must have been some reason? But what was the reason for the dead souls? There even was no reason. It was all a mere cock-and-bull story, nonsense, balderdash, soft-boiled boots! Mere devil take it! ... In short, there was talk and more talk, and the whole town started chattering about the dead souls and the governor's daughter, about Chichikov and the dead souls, about the governor's daughter and Chichikov, and everything there arose. Like a whirlwind the hitherto apparently slumbering town blew up! Out of their holes crept all the sluggards and sloths, who had been lying at home in their dressing gowns for several years, shifting the blame now onto the cobbler for making their boots too tight, now onto the tailor, now onto the drunken coachman. All those who had long since stopped all acquaintances and kept company only with the landowners Zavalishin and Polezhaev (well-known terms derived from the verbs *polezhat*, "to lie down," and *zavalitsa*, "to slump into bed," which are very popular in our Russia, as is the phrase about stopping to see Sopikov and Khrapovitsky, meaning all sorts of dead sleep – on your side, on your back, and in every other position, with snorting, nose whistling, and other accessories); all those who could not be lured out of the house even by an invitation to slurp up a five-hundred-rouble fish soup with a five-foot-long sterlet and various savory, melt-in-the-mouth pies; in short, it turned out that the town was populous, and big, and well inhabited. Some Sysoy Pafnutievich and Makdonald Karlovich appeared, of whom no one had ever heard; in the drawing rooms some long, long fellow with a bullet through his arm began sticking up, so tall that no one had ever seen the like. On the streets covered droshkies appeared, wagonettes previously unknown, rattletraps, wheel-squeakers – and the pot began to boil. At another time and under other circumstances, such rumors would perhaps not have attracted any attention; but the town of N. had not heard any news at all for a long time. Over the past three months there had even been nothing of what are called *commérages*[45] in the capitals, which, as everyone knows, is the same for a town as the timely delivery of food supplies. It suddenly turned out that the town's wits were divided into two completely opposite opinions, and suddenly two opposite parties were formed – the men's party and the women's party. The men's party, the more witless of the two, paid attention to the dead souls. The women's party occupied itself exclusively with the abduction of the governor's daughter. It must be noted to the ladies' credit that there was incomparably more order and circumspection in their party. Clearly, it is their very function to be good mistresses and managers. Everything with them soon took on a lively, definite look, was clothed in clear and obvious forms, explained, purified – in short, the result was a finished picture. It turned out that Chichikov had long been in love, and that they met in the garden by moonlight, that the governor would even have given him his daughter in marriage, because Chichikov was rich as a Jew, had it not been for the wife he had abandoned (where they found out that Chichikov was married – of this no one had any idea), that his wife, suffering from hopeless love, had written a most moving letter to the governor, and that Chichikov, seeing that the father and mother would never give their consent, had resolved on abduction. In other houses, it was told somewhat differently: that Chichikov did not have any wife, but, being a subtle man who acted only when certain of himself, he had undertaken, in order to win the hand of the daughter, to start an affair with the mother, had had a secret amorous liaison with her, and afterwards had made a declaration concerning the daughter's hand; but the mother, frightened that a crime against religion might be committed, and feeling pangs of conscience, had flatly refused, and this was why Chichikov had resolved on abduction. Many explanations and emendations were added to all this as the rumors finally penetrated into the remotest back alleys. In Russia, the lower society likes very much to discuss the gossip that occurs in high society, and so people started discussing it all in such hovels as had never known or set eyes on Chichikov, and there were additions and still further explanations. The subject became more entertaining every moment, assumed more definitive forms every day, and finally, just as it was, in all its definitiveness, was delivered into the very ears of the governor's wife. The governor's wife, as the mother of a family, as the first lady of the town, and finally as a lady who had never suspected anything of the sort, was thoroughly insulted by such stories, and felt an indignation in all respects justified. The poor blonde endured the most disagreeable tête-à-tête any sixteen-year-old girl had ever endured. Whole streams of queries, inquiries, reprimands, threats, reproaches, and admonishments poured out, so that the girl burst into tears, sobbed, and could not understand a single word; the door-keeper was given the strictest orders not to admit Chichikov at any time or on any account.

Having done their bit with regard to the governor's wife, the ladies put pressure on the men's party, trying to win them over to their side and insisting that the dead souls were only an invention employed with the sole purpose of diverting all suspicion and carrying out the abduction more successfully. Many of the men were even seduced and joined their party, despite their being subjected to strong disapprobation by their own comrades, who berated them as old women and skirts – names known to be most offensive for the male sex.

But, however the men armed themselves and resisted, their party still lacked the order of the women's. Everything with them was somehow crude, unpolished, unformed, uncomely, unattuned, none too good, in their heads a jumble, a muddle, a scramble, untidiness in their thoughts – in short, everything pointed to man's empty nature, his coarse, heavy nature, incapable of good management, or of heartfelt convictions, pusillanimous, lazy, filled with ceaseless doubt and eternal fear. They said it was all nonsense, that the abduction of the governor's daughter was more a hussar's affair than a civilian's, that Chichikov would not do it, that the women were lying, that a woman is like a sack – it holds whatever you put in it, that the main subject to pay attention to was the dead souls, which, however, meant devil knows what, but anyhow there was something quite nasty and none too good about them. Why it seemed to the men that there was something nasty and none too good about them, we shall learn at once: a new governor-general had been appointed to the province – an event known to put officials into a state of alarm: there would be reshuffling, reprimanding, lambasting, and all the official belly-wash to which a superior treats his subordinates. "And what," thought the officials, "if he just simply finds out the strange sort of rumors that are going around town, for that alone he can give us a boiling that'll be the life of us." The inspector of the board of health suddenly turned pale: he imagined God knows what: might the "dead souls" not refer to the sick who had died in considerable numbers in the infirmaries and other places from epidemic fever, against which due measures had not been taken, and might not Chichikov be an official sent from the governor-general's office to conduct a secret investigation? He informed the head magistrate of this. The magistrate replied that it was nonsense, and then suddenly he, too, turned pale, having asked himself the question: "And what if the souls bought by Chichikov are indeed dead, and he had allowed the deed to be drawn up for them and had himself acted as Plyushkin's agent, and it should come to the knowledge of the governor-general – what then?" He did no more than tell this to one or two others, and suddenly the one or two others turned pale – fear is more catching than the plague and communicates itself instantly. Everybody suddenly discovered in themselves such sins as did not even exist. The words "dead souls" sounded so indefinite that there was even a suspicion that they might contain an allusion to some bodies hastily buried following two quite recent incidents. The first incident had occurred with some Solvychegodsk merchants, who came to town for the fair and when their dealings were finished threw a party for their friends, the merchants from Ustsysolsk, a party on a real Russian footing, with German trimmings: orgeats, punches, cordials, and so on. The party ended, as usual, with a fight. The Solvychegodsks did in the Ustsysolsks, though they, too, suffered a good drubbing on the sides, under

the ribs, and in the solar plexus, which testified to the inordin-
ate size of the fists with which the deceased were furnished.
One of the triumphant even "had his pump lopped off entirely," as the combatants put it, meaning that his nose was
smashed to a pulp, so that there was not even a half finger's
width of it left on his face. The merchants confessed to the
affair, explaining that they had been up to a bit of mischief;
rumor had it that they added four thousand each to their
confession; however, the affair was all too obscure; it turned
out from the inquest and investigation undertaken that the
Ustsysolsk boys had died of fume poisoning, and so as fume-
poisoned they were buried. The other incident that had occurred recently was the following: the state peasants of the
hamlet called Lousy Arrogance, joining with their fellows from
the hamlet of Borovki, alias Cockyville, supposedly wiped
from the face of the earth the local police force, in the person
of the assessor, a certain Drobyazhkin, this local police force –
that is, the assessor Drobyazhkin – having gotten into the habit
of coming to their village far too often, which in some cases is
as good as epidemic fever, and the reason for it, they said, was
that the local police force, owing to certain weaknesses on the
amorous side, had his eyes on the women and village girls. This
was not known for certain, however, though the peasants
stated directly in their evidence that the local police force
was as lecherous as a tomcat, and had already been spared
more than once, and on one occasion had even been driven
naked out of some cottage he had made his way into. Of
course, the local police force deserved to be punished for his
amorous weaknesses, but the muzhiks of Lousy Arrogance and
alias-Cockyville could not be justified for such summary justice, if they had indeed participated in the slaying. But the affair
was obscure; the local police force was found on the road, the
uniform or frock coat on the local police force was worse than
a rag, and his physiognomy was utterly beyond recognition.
The case went through the courts and finally came to the

chancellery, where the intimate deliberations took the following line: since it was not known precisely who among the peasants had participated, and there were many of them, and since Drobyazhkin was a dead man, meaning that it would not be much use to him even if he did win the case, while the muzhiks were still alive, meaning that for them it was quite important that the decision be in their favor, it was therefore decided thus: the assessor Drobyazhkin was himself the cause, having unjustly oppressed the peasants of Lousy Arrogance and alias-Cockyville, and he had died of apoplexy while returning home in a sleigh. The case, it seemed, had been handled squarely, but the officials, for some unknown reason, began to think that these were the dead souls now in question. It also happened, as if by design, that just when the gentlemen officials were in a difficult position to begin with, two documents came to the governor simultaneously. The content of one was that, according to evidence and reports received, there was in their province a maker of forged banknotes, hiding under various names, and that the strictest investigation should immediately be undertaken. The second document contained a request from the governor of a neighboring province concerning a robber fleeing legal prosecution, that if any suspicious man were to turn up in their province, unable to produce any certificates or passports, he should be detained without delay. These two documents simply stunned everyone. Former conclusions and surmises were completely confounded. Of course, it was quite impossible to suppose that anything here referred to Chichikov; nevertheless, once they reflected, each for his own part, once they recalled that they still did not know who in fact Chichikov was, that he himself had given a rather vague account concerning his own person – true, he said he had suffered for the truth in the service, but this was all somehow vague – and when they also remembered that, as he had even said himself, he had many adversaries who had made attempts on his life, they pondered still more: so his life was in danger, so he was being pursued, so he must have done something or other...but who in fact could he be? Of course, it was impossible to think of him as a maker of forged bills, still less as a robber: his appearance was trustworthy; but still, for all that, who in fact could he be? And so the gentlemen officials now asked themselves the question they ought to have asked themselves in the beginning – that is, in the first chapter of our poem. It was decided to make a few more inquiries of those from whom the souls had been bought, in order to find out at least what sort of purchases they were, and what precisely these dead souls could mean, and whether he had somehow ex-plained to anyone, be it only by chance, in passing, his true intentions, and had told anyone who he was. First of all they addressed themselves to Korobochka, but there they gleaned little: he bought fifteen roubles' worth, she said, and was also buying bird feathers, and promised to buy a lot of everything, and also supplied the state with lard, and therefore was un-doubtedly a crook, for there had already been one like him who used to buy bird feathers and supplied the state with lard, and then he deceived everybody and took the archpriest's wife for more than a hundred roubles. Whatever she said beyond that was a repetition of one and the same thing, and the officials saw only that Korobochka was simply a stupid old woman. Manilov answered that he was always ready to vouch for Pavel Ivanovich as for his own self, that he would sacrifice all he owned to have a hundredth part of Pavel Ivanovich's qualities, and in general spoke of him in the most flattering terms, appending a few thoughts about friendship, with his eyes now tightly shut. These thoughts, of course, explained satis-factorily the tender impulse of his heart, but they did not explain to the officials the truth of the matter. Sobakevich answered that Chichikov was, in his opinion, a good man, and that he had sold him some choice peasants, folk alive in all respects; but that he could not vouch for what would happen later on, that if they died off a bit during the difficulties of resettlement, on the road, he was not to blame, since that was in God's power, and there were not a few fevers and various deadly diseases in the world, and there were examples when whole villages had died out. The gentlemen officials resorted to yet another method, not altogether noble, but which nevertheless is sometimes employed – that is, making inquiries in a roundabout way, through various lackey acquaintances, of Chichikov's servants, whether they knew any details concerning their master's former life and circumstances, but again they heard little. From Petrushka they got only the smell of living quarters, and from Selifan that he had been in the goverman's service and once worked in customs, and nothing else. This class of people has a very strange habit. If you ask one of them directly about anything, he will never remember, nothing will come to his head, and he will even say he simply does not know, but if you ask about something else, then he will spin his yarn and tell such details as you would not even want to know. The whole search carried out by the officials revealed to them only that they did not know for certain what Chichikov was, and that all the same Chichikov must certainly be something. They resolved finally to have a final discussion of the subject and decide at least what they were to do and how, and what measures to take, and what he was precisely: the sort of man to be detained and arrested as untrustworthy, or else the sort of man who might himself detain and arrest all of them as untrustworthy. To do all this it was proposed that they gather specially at the house of the police chief, known to the reader already as the father and benefactor of the town.

CHAPTER TEN

HAVING GATHERED AT the house of the police chief, known to the reader already as the father and benefactor of the town, the officials had occasion to observe to each other that they had even grown thinner as a result of all these cares and anxieties. Indeed, the appointment of the new governor-general, and the receipt of those documents of such serious content, and those God-knows-what rumors – all this left a visible imprint on their faces, and the frock coats of many of them had become visibly looser. Everything gave way: the head magistrate got thinner, the inspector of the board of health got thinner, the prosecutor got thinner, and some Semyon Ivanovich, who was never called by his last name, and who wore on his index finger a seal ring that he used to let the ladies look at – even he got thinner. Of course, as happens everywhere, there turned up some who did not quail or lose their presence of mind, but they were very few. Just the postmaster alone. He alone was unchanged in his constantly even character and had the custom of always saying on such occasions: "We know about you, governor-general! There's maybe three or four of you have come to replace each other, but as for me, my dear sir, I've been sitting in the same place for thirty years now." To this the other officials usually observed: "That's fine for you, Spre-chen-sie-Deych Ivan Andreych, yours is a mailing business: receiving and sending correspondence; so you might cheat on occasion by locking the office an hour early, or bilk some merchant for sending a letter at the wrong time, or else send some package that oughtn't to be sent – here, of course,

anyone can be a saint. But just let the devil start turning up
under your hands every day, so that you don't want to take it,
but he just sticks it there. You, naturally, couldn't care less, you
have just one boy, but we, brother, have the much-blessed
Praskovya Fyodorovna, so that every year brings something:
now a Praskushka, now a Petrusha – here, brother, it's a
different tune." So spoke the officials, but whether it is indeed
possible to hold out against the devil is not for the author to
judge. In the council that gathered this time, the absence of
that necessary thing which simple folk call sense was very
noticeable. Generally we are somehow not made for representative meetings. In all our gatherings, from the peasant com-
munity level up to all possible learned and other committees,
unless they have one head to control everything, there is a
great deal of confusion. It is even hard to say why this is so;
evidently the nation is like that, since the only meetings that
succeed are those arranged for the sake of carousing or dining,
to wit: clubs and all sorts of vauxhalls on a German footing.[46]
Yet there is a readiness for anything, you might say, at any
moment. Suddenly, as the wind blows, we start societies,
charitable or for the encouragement of God knows what.
The goal may be beautiful, but nothing will come of it for all
that. Maybe it is because we are suddenly satisfied at the very
beginning, and think that everything has already been done.
For instance, having started some charitable society for the
poor and donated considerable sums, we at once give a dinner
for all the foremost dignitaries of the town to celebrate this
praiseworthy action, spending, of course, half of all the
donated money on it; the rest goes straightaway to rent a
splendid apartment for the committee, with heating and door-
keepers, and then there are five and a half roubles left for the
poor from the entire sum, and even here not all the members
agree about their distribution, and each one trots out some
gammer of his own. However, the meeting that gathered this
time was of a completely different sort; it was formed as a result

of necessity. The matter did not concern some poor people or strangers, the matter concerned each official personally, it was the matter of a calamity that threatened them all equally; which meant that, willy-nilly, there had to be more unanimity, closeness. But, for all that, it ended with devil knows what. Not to speak of the disagreement common to all councils, the opinions of those assembled displayed some even inconceivable indecisiveness: one said that Chichikov was a forger of government banknotes, and then himself added, "Or maybe he's not"; another affirmed that he was an official of the governor-general's chancellery, and immediately went on, "Though, devil knows, it's not written on his forehead." Against the conjecture that he was a robber in disguise, everyone rose up in arms; they found that besides an appearance that in itself was trustworthy to begin with, there was nothing in his conversation to suggest a man of violent behavior. All at once the postmaster, who had stood for a few moments immersed in some reflection, cried out unexpectedly, either as a result of a sudden inspiration that visited him, or something else:

"Do you know who he is, gentlemen?"

The voice in which he uttered it contained in itself something so stupendous that it made them all cry out simultaneously:

"Who?"

"He, gentlemen, my dear sir, is none other than Captain Kopeikin!"[47]

And when straightaway they all asked with one voice: "Who is this Captain Kopeikin?" the postmaster said:

"So you don't know who Captain Kopeikin is?"

They all replied that they had no knowledge of who Captain Kopeikin was.

"Captain Kopeikin," the postmaster said, opening his snuff-box only halfway for fear one of his neighbors might get into it with his fingers, in the cleanness of which he had little faith and even had the custom of muttering: "We know, my dear, you may go visiting God knows what parts with your fingers, and snuff is a thing requiring cleanliness" – "Captain Kopeikin," the postmaster said, after taking a pinch, "no, but as a matter of fact, if someone was to tell it, it would, in a certain way, make a whole poem, quite amusing for some writer."

All those present expressed a desire to know this story, or, as the postmaster put it, in a certain way, whole poem, quite amusing for some writer, and he began thus:

THE TALE OF CAPTAIN KOPEIKIN

"After the campaign of the year 'twelve, my good sir," thus the postmaster began, though sitting in the room were not one sir but a whole six, "after the campaign of the year 'twelve, Captain Kopeikin was sent back along with the other wounded. It was either at Krasny or else at Leipzig, but anyway, if you can imagine, he had an arm and a leg blown off. Well, they hadn't yet made any of those, you know, arrangements for the wounded; this invalid fund or whatever, if you can picture it, was, in a certain way, introduced much later. Captain Kopeikin sees he ought to work, only, you understand, all he's got is his left hand. He tried going home to his father; the father says, 'I've got nothing to feed you with' – if you can picture it – 'I barely have bread for myself.' So my Captain Kopeikin decided to set out for Petersburg, my good sir, to petition the sovereign and see if he could obtain some imperial charity, 'because look, thus and so, in a certain way, so to speak, I sacrificed my life, spilled my blood...' Well, anyway, you know, with some government transport or wagon train – in short, my good sir, he somehow dragged himself to Petersburg. Well, if you can picture it, this some such one – Captain Kopeikin, that is – suddenly found himself in a capital the likes of which, so to speak, doesn't exist on earth! Suddenly there's a world before him, so to speak, a sort of field of life, a fairytale Scheherazade. Suddenly, if you can

picture it, there's some such Nevsky Prospect, or, you understand, some Gorokhovy Street, devil take it! or some such
Liteiny Street; there's some such spire sticking up in the air;
the bridges there hang like the devil, if you can picture it, that
is, not touching anywhere – in short, it's Semiramis, sir,[48] that's
the whole of it! He knocked about trying to rent a place, only
it all put too much of a pinch on him – all those curtains,
shades, devilish stuff, you understand, rugs – a whole Persia;
trampling on capitals with your feet, so to speak. Well, it's just,
I mean, you go down the street and your nose can simply smell
the thousands; and my Captain Kopeikin's bank account consists, you understand, of some ten fivers. Well, he somehow
got himself sheltered in a Revel inn[49] for one rouble a day;
dinner was cabbage soup and a piece of chopped beef. He sees
there's no point in overstaying. He makes inquiries about
where to address himself. There is, they say, a kind of high
commission, a board or whatever, you understand, and the
head of it is general-in-chief so-and-so. And you should know
that the sovereign was not yet in the capital then; the army, if
you can picture it, hadn't come back from Paris yet, everything
was abroad. My Kopeikin got up early, scraped at his beard
with his left hand – because to pay a barber would, in a certain
way, run up a bill – pulled on his wretched uniform, and went
on his wooden leg, if you can imagine, to see the chief himself,
the great man. He made inquiries about his lodgings. 'There,'
they say, pointing to a house on the Palace Embankment.
A right little peasant cottage, you understand: shiny glass ten
feet wide in the windows, if you can picture it, so the vases and
whatnot in the rooms seem as if they're outside – you could, in
a certain way, reach them from the street with your hand;
precious marbles on the walls, metal gewgaws, the sort of
handle on the door, you know, that you'd have to stop at the
grocer's first and buy a half-kopeck's worth of soap and rub
your hands with it for two hours before you dared take hold of
it – in short, there's such lacquers all over everything, in a

certain way, it boggles the mind. The doorkeeper alone already looks like a generalissimo: a gilded mace, a count's physiognomy, like some sort of fat, overfed pug; cambric collars, rascality! ... My Kopeikin somehow dragged himself with his wooden leg up to the reception room and flattened himself into a corner, so as not to shove his elbow, if you can picture it, into some America or India – some such gilded porcelain vase, you understand. Well, naturally, he got his full share of standing there, because, if you can picture it, he came when the general had, in a certain way, barely gotten up and his valet had just brought him some silver basin, you understand, for various sorts of ablutions. So my Kopeikin had been waiting for about four hours when, finally, in comes an adjutant or some other official on duty. 'The general,' he says, 'will now come out to the reception room.' And the reception room's chock-full of people by then, like beans on a plate. None of it like our kind, simple churls, it's all fourth or fifth rank, colonels, and an occasional fat noodle shining on an epaulette – in short, some generalty. Suddenly a barely noticeable stir passed over the room, you understand, like some fine ether. There was a 'sh, sh' here and there, and finally a terrible silence fell. The great man enters. Well ... if you can picture it: a statesman! His face, so to speak ... well, in keeping with the position, you understand ... with high rank ... the same for his expression, you understand. Whatever was in the waiting room, naturally, stands at attention that instant, trembling, expectant, anticipating, in a certain way, the deciding of their fate. The minister, the great man, goes up to one, then another: 'What is it? What is it? What do you want? What is your business?' Finally, my good sir, it's Kopeikin's turn. Kopeikin plucks up his courage: 'Thus and so, Your Excellency: I spilled my blood, lost an arm and a leg, in a certain way, can't work, and I make so bold as to ask for the sovereign's charity.' The minister sees: the man has a wooden leg, and his empty right sleeve is pinned to his uniform. 'Very well,' he says, 'come by in a few days.' My

Kopeikin goes out all but enraptured: for one thing, he was deemed worthy of an audience with a, so to speak, foremost great man; and for another, now the matter of the pension would, in a certain way, finally be settled. In this mood, you understand, he goes hopping along the sidewalk. He stopped at Palkin's tavern for a glass of vodka, had dinner, my good sir, in the 'London,' ordered a cutlet with capers, asked for poulard with all the frills; asked for a bottle of wine, went to the theater in the evening – in short, you understand, a little spree. He sees some trim English woman going down the sidewalk, if you can picture it, like some such swan. My Kopeikin – his blood, you know, was acting up in him – started after her, hump-hump, on his wooden leg – 'but no,' he thought, 'later, when I have my pension, I'm getting too carried away now.' So, my good sir, in some three or four days my Kopeikin again comes to the minister, waits for his appearance. 'Thus and so,' he says, 'I've come to hear Your Excellency's orders,' he says, 'being over- come with illness and owing to my wounds . . . ,' and so on, you understand, in official style. The great man, if you can imagine, recognized him at once. 'Ah,' he says, 'very well,' he says, 'this time I can tell you nothing except that you must wait for the sovereign's arrival; then, undoubtedly, arrangements will be made concerning the wounded, but without the im- perial will, so to speak, I can do nothing.' A bow, you under- stand, and – good-bye. Kopeikin, if you can imagine, walked out in a most uncertain position. He was already thinking he'd just be handed money the next day: 'Here, take it, dear boy, drink and make merry.' And instead of that he was told to wait, and the time was not specified. So he goes owlish down the steps, like a poodle, you understand, that the cook has doused with water – tail between his legs, ears drooping. 'Ah, no,' he thinks to himself, 'I'll go one more time and explain that I'm finishing my last crust – unless you help me, I'm sure to die, in a certain way, of hunger.' In short, my good sir, he comes to the Palace Embankment again; they say, 'Impossible, he's not receiving, come tomorrow.' Next day, same thing; and the doorkeeper just doesn't want to look at him anymore. And meanwhile in his pocket, you understand, there's only one of those fivers left. He used to eat cabbage soup, a piece of beef, and now he picks up some sort of herring or pickle in a food shop, and two groats' worth of bread – in short, the poor devil is starving, and yet he's got a wolf's appetite. He walks past some such restaurant – the cook there, if you can picture it, is a foreigner, some Frenchman or other with an open physiognomy, dressed in Holland linen, apron white as snow, preparing some finzerb or cutlets with truffles – in short, such a soup-super delicacy, you could almost eat yourself up, it's so appetizing. He goes past Milyutin's shops, there's this salmon peeking, in a certain way, out the window, cherries – five roubles apiece, a giant watermelon, a regular stagecoach, sticking out the window and looking, so to speak, for some fool willing to pay a hundred roubles – in short, such temptation at every step, it makes your mouth water, and meanwhile all he hears is 'tomorrow.' So that was his position, if you can imagine: here, on the one hand, so to speak, salmon and watermelon, and on the other they keep offering him one and the same dish: 'tomorrow.' In the end the poor devil, in a certain way, couldn't take it; he decided to get through by storm, you understand, whatever the cost. He waited at the entrance for some petitioner to come, and along with some general, you understand, he slipped in with his wooden leg to the reception room. The great man comes out as usual: 'What is your business? And yours? Ah!' he says, seeing Kopeikin, 'I already told you, you must wait for a decision.' 'For pity's sake, Your Excellency, I don't even have a crust of bread, so to speak . . . ' 'No help for it. I can do nothing for you; try to take care of yourself for the time being, look for some means.' 'But, Your Excellency, you can judge for yourself, in a certain way, what means I'll be able to find without an arm and a leg.' 'But,' says the dignitary, 'you must agree that I cannot, in a certain way, support you out of my own pocket; I have many wounded, they all have an equal right...Fortify yourself with patience. The sovereign will come, and I give you my word of honor that his imperial charity will not abandon you.' 'But, Your Excellency, I can't wait,' says Kopeikin, and he says it somehow rudely. The great man is already annoyed, you understand. In fact, there are generals on all sides waiting for decisions, orders; important, so to speak, state business, calling for the swiftest execution – a moment's neglect could be important – and here's this devil clinging to him and won't get unclung. 'Excuse me,' he says, 'I have no time ... there is more important business waiting for me.' He reminds him, in a subtle way, so to speak, that it's finally time to get out. But my Kopeikin – hunger spurred him on, you understand: 'As you will, Your Excellency,' he says, 'I'm not leaving this spot until you give me the decision.' Well ... you can imagine: to give such an answer to a great man, who has only to say a word and you go flying head over heels so that the devil himself will never find you ... Here, if an official just one step lower in rank says such a thing to one of us, it's already rudeness. But in this case, the size, the size of it! A general-in-chief and some Captain Kopeikin! Ninety roubles and a zero! The general, you understand, did nothing but glare at him, but that glare – firearms! No heart left – it's sunk into your heels. But my Kopeikin, if you can imagine, doesn't budge, he stands as if rooted to the spot. 'Well, man?' says the general, and he gave it to him, as they say, in spades. However, to tell the truth, he still treated him rather mercifully; another man would have thrown such a scare into him that the street would have been spinning upside down for three days afterwards, but all he said was: 'Very well, if it is too expensive for you to live here, and you cannot wait quietly in the capital for the deciding of your fate, then I'll send you away at government expense. Call the courier! Dispatch him to his place of residence!' And the courier, you see, is already standing there: a sort of hulk of a man, seven feet tall, with huge hands on him, if you can imagine, made by nature herself for dealing with coachmen – in short, some sort of tooth doctor . . . And so, my good sir, this servant of God was seized and put into a cart along with the courier. 'Well,' Kopeikin thinks, 'at least I won't have to pay for the trip, and thanks for that.' And so, my good sir, he rides on the courier, and as he rides on the courier, he, in a certain way, reasons with himself, so to speak: 'Since the general says I myself must look for means of taking care of myself – very well,' he says, 'I'll find those means!' he says. Well, just how he was delivered to the place and precisely where he was taken, none of that is known. So, you understand, the rumors about Captain Kopeikin sank into the river of oblivion, into some such Lethe, as the poets call it. But, forgive me, gentlemen, here begins the thread, one might say, the intrigue of the novel. And so, where Kopeikin got to is unknown; but before two months had passed, if you can picture it, a band of robbers appeared in the Ryazan forests, and the leader of the band, my good sir, was none other than . . . "

"Only, forgive me, Ivan Andreevich," the police chief said suddenly, interrupting him, "you yourself said that Captain Kopeikin was missing an arm and a leg, while Chichikov . . . "

Here the postmaster cried out, slapped himself roundly on the forehead, and publicly in front of them all called himself a hunk of veal. He could not understand how it was that this circumstance had not occurred to him at the very beginning of his account, and admitted that the saying, "Hindsight is the Russian man's forte," was perfectly correct. However, a minute later he straightaway began dodging and tried to get out of it by saying that, anyhow, mechanics was very advanced in England, and one could see from the newspapers that someone there had devised wooden legs in such a way that, at the mere touch of a concealed spring, the legs would take a man into God knows what parts, so that afterwards it was even impossible to find him anywhere.

But they all had great doubts about Chichikov being Captain Kopeikin, and found that the postmaster had way overshot his mark. However, they, for their part, also had no flies on them, and, prompted by the postmaster's sharp-witted surmise, went perhaps even further afield. Among the many shrewd suggestions of a sort, there was finally one – it is even strange to say it – that Chichikov might be Napoleon in disguise, that the English had long been envious of the greatness and vastness of Russia, and that several caricatures had even been published in which a Russian is shown talking with an Englishman. The Englishman stands and holds a dog behind him on a rope, and the dog represents Napoleon: "Watch out," he seems to be saying, "if there's anything wrong, I'll set this dog on you!" – and so now it might be that they let him go from the island of St. Helena, and now here he is sneaking into Russia as if he were Chichikov, when in fact he is not Chichikov at all.

Of course, as far as believing it went, the officials did not believe it, but nevertheless they did fall to thinking and, each considering the matter in himself, found that Chichikov's face, if he turned and stood sideways, looked a lot like Napoleon's portrait. The police chief, who had served in the campaign of the year 'twelve and had seen Napoleon in person, also could not help admitting that he was no whit taller than Chichikov, and that, concerning his build, it was impossible to say he was too fat, and yet neither was he so very thin. Perhaps some readers will call all this incredible; to please them, the author is also ready to call all this incredible; but, unfortunately, it all happened precisely as it is being told, and what makes it more amazing still is that the town was not in some backwoods, but, on the contrary, no great distance from the two capitals.[50] However, it must be remembered that all this happened shortly after the glorious expulsion of the French. At that time all our landowners, officials, merchants, shop clerks, literate and even illiterate folk of every sort became sworn politicians for a good eight years at least. The *Moscow Gazette* and the *Son of the Fatherland* were mercilessly read to pieces and reached their last reader in shreds unfit for any use whatsoever. Instead of such questions as: "Well, my dear, how much did you get for a measure of oats?" or "Did you avail yourself of yesterday's snowfall?" people would say: "And what are they writing in the papers, has Napoleon been let go from his island again?" The merchants were very much afraid of that, because they believed completely in the prediction of a certain prophet who had been put in jail three years before; the prophet had come from no one knew where, in bast shoes and a raw sheepskin coat that stank terribly of rotten fish, and announced that Napoleon was the Antichrist and was kept on a chain of stone beyond the six walls and the seven seas, but afterwards he would break the chain and take possession of the whole world. For this prediction the prophet had landed, quite properly, in jail, but he had done his bit all the same and completely disturbed the merchants. For a long time after, even during the most profitable dealings, as they went to the tavern to wash them down with tea, the merchants kept muttering about the Antichrist. Many of the officials and nobility also kept thinking about it inadvertently and, infected with mysticism, which, as we know, was in great vogue then, saw some special meaning in every letter that made up the word "Napoleon"; many even discovered Apocalyptic numbers in it.[51] And so it is nothing surprising that our officials inadvertently kept pondering this point; soon, however, they checked themselves, noticing that their imaginations were galloping away with them, and that all this was not it. They thought and thought, talked and talked, and finally decided that it would not be a bad idea to question Nozdryov a little better. Since he was the first to bring out the story of the dead souls and was, as they say, in some close relationship with Chichikov, he therefore undoubtedly knew something about the circumstances of his life, so why not try again what Nozdryov would say.

Strange people these gentlemen officials, and all other degrees along with them: they knew very well that Nozdryov was a liar, that not a single word of his could be trusted, not the least trifle, and nevertheless they resorted precisely to him. What are you going to do with man? He does not believe in God, yet he believes that if the bridge of his nose itches he is sure to die; he will pass by a poet's work, clear as day, all pervaded with harmony and the lofty wisdom of simplicity, and throw himself precisely on one in which some brave fellow bemuddles, befuddles, distorts, and perverts nature, and he likes it, and he starts shouting: "Here it is, the true knowledge of the heart's secrets!" All his life he cares not a penny for doctors, and it ends up with him turning finally to some village wench, who treats him with mumbling and spittle, or, better still, he himself invents some decoction of God knows what trash, which, lord knows why, he fancies is precisely the remedy for his ailment. Of course, the gentlemen officials can be partly excused by their truly difficult situation. A drowning man, they say, clutches even at a little splinter, and does not have sense enough at that moment to reflect that perhaps only a fly could go riding on a splinter, while he weighs as much as a hundred and fifty pounds, if not a full two hundred; but the thought does not enter his head at that moment, and he clutches at the splinter. So, too, our gentlemen clutched finally at Nozdryov. The police chief at once wrote him a little note kindly inviting him to a soirée, and a policeman in top boots and with an attractive glow to his cheeks ran off at once, holding his sword in place, skipping to Nozdryov's. Nozdryov was occupied with something very important; for a whole four days he had not left his room, would not let anyone in, and took his dinner through a little window – in short, he had even grown thin and green. The matter called for great attentiveness: it consisted of selecting from some tens of dozens of cards one pack, but the choicest, which could be relied upon like the most faithful friend. There was still at least two weeks of work to go; during all this time, Porfiry was to clean the mastiff pup's navel with a special brush and wash him with soap three times a day. Nozdryov was very angry that his solitude had been disturbed; first of all he sent the policeman to the devil, but, when he read in the police chief's note that there might be some pickings in it, because some novice was expected at the soirée, he softened at once, hastily locked his door with a key, got dressed haphazardly, and went to them. The evidence, testimony, and suppositions of Nozdryov presented such a sharp contrast to those of the gentlemen officials that even the last of their surmises were confounded. This was decidedly a man for whom there was no such thing as doubt; and as much as they were noticeably wavering and timid in their suppositions, so much was he firm and confident. He responded to all points without faltering in the least, declared that Chichikov had bought up several thousands' worth of dead souls, and that he himself had sold him some, because he saw no reason not to; to the question whether he was a spy and was trying to sniff something out, Nozdryov replied that he was a spy, that even at school, where they had studied together, he had been known as a tattletale, and that their comrades, himself included, had given him a bit of a drubbing for it, so that afterwards he had had to have two hundred and forty leeches put to his temples – that is, he meant to say forty, but the two hundred got said somehow of itself. To the question whether he was a maker of forged bills, he replied that he was, and used the occasion to tell an anecdote about Chichikov's remarkable adroitness: how it had been found out once that there were in his house two million in forged banknotes, the house was sealed and a guard set on it, two soldiers for each door, and how Chichikov replaced them all in one night, so that the next day, when the seals were removed, they found that all the notes were genuine. To the question whether Chichikov indeed had the intention of carrying off the governor's daughter and was it true that he himself had undertaken to help and participate in the affair, Nozdryov replied that he had helped, and that if it had not been for him, nothing would have come of it – here he tried to check himself, seeing that he had lied quite needlessly and could thereby invite trouble, but he was no longer able to hold his tongue. However, it would also have been difficult to do so, because such interesting details emerged of themselves that it was simply impossible to give them up: the village was even mentioned by name, wherein was located the parish church in which the wedding was to take place – namely, the village of Trukhmachevka; the priest – Father Sidor; the fee for the wedding – seventy-five roubles, and he would not have agreed even for that had he not been frightened by the threat of a denunciation for having married the flour dealer Mikhailo and his *kuma*;[52] and that he had even given them his carriage and prepared a change of horses for each station. The details went so far that he was already beginning to give the names of the coachmen. They tried mentioning Napoleon, but were not happy they did, because Nozdryov began pouring out such drivel as not only had no semblance of truth, but had no semblance of anything whatsoever, so that the officials all sighed and walked away; only the police chief went on listening for a long time, thinking there might at least be something further on, but finally he waved his hand, saying: "Devil knows what it is!" And they all agreed that, however you push and pull, you'll never get milk from a bull. And the officials were left in a still worse position than they were in before, and the upshot of it was that there was simply no way of finding out what Chichikov was. And it became clear what sort of creature man is: wise, intelligent, and sensible in all that concerns others than himself; what discreet, firm advice he provides in life's difficult occasions! "What an efficient head!" cries the crowd. "What staunch character!" But let some trouble befall this efficient head, let him be put into one of life's difficult occasions himself, and what becomes of his character, the staunch fellow is all at a loss, he turns into a pathetic little coward, a nonentity, a weak child, or simply a foozle, as Nozdryov put it.

All these discussions, opinions, and rumors, for some un-known reason, affected the poor prosecutor most of all. They affected him to such a degree that, on coming home, he started thinking and thinking, and suddenly, without a by-your-leave, as they say, he died. Whether he was seized by paralysis or by something else, in any case, as he sat there, he simply flopped off his chair onto his back. Clasping their hands, they cried out, as is customary: "Oh, my God!" and sent for the doctor to let his blood, but saw that the prosecutor was already a mere soulless body. Only then did they learn with commiseration that the deceased indeed had had a soul, though in his modesty he had never shown it. And yet the appearance of death was as terrible in a small as in a great man: he who not so long ago had walked, moved, played whist, signed various papers, and was seen so often among the officials with his bushy eyebrows and winking eye, was now lying on the table, his left eye not winking at all, but one eyebrow still raised with some quizzical expression. What the deceased was asking – why he had died, or why he had lived – God alone knows.

But this, however, is incongruous! this is incompatible with anything! this is impossible – that officials should scare them-selves so; to create such nonsense, to stray so far from the truth, when even a child could see what the matter was! So many readers will say, reproaching the author for incongruousness or calling the poor officials fools, because man is generous with the word "fool" and is ready to serve it up to his neighbor twenty times a day. It is enough to have one stupid side out of ten to be accounted a fool, aside from the nine good ones. It is easy for the reader to judge, looking down from his comfort-able corner at the top, from which the whole horizon opens out, upon all that is going on below, where man can see only the nearest object. And in the world chronicle of mankind there are many whole centuries which, it would seem, should be crossed out and abolished as unnecessary. There have been many errors in the world which, it would seem, even a child would not make now. What crooked, blind, narrow, impassable, far-straying paths mankind has chosen, striving to attain eternal truth, while a whole straight road lay open before it, like the road leading to a magnificent dwelling meant for a king's mansions! Broader and more splendid than all other roads it is, lit by the sun and illumined all night by lamps, yet people have flowed past it in the blind darkness. So many times already, though guided by a sense come down from heaven, they have managed to waver and go astray, have managed in broad daylight to get again into an impassable wilderness, have managed again to blow a blinding fog into each other's eyes, and, dragging themselves after marsh-lights, have managed finally to reach the abyss, only to ask one another in horror: where is the way out, where is the path? The current generation now sees everything clearly, it marvels at the errors, it laughs at the folly of its ancestors, not seeing that this chronicle is all overscored by divine fire, that every letter of it cries out, that from everywhere the piercing finger is pointed at it, at this current generation; but the current generation laughs and presumptuously, proudly begins a series of new errors, at which their descendants will also laugh afterwards.

Chichikov knew nothing whatsoever about all that. As luck would have it, he had caught a slight cold at the time – a swollen tooth and a minor throat infection, which the climate of many of our provincial towns is so generous in dispensing. So that his life should not, God forbid, somehow cease without posterity, he decided he had better stay home for about three days. During these days he constantly rinsed his throat with milk and fig, eating the fig afterwards, and went around with a camomile- and camphor-filled compress tied to his cheek. Wishing to occupy his time with something, he made several new and detailed lists of all the purchased peasants, even read some tome of the Duchess de La Vallière[53] that turned up in his trunk, looked through all the objects and little notes in the chest, read some over again, and all of it bored him greatly. He was simply unable to understand what it could mean that not one of the town officials had come even once to inquire after his health, whereas still recently there was a droshky constantly standing in front of the inn – now the postmaster's, now the prosecutor's, now the head magistrate's. He merely shrugged his shoulders as he paced the room. At last he felt better and was God knows how glad when he saw it was possible to go out into the fresh air. Without delay, he set about immediately with his toilet, unlocked his chest, poured hot water into a glass, took out brush and soap, and got down to shaving, for which, incidentally, it was high time and season, because, having felt his chin with his hand and glanced in the mirror, he had declared: "Eh, quite a forest scrawling there!" And, indeed, forest or not, there was a rather thick crop coming up all over his cheeks and chin. After shaving, he turned to dressing, so briskly and quickly that he all but jumped out of his trousers. Finally, dressed, sprinkled with eau de cologne, and wrapped up warmly, he took himself outside, having bound up his cheek as a precaution. His going out, as with any man who has recovered from an illness, was indeed festive. Whatever came his way acquired a laughing look: the houses, the passing muzhiks – who, incidentally, were rather serious, one of them having just managed to give his fellow a cuffing. He intended to pay his first call on the governor. On the way many different thoughts came to his mind; the blonde was whirling through his head, his imagination was even beginning to frolic slightly, and he himself was already starting to joke and chuckle at himself a bit. In this mood he found himself before the governor's entrance. He was already in the front hall, hastily throwing off his overcoat, when the doorkeeper stunned him with the totally unexpected words:

"I am ordered not to admit you!"

"How? what's that? you obviously didn't recognize me? Take a closer look at my face!" Chichikov said to him.

"How should I not recognize you, it's not the first time I'm seeing you," the doorkeeper said. "No, it's precisely you alone that I'm not to let in, all the rest are allowed."

"Look at this, now! But why? What for?"

"Them's the orders, so obviously it's proper," said the doorkeeper, adding to it the word "Yes." After which he stood before him totally at ease, not keeping that benign look with which he formerly used to hasten and take his overcoat from him. He seemed to be thinking, as he looked at him: "Oho! if the masters are showing you the door, then clearly you're some kind of riffraff!"

"Incomprehensible!" Chichikov thought to himself, and set off straightaway for the head magistrate's, but the magistrate got so embarrassed on seeing him that he could not put two words together, and talked such rot that they both even felt ashamed. On leaving him, Chichikov tried his best as he went along to explain and make some sense of what the magistrate had meant and what his words might have referred to, but he was unable to understand anything. After that he called on others – the police chief, the vice-governor, the postmaster – but they all either did not receive him or received him so strangely, made such forced and incomprehensible conversation, were so much at a loss, and such a muddle came of it all, that he doubted the soundness of their brains. He tried calling on one or two others, to find out the reason at least, but he did not get at any reason. Like one half asleep, he wandered the town aimlessly, unable to decide whether he had gone out of his mind or the officials had lost their wits, whether it was all happening in a dream or reality had cooked up a folly worse than any dream. Late, almost at dusk, he returned to his inn, which he had left in such good spirits, and out of boredom ordered tea to be brought. Deep in thought and in some senseless reflection on the strangeness of his position, he began pouring tea, when suddenly the door of his room opened and there, quite unexpectedly, stood Nozdryov.

"As the proverb says, 'For a friend five miles is not a long way around!'" he said, taking off his peaked cap. "I was passing by, saw a light in the window, why don't I stop in, I thought, he can't be asleep. Ah! that's good, you've got tea on the table, I'll have a little cup with pleasure – today at dinner I overfed on all sorts of trash, I feel a turmoil starting in my stomach. Order me a pipefull! Where's your pipe?"

"But I don't smoke a pipe," Chichikov said dryly.

"Nonsense, as if I don't know you're a whiffer. Hey! what'd you say your man's name was? Hey, Vakhramey!"

"Not Vakhramey – Petrushka."

"How's that? You used to have a Vakhramey."

"I never had any Vakhramey."

"Right, exactly, it's Derebin who has a Vakhramey. Imagine Derebin's luck: his aunt quarreled with her son for marrying a serf girl, and now she's willed him her whole estate. I'm thinking to myself, it wouldn't be bad to have such an aunt for further on! But what's with you, brother, you're so withdrawn from everybody, you don't go anywhere? Of course, I know you're sometimes occupied with learned subjects, you like to read" (what made Nozdryov conclude that our hero occupied himself with learned subjects and liked to read, we must confess, we simply cannot say, and still less could Chichikov). "Ah, brother Chichikov, if only you'd seen it . . . that really would have been food for your satirical mind" (why Chichikov should have a satirical mind is also unknown). "Imagine, brother, we were playing a game of brag at the merchant Likhachev's, and how we laughed! Perependev, who was with me, 'You know,' he says, 'if it was Chichikov now, you know, he'd really..." " (while never in his born days did Chichikov know any Perependev). "And confess, brother, you really did me the meanest turn that time, remember, when we were playing checkers, because I really did win... Yes, brother, you just diddled me out of it. But, devil knows what it is with me, I can never be angry. The other day with the magistrate... Ah, yes! I must tell you, the whole town's against you; they think you make forged bills, they started pestering me, but I stood up for you like a rock, I told them a heap of things, that I went to school with you and knew your father; well, needless to say, I spun them a good yarn."

"I make forged bills?" cried Chichikov, rising from his chair.

"All the same, why did you frighten them so?" Nozdryov went on. "Devil knows, they've lost their minds from fear: they've got you dressed up as a robber and a spy... And the prosecutor died of fright, the funeral's tomorrow. You're not going? To tell you the truth, they're afraid of the new governor-general, in case something comes out on account of you; and my opinion about the governor-general is that if he turns up his nose and puts on airs, he'll get decidedly nowhere with the nobility. The nobility demand cordiality, right? Of course, one can hide in one's study and not give a single ball, but what then? Nothing's gained by it. You, though, it's a risky business you're undertaking, Chichikov."

"What risky business?" Chichikov asked uneasily.

"Why, carrying off the governor's daughter. I confess, I expected it, by God, I did! The first time, as soon as I saw you together at the ball, well now, Chichikov, I thought to myself, surely there's some purpose... However, it's a poor choice you've made, I don't find anything good in her. But there is one, Bikusov's relative, his sister's daughter, now there's a girl! a lovely bit of chintz!"

"But what is this, what are you blathering about? How, carry off the governor's daughter, what's got into you?" Chichikov said, his eyes popping out.

"Well, enough, brother, what a secretive man! I confess, that's what I came to you for: if you like, I'm ready to help you. So be it: I'll hold the crown,[54] the carriage and change of horses are mine, only on one condition – you must lend me three thousand. Damn me, brother, if I don't need it!"

In the course of all Nozdryov's babble, Chichikov rubbed his eyes several times, wanting to be sure he was not hearing it all in a dream. The making of forged banknotes, the carrying off of the governor's daughter, the death of the prosecutor, of which he was supposedly the cause, the arrival of the governor-general – all this produced quite a decent fright in him. "Well, if things have come to that," he thought to himself, "there's no point in lingering, I must get myself out of here."

He got Nozdryov off his hands as quickly as he could, summoned Selifan at once, and told him to be ready at daybreak, so that the next day at six o'clock in the morning they could leave town without fail, and that everything should be looked over, the britzka greased, and so on and so forth. Selifan said, "Right, Pavel Ivanovich!" and nevertheless stood for some time by the door, not moving from the spot. The master at once told Petrushka to pull the trunk, already quite covered with dust, from under the bed, and together with him began to pack, without much sorting out, stockings, shirts, underwear washed and unwashed, boot trees, a calendar . . . All this was packed haphazardly; he wanted to be ready that evening without fail, so that no delay should occur the next day. Selifan, having stood for some two minutes by the door, finally walked very slowly out of the room. Slowly, as slowly as one could only imagine, he went down the stairs, stamping traces with his wet boots on the worn-down, descending steps, and for a long time he scratched the back of his head with his hand. What did this scratching mean? and what does it generally mean? Was it vexation that now the planned meeting next day with his chum in the unseemly sheepskin coat tied with a belt, somewhere in a pot-house, would not come off, or had some little heartthrob started already in the new place, and he had to abandon the evening standing by the gate and the politic holding of white hands, at the hour when twilight pulls its brim down over the town, a strapping lad in a red shirt is strumming his balalaika before the household servants, and people, having finished work, weave their quiet talk? Or was he simply sorry to leave his already warmed-up place in the servants' kitchen, under a coat, next to the stove, and the cabbage soup with tender town-baked pies, and drag himself out again into the rain and sleet and all the adversities of the road? God knows, there's no guessing. Many and various among the Russian people are the meanings of scratching one's head.

CHAPTER ELEVEN

NOTHING, HOWEVER, HAPPENED the way Chichikov had intended. In the first place, he woke up later than he thought – that was the first unpleasantness. Having gotten up, he sent at once to find out if the britzka was harnessed and everything was ready; but was informed that the britzka was not yet harnessed and nothing was ready. That was the second unpleasantness. He got angry, even prepared himself to give our friend Selifan something like a thrashing, and only waited impatiently to see what reason he, for his part, would give to justify himself. Soon Selifan appeared in the doorway, and the master had the pleasure of hearing the same talk one usually hears from domestics when it is a case of needing to set off quickly.

"But, Pavel Ivanovich, we'll have to shoe the horses."

"Ah, you pig! you fence post! Why didn't you say so before? Didn't you have time enough?"

"Time, yes, I did have...And the wheel, too, Pavel Ivanovich, we'll have to put a new tire on it, because the road's bumpy now, such potholes all over...And, allow me to say: the front end of the britzka is quite loose, so that we maybe won't even make two stations."

"You scoundrel!" cried Chichikov, clasping his hands, and he came up so close to him that Selifan, for fear the master might make him a little gift, backed off a bit and stepped aside. "So you're going to kill me, eh? want to put a knife in me? knife me on the high road, you robber, you cursed pig, you sea monster! eh? eh? Sat here for three weeks, eh? If you'd only

248

made a peep, you wastrel – and now you've pushed it right up
to the final hour! when everything's almost set – just get in and
go, eh? and it's here that you muck it up, eh? eh? Didn't you
know before? didn't you, eh? eh? Answer! Didn't you know?"

"I knew," Selifan replied, hanging his head.

"Then why didn't you say so, eh?"

To this question Selifan made no reply, but, hanging his
head, seemed to be saying to himself: "You see what a tricky
thing it is: I knew, and I just didn't say!"

"So, now go and fetch the blacksmith, and see that everything's done in two hours. Do you hear? in two hours without
fail, and if it's not, I'll . . . I'll bend you double and tie you in a
knot!" Our hero was very angry.

Selifan made as if to turn for the door, to go and carry out
the order, but stopped and said:

"Another thing, sir, the dapple-gray horse, he really ought
to be sold, because he's a downright scoundrel, Pavel Ivanovich; he's that kind of horse, God help us, nothing but a
hindrance."

"Oh, yes! I'll just up and run to the market to sell him!"

"By God, Pavel Ivanovich, not but he looks right enough,
only in fact he's a sly horse, such a horse as never . . ."

"Fool! When I want to sell him, I'll sell him. Look at the
man reasoning! I'll see: if you don't bring me the blacksmiths
and if everything's not ready in two hours, I'll give you such
a thrashing . . . you won't know your own face! Go! Off
with you!"

Selifan left.

Chichikov was completely out of sorts and flung down on
the floor the sword that traveled with him for inspiring due fear
in those who needed it. He fussed with the blacksmiths for a
good quarter of an hour before he could come to terms with
them, because the blacksmiths, as is their wont, were inveterate scoundrels, and, having grasped that the job was an urgent
one, struck him with six times the price. He got all fired up,

called them crooks, thieves, highway robbers, even hinted at the Last Judgment, but nothing fazed them: the blacksmiths stayed absolutely in character – not only did not yield on the price, but even fussed over the work for a whole five and a half hours instead of two. During that time he had the pleasure of experiencing those agreeable moments, familiar to every traveler, when the trunk is all packed and only strings, scraps of paper, and various litter are strewn about the room, when a man belongs neither to the road nor to sitting in place, and from the window sees people plodding by, discussing nickels and dimes, lifting their eyes with some stupid curiosity to glance at him and then continuing on their way, which further aggravates the low spirits of the poor non-departing traveler. Everything there, everything he sees – the little shop across from his windows, the head of the old woman who lives in the house opposite, and who keeps coming up to the window with its half-curtains – everything is loathsome to him, and yet he will not leave the window. He stands, now oblivious, now dimly attentive again to everything moving and not moving in front of him, and in vexation stifles under his finger some fly which at the moment is buzzing and beating against the glass. But there is an end to all things, and the longed-for moment came: everything was ready, the front end of the britzka was set to rights, the wheel was fitted with a new tire, the horses were brought from the watering place, and the robber-blacksmiths went off counting the roubles they had made and wishing him all their blessings. Finally the britzka, too, was harnessed, and two hot *kalatchi*, only just bought, were put in, and Selifan stuck something for himself into the pouch in the coachman's box, and finally the hero himself, to the waving cap of the floorboy, who stood there in the same half-cotton frock coat, in the presence of the tavern servants and other lackeys and coachmen, who gathered to gape at someone else's master departing, and with all the other circumstances that accompany a departure, got into the carriage – and the britzka such as bachelors drive around in, which had stood so long in town and which the reader is so sick of, finally drove out the gates of the inn. "Thank God for that!" thought Chichikov, crossing himself. Selifan cracked his whip; Petrushka, having first hung from the footboard for a while, sat down next to him, and our hero, settling himself better on the Georgian rug, put a leather cushion behind his back and squashed the two *kalatchi*, as the carriage again started its jigging and jolting, owing to the pavement, which, as we know, possessed a bouncing force. With a sort of indefinite feeling he gazed at the houses, walls, fences, and streets, which, also as if hopping for their own part, were slowly moving backwards, and which God knows if he was destined to see again in the course of his life. At a turn down one of the streets the britzka had to stop, because an endless funeral procession was passing the whole length of it. Chichikov, having peeked out, told Petrushka to ask who was being buried, and learned that it was the prosecutor. Filled with unpleasant sensations, he at once hid himself in a corner, covered himself with the leather apron, and closed the curtains. All the while the carriage was stopped in this way, Selifan and Petrushka, piously doffing their hats, were looking at who drove how, in what, and on what, counting the number of all those on foot and on wheels, while the master, ordering them not to acknowledge or greet any servants they knew, also began timidly looking through the glass in the leather curtains: behind the coffin, hats off, walked all the officials. He began to be a bit afraid that they might recognize his carriage, but they could not be bothered with that. They were not even occupied with the various mundane conversations that are usually conducted among those accompanying the deceased. All their thoughts at that time were concentrated on their own selves: they thought about what sort of man the new governor-general would be, how he would get down to business, and how he would receive them. After the officials, who went on foot, came carriages out of which peeked ladies in mourning caps. By the movement of their lips and hands one could see that they were engaged in lively conversation; perhaps they, too, were talking about the arrival of the new governor-general, making speculations concerning the balls he would give, and worrying about their eternal festoons and appliqués. Finally, after the carriages, came several empty droshkies, strung out in single file, and finally there was nothing more left, and our hero could go. Opening the leather curtains, he sighed, saying from the bottom of his heart: "So, the prosecutor! He lived and lived, and then he died! And so they'll print in the newspapers that there passed away, to the sorrow of his subordinates and of all mankind, a respectable citizen, a rare father, an exemplary husband, and they'll write all sorts of stuff; they'll add, maybe, that he was accompanied by the weeping of widows and orphans; but if one looks into the matter properly, all you had, in fact, was bushy eyebrows." Here he told Selifan to drive faster, and meanwhile thought to himself: "It's a good thing, however, that I met the funeral; they say it's a lucky sign when you meet a dead man."

The britzka meanwhile turned onto more deserted streets; soon there were only long stretches of wooden fence, heralding the end of town. Now the pavement has already ended, and the tollgate, and the town is behind, and there is nothing, and it is the road again. And again both sides of the high road are scrawled once more with mileposts, stationmasters, wells, wagon trains, gray villages with samovars, women, and a brisk, bearded innkeeper running out of the inn yard with an armful of oats, a passerby in worn bast shoes trudging on foot from eight hundred miles away, little towns slapped together, with little wooden shops, flour barrels, bast shoes, *kalatchi*, and other small stuff, rippling tollgates, bridges under repair, fields beyond view on this side and that, landowners' coaches, a soldier on horseback carrying a green box of leaden peas and the words "Such-and-such Artillery Battery," green, yellow, and freshly ploughed black stripes flashing over the steppes, a song struck up afar, pine tops in the mist, a ringing bell fading far off, crows like flies, and a horizon without end...Rus! Rus! I see you, from my wondrous, beautiful distance I see you:[55] it is poor, scattered, and comfortless in you; not gladdened, not frightened will one's gaze be at bold wonders of nature, crowned by bold wonders of art, cities with high, many-windowed palaces grown into the cliffs, picturesque trees and ivy grown into the houses, with the noise and eternal mist of waterfalls; the head will not be thrown back to look at great boulders heaped up endlessly above it and into the heights; through dark arches cast one upon the other, all entangled with vines and ivy and countless millions of wild roses, there will come no flash of the distant, eternal lines of shining mountains, soaring up into the bright silver heavens. In you all is openly deserted and level; like dots, like specks, your low towns stick up inconspicuously amidst the plains; there is nothing to seduce or enchant the eye. But what inconceivable, mysterious force draws one to you? Why do the ears hear and ring unceasingly with your melancholy song, coursing through the whole length and breadth of you from sea to sea? What is in it, in this song? What calls, and weeps, and grips the heart? What sounds so painfully caress and stream into the soul, and twine about my heart? Rus! what is it that you want of me? what inconceivable bond lies hidden between us? Why do you gaze so, and why is everything in you turned towards me with eyes full of expectation?...And still, all in perplexity, I stand motionless, but my head is already overshadowed by a menacing cloud, heavy with coming rains, and thought stands numb before your vastness. What prophecy is in this uncompassable expanse? Is it not here, in you, that the boundless thought is to be born, since you yourself are without end? Is it not here that the mighty man is to be, where there is room for him to show himself and walk about? And menacingly the mighty vastness envelops me, reflected with terrible force in my depths; my eyes are lit up by an unnatural power: ohh! what a shining, wondrous yonder, unknown to the world! Rus! . . .

"Hold up, hold up, you fool!" Chichikov shouted to Selifan.

"You'll get a taste of my saber!" shouted a courier with yard-long mustaches, galloping in the opposite direction. "The hairy devil take your soul: don't you see it's a government carriage?" And like a phantom, the troika disappeared in thunder and dust.

What a strange, and alluring, and transporting, and wonderful feeling is in the word: road! and how wondrous is this road itself: the bright day, the autumn leaves, the chill air . . . wrap up tighter in your traveling coat, pull your hat over your ears, squeeze closer and more cozily into the corner! A shiver runs through your limbs for a last time, yielding now to the pleasant warmth. The horses fly . . . drowsiness steals up so temptingly, and your eyes are closing, and now through sleep you hear "'Tis not the white snows . . ." and the breathing of the horses, and the noise of the wheels, and you are already snoring, having squeezed your neighbor into the corner. You wake up: five stations have raced by; the moon, an unknown town, churches with ancient wooden cupolas and black spires, houses of dark logs or white stone. The crescent moon shines there and there, as if white linen kerchiefs were hung on the walls, the pavement, the streets; they are crossed by slant shadows, black as coal; the slantly lit wooden roofs gleam like shining metal, and not a soul anywhere – everything sleeps. Perhaps, all by itself somewhere, a light glimmers in a window: a town tradesman mending his pair of boots, a baker poking in his little oven – what of them? But the night! heavenly powers! what a night is transpiring in the heights! And the air, and the sky, far off, far up, spreading so boundlessly, resoundingly, and brightly, there, in its inaccessible depths! . . . But the cold breath of night breathes fresh in your eyes and lulls you, and now you are dozing, and sinking into oblivion, and snoring, and your poor neighbor, pressed into the corner, turns angrily, feeling your weight on him. You wake up – again there are fields and steppes before you, nothing anywhere – everywhere emptiness, all wide open. A milestone with a number flies into your eyes; day is breaking; on the cold, whitening curve of the sky a pale golden streak; the wind turns fresher and sharper: wrap up tighter in your overcoat! ... what fine cold! what wonderful sleep enveloping you again! A jolt – and again you wake up. The sun is high in the sky. "Easy! easy!" a voice is heard, a cart is coming down a steep hill: below, a wide dam and a wide, bright pond shining like a copper bottom in the sun; a village, cottages scattered over the slope; to one side, the cross of the village church shines like a star; the chatter of muzhiks and an unbearable appetite in your stomach ... God! how good you are sometimes, you long, long road! So often, perishing and drowning, I have clutched at you, and each time you have magnanimously brought me through and saved me! And there were born of you so many wonderful designs, poetical reveries, so many delightful impressions were felt! ... But our friend Chichikov was also feeling some not altogether prosaic reveries at that time. Let us have a look at what he was feeling. At first he felt nothing, and only kept glancing behind him, wishing to make certain that he had indeed left the town; but when he saw that the town had long disappeared, that neither smithies, nor windmills, nor anything found around towns were to be seen, and even the white tops of the stone churches had long sunk into the ground, he occupied himself only with the road, kept looking only to right and left, and the town of N. was as if it had never been in his memory, as if he had passed by it long ago, in childhood. Finally, the road, too, ceased to occupy him, and he began to close his eyes slightly and lean his head towards the cushion. The author even confesses to being glad of it, finding, in this way, an occasion for talking about his hero; for up to now, as the reader has seen, he has constantly been hindered, now by Nozdryov, now by the balls, the ladies, the town gossip, and finally by thousands of those trifles that only seem like trifles when they are set down in a book, but while circulating in the world are regarded as very important matters. But now let us put absolutely everything aside and get straight to business.

It is highly doubtful that readers will like the hero we have chosen. The ladies will not like him, that can be said positively, for the ladies demand that a hero be a decided perfection, and if there is any little spot on his soul or body, it means trouble! However deeply the author peers into his soul, reflecting his image more purely than a mirror, it will be of no avail. The very plumpness and middle age of Chichikov will do him great harm: plumpness will in no way be forgiven a hero, and a great many ladies will turn away, saying: "Fie, ugly thing!" Alas! all this is known to the author, yet for all that he cannot take a virtuous man as his hero, but . . . perhaps in this same story some other, as yet untouched strings will be felt, the inestimable wealth of the Russian spirit will step forth, a man endowed with divine valor will pass by, or some wondrous Russian maiden such as can be found nowhere in the world, with all the marvelous beauty of a woman's soul, all magnanimous aspiration and self-denial. And all virtuous people of other tribes will seem dead next to them, as a book is dead next to the living word! Russian movements will arise . . . and it will be seen how deeply that which has only grazed the nature of other peoples has sunk into the Slavic nature . . . But wherefore and why speak of what lies ahead? It is unbecoming for the author, a man long since taught by a stern inner life and the refreshing sobriety of solitude, to forget himself like a youth. Everything in its turn, its place, its time! But all the same the virtuous man has not been taken as a hero. And it is even possible to say why he has not been taken. Because it is time finally to give the poor virtuous man a rest, because the phrase "virtuous man" idly circulates on all lips; because

the virtuous man has been turned into a horse, and there is no
writer who has not driven him, urging him on with a whip and
whatever else is handy; because the virtuous man has been so
worn out that there is not even the ghost of any virtue left in
him, but only skin and ribs instead of a body; because the
virtuous man is invoked hypocritically; because the virtuous
man is not respected! No, it is time finally to hitch up a
scoundrel. And so, let us hitch up a scoundrel.

Obscure and modest was our hero's origin. His parents
were of the nobility, but whether ancient or honorary – God
knows; in appearance he did not resemble them: at least the
relation who was present at his birth, a short, brief woman of
the kind usually called a wee thing, on taking the child in her
arms, exclaimed: "Quite different than I thought! He should
have taken after his grandmother on his mother's side, that
would have been best, but he came out just as the saying goes:
'Not like mother, not like father, but like Roger the lodger.' "
Life, at its beginning, looked upon him somehow sourly,
inhospitably, through some dim, snow-covered window: not
one friend, not one childhood companion. A small room with
small windows, never opened winter or summer, the father an
ailing man, in a long frock coat trimmed with lambskin and
with knitted slippers on his bare feet, who sighed incessantly as
he paced the room, spitting into a box of sand that stood in the
corner, the eternal sitting on the bench, pen in hand, ink-
stained fingers and even lips, the eternal maxim before his eyes:
"Do not lie, obey your elders, keep virtue in your heart"; the
eternal shuffling and scraping of the slippers in the room, the
familiar but ever stern voice: "Fooling again!" that resounded
whenever the child, bored with the monotonous work, attached some flourish or tail to a letter; and the eternally
familiar, ever unpleasant feeling when, after these words, the
edge of his ear was rolled up very painfully by the nails of long
fingers reaching from behind: this is the poor picture of his
early childhood, of which he barely preserved a pale memory.

But in life everything changes swiftly and livelily: and one day, with the first spring sun and the flooding streams, the father, taking his son, drove off with him in a cart, dragged by a runty piebald horse known among horse traders as a magpie; she was driven by a coachman, a hunchbacked little man, progenitor of the only serf family belonging to Chichikov's father, who filled almost all the positions in the house. This magpie dragged them for a little over a day and a half; they slept on the road, crossed a river, lunched on cold pie and roast lamb, and only on the morning of the third day did they reach town. In unsuspected magnificence the town streets flashed before the boy and left him gaping for a few minutes. Then the magpie plopped together with the cart into a hole at the head of a narrow lane, all straining downhill and clogged with mud; she toiled there for a long time, using all her strength and kneading away with her legs, urged on by the hunchback and by the master himself, and finally dragged them into a little yard that sat on a slope, with two flowering apple trees in front of a little old house, and with a garden behind, low, puny, consisting only of a mountain ash, an elder, and, hidden in its depths, a little wooden shed, roofed with shingles, with a narrow matte window. Here lived their relative, a wobbly little crone, who still went to market every morning and then dried her stockings by the samovar. She patted the boy on the cheek and admired his plumpness. Here he was to stay and go every day to study at the town school. The father, after spending the night, set out on the road the very next day. On parting, the parental eyes shed no tears; fifty kopecks in copper were given for expenses and treats, and, which was more important, a wise admonition: "Watch out, then, Pavlusha, study, don't be a fool or a scapegrace, and above all try to please your teachers and superiors. If you please your superior, then even if you don't succeed in your studies and God has given you no talent, you will still do well and get ahead of everybody. Don't keep company with your schoolmates, they won't teach you any good; but if you do, then keep company with the richer ones, on the chance that they may be useful to you. Do not regale or treat anyone, but rather behave in such a way that they treat you, and above all keep and save your kopeck: it is the most reliable thing in the world. A comrade or companion will cheat you and be the first to betray you in trouble; but a kopeck will never betray you, whatever trouble you get into. You can do everything and break through everything with a kopeck." Having delivered this admonition, the father parted from his son and dragged himself back home with his magpie, and after that he never saw him again, but his words and admonitions sank deeply into his soul.

Pavlusha started going to school the very next day. It turned out that there were no special abilities in him for any subject; he was rather distinguished for his diligence and neatness; but instead there turned out to be great intelligence in him on the other side, the practical one. He suddenly grasped and under-stood things and behaved himself with regard to his comrades precisely in such a way that they treated him, while he not only never treated them, but even sometimes stashed away the received treat and later sold it to them. While still a child he knew how to deny himself everything. Of the fifty kopecks his father had given him, he did not spend even one; on the contrary, that same year he already made additions to them, showing a resourcefulness that was almost extraordinary: he made a bullfinch out of wax, painted it, and sold it for a good profit. Then, over a certain course of time, he got into other speculations, namely the following: having bought some food at the market, he would sit in class near those who were better off, and as soon as he noticed some queasiness in his comrade – a sign of approaching hunger – he would show him from under the bench, as if accidentally, a wedge of gingerbread or a roll, and, after getting him all excited, would charge a price com-mensurate with his appetite. He spent two months in his room fussing tirelessly over a mouse that he kept in a small wooden cage, and finally managed to get the mouse to stand on its hind legs, lie down and get up on command, and then he sold it, also for a good profit. When he had accumulated as much as five roubles, he sewed up the little bag and started saving in another one. With respect to the authorities he behaved still more cleverly. No one could sit so quietly on a bench. It should be noted that the teacher was a great lover of silence and good conduct and could not stand clever and witty boys; it seemed to him that they must certainly be laughing at him. It was enough for one who had drawn notice with regard to wit, it was enough for him merely to stir or somehow inadvertently twitch his eyebrow, to suddenly fall under his wrath. He would persecute him and punish him unmercifully. "I'll drive the defiance and disobedience out of you, my boy!" he would say. "I know you through and through, as you hardly know yourself. You're going to go on your knees for me! You're going to go hungry for me!" And the poor lad, not knowing why himself, would get sores on his knees and go hungry for days. "Abilities and talents? That's all nonsense," he used to say. "I look only at conduct. I'll give top grades in all subjects to a boy who doesn't know *a* from *b*, if his conduct is praiseworthy; and if I see a bad spirit or any mockery in a one of you, I'll give him a zero, even if he outshines Solon himself!" So spoke the teacher, who had a mortal hatred of Krylov for saying: "Better a drunken slob, if he knows his job,"[56] and always used to tell, with delight in his face and eyes, that in the school where he taught previously there was such silence that you could hear a fly buzz; that not one pupil the whole year round either coughed or blew his nose in class, and until the bell rang it was impossible to tell whether anyone was there or not. Chichikov suddenly comprehended the superior's spirit and how to behave accordingly. He never moved an eye or an eyebrow all through class time, however much he was pinched from behind; as soon as the bell rang, he rushed headlong and was the first to offer the teacher his fur hat (the teacher wore a fur hat with ear flaps); after offering him the hat, he left class ahead of him, trying two or three times to cross paths with him, incessantly tipping his cap. The thing was a complete success. All the while he was at school, he was in excellent repute, and at graduation he received full honors in all subjects, a diploma, and an album with *For Exemplary Diligence and Good Conduct* stamped on it in gold. On leaving school, he turned out to be already a young man of rather attractive appearance, with a chin calling for a razor. Just then his father died. The inheritance was found to consist of four irretrievably worn-out jerkins, two old frock coats trimmed with lambskin, and an insignificant sum of money. The father evidently was competent only to advise on saving kopecks, but saved very few himself. Chichikov straightaway sold the decrepit little farmstead with its worthless bit of land for a thousand roubles, and moved with his family of serfs to town, intending to settle there and enter the civil service. Just at that time the poor teacher, the lover of silence and praiseworthy conduct, was thrown out of the school for stupidity or some other fault. He took to drinking from grief; in the end he had nothing left even to buy drink with; ill, helpless, without a crust of bread, he was perishing somewhere in an unheated, abandoned hovel. His former pupils, the clever and witty, whom he had constantly suspected of disobedience and defiant conduct, on hearing of his pitiful plight, straightaway collected money for him, even selling much that was needed; only Pavlusha Chichikov pleaded want and gave them a silver five-kopeck piece, which his comrades there and then threw back at him, saying: "Eh, you chiseler!" The poor teacher buried his face in his hands when he heard of this act of his former pupils; tears gushed from his fading eyes, as if he were a strengthless child. "On my deathbed God has granted me to weep!" he said in a weak voice, and on hearing about Chichikov, he sighed deeply, adding straightaway: "Eh, Pavlusha! how a man can change! He was so well-behaved, no rowdiness, like silk! Hoodwinked, badly hoodwinked . . ."

It is impossible, however, to say that our hero's nature was so hard and callous and his feelings were so dulled that he did not know either pity or compassion; he felt both the one and the other, he would even want to help, but only provided it was not a significant sum, provided the money he had resolved not to touch remained untouched; in short, the fatherly admonition – "Keep and save your kopeck" – proved beneficial. But he was not attached to money for its own sake; he was not possessed by stinginess and miserliness. No, they were not what moved him: he pictured ahead of him a life of every comfort, of every sort of prosperity; carriages, an excellently furnished house, tasty dinners – this was what constantly hovered in his head. So as to be sure ultimately, in time, to taste all that – this was the reason for saving kopecks, stingily denied in the meantime both to himself and to others. When a rich man raced by him in a pretty, light droshky, his trotters richly harnessed, he would stand rooted to the spot, and then, coming to, as if after a long sleep, would say: "Yet he used to be a clerk and had a bowl haircut!" And whatever there was that smacked of wealth and prosperity produced an impression on him inconceivable to himself. On leaving school he did not even want to rest: so strong was his desire to get quickly down to business and start in the service. However, despite his honors diploma, it was with great difficulty that he found himself a place in the treasury. Even in a remote backwoods one needs patronage! The little post he got was a wretched one, the salary thirty or forty roubles a year. But he resolved to engage himself ardently in his service, to conquer and overcome all. And indeed he displayed unheard-of self-denial, patience, and restriction of needs. From early morning till late evening, tireless of both body and soul, he kept writing, all buried in office papers, did not go home, slept on tables in office rooms, ate on occasion with the caretakers, and for all that managed to keep himself tidy, to dress decently, to give his face an agreeable expression, and even a certain nobility to his gestures. It must be said that the treasury clerks were particularly distinguished by their unsightliness and unattractiveness. Some had faces like badly baked bread: a cheek bulging out on one side, the chin skewed to the other, the upper lip puffed into a blister, and cracked besides – in short, quite ugly. They all talked somehow harshly, in such tones as if they were about to give someone a beating; sacrifices were frequently offered to Bacchus, thereby showing that many leftovers of paganism still persist in the Slavic nature; occasionally they even came to the office soused, as they say, for which reason the office was not a very nice place and the air was far from aromatic. Among such clerks Chichikov could not fail to be noticed and distinguished, presenting a complete contrast to them in all ways, by the attractiveness of his face, and the amiableness of his voice, and his total abstention from all strong drink. Yet, for all that, his path was difficult; his superior was an elderly department chief, who was the image of some stony insensibility and unshakableness: eternally the same, unapproachable, never in his life showing a smile on his face, never once greeting anyone even with an inquiry after their health. No one had ever seen him, even once, be other than he always was, either in the street or at home; if only he had once shown sympathy for something or other, if only he had gotten drunk and in his drunkenness burst out laughing; if only he had even given himself to wild gaiety, as a robber will in a drunken moment – but there was not even a shadow of anything of the sort in him. There was precisely nothing in him, neither villainy nor goodness, and something frightful showed itself in this absence of everything. His callously marble face, with no sharp irregularity, did not hint at any resemblance; his features were in strict proportion to each other. Only the quantity of pocks and pits that mottled it included it in the number of those faces on which, according to the popular expression, the devil comes at night to thresh peas. It seemed beyond human power to suck up to such a man and win his favor, but Chichikov tried. To begin with, he set about pleasing him in various inconspicuous trifles: he made a close study of how the pens he wrote with were sharpened, and, preparing a few in that way, placed them at his hand each day; he blew and brushed the sand and tobacco from his desk; he provided a new rag for his inkstand; he found his hat somewhere, the vilest hat that ever existed in the world, and placed it by him each day a minute before the end of office hours; he cleaned off his back when he got whitewash on it from the wall – but all this went decidedly unnoticed, the same as if none of it had been done. Finally he sniffed out his home and family life, and learned that he had a grown-up daughter whose face also looked as if the threshing of peas took place on it nightly. It was from this side that he decided to mount his assault. Learning what church she went to on Sundays, he would stand opposite her each time, in clean clothes, his shirtfront stiffly starched – and the thing proved a success: the stern department chief wavered and invited him to tea! And before anyone in the office had time to blink, things got so arranged that Chichikov moved into his house, became a necessary and indispensable man, purchased the flour and the sugar, treated the daughter as his fiancée, called the department chief papa, and kissed his hand; everyone in the office decided that at the end of February, before the Great Lent, there would be a wedding.[57] The stern department chief even began soliciting the authorities, and in a short time Chichikov himself was installed as a department chief in a vacancy that had come open. In this, it seemed, the main purpose of his connection with the old department chief consisted, because he straight-away sent his trunk home in secret, and the next day was already settled in other quarters. He stopped calling the depart-ment chief papa and no longer kissed his hand, and the matter of the wedding was hushed up, as if nothing had ever happened. However, on meeting him, he amiably shook his hand each time and invited him to tea, so that the old department chief, despite his eternal immobility and callous indifference, shook his head each time and muttered under his breath: "Hoodwinked, hoodwinked – that devil's son!"

This was the most difficult threshold he had to cross. After that it went more easily and successfully. He became a man of note. There was everything in him needed for this world: agreeableness of manner and behavior, and briskness in the business of doing business. By these means he obtained before too long what is known as a cushy billet, and he made excellent use of it. It should be known that at that very time the strictest persecution of every sort of bribery was begun; he did not let the persecution frighten him, but at once turned it to his own profit, thereby showing a truly Russian inventiveness, which emerges only under pressure. This is how it was set up: as soon as a petitioner appeared and thrust his hand into his pocket to produce from it the familiar letters of reference from Prince Khovansky, as we say in Russia[58] – "No, no," he would say with a smile, restraining his hand, "you think that I . . . no, no. This is our duty, our responsibility, we must do it without any rewards! Rest assured in that regard: by tomorrow everything will be done. Give me your address, please, no need to trouble yourself, everything will be brought to your house." The charmed petitioner would return home almost in ecstasy, thinking: "Here at last is the sort of man we need more of – simply a priceless diamond!" But the petitioner waits a day, then another day, nothing is brought to his house, nor on the third day. He comes to the office, nothing has even begun yet: he goes to the priceless diamond. "Ah, forgive me!" Chichikov would say very politely, seizing both his hands, "we've been so busy; but by tomorrow everything will be done, tomorrow without fail, really, I'm so ashamed!" And all this would be accompanied by the most charming gestures. If the flap of some caftan should fly open just then, a hand would try at the same moment to set things straight and hold the flap. But neither the next day, nor the day after, nor the third day is anything brought to the house. The petitioner reconsiders:

really, maybe there's something behind it? He makes inquiries; they say you must give something to the scriveners. "Why not? I'm prepared to give twenty-five kopecks or so." "No, not twenty-five kopecks, but twenty-five roubles each." "Twenty-five roubles to each scrivener!" the petitioner cries out. "Why get so excited," comes the reply, "it amounts to the same thing – the scriveners will get twenty-five kopecks each, and the rest will go to the superiors." The slow-witted petitioner slaps himself on the forehead, calls down all plagues upon the new order of things, the persecution of bribery, and the polite, gentilized manners of the officials. Before, one at least knew what to do: bring the chief clerk a ten-rouble bill and the thing was in the bag, but now it's a twenty-fiver and a week of fussing besides before you figure it out – devil take disinterestedness and official gentility! The petitioner, of course, is right, but, on the other hand, now there are no more bribe takers: all the chief clerks are most honest and genteel people, only the secretaries and scriveners are crooks. Soon a much vaster field presented itself to Chichikov: a commission was formed for the building of some quite capital government building. He, too, got himself into this commission and ended up being one of its most active members. The commission immediately set to work. For six years they fussed over the edifice; but maybe the climate interfered, or there was something about the materials, in any case the government edifice simply would not get higher than its foundations. And meanwhile, in other parts of town, each of the members turned out to have a beautiful house of civil architecture: evidently the subsoil was somewhat better there. The members were already beginning to prosper and started raising families. Only here and only now did Chichikov begin gradually to extricate himself from the stern law of temperance and his own implacable self-denial. Only here was his long-lasting fast finally relaxed, and it turned out that he had never been a stranger to various pleasures, from which he had been able to abstain in the years of his ardent youth, when no man is completely master of himself. Some indulgences turned up: he acquired a rather good cook, fine Holland shirts. Already he had bought himself such flannel as no one in the entire province wore, and from then on began keeping more to brown and reddish colors, with flecks; already he had acquired an excellent pair of horses, and would hold one of the reins himself, making the outrunner twist and turn; already he had begun the custom of sponging himself with water mixed with eau de cologne; already he had bought himself a certain far-from-inexpensive soap for imparting smoothness to his skin, already...

But suddenly, to replace the former old doormat, a new superior was sent, a military man, strict, the enemy of bribe takers and of everything known as falsehood. The very next day he threw a scare into one and all, demanded the accounts, found missing amounts, sums omitted at every step, noticed straight off the houses of beautiful civil architecture, and the sorting out began. The officials were dismissed from their posts; the houses of civil architecture were made government property and turned into various almshouses and schools for cantonists;[59] everywhere the feathers flew, and with Chichikov more than the rest. Despite its agreeableness, the superior suddenly took a dislike to his face, God knows why exactly – sometimes it is even simply for no reason at all – and conceived a mortal hatred for him. And to everyone this implacable superior was a great terror. But since he was anyhow a military man, and consequently did not know all the subtleties of civilian capers, in a short time certain other officials wormed their way into his graces, by means of a truthful appearance and a skill in ingratiating themselves with everyone, and the general soon wound up in the hands of still greater crooks, whom he by no means regarded as such; he was even pleased that he had finally made a proper choice of people, and seriously boasted of his fine skill in discerning abilities. The officials suddenly comprehended his spirit and character. All that were under his command became terrible persecutors of falsehood; everywhere, in all things, they pursued it as a fisherman with a harpoon pursues some meaty sturgeon, and they pursued it so successfully that in a short while each of them turned out to have several thousand in capital. At that time many of the former officials returned to the right way and were taken back into the service. But Chichikov simply could not worm his way in, despite all the efforts of the general's first secretary to stand up for him, instigated by letters from Prince Khovansky, for though he comprehended perfectly the art of directing the general's nose, in this case he could do decidedly nothing. The general was the kind of man who, while he could be led by the nose (though without his knowing it), yet if some thought lodged itself in his head, it was the same as an iron nail: there was no way of getting it out. All that the clever secretary managed to do was to have the tarnished service record destroyed, and he moved the superior to that only by compassion, portraying for him in vivid colors the touching plight of Chichikov's unfortunate family, which he, fortunately, did not have.

"Well, so what!" said Chichikov. "There was a nibble – I pulled, lost it – no more questions. Crying won't help, I must get to work." And so he decided to start his career over again, fortify himself again with patience, limit himself again in everything, however freely and fully he had expanded before. He had to move to another town, and still make himself known there. Somehow nothing worked. In a very short period of time he had to change posts two or three times. The posts were somehow dirty, mean. It should be known that Chichikov was the most decent man who ever existed in the world. Although he did have to start by working himself through dirty society, in his soul he always maintained cleanliness, liked office desks to be of lacquered wood and everything to be genteel. He never allowed himself an indecent word in his speech and always became offended when he noticed in the words of others an absence of due respect for rank or title. The reader will, I think, be pleased to know that he changed his linen every other day, and in summer, when it was hot, even every day: every unpleasant smell, however slight, offended him. For this reason, every time Petrushka came to undress him and take his boots off, he put a clove in his nose, and in many cases his nerves were as ticklish as a girl's; and therefore it was hard finding himself again in those ranks where everything smacked of cheap vodka and unseemly behavior. However firm he was in spirit, he grew thin and even turned green in this time of such adversities. Already he had begun to gain weight and to acquire those round and seemly forms in which the reader found him on first making his acquaintance, and already more than once, glancing in the mirror, he had had thoughts of many pleasant things – a little woman, a nursery – and these thoughts would be followed by a smile; but now, when he once accidentally glanced at himself in the mirror, he could not help crying out: "Holy mother mine! how repulsive I've become!" And then for a long time he would not look at himself. But our hero endured it all, endured staunchly, patiently endured, and – at last went to work in customs. It must be said that this work had long constituted the secret object of his thoughts. He saw what stylish foreign things the customs officials acquired, what china and cambric they sent to their sweeties, aunties, and sisters. Long since he had said more than once with a sigh: "That's the place to get to: the border's close, the people are enlightened, and what fine Holland shirts one can acquire!" It should be added that at the same time he was also thinking about a particular kind of French soap that imparted an extraordinary whiteness to the skin and freshness to the cheeks; what it was called, God only knows, but, by his reckoning, it was sure to be found at the border. And so he had long wanted to work in customs, but was kept from it by the various ongoing profits of the building commission, and he rightly reasoned that, in any case, customs was no more than two birds in the bush, while the commission was already one in the hand. But now he resolved at all costs to get into customs, and get there he did. He tackled his work with extraordinary zeal. It seemed that fate itself had appointed him to be a customs official. Such efficiency, perceptivity, and perspicacity had been not only never seen, but never even heard of. In three or four weeks he became such a skilled hand at the customs business that he knew decidedly everything: he did not weigh or measure, but could tell by the feel of it how many yards of flannel or other fabric were in each bolt; taking a parcel in his hand, he could say at once how much it weighed. As for searches, here, as even his colleagues put it, he simply had the nose of a hound: one could not help being amazed, seeing him have patience enough to feel every little button, and all of it performed with deadly coldbloodedness, polite to the point of incredibility. And while those being searched became furious, got beside themselves, and felt a spiteful urge to give the back of their hand to his agreeable appearance, he, changing neither his countenance nor his polite demeanor, merely kept murmuring: "Would you kindly take the trouble to get up a little?" or "Would you kindly proceed to the other room, madam? The spouse of one of our officials will speak with you there" or "Excuse me, I'll just unstitch the lining of your overcoat a bit with my penknife" – and, so saying, he would pull shawls and kerchiefs out of it as coolly as out of his own trunk. Even his superiors opined that this was a devil, not a man: he found things in wheels, shafts, horses' ears, and all sorts of other places where no author would even dream of going, and where no one but customs officials are allowed to go. So that the poor traveler, once past the border, would not recover himself for several minutes, and, mopping the sweat that had broken out in small droplets all over his body, could only cross himself, murmuring: "My, oh, my!" His position rather resembled that of a schoolboy who comes running from a private room to which the headmaster summoned him in order to deliver some admonition, instead of which he quite unexpectedly gave him a caning. In a short while he made life simply impossible for the smugglers. He was the terror and despair of all Polish Jewry. His honesty and incorruptibility were insurmountable, almost unnatural. He did not even amass a small capital for himself from various confiscated goods and objects of all sorts, seized but not turned over to the treasury so as to save unnecessary paperwork. Such zealously unmercenary service could not but become an object of general amazement and be brought finally to the notice of the superiors. He was given more rank and promotion, after which he presented a plan for catching all the smugglers, asking only for the means of implementing it himself. He was straightaway given command and an unlimited authority to perform all searches. This was just what he wanted. At that time a powerful company of smugglers had been formed in a carefully planned way; the bold undertaking promised millions in profit. He had long been informed of it and had even turned away those sent to bribe him, saying dryly: "It's not time yet." Once everything was put at his disposal, he immediately sent word to the company, saying: "The time has now come." The calculation was only too correct. Here he could get in one year what he could not gain in twenty years of the most zealous service. Prior to this he had not wanted to enter into any relations with them, because he was no more than a mere pawn, which meant that he would not get much; but now...now it was quite a different matter: he could offer any conditions he liked. To smooth the way, he won over another official, a colleague of his, who could not resist the temptation despite his gray hairs. The conditions were agreed to, and the company went into action. The action began brilliantly: the reader has undoubtedly heard the oft-repeated story of the clever journey of the Spanish sheep that crossed the border in double fleeces, carrying in between a million roubles' worth of Brabant lace.

This event occurred precisely when Chichikov was serving in customs. If he himself had not participated in this undertaking, no Jews in the world could have succeeded in bringing off such a thing. After three or four sheep-crossings at the border, each of the officials found himself with four hundred thousand in capital. With Chichikov, they say, it even went over five hundred thousand, because he was a bit quicker. God knows what enormous figures the blessed sums might have grown to, if some deuced beast had not crossed paths with it all. The devil befuddled both officials; to speak plainly, the officials went berserk and quarreled over nothing. Once, in a heated conversation, and perhaps being a bit tipsy, Chichikov called the other official a parson's kid, and the man, though he was indeed a parson's kid, for no reason at all became bitterly offended and straightaway answered him strongly and with extraordinary sharpness, namely thus: "No, lies, I'm a state councillor, not a parson's kid, it's you who are a parson's kid!" And then added, to pique him to greater vexation: "So there!" Although he told him off thus roundly, turning back on him the very title he had bestowed, and although the expression "So there!" may have been a strong one, he was not satisfied with that and also sent in a secret denunciation against him. However, they say that, to begin with, they had quarreled over some wench, fresh and firm as a ripe turnip, in the custom officials' expression; that some people were even paid to give our hero a little beating at night in a dark alley; but that both officials were played for fools, and the wench went to the use of a certain Captain Shamsharev. How it was in reality, God only knows; better let the inventive reader think up his own ending. The main thing was that the secret connections with the smugglers became manifest. The state councillor, though ruined himself, also cooked his colleague's goose. The officials were brought to trial, everything they had was confiscated, perquisitioned, and it all suddenly broke like thunder over their heads. They recovered as if from a stupor and saw with horror what they had done. The state councillor, following Russian custom, took to drinking from grief, but the collegiate one withstood. He managed to hide away part of the cash, despite the keen scent of the authorities who came for the investigation. He used all the subtle wiles of his mind, only too experienced by then, only too knowledgeable of people: at one point he acted by means of an agreeable manner, at another by moving speeches, at another by the incense of flattery, which never does any harm, at another by dropping a bit of cash – in short, he handled things so as to be retired with less dishonor than his colleague, and to dodge criminal proceedings. But no capital, no foreign-made trinkets, nothing was left to him; other lovers of such things had come along. All that remained to him was some ten thousand stashed away for a rainy day, that and two dozen Holland shirts, and a small britzka such as bachelors drive around in, and two serfs – the coachman Selifan and the lackey Petrushka – and the customs officials, out of the kindness of their hearts, left him five or six pieces of soap for preserving the freshness of his cheeks – that was all. And so, this was the position our hero again found himself in! This was the immense calamity that came crashing down on his head! This was what he called suffering for the truth in the service. Now it might be concluded that after such storms, trials, vicissitudes of fate, and sorrows of life, he would retire with his remaining ten thousand to the peaceful back-woods of some provincial town and there wither away forever in a chintz dressing gown at the window of a low house, on Sundays sorting out a fight between muzhiks that started up outside his windows, or refreshing himself by going to the chicken coop and personally inspecting the chicken destined for the soup, thus passing his none-too-noisy but in its own way also not quite useless life. But it did not happen so. One must do justice to the invincible force of his character. After all this, which was enough, if not to kill, then at least to cool down and subdue a man forever, the inconceivable passion did not die in him. He was aggrieved, vexed, he murmured against the whole world, was angry at the injustice of fate, indignant at the injustice of men, and, nevertheless, could not renounce new attempts. In short, he showed a patience compared with which the wooden patience of the German is nothing, consisting as it does of a slow, sluggish circulation of the blood. Chichikov's blood, on the contrary, ran high, and much reasonable will was needed to bridle all that would have liked to leap out and play freely. He reasoned, and a certain aspect of justice could be seen in his reasoning: "Why me? Why should the calamity have befallen me? Who just sits and gapes on the job? – everybody profits. I didn't make anyone unhappy: I didn't rob a widow, I didn't send anyone begging, I made use of abundance, I took where anyone else would have taken; if I hadn't made use of it, others would have. Why, then, do others prosper, and why must I perish like a worm? What am I now? What good am I? How will I look any respectable father of a family in the eye now? How can I not feel remorse, knowing that I'm a useless burden on the earth, and what will my children say later? There, they'll say, is a brute of a father, he didn't leave us any inheritance!"

It is already known that Chichikov was greatly concerned with his posterity. Such a sensitive subject! A man would, perhaps, not be so light of finger, were it not for the question which, no one knows why, comes of itself: "And what will the children say?" And so the future progenitor, like a cautious cat casting a sidelong glance with one eye to make sure his master is not watching, hastily grabs everything close to him – soap, a candle, lard, a canary that turns up under his paw – in short, he does not miss a thing. So our hero complained and wept, and meanwhile the activity in his head refused to die; it was all concentrated on building something and only waited for a plan. Again he shrank, again he began to lead a hard life, again limited himself in everything, again sank from cleanliness and a decent situation into mire and low life. And, in expectation of better things, was even forced to occupy himself with the calling of solicitor, a calling which has not yet acquired citizenship among us, is pushed around on all sides, is little respected by petty clerkdom, or even by the clients themselves, which is condemned to groveling in hallways, to rudeness, and all the rest of it, but need made him resolve on it all. Among other cases there was one in which he had to solicit for the taking in custody of several hundred peasants. The estate was in the last degree of disorder. The disorder had been caused by loss of cattle, swindling stewards, bad crops, epidemic diseases that killed off the best workers, and finally by the witlessness of the landowner himself, who was decorating his Moscow house in the newest taste and in the process destroying his entire fortune to the last kopeck, so that there was no longer enough to eat. And this was the reason why it was finally necessary to mortgage what remained of the estate. Mortgaging to the treasury was a new thing then, which was not ventured upon without fear. As a solicitor, Chichikov, having first gained everyone's favor (without gaining favor beforehand, as we all know, even the simplest document or certificate cannot be obtained; a bottle of Madeira must at least be poured down every gullet) – and so, having gained the favor of everyone he needed, he explained that there was, incidentally, this circumstance, that half the peasants had died off – just so there should be no quibbling later on . . .

"But aren't they listed in the census reports?" said the secretary.

"They are," replied Chichikov.

"Well, then why be so timid?" said the secretary. "One dies, another gets born, there's nothing to mourn."

The secretary, as you see, could also talk in rhyme. And meanwhile the most inspired thought that ever entered a human head dawned on our hero. "Ah, what a Simple Simon I am," he said to himself, "hunting for my mittens when they're tucked right under my belt! No, if I were to buy up all the ones that have died before the new census lists are turned in, to acquire, say, a thousand of them, and get, say, two hundred roubles per soul – that's already two hundred thousand in capital! And now is a good time, there were epidemics recently, thank God, quite a lot of folk died off. The landowners have gambled away everything at cards, caroused and squandered the lot well and good; everything goes off to government service in Petersburg; estates are abandoned, managed haphazardly, the taxes are harder to pay each year, so everyone will be glad to let me have them, if only so as not to pay the soul tax for them; chances are I may occasionally pick up a kopeck or two on it. Of course, it's difficult, worrisome, frightening, because I might get in trouble again for it, some scandal might come of it. Well, but after all, man hasn't been given brains for nothing. And the best part of it is that the thing will seem incredible to them all, no one will believe it. True, it's impossible to buy or mortgage them without land. So I'll buy them for relocation, that's what; land in the Taurida and Kherson provinces is being given away now, just go and settle on it. I'll resettle them all there! to Kherson with them! let them live there! And the resettlement can be done legally, through the proper court procedures. If they want to verify the peasants: go ahead, I have no objections, why not? I'll provide a certificate signed by the district captain of police with his own hand. The village can be called Chichikov Hamlet, or by the name I was baptized with: Pavlovsk Settlement." And that was how this strange subject formed itself in our hero's head, for which I do not know whether readers will be grateful to him, but how grateful the author is, it is even difficult to express. For, say what you will, if this thought had not entered Chichikov's head, the present poem would never have come into being.

After crossing himself, as Russians do, he went into action. In the guise of looking for a place to live and on other pretexts, he undertook to peek into various corners of our state, mostly those that had suffered more than others from calamities, bad harvests, mortalities, and so on and so forth – in short, where he could more readily and cheaply buy up the sort of folk he wanted. He did not turn at random to just any landowner, but selected people more to his taste or those with whom he would have less difficulty concluding such deals, and he tried first to strike up an acquaintance, to gain favor, so as to acquire the muzhiks, if possible, more through friendship than by purchase. And so, readers ought not to be indignant with the author if the characters who have appeared so far are not to their liking: it is Chichikov's fault, he is full master here, and wherever he decides to go, we must drag ourselves after him. For our part, if indeed there should fall an accusation of paleness and unsightliness in our characters and persons, we shall say only that in the beginning one never sees the whole broad flow and volume of a thing. The entrance to any town whatever, even a capital, is always somehow pale; at first everything is gray and monotonous: mills and factories all smudged with smoke stretch out endlessly, and only later appear the corners of six-storied buildings, shops, signboards, the immense perspectives of streets, steeples everywhere, columns, statues, towers, with city splendor, noise and thunder, and all that the hand and mind of man have so marvelously brought about. How the first purchases were brought about, the reader has already seen; how matters will develop further, what fortunes and misfortunes await our hero, how he is to solve and surmount more difficult obstacles, how colossal images will emerge, how the secret levers of the vast narrative will work, how its horizon will extend far and wide, and all of it become one majestic lyrical flow – this he will see later. There is still a long way ahead of the whole traveling outfit, consisting of a gentleman of middle age, a britzka such as bachelors drive around in, a lackey Petrushka, a coachman Selifan, and three horses already known by name, from Assessor to the scoundrelly dapple-gray. And so, there you have the whole of our hero, just as he is! But perhaps there will be a demand for a conclusive definition, in one stroke: what is he as regards moral qualities? That he is no hero filled with perfections and virtues is clear. What is he – a scoundrel, then? Why a scoundrel, why be so hard on others? Nowadays we have no scoundrels, we have well-meaning, agreeable people, and of those who, for general disgrace, would offer their physiognomies to be publicly slapped, one can count no more than some two or three men, and they, too, have started talking about virtue. It would be most correct to call him an owner, an acquirer. Acquisition is to blame for everything; because of it things have been done which the world dubs *not quite clean*. True, there is something repulsive in such a character, and the same reader who on his journey through life would make friends with such a person, welcome him at his table, and pass the time pleasantly, will look askance at him once he becomes the hero of a drama or a poem. But he is wise who does not scorn any character, but, fixing a piercing eye on him, searches out his primary causes. Everything transforms quickly in man; before you can turn around, a horrible worm has grown inside him, despotically drawing all life's juices to itself. And it has happened more than once that some passion, not a broad but a paltry little passion for some petty thing, has spread through one born for better deeds, making him forsake great and sacred duties and see the great and sacred in paltry baubles. Numberless as the sands of the sea are human passions, and no one resembles another, and all of them, base or beautiful, are at first obedient to man and only later become his dread rulers. Blessed is he who has chosen the most beautiful passion; his boundless bliss grows tenfold with every hour and minute, and he goes deeper and deeper into the infinite paradise of his soul. But there are passions that it is not for man to choose. They are born with him at the moment of his birth into this world, and he is not granted the power to refuse them. They are guided by a higher destiny, and they have in them something eternally calling, never ceasing throughout one's life. They are ordained to accomplish a great earthly pursuit: as a dark image, or as a bright apparition sweeping by, gladdening the world – it makes no difference, both are equally called forth for the good unknown to man. And it may be that in this same Chichikov the passion that drives him comes not from him, and that his cold existence contains that which will later throw man down in the dust and make him kneel before the wisdom of the heavens. And it is still a mystery why this image has appeared in the poem that is presently coming into being.

But the hard thing is not that readers will be displeased with my hero, what is hard is that there lives in my soul an irrefutable certainty that they might have been pleased with this same hero, this same Chichikov. If the author had not looked deeply into his soul, had not stirred up from its bottom that which flees and hides from the light, had not revealed his secret thoughts which no man entrusts to another, but had shown him such as he appeared to the whole town, to Manilov and the others, everyone would have been happy as can be and would have taken him for an interesting man. Never mind that neither his face nor his whole image would have hovered as if alive before their eyes; instead, once the reading was over, the soul would not be troubled by anything, and one could turn back to the card table, the solace of all Russia. Yes, my good readers, you would prefer not to see human poverty revealed. Why, you ask, what for? Do we not know ourselves that there is much in life that is contemptible and stupid? Even without that, one often chances to see things which are by no means comforting. Better present us with something beautiful, captivating. Better let us become oblivious! "Why, brother, are you telling me that things aren't going well with the management of the estate?" says the landowner to his steward. "I know that without you, brother, haven't you got something else to talk about? You ought to let me forget it, not know it, then I'll be happy." And so the money that would have helped somehow to straighten things out is spent on the means for making oneself oblivious. The mind sleeps, the mind that might find some unexpected fount of great means; and then, bang! the estate gets auctioned, and the landowner takes his oblivion and goes begging, his soul ready in its extremity for such baseness as once would have horrified him.

Accusation will also fall upon the author from the side of the so-called patriots, who sit quietly in their corners, occupied with completely unrelated matters, and stash away small fortunes for themselves, arranging their lives at the expense of others; but as soon as something happens which in their opinion is insulting to the fatherland, if some book appears in which the sometimes bitter truth is told, they rush out of all corners like spiders seeing a fly tangled in their web, and suddenly raise a cry: "But is it good to bring it to light, to proclaim about it? Because all this that's written here, all this is ours – is that nice? And what will foreigners say? Is it cheery to hear a bad opinion of oneself? Do they think it doesn't hurt? Do they think we're not patriots?" To these wise observations, especially concerning the opinion of foreigners, I confess it is impossible to find an answer. Unless it is this: in a remote corner of Russia there lived two inhabitants. One was a father of a family, Kifa Mokievich by name, a man of meek character who spent his life in a dressing-gown way. He did not occupy himself with his family; his existence was turned more in a contemplative direction and was occupied with the following, as he called it, philosophical question: "Take, for instance, a beast," he would say, pacing the room, "a beast is born naked. And why precisely naked? Why not like a bird, why not hatched from an egg? So you see: the deeper you go into nature, the less you understand her!" Thus reasoned the inhabitant Kifa Mokievich. But that is still not the main thing. The other inhabitant was Moky Kifovich, his own son. He was what is known in Russia as a mighty man, and all the while that his father was occupied with the birth of a beast, his broad-shouldered twenty-year-old nature kept wanting to display itself. He could not go about anything lightly: it was always someone's arm broken or a bump swelling on someone's nose. In and around the house everything, from the serf wench to the yard bitch, ran away from him on sight; he even broke his own bed to pieces in the bedroom. Such was Moky Kifovich, who nevertheless had a good heart. But that is still not the main thing. The main thing is the following: "For pity's sake, dear master, Kifa Mokievich," his own and other house serfs used to say to the father, "what's with your Moky Kifovich? He won't leave anyone in peace, he's such a roughneck." "Yes, a prankster, a prankster," the father usually replied to that, "but what can I do? It's too late to beat him, and I'd be the one accused of cruelty; then, too, he's a proud man, if I reproached him in front of just a couple of people, he'd calm down, but publicity – there's the trouble! They'd find out in town and call him a downright dog. What do they think, really, that it doesn't hurt me? that I'm not a father? That I occupy myself with philosophy and sometimes have no time, and so I'm not a father anymore? No, I'm a father all right! a father, devil take them, a father! I've got Moky Kifovich sitting right here in my heart!" Here Kifa Mokievich beat himself quite hard on the breast with his fist and flew into a complete passion. "Let him even remain a dog, but let them not find it out from me, let it not be me who betrays him." Then, having shown such paternal feeling, he would leave Moky Kifovich to go on with his mighty deeds, and himself turn again to his favorite subject, suddenly asking himself some such question as: "Well, and if an elephant was born from an egg, then I suppose the shell would be mighty thick, a cannonball couldn't break it; some new firearms would have to be invented." So they spent their life, these two inhabitants of a peaceful corner, who have suddenly peeked out, as from a window, at the end of our poem, peeked out in order to respond modestly to accusations on the part of certain ardent patriots, who for the moment are quietly occupied with some sort of philosophy or with augmentations at the expense of their dearly beloved fatherland, and think not about not doing wrong, but only about having no one say they are doing wrong. But no, neither patriotism nor primal feeling is the cause of these accusations, something else is hidden behind them. Why conceal the word? Who, then, if not an author, must speak the sacred truth? You fear the deeply penetrating gaze, you are afraid to penetrate anything deeply with your own gaze, you like to skim over everything with unthinking eyes. You will even have a hearty laugh over Chichikov, will perhaps even praise the author, saying: "He did cleverly catch a thing or two, though; must be a man of merry temperament!" And after these words you will turn to yourself with redoubled pride, a self-satisfied smile will appear on your face, and you will add: "One can't help agreeing, the most strange and ridiculous people turn up in some provinces, and no small scoundrels at that!" And who among you, filled with Christian humility, not publicly, but in quiet, alone, in moments of solitary converse with himself, will point deeply into his own soul this painful question: "And isn't there a bit of Chichikov in me, too?" Perish the thought! But if some acquaintance of yours should pass by just then, a man of neither too high nor too low a rank, you will straightaway nudge your neighbor and tell him, all but snorting with laughter: "Look, look, there goes Chichikov, it's Chichikov!" And then, like a child, forgetting all decorum incumbent upon your age and station, you will run after him, taunting him from behind and repeating: "Chichikov! Chichikov! Chichikov!"

But we have begun talking rather loudly, forgetting that our hero, asleep all the while his story was being told, is now awake and can easily hear his last name being repeated so often. He is a touchy man and does not like it when he is spoken of disrespectfully. The reader can hardly care whether Chichikov gets angry with him or not, but as for the author, he must in no case quarrel with his hero: they still have many a road to travel together hand in hand; two big parts lie ahead − no trifling matter.

"Hey, hey! what's with you!" said Chichikov to Selifan, "eh?"

"What?" said Selifan in a slow voice.

"What do you mean, what? You goose! is that any way to drive? Get a move on!"

And indeed Selifan had long been driving with his eyes closed, only occasionally, through sleep, snapping the reins against the flanks of the horses, who were also dozing; and Petrushka's cap had long since flown off at some unknown place, and he himself was leaning back, resting his head on Chichikov's knee, so that he had to give it a flick. Selifan perked up and, slapping the dapple-gray on the back a few times, which made him break into a trot, and brandishing his whip over them all, added in a thin, singsong voice: "Never fear!" The horses got moving and pulled the light britzka along like a bit of fluff. Selifan just kept brandishing and shouting "Hup! hup! hup!" bouncing smoothly on his box, as the troika now flew up and now rushed full-tilt down a hummock, such as were scattered the whole length of the high road, which ran down a barely noticeable slope. Chichikov just smiled, jouncing slightly on his leather cushion, for he loved fast driving. And what Russian does not love fast driving? How can his soul, which yearns to get into a whirl, to carouse, to say sometimes: "Devil take it all!" − how can his soul not love it? Not love it when something ecstatically wondrous is felt in it? It seems an unknown force has taken you on its wing, and you are flying, and everything is flying: milestones go flying by, merchants come flying at you on the boxes of their kibitkas, the forest on both sides is flying by with its dark ranks of firs and pines, with axes chopping and crows cawing, the whole road is flying off no one knows where into the vanishing distance, and there is something terrible in this quick flashing, in which the vanishing object has no time to fix itself – only the sky overhead, and the light clouds, and the moon trying to break through, they alone seem motionless. Ah, troika! bird troika, who invented you? Surely you could only have been born among a brisk people, in a land that cares not for jokes, but sweeps smoothly and evenly over half the world, and you can go on counting the miles until it all dances before your eyes. And you are no clever traveling outfit, it seems, held together by an iron screw, but some dextrous Yaroslav muzhik fitted you out and put you together slapdash, with only an axe and a chisel. The driver wears no German top boots: a beard, mittens, and devil knows what he sits on; but when he stands up, waves, and strikes up a song – the steeds go like the wind, the spokes of the wheels blend to a smooth disc, the road simply shudders, and the passerby stops and cries out in fright – there she goes racing, racing, racing! . . . And already far in the distance you see something raising dust and drilling the air.

And you, Rus, are you not also like a brisk, unbeatable troika racing on? The road smokes under you, bridges rumble, everything falls back and is left behind. Dumbstruck by the divine wonder, the contemplator stops: was it a bolt of lightning thrown down from heaven? what is the meaning of this horrific movement? and what unknown force is hidden in these steeds unknown to the world? Ah, steeds, steeds, what steeds! Are there whirlwinds in your manes? Is a keen ear burning in your every nerve? Hearing the familiar song from above, all in one accord you strain your bronze chests and, hooves barely touching the ground, turn into straight lines flying through the air, and all inspired by God it rushes on! . . . Rus, where are you racing to? Give answer! She gives no answer. Wondrously the harness bell dissolves in ringing; the air rumbles, shattered to pieces, and turns to wind; everything on earth flies by, and, looking askance, other nations and states step aside to make way.

VOLUME TWO

CHAPTER ONE

WHY, THEN, MAKE a show of the poverty of our life and our sad imperfection, unearthing people from the backwoods, from remote corners of the state? But what if this is in the writer's nature, and his own imperfection grieves him so, and the makeup of his talent is such, that he can only portray the poverty of our life, unearthing people from the backwoods, from remote corners of the state! So here we are again in the backwoods, again we have come out in some corner!

Yes, but what a backwoods and what a corner!

Over a thousand miles and more raced the meandering mountain heights. Like the giant rampart of some endless fortress they rose above the plains, now as a yellowish cliff, a gullied and pitted wall in appearance, now as a rounded green prominence covered, as if with lambswool, with young shrubs growing from the stumps of cut trees, or, finally, with dark forest so far spared the axe. The river, sometimes faithful to its high banks, followed them in their angles and bends over the whole expanse, but at other times abandoned them to go into the meadows, meandering there through several meanders, flashing like fire in the sun, then vanished in groves of birches, aspens, and alders, to rush out again in triumph, accompanied by bridges, mills, and dams that seemed to pursue it at every turn.

In one place the steep side of the heights heaved itself higher than the rest, and was decked out from top to bottom in a greenery of thickly crowding trees. Everything was there together: maples, pear trees, low-growing willows, gorse, birches, firs, and mountain ash all twined with hops; here flashed the red roofs of manor buildings, the fretwork cornices of cottages hiding behind them, and the upper story added to the manor house itself, and over this whole heap of trees and roofs the ancient church raised aloft its five gleaming tops. On each of them stood a gold openwork cross, attached to the cupola by gold openwork chains, so that the gold shone from afar as if it were suspended in air, not attached to anything. And this whole heap of trees and roofs, together with the church, turned upside down, was reflected in the river, where picturesquely ugly old willows, some standing on the bank, some right in the water, trailing their branches and leaves in it, were as if gazing at this picture, which they could not get their fill of admiring through all their long lives.

The view was not bad at all, but the view from above, from the upper story of the house, onto the plains and the distance, was better still. No guest or visitor could long stand indifferently on the balcony. His breath would be taken away, and he would only be able to say: "Lord, how spacious it is!" The space opened out endlessly. Beyond the meadows strewn with copses and water mills, thick forests stood green and blue, like seas or mist spreading far away. Beyond the forests, through the hazy air, showed yellowing sands. Beyond the sands, a ridge against the far curve of the sky, lay chalk mountains, their dazzling whiteness gleaming even in rainy spells, as if an eternal sun shone on them. Here and there upon them, light misty blue spots smoked. These were remote villages, but the human eye could no longer make them out. Only the golden dome of a church, flashing like a spark, made known that it was a large, populous village. All this was wrapped in imperturbable silence, which was not broken even by the barely audible echoes of the aerial singers that filled the air. In short, no guest or visitor could long stand indifferently on the balcony, and after some two hours of contemplation he would utter the same exclamation as in the first minute: "Heavenly powers, how spacious it is!"

Who, then, was the occupant of this estate, which, like an impregnable fortress, could not even be approached from here, but had to be approached from the other side – through meadows, wheat fields, and, finally, a sparse oak grove, spread picturesquely over the green, right up to the cottages and the master's house? Who was the occupant, the master and owner of this estate? To what happy man did this remote corner belong?

To Andrei Ivanovich Tentetnikov, landowner of the Tremalakhan district, a young gentleman, thirty-three years old, a collegiate secretary, an unmarried man.

And what sort of man, then, of what disposition, what qualities and character, was the landowner Andrei Ivanovich Tentetnikov?

To be sure, these inquiries ought to be addressed to his neighbors. One neighbor, who belonged to the race of retired staff officers and firebrands, expressed himself about him in a laconic expression: "A natural-born brute!" The general who lived six miles away used to say: "A young man, no fool, but with too many ideas in his head. I could be useful to him, because I have in Petersburg, and even at the . . . " The general never finished his speech. The district captain of police observed: "No, but his rank is – trash; and what if I come by tomorrow to collect the arrears!" A muzhik from his estate, if asked what sort of master he had, usually gave no answer. In short, the public opinion of him was rather unfavorable than favorable.

And yet in his essence Andrei Ivanovich was neither a good nor a bad being, but simply – a burner of the daylight. Since there are already not a few people in the world occupied with burning the daylight, why should Tentetnikov not burn it as well? However, here in a few words is the full journal of his day, and from it the reader himself can judge what his character was.

In the morning he awoke very late and, sitting up, stayed in bed for a long time rubbing his eyes. His eyes, as ill luck would have it, were small, and therefore the rubbing of them was performed for an extraordinarily long time. All the while the servant Mikhailo would be standing at the door with a wash-basin and a towel. This poor Mikhailo would stand there for one hour, two hours, then go to the kitchen, come back again – the master would still be rubbing his eyes and sitting on his bed. Finally he would get up, wash himself, put on his dressing gown, and come out to the drawing room to have tea, coffee, cocoa, and even fresh milk, taking little sips of each, crumbling his bread unmercifully, and shamelessly scattering pipe ashes everywhere. Two hours he would spend over his tea; what's more, he would take a cold cup and with it move to the window looking out on the yard. And at the window the following scene would take place each time.

First of all, the unshaven butler Grigory would bellow, addressing himself to the housekeeper, Perfilyevna, in the following terms:

"You wretched petty-landowning soul, you nonentity! You'd better shut up, vile wench, and that's all!"

"I take no orders from the likes of you, you guzzling gullet!" the nonentity, that is, Perfilyevna, would shout back.

"Nobody can get along with you, you even scrap with the steward, you barnyard piddler!" Grigory would bellow.

"The steward's a thief, just like you!" the nonentity would shout back, so that it could be heard in the village. "You're both drunkards, you're ruining the master, you bottomless barrels! You think the master doesn't know it? There he is, and he can hear you."

"Where is he?"

"He's sitting there in the window; he can see everything."

And indeed the master was sitting in the window and could see everything.

To crown it all, a house serf's brat was yelling his head off, having received a whack from his mother; a borzoi hound was whimpering, crouched on the ground, for reason of being scalded with boiling hot water by the cook, who was peeking out from the kitchen. In short, everything was howling and squealing insufferably. The master could see and hear it all. And only when it became so unbearable that it even prevented the master from doing nothing, would he send to tell them to make their noise more quietly.

Two hours before dinner, Andrei Ivanovich would go to his study in order to occupy himself truly and seriously. The occupation was indeed a serious one. It consisted in pondering a work which had been long and continuously pondered. This work was to embrace Russia from all viewpoints – civic, political, religious, philosophical; to resolve the difficult problems and questions posed for her by the times; and to define clearly her great future – in short, a work of vast scope. But so far it had all ended with the pondering; the pen got well chewed, doodles appeared on the paper, then it was all pushed aside, a book was taken up instead and not put down until dinnertime. The book was read with the soup, the sauce, the stew, and even the pastry, so that some dishes got cold as a result, while others were sent back quite untouched. Then came a pipe and the sipping of a cup of coffee, then a game of chess with himself. What was done from then until suppertime it is really quite difficult to say. It seems that simply nothing was done.

And thus, as alone as could be in the whole world, this young man of thirty-three spent his time, sitting around in a dressing gown without a tie. He did not feel like strolling, like walking, did not even want to go upstairs and have a look at the distances and views, did not even want to open the windows and let some fresh air into his room, and the beautiful view of the countryside, which no visitor could admire with indifference, was as if it did not exist for the owner himself.

From this journal the reader can see that Andrei Ivanovich Tentetnikov belonged to that race of people, so numerous in

Russia, who are known as sluggards, lie-abeds, sloths, and the like.

Whether such characters are born that way or become that way later on – who can answer? I think that, instead of an answer, it would be better to tell the story of Andrei Ivanovich's childhood and upbringing.

In childhood he was a clever, talented boy, now lively, now pensive. By a lucky or unlucky chance, he landed in a school of which the director was, in his own way, a remarkable man, despite certain whimsicalities. Alexander Petrovich possessed the gift of sensing the nature of the Russian man and knew the language in which to speak to him. No child left his presence crestfallen; on the contrary, even after a severe reprimand, he would feel a certain cheerfulness and a desire to smooth over the nastiness or trespass committed. The crowd of his charges seemed to look so mischievous, casual, and lively that one might have taken them for disorderly, unbridled freebooters. But that would have been a mistake: one man's power was felt only too well by these freebooters. There was no mischief maker or prankster who would not come to him on his own and tell all the mischief he had done. The least movement of their thoughts was known to him. In all things he acted extraordinarily. He used to say that one ought first of all to awaken ambition in a man – he called ambition the force that pushes a man forward – without which he cannot be moved to activity. Many times he did not restrain playfulness and prankishness at all: in elementary playfulness he saw the awakening development of the soul's qualities. He needed it in order to see precisely what lay hidden in a child. So an intelligent doctor looks calmly at the temporary fits approaching and the rashes appearing on the body, not combatting them, but studying them attentively, so as to find out for certain precisely what is concealed inside the man.

He did not have many teachers: the majority of the subjects he taught himself. And, truth to tell, he knew how to convey the very soul of a subject in a few words, without any of the pedantic terminology, the enormous views and opinions that young professors like to flaunt, so that even a young child could see clearly the precise need for this subject. He maintained that what man needed most was the science of life, that once he knew that, he would then know for himself what he must occupy himself with predominantly.

This science of life he made the subject of a separate course of study, to which he admitted only the most excellent. Those of small ability he let go into government service after the first year, maintaining that there was no need to torment them too much: it was enough for them if they learned to be patient, industrious workers, without acquiring presumptuousness or any long-range views. "But with the clever ones, the gifted ones, I must take a lot more trouble," he used to say. And in this course he became a totally different Alexander Petrovich, who from the first announced to them that so far he had demanded simple intelligence from them, but now he would demand a higher intelligence. Not the intelligence that knows how to taunt a fool and laugh at him, but one that knows how to endure any insult, ignore the fool – and not become irritated. It was here that he started to demand what others demand of children. It was this that he called the highest degree of intelligence! To preserve the lofty calm in which man must abide eternally amid any griefs whatever – it was this that he called intelligence! It was in this course that Alexander Petrovich showed that he indeed knew the science of life. Of subjects those alone were selected which were able to form a man into a citizen of his country. The majority of the lectures consisted of accounts of what lay ahead for a man in all careers and steps of government service and private occupations. All the troubles and obstacles that could be set up on a man's path, all the temptations and seductions lying in wait for him, he gathered before them in all their nakedness, concealing nothing. Everything was known to him, just as if he himself had filled every rank and post. In short, what he outlined for them was not at all a bright future. Strangely enough, whether because ambition was already so strongly awakened in them, or because there was something in the very eyes of their extraordinary mentor that said to a young man: Forward! – that word which produces such miracles in the Russian man – in any case, the young men sought only difficulties from the very start, longing to act only where it was difficult, where one had to show great strength of soul. There was something sober in their life. Alexander Petrovich did all sorts of experiments and tests with them, inflicting palpable insults on them either himself or by means of their comrades, but, perceiving as much, they would become still more prudent. Few finished this course, but those few were stalwarts, people who had been under fire. In the service they held out in the most unstable posts, while many far more intelligent men, not able to endure, quit the service on account of petty personal troubles, quit altogether, or, quite unawares, wound up in the hands of bribe takers and crooks. But those educated by Alexander Petrovich not only did not waver, but, wise in their knowledge of man and the soul, acquired a lofty moral influence even over the bribe takers and bad people.

But poor Andrei Ivanovich did not manage to taste this learning. He had just been deemed worthy of moving on to this higher course as one of the very best, and suddenly – disaster; the extraordinary mentor, from whom one word of approval sent him into sweet tremors, unexpectedly died. Everything changed at the school: to replace Alexander Petrovich there came a certain Fyodor Ivanovich, a man both kind and diligent, but with a totally different view of things. He imagined something unbridled in the free casualness of the children in the first course. He began to introduce certain external rules among them, demanded that the young men remain somehow mutely silent, that they never walk otherwise than in pairs. He himself even began to measure the distance between pairs with a yardstick. At table, to improve appearances, he seated them all by height rather than by intelligence, so that the asses got the best portions, and the clever got only scraps. All this caused murmuring, especially when the new head, as if in defiance of his predecessor, announced that intelligence and success in studies meant nothing to him, that he looked only at conduct, that even if a person was a poor student, if his conduct was good, he would prefer him to a clever one. But Fyodor Ivanovich did not get exactly what he wanted. Secret pranks started, which, as everyone knows, are worse than open ones. Everything was tip-top during the day, but at night – a spree.

In his manner of teaching subjects he turned everything upside down. With the best intentions, he introduced all sorts of novelties – all of them inappropriate. He brought in new teachers with new opinions and new points of view. They taught learnedly, showered their listeners with a host of new words and terms. One could see the logical connection and the conformity with new discoveries, but, alas! there was simply no life in the subject itself. It all seemed like carrion in the eyes of listeners who had already begun to have some understanding. Everything was inside out. But the worst thing was the loss of respect for their superiors and for authority: they began to mock both mentors and teachers; the director came to be called Fedka, Breadroll, and various other names; such things got started that many boys had to be expelled and thrown out.

Andrei Ivanovich was of a quiet disposition. He did not participate in the nighttime orgies of his comrades, who, despite the strictest supervision, had got themselves a mistress on the side – one for eight of them – nor in other pranks that went as far as blasphemy and the mockery of religion itself, only because the director demanded frequent attendance at church and the priest happened to be a bad one. But he was downcast. Ambition had been strongly awakened in him, but there was no activity or career before him. It would have been better for him not to be awakened! He listened to the professors getting excited at the podium, and remembered his former mentor, who had known how to speak clearly without getting excited. He heard lectures in chemistry and the philosophy of law, and profound professional analyses of all the subtleties of political science, and the universal history of mankind on such an enormous scale that in three years the professor managed only to give an introduction and to speak on the development of communes in some German cities; but all this remained as some sort of misshapen scraps in his head. Thanks to his natural intelligence, he simply felt that that was not how to teach, but how to teach – he did not know. And he often remembered Alexander Petrovich, and it made him so sad that he did not know where to turn for sorrow.

But youth has a future. The closer he came to graduation, the more his heart beat. He said to himself: "This is still not life, this is only the preparation for life: real life is in the service. The great deeds are there." And without even a glance at the beautiful corner that so struck every visiting guest, without paying respects to his parents' remains, following the pattern of all ambitious men, he raced off to Petersburg, where, as is well known, our ardent youth flock from all ends of Russia – to serve, to shine, to make careers, or simply to skim the surface of our colorless, ice-cold, delusive higher education. Andrei Ivanovich's ambition was, however, brought up short from the very beginning by his uncle, the actual state councillor Onufry Ivanovich. He announced that the chief thing is good handwriting, that and nothing else, and without it one can become neither a minister nor a state councillor, whereas Tentetnikov's handwriting was the sort of which people say: "A magpie wrote it with her claw, and not a man."

With great difficulty, and with the help of his uncle's connections, after spending two months studying calligraphy, he finally found a position as a copying clerk in some department. When he entered the big, bright room, all filled with writing gentlemen, sitting at lacquered desks, scratching with their quills, and tilting their heads to one side, and when he himself was seated and straightaway handed some document to copy – an extraordinarily strange feeling came over him. For a moment it seemed to him that he was at some primary school, starting to learn his ABCs over again, as if on account of some delinquency he had been transferred from the upper grade to the lowest. The gentlemen sitting around him seemed to him so like pupils. Some of them were reading novels, holding them between the big pages of the case in hand, pretending to be busy with it and at the same time giving a start each time a superior appeared. His schooldays suddenly stood before him as an irretrievably lost paradise. So lofty did his studies suddenly become compared with this petty writing occupation. How much higher that school preparation for the service now seemed to him than the service itself. And suddenly in his thoughts Alexander Petrovich stood before him as if alive – his wonderful mentor, incomparable with anyone else, ir-replaceable by anyone else – and tears suddenly poured in streams from his eyes. The room spun, the desks moved, the officials all mixed together, and he almost fell down in a momentary blackout. "No," he said to himself, recovering, "I'll set to work, however petty it seems at the start!" Harness-ing his heart and spirit, he resolved to serve on the example of the others.

Where will one not find pleasures? They also live in Peters-burg, despite its stern, somber appearance. A biting twenty below zero outside, a witch-blizzard shrieking like a desperate demon, pulling the collars of fur coats and greatcoats over heads, powdering men's mustaches and animals' muzzles, but friendly is the light in a window somewhere high up, perhaps even on the fourth floor; in a cozy room, by the light of modest stearin candles, to the hum of the samovar, a heart- and soul-warming conversation goes on, a bright page from an inspired Russian poet, such as God has bestowed upon His Russia, is being read, and a youth's young heart flutters so ardently and loftily, as never happens in any other lands, even under splendid southern skies.

Tentetnikov soon got accustomed to the service, only it became not the first thing or aim, as he had thought at the start, but something secondary. It served to organize his time, making him better cherish the remaining minutes. The uncle, the actual state councillor, was already beginning to think that something good would come of his nephew, when the nephew suddenly mucked things up. It must be said that among Andrei Ivanovich's friends there were two of what are known as disgruntled men. They were the sort of troublesomely strange characters who are unable to bear with equanimity not only injustice, but even anything that in their eyes looks like injustice. Basically kind, but disorderly in their actions, they were full of intolerance towards others. Their ardent talk and loftily indignant manner influenced him greatly. Arousing the nerves and the spirit of vexation in him, they made him notice all the trifles he had never even thought of paying attention to before. He suddenly took a dislike to Fyodor Fyodorovich Lenitsyn, the head of the department he worked in, a man of most agreeable appearance. He began to find myriads of faults in him, and came to hate him for having such a sugary expression when talking to a superior, and straightaway becoming all vinegar when addressing a subordinate. "I could forgive him," said Tentetnikov, "if the change in his face did not occur so quickly; but it's right there in front of my eyes, both sugar and vinegar at once!" After that he started noticing every step. It seemed to him that Fyodor Fyodorovich gave himself far too many airs, that he had all the ways of a minor official, to wit: making note of all those who did not come to congratulate him on festive occasions, even taking revenge on all those whose names were not found on the doorkeeper's list, and a host of other sinful accessories which neither a good nor a wicked man can do without. He felt a nervous loathing for him. Some evil spirit prompted him to do something unpleasant to Fyodor Fyodorovich. He sought it out with some special enjoyment, and he succeeded. Once he exchanged such words with him that the authorities declared he must either apologize or retire. He sent in his resignation. His uncle, the actual state councillor, came to him all frightened and beseeching.

"For Christ's sake! have mercy, Andrei Ivanovich, what are you doing? Leaving a career that has begun so profitably, only because the superior happens to be not so . . . What is this? If one looked at such things, there would be no one left in the service. Be reasonable, be reasonable! There's still time! Renounce your pride and your amour propre, go and talk with him!"

"That's not the point, dear uncle," said the nephew. "It's not hard for me to apologize, the more so as I am indeed to blame. He is my superior, and I should never have spoken to him in that way. But the point is this: you forget that I have a different service; I have three hundred peasant souls, my estate is in disorder, and the steward is a fool. It will be no great loss to the state if someone else sits in the office copying papers instead of me, but it will be a great loss if three hundred men don't pay their taxes. I am a landowner: the title is not a worthless one. If I take care to preserve, protect, and improve the lot of the people entrusted to me, and present the state with three hundred fit, sober, and industrious subjects – will my service be in any way worse than the service of some department chief Lenitsyn?"

The actual state councillor stood gaping in astonishment. He had not expected such a torrent of words. After a moment's thought, he began in the following vein:

"But all the same . . . all the same . . . why go perish yourself in the country? What sort of society is there among muzhiks? Here, after all, you can come across a general or a prince in the street. If you wish, you can walk past some handsome public buildings, or else go and look at the Neva, but there whatever comes along is either a muzhik or a wench. Why condemn yourself to ignorance for the rest of your life?"

So spoke his uncle, the actual state councillor. He himself had never once in his life walked any other street than the one that led to his place of service, where there were no handsome public buildings; he never noticed anyone he met, either general or prince; he had not the foggiest notion of the fancies that are the attraction of a capital for people greedy for license, and had never once in his life even been in a theater. He said all this solely in order to stir up the young man's ambition and work on his imagination. In this, however, he did not succeed: Tentetnikov stubbornly held his own. He had begun to weary of the departments and the capital. The countryside had begun to appear as a sort of haven of freedom, a nourisher of thoughts and intentions, the only path for useful activity. Some two weeks after this conversation, he was already in the vicinity of the places where his childhood had flown by. How it all started coming back to him, how his heart began to beat when he felt he was nearing his father's estate! He had already completely forgotten many places and gazed curiously, like a newcomer, at the beautiful views. When the road raced through a narrow ravine into the thick of a vast, overgrown forest, and he saw above, below, over, and under himself three-century-old oaks of enormous girth, mixed with silver firs, elms, and black poplars that overtopped the white, and when, to the question, "Whose forest?" he was told, "Tentetnikov's"; when, emerging from the forest, the road raced across meadows, past aspen groves, willows, and vines young and old, with a view of the distant mountains, and flew over bridges which in various places crossed one and the same river, leaving it now to the right, now to the left of him, and when, to the question, "Whose fields and water meadows?" he was answered, "Tentetnikov's"; when, after that, the road went uphill and over a level elevation past unharvested fields of wheat, rye, and oats on one side, and on the other past all the places he had just driven by, which all suddenly appeared in the picturesque distance, and when, gradually darkening, the road started to enter and then did enter under the shade of wide-spreading trees, scattered over a green carpet right up to the estate, and before him peasant cottages and red-roofed manor buildings began to flash; when the ardently pounding heart knew even without asking where it had come to – the constantly accumulating feelings finally burst out in almost these words: "Well, haven't I been a fool all this while? Destiny appointed me the owner of an earthly paradise, a prince, and I got myself enslaved as a scrivener in an office! After studying, being educated, enlightened, laying up quite a large store of information necessary precisely in order to direct people, to improve the whole region, to fulfill the manifold duties of a landowner as judge, manager, keeper of order, I entrusted this place to an ignorant steward! And instead of that chose what? – copying papers, which a cantonist who never went to any school can do incomparably better!" And once again Andrei Ivanovich Tentetnikov called himself a fool.

And meanwhile another spectacle awaited him. Having learned of the master's arrival, the population of the entire village gathered by the porch. Gay-colored kerchiefs, head-bands, scarfs, homespun coats, beards of all sorts – spade, shovel, wedge-shaped, red, blond, and white as silver – covered the whole square. The muzhiks boomed out: "Our provider, we've waited so long!" The women wailed: "Gold, the heart's silver!" Those who stood further away even fought in their zeal to press forward. A wobbly crone who looked like a dried pear crept between the others' legs, accosted him, clasped her hands, and shrieked: "Our little runny-nose, what a weakling you are! the cursed Germans have starved you out!" "Away with you, granny!" the spade, shovel, and wedge-shaped beards all shouted at her. "Watch where you're shoving, you old scraggy one!" Someone tacked on a little word, at which only a Russian peasant could keep from laughing. The master could not help himself and laughed, but nevertheless he was deeply touched in his soul. "So much love! and what for?" he thought to himself. "For never having seen them, for never concerning myself with them! I give my word that henceforth I will share all your labors and concerns with you! I'll do everything to help you become what you ought to be, what the good nature that is in you meant you to be, so that your love for me will not be in vain, so that I will indeed be your provider!"

And in fact Tentetnikov began managing and giving orders in earnest. He saw on the spot that the steward was an old woman and a fool, with all the qualities of a rotten steward – that is, he kept a careful account of the hens and the eggs, of the yarn and linen the women brought, but did not know a blessed thing about harvesting and sowing, and on top of that suspected the peasants of making attempts on his life. He threw out the fool steward and chose another to replace him, a perky one. He disregarded trifles and paid attention to the main things, reduced the corvée, decreased the number of days the muzhiks had to work for him, added more time for them to work for themselves, and thought that things would now go most excellently. He began to enter into everything himself, to appear in the fields, on the threshing floor, in the barns, at the mills, on the wharf where barges and flatboats were loaded and sent off.

"He's a quick-stepper, that he is!" the muzhiks started saying, and even scratched their heads, because from long-standing womanish management they had turned into a rather lazy lot. But this did not last long. The Russian muzhik is clever and intelligent: they soon understood that though the master was quick and wanted to take many things in hand, yet precisely how, in what way to take them in hand – of this he still knew nothing, he spoke somehow too literately and fancifully, puzzling for a muzhik and beyond his ability. As a result, while there was not really a total lack of comprehension between master and muzhik, they simply sang to different tunes, never able to produce the same note. Tentetnikov began to notice that everything turned out somehow worse on the master's land than on the muzhik's: the sowing came earlier, the sprouting later. Yet it seemed they worked well: he himself was there and even ordered a reward of a noggin of vodka for diligent work. The muzhiks had long had rye in the ear, oats swelling, millet bushing out, while his grain was still in the shoot and the ears had not yet begun to form. In short, the master began to notice that the muzhiks were simply cheating him, despite all his good turns. He made an attempt to reproach them, but received the following answer: "How can it be, your honor, that we haven't been zealous for the master's profit? You yourself were pleased to see how diligently we ploughed and sowed: you ordered us given a noggin of vodka each." What objection could he make to that? "But why has it turned out so badly now?" the master persisted. "Who knows! Must be worms gnawed it from below, and just look at this summer: no rain at all." But the master could see that worms had not gnawed the muzhiks' crops from below, and it rained somehow oddly, in strips: the muzhiks got it, while the master's fields did not get so much as a single drop. It was harder still for him to get along with the women. They asked so often to be excused from work, complaining about the heaviness of the corvée. How strange! He had abolished outright all bringing in of linen, berries, mushrooms, and nuts, and reduced the other tasks by half, thinking that the women would spend this time on housework, sewing, making clothes for their husbands, improving their kitchen gardens. Not a bit of it! Such idleness, fights, gossip, and all sorts of quarrels set in among the fair sex that the husbands kept coming to him with such words as: "Master, quiet down this demon of a woman! Just like some devil! she won't let me live!" Several times, with heavy heart, he wanted to introduce severity. But how could he be severe? The woman would come as such a woman, get into such shrieking, was so sick, so ailing, would wrap herself up in such poor, vile rags – God only knows where she got them. "Go, just leave my sight, God be with you!" poor Tentetnikov would say, after which he would have the pleasure of seeing how the sick woman, coming out, would start squabbling with a neighbor over some turnip and give her such a drubbing as even a healthy man would not be capable of. He decided to try and start some sort of school among them, but such nonsense came out of it that he even hung his head – it would be better not to think about it! All this significantly chilled his enthusiasm both for management and for acting as judge, and generally for all activity. He was present at the field work almost without noticing it: his thoughts were far away, his eyes searched for extraneous objects. During the mowing he did not watch the quick raising of sixty scythes at once, followed by the measured fall, with a faint sound, of rows of tall grass; instead he looked off to the side at some bend of the river, on the bank of which walked some red-nosed, red-legged stalker – a stork, of course, not a man; he watched the stork catch a fish and hold it crosswise in its beak, as if considering whether to swallow it or not, and at the same time looking intently up the river, where, some distance away, another stork could be seen who had not yet caught a fish, but was looking intently at the one who already had. During the harvest, he did not look at how the sheaves were piled in shocks, in crosses, or sometimes simply in heaps. He hardly cared whether the piling and stacking was done lazily or briskly. Eyes closed, face lifted up to the spacious sky, he allowed his nose to imbibe the scent of the fields and his ears to be struck by the voices of the songful populace of the air, when it comes from everywhere, heaven and earth, to join in one harmonious chorus with no discord among themselves. The quail throbs, the corncrake crakes in the grass, linnets warble and twitter as they fly from place to place, the trilling of the lark spills down an invisible stairway of air, and the whooping of cranes rushing in a line off to one side – just like the sounding of silver trumpets – comes from the emptiness of the resoundingly vibrant airy desert. If the field work was close to him, he was far away from it; if it was far away, his eyes sought out things that were close. And he was like the distracted schoolboy who, while looking into his book, sees only the snook his comrade is cocking at him at the same time. In the end he stopped going out to the field work altogether, dropped entirely all administering of justice and punishments, firmly ensconced himself inside, and even stopped receiving the steward with his reports.

From time to time a neighbor would stop by, a retired lieutenant of the hussars, a thoroughly smoke-saturated pipe smoker, or the firebrand colonel, a master and lover of talking about everything. But this, too, began to bore him. Their conversation began to seem to him somehow superficial; lively, adroit behavior, slappings on the knee, and other such casualness began to seem much too direct and overt to him. He decided to break off all his acquaintances and even did it quite abruptly. Namely, when that representative of all firebrand colonels, he who was most pleasant in all superficial conversations about everything, Barbar Nikolaych Vishnepokromov, came calling precisely in order to talk his fill, touching on politics, and philosophy, and literature, and morality, and even the state of England's finances, he sent word that he was not at home, and at the same time was so imprudent as to appear in the window. The guest's and host's eyes met. One, of course, grumbled "Brute!" through his teeth, while the other also sent after him something like a swine. Thus ended their acquaintance. After that no one came to see him. Total solitude installed itself in the house. The master got permanently into his dressing gown, giving his body over to inaction and his mind – to pondering a big work about Russia. How this work was being pondered, the reader has already seen. The day came and went, monotonous and colorless. It cannot be said, however, that there were not moments when he seemed to awaken from his sleep. When the mail brought newspapers, new books, and magazines, and in the press he came across the familiar name of a former schoolmate, who had already succeeded in some prominent post of the government service, or made a modest contribution to science and world knowledge, a secret, quiet sadness would come to his heart, and a doleful, wordlessly sad, quiet complaint at his own inactivity would involuntarily escape him. Then his life seemed revolting and vile to him. Before him his past schooldays rose up with extraordinary force and suddenly Alexander Petrovich stood before him as if alive . . . A flood of tears poured from his eyes, and his weeping continued for almost the whole day.

What was the meaning of this weeping? Was his aching soul thereby revealing the doleful mystery of its illness – that the lofty inner man who was beginning to be built in him had had no time to form and gain strength; that, not tried from early years in the struggle with failure, he had never attained the lofty ability to rise and gain strength from obstacles and barriers; that, having melted like heated metal, the wealth of great feelings had not been subjected to a final tempering, and now, lacking resilience, his will was powerless; that an extraordinary mentor had died too soon, and there was no longer anyone in the whole world capable of raising and holding up those forces rocked by eternal vacillation and that feeble will lacking in resilience – who could cry out in a live and rousing voice – cry out to his soul the rousing word: *forward!* – which the Russian man everywhere, at every level of rank, title, and occupation, yearns for?

Where is he who, in the native tongue of our Russian soul, could speak to us this all-powerful word: *forward*? who, knowing all the forces and qualities, and all the depths of our nature, could, by one magic gesture, point the Russian man towards a lofty life? With what words, with what love the grateful

Russian man would repay him! But century follows century, half a million loafers, sluggards, and sloths lie in deep slumber, and rarely is a man born in Russia who is capable of uttering it, this all-powerful word.

One circumstance, however, nearly roused Tentetnikov and nearly caused a turnabout in his character. Something resembling love occurred, but here, too, the matter somehow came to nothing. In the neighborhood, six miles from his estate, lived a general, who, as we have already seen, spoke not altogether favorably of Tentetnikov. The general lived like a general, was hospitable, liked his neighbors to come and pay their respects; he himself, naturally, paid no visits, spoke hoarsely, read books, and had a daughter, a strange, incomparable being, who could be regarded more as some fantastic vision than as a woman. It happens that a man sometimes sees such a thing in a dream, and afterwards he dwells on this dream all his life, reality is lost to him forever, and he is decidedly good for nothing anymore. Her name was Ulinka. Her upbringing had been somehow strange. She was brought up by an English governess who did not know a word of Russian. She had lost her mother while still a child. The father had no time. Anyway, loving his daughter to distraction, he would only have spoiled her. It is extraordinarily difficult to paint her portrait. This was something as alive as life itself. She was lovelier than any beauty; better than intelligent; trimmer and more ethereal than a classical woman. It was simply impossible to tell what country had set its stamp on her, because it was difficult to find such a profile and facial form anywhere, except perhaps on antique cameos. As a child brought up in freedom, everything in her was willful. Had anyone seen the sudden wrath all at once gather wrinkles on her beautiful brow, as she ardently disputed with her father, he would have thought she was a most capricious being. Yet she was wrathful only when she heard of some injustice or cruel act done to anyone. But how this wrath would suddenly vanish, if she saw misfortune overtake the one against whom she was wrathful, how she would suddenly throw him her purse, without reflecting on whether it was smart or stupid, or tear up her own dress for bandages if he were wounded! There was something impetuous in her. When she spoke, everything in her seemed to rush after her thought: the expression of her face, the expression of her speech, the movements of her hands, the very folds of her dress seemed to rush in the same direction, and it seemed as if she herself were about to fly off after her own words. Nothing in her was hidden. She would not have been afraid of displaying her thoughts before anyone, and no power could have forced her to be silent if she wished to speak. Her charming, peculiar gait, which belonged to her alone, was so dauntlessly free that everything inadvertently gave way to her. In her presence a bad man became somehow embarrassed and speechless, and a good one, even of the shyest sort, could get to talking with her as never with anyone in his life before, and – strange illusion! – from the first moments of the conversation it would seem to him that he had known her sometime and somewhere, that it had been in the days of some immemorial infancy, in his own home, on a gay evening, with joyful games amid a crowd of children, and after that for a long time he would remain somehow bored with sensible adulthood.

Andrei Ivanovich Tentetnikov could by no means have said how it happened that from the very first day he felt as if he had known her forever. An inexplicable new feeling entered his soul. His dull life became momentarily radiant. The dressing gown was abandoned for a while. He did not linger so long in bed, Mikhailo did not stand for so long holding the washbasin. The windows got opened in the rooms, and the owner of the picturesque estate would spend a long time strolling along the shady, winding paths of his garden, standing for hours before the enchanting views in the distance.

The general at first received Tentetnikov rather nicely and cordially; but they could not become completely close. Their

conversations always ended with an argument and some unpleasant feeling on both sides. The general did not like to be
contradicted or objected to, though at the same time he liked
to talk even about things of which he had no knowledge.
Tentetnikov, for his part, was also a ticklish man. However, a
great deal was forgiven the father for the daughter's sake, and
their peace held until some of the general's relatives came for a
visit, the countess Boldyrev and the princess Yuzyakin – one a
widow, the other an old maid, both erstwhile ladies-in-
waiting, both chatterboxes, both gossips, of not entirely
charming amiability, yet with important connections in Petersburg, and upon whom the general even fawned a bit. It seemed
to Tentetnikov that since the very day of their arrival, the
general had become somehow colder with him, scarcely
noticed him, and treated him as a mute extra or a clerk
employed for copying, the lowest sort. He called him now
"brother," now "my dear fellow," and once even addressed
him as "boy." Andrei Ivanovich exploded; the blood rushed to
his head. Teeth clenched and heart contrary, he nevertheless
had enough presence of mind to say in an unusually courteous
and gentle voice, as spots of color came to his cheeks and
everything seethed inside him:

"I must thank you, General, for your good disposition. By
your manner of address you invite me and summon me to the
most intimate friendship, obliging me, too, to address you
similarly. But allow me to observe that I am mindful of our
difference in age, which utterly rules out such familiarity
between us."

The general was embarrassed. Collecting his words and
thoughts, he began to say, albeit somewhat incoherently, that
the familiarity had not been used in that sense, that it was
sometimes permissible for an old man to address a young one
in such fashion (he did not mention a word about his rank).

Naturally, after that their acquaintance ceased, and love
ended at its very beginning. Out went the light that had

gleamed before him momentarily, and the gloom that followed became still gloomier. The sloth got into his dressing gown once again. Everything steered itself once again towards prostration and inaction. Nastiness and disorder came to the house. A broom stood for days on end in the middle of the room together with its sweepings. His trousers sometimes even stopped for a visit in the drawing room. On an elegant table in front of the sofa lay a pair of greasy suspenders, as a sort of treat for a guest, and so worthless and drowsy did his life become that not only did the house serfs stop respecting him, but even the barnyard chickens all but pecked him. He spent long hours impotently tracing doodles on paper – little houses, cottages, carts, troikas – or else writing "Dear Sir!" with an exclamation point in all sorts of hands and characters. And sometimes, all oblivious, the pen would trace of itself, without the master's knowledge, a little head with fine, sharp features, with light, combed-up tresses, falling from behind the comb in long, delicate curls, young bared arms, as if flying off somewhere – and with amazement the master saw emerging the portrait of her whose portrait no artist could paint. And he would feel still sadder after that, and, believing that there was no happiness on earth, would remain dull and unresponsive for the rest of the day.

Such were the circumstances of Andrei Ivanovich Tentetnikov. Suddenly one day, going up to the window in his usual way, with pipe and cup in hand, he noticed movement and a certain bustle in the yard. The scullion and the charwoman were running to open the gates, and in the gates horses appeared, exactly as they are sculpted or drawn on triumphal arches: a muzzle to the right, a muzzle to the left, a muzzle in the middle. Above them, on the box – a coachman and a lackey in a loose frock coat with a bandana tied around his waist. Behind them a gentleman in a peaked cap and an overcoat, wrapped in a rainbow-colored scarf. When the carriage wheeled around in front of the porch, it turned out to be nothing other than a light spring britzka. A gentleman of remarkably decent appearance jumped out onto the porch with the swiftness and adroitness of an almost military man.

Andrei Ivanovich quailed. He took him to be an official from the government. It must be mentioned that in his youth he had been mixed up in a certain unreasonable affair. Some philosophers from the hussars, plus a former student and a ruined gambler, started a sort of philanthropic society, under the supreme leadership of an old crook – a mason, a cardsharper, a drunkard, and a most eloquent man. The society was set up with the purpose of bestowing solid happiness on all mankind from the banks of the Thames to Kamchatka. The cashbox required was enormous, the donations collected from magnanimous members were unbelievable. Where it all went, only the supreme leader knew. Tentetnikov had been drawn into it by two friends who belonged to the class of disgruntled men – good men, but who, from the frequent toasting of science, enlightenment, and progress, eventually became certified drunkards. Tentetnikov soon thought better of it and left this circle. But the society had already managed to get entangled in some other actions, even not entirely befitting a nobleman, so that later they also had to deal with the police . . . And so it was no wonder that, though he had left and broken all relations with the benefactor of mankind, Tentetnikov nevertheless could not remain at peace. His conscience was somewhat uneasy. Not without fear did he now watch the door opening.

His fear, however, passed suddenly, as the visitor made his bows with unbelievable adroitness, keeping his head slightly inclined to one side in a respectful attitude. In brief but definite words he explained that he had long been traveling over Russia, urged both by necessity and by inquisitiveness; that our state abounds in remarkable objects, to say nothing of the beauty of places, the abundance of industries, and the diversity of soils; that he was attracted by the picturesque setting of his estate; that nevertheless, notwithstanding the picturesqueness of the setting, he would not have ventured to trouble him by his inopportune visit, if something had not happened to his britzka which called for a helping hand from blacksmiths and artisans; that for all that, nevertheless, even if nothing had happened to his britzka, he would have been unable to deny himself the pleasure of personally paying his respects.

Having finished his speech, the visitor, with charming agreeableness, scraped with his foot, and, despite the plumpness of his body, straightaway made a little leap backwards with the lightness of a rubber ball.

Andrei Ivanovich thought that this must be some inquisitive scholar and professor, who traveled over Russia with the purpose of collecting some sort of plants or even minerals. He expressed all possible readiness to be of assistance; offered his artisans, wheelwrights, and blacksmiths to repair the britzka; begged him to make himself at home; seated his courteous visitor in a big Voltaire armchair, and prepared himself to listen to him talk, doubtless on subjects of learning and natural science.

The visitor, however, touched more upon events of the inner world. He started speaking about the adversities of fate; likened his life to a ship on the high seas, driven about by winds from every quarter; mentioned that he had had to change places and posts many times, that he had suffered much for the truth, that even his very life had more than once been in danger from enemies, and there was much else he said which let Tentetnikov see that his visitor was rather a practical man. In conclusion to it all he blew his nose into a white cambric handkerchief, so loudly that Andrei Ivanovich had never heard the like of it. Sometimes in an orchestra there is one rascally trumpet which, when it strikes up, seems to quack not in the orchestra but in one's own ear. Exactly the same noise resounded in the awakened rooms of the dozing house, and was immediately followed by the fragrance of eau de cologne,

invisibly diffused by an adroit shake of the cambric handkerchief.

The reader has perhaps already guessed that the visitor was
none other than our respected, long-abandoned Pavel Ivanovich Chichikov. He had aged slightly: one could see that the
time had not been without storms and anxieties for him. It
seemed as if the very tailcoat on him had aged slightly, and that
the britzka, and the coachman, and the servant, and the horses,
and the harness were all as if a bit more scuffed and worn. It
seemed as if the finances themselves were not in an enviable
state. But the expression of his face, the decency, the manners
had remained the same. He had even become as if still more
agreeable in his movements and ways, still more deftly tucked
his feet under when sitting in an armchair; there was still more
softness in the enunciation of his speech, more prudent moderation in his words and expressions, more skill in his comportment, and more tact in everything. Whiter and cleaner
than snow were his collar and shirtfront, and though he had
only just come from the road, there was not a bit of fluff on his
tailcoat – fit even for a party! His cheeks and chin were so
clean-shaven that only a blind man could fail to admire their
pleasant prominence and roundness.

In the house a transformation took place. Half of it, hitherto
abiding in blindness, with nailed shutters, suddenly recovered
its sight and lit up. Luggage began to be carried in from the
britzka. Everything began to settle itself in the lighted rooms,
and soon it all acquired the following look: the room that was
to be the bedroom accommodated the things necessary for the
evening toilet; the room that was to be the study . . . But first of
all it should be known that there were three tables in this room:
one a writing table in front of the sofa, the second a card table
between the windows by the wall, the third a corner table in
the corner between the door to the bedroom and the door to a
large, uninhabited room filled with disabled furniture. This
corner table accommodated the clothing taken from the trunk

– namely, trousers to go with a tailcoat, trousers to go with a frock coat, gray trousers, two velvet waistcoats and two of satin, a frock coat, and two tailcoats. (The white piqué waistcoats and summer trousers joined the linen in the chest of drawers.) All of this was stacked up in a little pyramid and covered with a silk handkerchief. In another corner, between the door and the window, boots were lined up side by side: boots that were not quite new, boots that were quite new, boots with new uppers, and patent leather shoes. These, too, were modestly curtained off by a silk handkerchief, as if they were not there. On the table between the two windows the little chest found a place for itself. On the writing table in front of the sofa – a briefcase, a bottle of eau de cologne, sealing wax, toothbrushes, a new calendar, and a couple of novels, both second volumes. The clean linen was put into a chest of drawers that was already in the room; the linen that was to go to the washerwoman was tied in a bundle and shoved under the bed. The trunk, once it was unpacked, was also shoved under the bed. The sword, too, found its place in the bedroom, hanging on a nail not far from the bed. Both rooms acquired a look of extraordinary cleanness and neatness. Not a scrap, not a speck, not a bit of litter. The very air became somehow ennobled. In it there was established the pleasant smell of a healthy, fresh man, who does not wear his linen long, goes to the bathhouse, and wipes himself with a wet sponge on Sundays. In a vestibule, the smell of the servant Petrushka first presumed to establish itself, but Petrushka was promptly relocated to the kitchen where he belonged.

For the first few days Andrei Ivanovich feared for his independence, lest his guest somehow bind him, hinder him with some changes in his way of life, and the order of his day, so happily established, be violated – but his fears were in vain. Our Pavel Ivanovich showed an extraordinary flexibility in adapting to everything. He approved of the philosophical unhurriedness of his host, saying that it promised a hundred-year life. About solitude he expressed himself rather felicitously – namely, that it nursed great thoughts in a man. Having looked at the library and spoken with great praise of books in general, he observed that they save a man from idleness. In short, he let fall few words, but significant. In his actions, he acted still more appropriately. He came on time, and he left on time; he did not embarrass his host with questions during the hours of his taciturnity; with pleasure he would play chess with him, with pleasure he would be silent. While the one was sending up curly clouds of pipe smoke, the other, not a pipe smoker, nevertheless invented a corresponding activity: he would, for instance, take from his pocket a silver niello snuff-box and, placing it between two fingers of his left hand, spin it quickly with a finger of the right, just as the earthly sphere spins on its axis, or else he would simply drum on the snuffbox with his fingers, whistling some tune or other. In short, he did not hinder his host in any way. "For the first time I see a man one can get along with," Tentetnikov said to himself. "Generally we lack this art. There are plenty of people among us who are intelligent, and educated, and kind, but people who are constantly agreeable, people of a constantly even temper, people with whom one can live for ages without quarreling – I don't know that we can find many such people! Here is the first, the only man I've seen!" Such was Tentetnikov's opinion of his guest.

Chichikov, for his part, was very glad to have settled for a while with such a peaceful and placid host. He was sick of the gypsy life. To have a bit of rest, at least for a month, on a wonderful estate, in view of the fields and the approaching spring, was useful even in the hemorrhoidal respect. It would have been hard to find a more reposeful little corner. Spring adorned it with an unutterable beauty. What brightness of green! What freshness of air! What birdcalls in the garden! Paradise, mirth, and exultant rejoicing in everything. The countryside resounded and sang as if newborn.

Chichikov walked a lot. Sometimes he directed his steps over the flat top of the heights, with a view of the valleys spreading out below, where flooding rivers left big lakes everywhere; or else he would go into the ravines, where the trees, barely beginning to be adorned with leaves, were laden with birds' nests – and be deafened by the cawing of crows, the chatter of jackdaws, and the croaking of rooks that darkened the sky with their crisscross flight; or else he went down to the water meadows and burst dams, to watch the water rush with a deafening noise and fall upon the wheels of a mill; or else he made his way further to the pier, from which, borne along by the current, the first boats rushed, laden with peas, oats, barley, and wheat; or he set out for the first spring work in the fields, to watch the freshly ploughed furrow cutting a black stripe through the green, or the deft sower casting handfuls of seed evenly, accurately, not letting a single seed fall to one side or the other. He had discussions with the steward, the muzhiks, the miller, talking of what and of how, and of whether the harvest would be good, and how the ploughing was going, and how much grain they sell, and what they charged for grinding flour in the spring and fall, and what was the name of each muzhik, and who was related to whom, and where he had bought his cow, and what he fed his sow on – in short, everything. He also found out how many muzhiks had died. Not many, it turned out. Being an intelligent man, he noticed at once that Andrei Ivanovich's estate was not in good shape. Everywhere there was negligence, carelessness, theft, and not a little drunkenness. And mentally he said to himself: "What a brute Tentetnikov is, though! To so neglect an estate that could bring in at least fifty thousand a year!" And, unable to restrain his righteous indignation, he kept repeating: "Decidedly a brute!" More than once in the middle of these walks the thought occurred to him of himself becoming someday – that is, of course, not now but later on, when the main business was taken care of, and the means were in hand – of himself becoming the peaceful owner of such an estate. Here he usually pictured a young mistress, a fresh, fair-skinned wench, perhaps even of merchant class, though nonetheless educated and brought up like a gentlewoman – so that she also understood music, for, while music is, of course, not the main thing, still, since that is the custom, why go against the general opinion? He also pictured the younger generation that was to perpetuate the name of the Chichikovs: a frolicsome lad and a beautiful daughter, or even two boys, two or even three girls, so that everyone would know that he had indeed lived and existed, and had not merely passed over the earth like some shadow or ghost – so that there would be no shame before the fatherland. He even pictured that a certain addition to his rank would not be amiss: state councillor, for instance, is a venerable and respectable rank ... And much came into his head of the sort that so often takes a man away from the dull present moment, frets him, teases him, stirs him, and gives him pleasure even when he himself is sure that it will never come true.

Pavel Ivanovich's servants also liked the estate. Like him, they made themselves at home there. Petrushka very soon made friends with the butler Grigory, though at first they both put on airs and blustered before each other insufferably. Petrushka threw dust in Grigory's eyes by saying that he had been in Kostroma, Yaroslavl, Nizhni Novgorod, and even Moscow; Grigory immediately pulled him up short with Petersburg, where Petrushka had never been. The latter tried to rise and get his own back with the considerable remoteness of the places he had been; but Grigory named a place for him such as could not be found on any map, and reckoned it was over twenty thousand miles away, so that Petrushka stood like an owl, gaping, and was immediately laughed at by all the servants. However, matters ended between them in the closest friendship: bald Uncle Pimen kept a well-known pot-house at the end of the village, called "Akulka"; in this establishment they could be seen at all hours of the day. There they became fast friends, or what is known among the people as – pot-house fixtures.

Selifan took a different sort of bait. Every evening in the village songs were sung, and spring round dances twined and untwined. Trim, well-built wenches, such as can hardly be found elsewhere, made him stand gawking for several hours. It was hard to say which one was better: they were all white-bosomed, white-necked, all with eyes like turnips, languishing, strutting like peacocks, with braids down to their waists. When, holding white hands in his own, he slowly moved in a circle with them, or came towards them in a wall with the other lads, while the hotly glowing evening died out, and the surrounding neighborhood slowly faded, and from away across the river came the faithful echo of an inevitably sad tune – he did not know himself what was happening to him. Long afterwards, in sleep or in waking, at dawn and at dusk, he kept imagining his hands holding those white hands and moving with them in a round dance. With a wave of the hand he would say: "Cursed wenches!"

Chichikov's horses also liked their new abode. The shaft horse and the chestnut outrunner called Assessor, and that same dapple-gray which Selifan referred to as "a scoundrel of a horse," found their stay at Tentetnikov's far from dull, the oats of excellent quality, and the layout of the stables uncommonly convenient. Each stable was partitioned off, yet over the partitions one could see the other horses, so that if any of them, even the furthest off, suddenly got a notion to start whinnying, it was possible to respond in kind straightaway.

In short, everyone settled as if into their own home. The reader may be astonished that Chichikov had so far not made a peep about the notorious souls. Perish the thought! Pavel Ivanovich had become very cautious with regard to the subject. Even if he had been dealing with perfect fools, he would not have started suddenly on it. And Tentetnikov, after all, reads books, philosophizes, tries to explain to himself the various reasons for everything – why and how... "No, devil take him! maybe I should start from the other end?" So thought Chichikov. Chatting frequently with the servants, he found out from them, among other things, that the master once used to visit his neighbor the general quite often, that there was a young miss at the general's, that the master had been sweet on the young miss, and the young miss on the master, too... but then suddenly they had a falling out over something and parted. He himself noticed that Andrei Ivanovich kept drawing some sort of heads with pencil or pen, all looking the same. Once, after dinner, spinning the silver snuffbox on its axis with his finger, as usual, he spoke thus:

"You have everything, Andrei Ivanovich; only one thing is missing."

"What is that?" the other responded, letting out curls of smoke.

"A life's companion," said Chichikov.

No reply came from Andrei Ivanovich. And with that the conversation ended.

Chichikov was not embarrassed, he chose another moment, this time just before supper, and while talking about one thing and another, said suddenly:

"But really, Andrei Ivanovich, it wouldn't do you any harm to get married."

Not a word of reply came from Tentetnikov, as if the very mention of the subject was disagreeable to him.

Chichikov was not embarrassed. For the third time he chose a moment, this time after supper, and spoke thus:

"But all the same, whichever way I turn your circumstances, I see that you must get married: you'll fall into hypochondria."

Whether it was that Chichikov's words this time were so convincing, or that Andrei Ivanovich's mood was somehow especially inclined to frankness, he sighed and said, sending up smoke from his pipe: "For all things one needs to be born lucky, Pavel Ivanovich," and he told everything as it had been, the whole story of his acquaintance with the general and its breakup.

As Chichikov listened, word by word, to the whole affair and saw that because of one word such an incident had occurred, he was dumbfounded. For several minutes he looked intently into Tentetnikov's eyes and concluded: "Why, he's simply a perfect fool!"

"Andrei Ivanovich, for pity's sake!" he said, taking both his hands. "Where's the insult? what's insulting in one familiar word?"

"There's nothing insulting in the word itself," said Tentetnikov, "but the sense of the word, the voice in which it was uttered, that's where the insult lies. The word means: 'Remember, you're trash; I receive you only because there's no one better, but if some Princess Yuzyakin comes – you know your place, you stand by the door.' That's what it means!"

As he said this, the placid and meek Andrei Ivanovich flashed his eyes, and in his voice the irritation of offended feelings could be heard.

"But even if that is the sense of it – what matter?" said Chichikov.

"What?" said Tentetnikov, looking intently into Chichikov's eyes. "You want me to continue visiting him after such an action?"

"But what sort of action is that? It's not an action at all!" said Chichikov.

"What a strange man this Chichikov is!" Tentetnikov thought to himself.

"What a strange man this Tentetnikov is!" Chichikov thought to himself.

"It's not an action, Andrei Ivanovich. It's simply a general's habit: they call everyone 'boy.' And, incidentally, why not allow it in a venerable, respectable man?"

"That's another matter," said Tentetnikov. "If he were an old man, a poor man, not proud, not conceited, not a general, I would allow him to address me that way and even take it respectfully."

"He's an utter fool!" Chichikov thought to himself. "To allow it to a ragamuffin, and not to a general!" And, following this reflection, he objected to him aloud, thus:

"Very well, suppose he did insult you, but you also got even with him; he you, and you him. But to part forever on account of a trifle – for pity's sake, that's beyond anything! Why abandon an affair that's just begun? Once the goal has been chosen, one must push one's way through. No point in looking at a man who spits! Men are always spitting; you won't find anyone in the whole world who doesn't spit."

Tentetnikov was completely taken aback by these words; dumbfounded, he stared into Pavel Ivanovich's eyes, thinking to himself: "A most strange man, though, this Chichikov!"

"What an odd duck, though, this Tentetnikov!" Chichikov thought meanwhile.

"Allow me to do something about this matter," he said aloud. "I could go to His Excellency and explain that on your part it occurred owing to misunderstanding, youth, an ignorance of men and the world."

"I have no intention of groveling before him!" Tentetnikov said strongly.

"God forbid you should grovel!" said Chichikov, crossing himself. "To influence with a word of admonition, like a sensible mediator, yes, but to grovel . . . Excuse me, Andrei Ivanovich, for my good will and devotion, I never expected that you would take my words in such an offensive sense!"

"Forgive me, Pavel Ivanovich, I am to blame!" Tentetnikov said, touched, and seizing both his hands in gratitude. "Your kind sympathy is precious to me, I swear! But let's drop this conversation, let's never speak of it again!"

"In that case I'll simply go to the general without any reason," said Chichikov.

"What for?" asked Tentetnikov, looking at Chichikov in bewilderment.

"To pay my respects," said Chichikov.

"What a strange man this Chichikov is!" thought Tentetnikov.

"What a strange man this Tentetnikov is!" thought Chichikov.

"Since my britzka," said Chichikov, "has not yet attained the proper condition, allow me to take your coach. I'll go and visit him tomorrow at around ten o'clock or so."

"Good gracious, what a request! You are full master, choose any carriage you like, everything's at your disposal."

They said good night and went to bed, not without reflecting on each other's strangeness.

An odd thing, however: the next day, when Chichikov's horses were ready, and he leaped into the carriage with the ease of an almost military man, dressed in a new tailcoat, a white tie and waistcoat, and drove off to pay his respects to the general, Tentetnikov felt an agitation in his soul such as he had not experienced for a long time. All the rusty and drowsy course of his thoughts turned into an actively troubled one. A nervous excitement came over all the feelings of the sloth who hitherto had been sunk in careless indolence. Now he sat down on the sofa, now he went to the window, now he would take up a book, now he wanted to think – futile wanting! – thought refused to come into his head. Now he attempted not to think about anything – futile attempt! – scraps of something resembling thoughts, odds and ends of thoughts, kept creeping and pecking into his head from everywhere. "A strange state!" he said and moved to the window to gaze at the road cutting through the grove, at the end of which the clouds of dust raised by the departing carriage had not yet had time to settle. But let us leave Tentetnikov and follow Chichikov.

CHAPTER TWO

IN A LITTLE over half an hour the horses carried Chichikov across the six-mile space – first through the grove, then through wheat fields already beginning to green amid the freshly ploughed earth, then over the skirts of the hills, from which views of the distance opened every minute – and along a wide avenue of spreading lindens leading to the general's estate. The avenue of lindens turned into an avenue of poplars, fenced at the base with wicker boxes, and ran up to wrought-iron gates through which appeared the splendidly ornate carved façade of the general's house, resting on eight columns with Corinthian capitals. Everywhere there was a smell of oil paint, with which everything was renewed, allowing nothing to get old. The yard was as clean as parquet. Having rolled up to the front entrance, Chichikov respectfully jumped off onto the porch, asked to be announced, and was introduced directly into the general's study.

The general struck him with his majestic appearance. He was, at that moment, dressed in a raspberry satin dressing gown. An open look, a manly face, grizzled side-whiskers and a big mustache, hair cut short and even shaved at the nape, a thick, broad neck, in three stories, as they say, or three folds with a crease across the middle, the voice a bass with some huskiness, the movements those of a general. Like all of us sinners, General Betrishchev was endowed with many virtues and many defects. Both the one and the other were scattered through him in a sort of picturesque disorder. Self-sacrifice, magnanimity in decisive moments, courage, intelligence – and with all that, a generous mixture of self-love, ambition, vanity, petty personal ticklishness, and a good many of those things which a man simply cannot do without. He disliked all those who got ahead of him in the service, spoke of them caustically, in pointed, sardonic epigrams. Most of it hit at a former colleague, whom he considered his inferior in intelligence and abilities, but who had nevertheless outstripped him and was already the governor-general of two provinces, and, as if by design, of the very ones in which his own estates were located, so that he found himself as if dependent on him. In revenge, he derided him at every opportunity, criticized his every directive, and looked upon all his measures and actions as the height of folly. Despite his good heart, the general was given to mockery. Broadly speaking, he liked being first, liked incense, liked to shine and display his intelligence, liked knowing things that others did not know, and did not like those who knew something he did not know. Brought up with a half-foreign upbringing, he wanted at the same time to play the role of a Russian squire. With such unevenness of character, with such big, striking contrasts, he was inevitably bound to meet with a heap of troubles in the service, as a result of which he took his retirement, accusing some enemy party of everything and not having enough magnanimity to blame himself for any of it. In retirement he preserved the same picturesque, majestic bearing. In a frock coat, a tailcoat, or a dressing gown – he was the same. From his voice to his least gesture, everything in him was imperious, commanding, inspiring, if not respect, then at least timidity in the lower ranks.

Chichikov felt both the one and the other: both respect and timidity. Inclining his head respectfully to one side, he began thus:

"I felt it my duty to introduce myself to Your Excellency. Nursing the greatest respect for the men of valor who have saved the fatherland on the field of battle, I felt it my duty to introduce myself personally to Your Excellency."

The general obviously did not dislike this sort of assault. With a rather gracious motion of his head, he said:

"Very glad to meet you. Pray be seated. Where did you serve?"

"My career in the service," said Chichikov, sitting down not in the center of the armchair, but obliquely, and grasping the armrest with his hand, "began in the treasury department, Your Excellency; and the further course of same was pursued in various places: I was in the civil courts, on a building commission, and in customs. My life may be likened to a ship amidst the waves, Your Excellency. I grew up, one might say, on patience, nursed by patience, swaddled by patience, and am myself, so to speak, nothing but patience. And how much I have suffered from enemies no words or colors can tell. And now, in the evening, so to speak, of my life, I am searching for a little corner in which to pass the rest of my days. And I am staying meanwhile with a near neighbor of Your Excellency's . . . "

"Who is that?"

"Tentetnikov, Your Excellency."

The general winced.

"He greatly regrets, Your Excellency, his not having paid due respect . . . "

"To what?"

"To Your Excellency's merits. Words fail him. He says: 'If only I could somehow . . . because really,' he says, 'I know how to value the men who have saved the fatherland,' he says."

"Good gracious, what's the matter with him? . . . Why, I'm not angry!" the softened general said. "In my heart I sincerely loved him, and I'm sure that in time he will become a most useful man."

"Quite correctly put, Your Excellency, if you please, a most useful man, with a gift for eloquence, and wielding a skillful pen."

"But he writes trifles, I suppose, some sort of verses?"

"No, Your Excellency, not trifles . . . "

"What, then?"

"He writes . . . history, Your Excellency."

"History! The history of what?"

"The history . . . " here Chichikov paused, and either because there was a general sitting before him, or simply to give more importance to the subject, added: " . . . the history of generals, Your Excellency."

"How, of generals? of what generals?"

"Of generals in general, Your Excellency, overall . . . that is, as a matter of fact, the generals of the fatherland," Chichikov said, and thought to himself: "What drivel I'm pouring out!"

"Excuse me, I don't quite understand . . . would that mean a history of some period, or separate biographies, and is it all of them, or only those who took part in the year 'twelve?"

"That's right, Your Excellency, those who took part in the year 'twelve!" Having said which, he thought to himself: "Strike me dead if I understand."

"But why doesn't he come to me, then? I could gather quite a bit of curious material for him."

"He doesn't dare, Your Excellency."

"What nonsense! Because of some trifling word . . . But I'm not that sort of man at all. I might even be ready to call on him myself."

"He wouldn't allow that, he'll come to you," Chichikov said, and at the same time thought to himself: "The generals came in nicely; and yet my tongue just stupidly blurted it out."

A rustling was heard in the study. The walnut door of a carved wardrobe opened by itself. On the other side of the open door, her wonderful hand grasping the door handle, a live little figure appeared. If a transparent painting, lit from behind, were suddenly to shine in a dark room, it would not be so striking as this little figure radiant with life appearing as if in order to light up the room. It seemed as though along with her a ray of sunlight flew into the room, suddenly illumining its ceiling, its moldings, and its dark corners. She seemed to be of glorious height. This was an illusion; it came from her extraordinary slenderness and the harmonious relation of all the parts of her body, from head to little toe. The solid–color dress that was thrown on her was thrown on with such taste that it seemed as if all the seamstresses of the capital had held a council among themselves on how best to adorn her. But it only seemed so. She made her own dresses, haphazardly; gathered an uncut piece of fabric in two or three places, and it clung and arranged itself around her in such folds as a sculptor could at once transfer to marble, and the young ladies who dressed fashionably all looked like some sort of motley hens beside her. Though her face was almost familiar to Chichikov from Andrei Ivanovich's drawings, he looked at her as if stunned, and only later, having come to his senses, did he notice that she lacked something very essential – namely, plumpness.

"Allow me to introduce my naughty little girl!" said the general, addressing Chichikov. "However, I still don't know your name."

"Though why should people know the name of a man not distinguished by deeds of valor?" said Chichikov.

"Still, however, one must know . . . "

"Pavel Ivanovich, Your Excellency," said Chichikov, inclining his head slightly to one side.

"Ulinka! Pavel Ivanovich has just told me the most interesting news. Our neighbor Tentetnikov is not at all as stupid a man as we thought. He's occupied with something rather important: the history of the generals of the year 'twelve."

Ulinka suddenly seemed to flush and became animated.

"But who thought he was a stupid man?" she said quickly. "Maybe only Vishnepokromov could think that, whom you believe, papa, though he's both empty and mean."

"Why mean? He's a bit empty, it's true," said the general.

"He's a bit base, and a bit vile, not just a bit empty," Ulinka picked up promptly. "Whoever offends his own brothers like that, and throws his sister out of the house, is a vile man . . . "

"But that's just talk."

"There wouldn't be talk for no reason. You, father, have the kindliest soul and a rare heart, but the way you act could make people think quite otherwise about you. You'll receive a man who you yourself know is bad, only because he's a fancy talker and an expert at twining himself around you."

"But, dear heart! I couldn't really throw him out," said the general.

"Don't throw him out, then, but don't love him either!"

"Not so, Your Excellency," Chichikov said to Ulinka, inclining his head slightly, with a pleasant smile. "According to Christianity, it's precisely them that we ought to love."

And, straightaway turning to the general, he said with a smile, this time a somewhat coy one:

"If you please, Your Excellency, have you ever heard it said, in this regard – 'love us black, anyone can love us white'?"

"No, I haven't."

"It's a most singular anecdote," said Chichikov, with a coy smile. "There was, Your Excellency, on the estate of Prince Gukzovsky, whom Your Excellency is no doubt pleased to know . . . "

"I don't."

"There was a steward, Your Excellency, of German stock, a young man. He had to go to town for supplying recruits and on other occasions, and, of course, to grease the palms of the court clerks." Here Chichikov, narrowing one eye, showed with his face how court clerks' palms are greased. "However, they also liked him and used to wine and dine him. So once, at dinner with them, he said: 'You know, gentlemen, one day you must also visit me on the prince's estate.' They said: 'We will.' Soon after that the court happened to go to investigate a case that occurred on the domains of Count Trekhmetyev, whom Your Excellency is no doubt also pleased to know."

"I don't."

"They made no investigation properly speaking, but the whole court turned off at the steward's place, to visit the count's old steward, and for three days and nights they played cards nonstop. The samovar and punch, naturally, never left the table. The old man got sick of them. In order to get rid of them somehow, he says: 'Why don't you gentlemen go and visit the prince's steward, the German: he's not far from here, and he's expecting you.' 'Why not, in fact,' they say, and half-drunk, unshaven, and sleepy, just as they were, they got into their carts and went to the German . . . And the German, be it known to Your Excellency, had just gotten married at that time. He married a boarding-school girl, a genteel young thing" (Chichikov expressed genteelness with his face). "The two of them are sitting over their tea, not suspecting anything, when suddenly the doors open and the throng barges in."

"I can imagine – a pretty sight!" the general said, laughing.

"The steward was simply dumbfounded. 'What can I do for you?' he says. 'Ah!' they said, 'so that's how you are!' And all at once, with these words, there is a change of looks and physiognomies . . . 'To business! How much liquor is distilled on the premises? Show us the books!' The man hems and haws. 'Hey, witnesses!' They took him, bound him, dragged him to town, and the German actually spent a year and a half in jail."

"Well, now!" said the general.

Ulinka clasped her hands.

"The wife went around soliciting!" Chichikov continued. "But what can a young, inexperienced woman do? Luckily there happened to be some good people who advised her to settle peaceably. He got off with two thousand and dinner for all. And at the dinner, when they all got quite merry, and he as well, they said to him: 'Aren't you ashamed to have treated us the way you did? You'd like to see us always neat and shaven and in tailcoats. No, *you must love us black, anyone can love us white.*'"

The general burst out laughing; Ulinka groaned painfully.

"I don't understand how you can laugh, papa!" she said quickly. Wrath darkened her beautiful brow... "A most dishonorable act, for which I don't know where they all ought to be sent..."

"My dear, I'm not justifying them in the least," said the general, "but what can I do if it's so funny? How did it go: 'Love us white...'?"

"Black, Your Excellency," Chichikov picked up.

"'Love us black, anyone can love us white.' Ha, ha, ha, ha!"

And the general's body began to heave with laughter. Those shoulders that had once borne thick epaulettes were shaking as if even now they bore thick epaulettes.

Chichikov also delivered himself of an interjection of laughter, but, out of respect for the general, he launched it with the letter *e*: "Heh, heh, heh, heh, heh!" And his body, too, began to heave with laughter, though his shoulders did not shake, having never borne thick epaulettes.

"I can picture what a sight that unshaven court was!" the general said, still laughing.

"Yes, Your Excellency, in any event it was... nonstop... a three-day vigil – the same as fasting: they wasted away, simply wasted away!" said Chichikov, still laughing.

Ulinka sank into an armchair and covered her beautiful eyes with her hand; as if vexed that there was no one to share her indignation, she said:

"I don't know, it's just that I'm so vexed."

Indeed, of extraordinarily strange contrast were the feelings born in the hearts of the three conversing people. One found amusing the awkward ineptitude of the German. Another found amusing the amusing way the crooks wriggled out of it. The third was saddened that an unjust act had been committed with impunity. There only lacked a fourth to ponder precisely such words as could produce laughter in one and sadness in another. What does it mean, however, that even in his fall, the perishing dirty man demands to be loved? Is it an animal instinct? or the faint cry of the soul smothered under the heavy burden of base passions, still trying to break through the hardening crust of abominations, still crying: "Save me, brother!" There lacked a fourth for whom the most painful thing of all would be his brother's perishing soul.

"I don't know," Ulinka said, taking her hand away from her face, "it's that I'm just so vexed."

"Only please don't be angry with us," said the general. "We're not to blame for anything. Give me a kiss and go to your room, because I'll be dressing for dinner now. You, my boy," the general said, suddenly turning to Chichikov, "will be dining with me?"

"If Your Excellency . . . "

"No ceremonies. There's cabbage soup."

Chichikov inclined his head agreeably, and when he raised it again, he no longer saw Ulinka. She had vanished. Instead of her there stood, in bushy mustache and side-whiskers, a giant of a valet, with a silver pitcher and basin in his hands.

"You'll allow me to dress in your presence, eh, my boy?" said the general, throwing off his dressing gown and rolling up the sleeves of his shirt on his mighty arms.

"Good gracious, not only to dress, you may do anything Your Excellency pleases in my presence," said Chichikov.

The general began to wash, splashing and snorting like a duck. Soapy water flew in all directions.

"How did it go?" he said, wiping his fat neck on all sides, " 'love us white . . . '?"

"Black, Your Excellency."

" 'Love us black, anyone can love us white.' Very, very good!"

Chichikov was in extraordinarily high spirits; he felt some sort of inspiration.

"Your Excellency!" he said.

"What?" said the general.

"There's another story."

"What sort?"

"Also an amusing story, only I don't find it amusing. Even if Your Excellency..."

"How so?"

"Here's how, Your Excellency!..." At this point Chichikov looked around and, seeing that the valet with the basin had left, began thus: "I have an uncle, a decrepit old man. He owns three hundred souls and has no heirs except me. He himself, being decrepit, cannot manage the estate, yet he won't hand it over to me. And he gives such a strange reason: 'I don't know my nephew,' he says, 'maybe he's a spendthrift. Let him first prove to me that he's a reliable man, let him first acquire three hundred souls himself, then I'll give him my three hundred souls as well.'"

"What a fool!"

"Quite a correct observation, if you please, Your Excellency. But imagine my position now..." Here Chichikov, lowering his voice, began speaking as if in secret: "He has a housekeeper in his house, Your Excellency, and she has children. Just you watch, everything will go to them."

"The stupid old man's gone dotty, that's all," said the general. "Only I don't see how I can be of use to you."

"Here's what I've thought up. Right now, before the new census lists have been turned in, the owners of big estates may have, along with their living souls, also some that are departed and dead... So that if, for instance, Your Excellency were to hand them over to me as if they were alive, with a deed of purchase, I could then present this deed to the old man, and he, dodge as he may, will have to give me my inheritance."

Here the general burst into such laughter as hardly a man has ever laughed: he collapsed just as he was into his armchair; he threw his head back and nearly choked. The whole house became alarmed. The valet appeared. The daughter came running in, frightened.

"Papa, what's happened to you?"

"Nothing, my dear. Ha, ha, ha! Go to your room, we'll come to dinner presently. Ha, ha, ha!"

And, having run out of breath several times, the general's guffaw would burst out with renewed force, ringing throughout the general's high-ceilinged, resonant apartments from the front hall to the last room.

Chichikov waited worriedly for this extraordinary laughter to end.

"Well, brother, excuse me: the devil himself got you to pull such a trick. Ha, ha, ha! To give the old man a treat, to slip him the dead ones! Ha, ha, ha, ha! And the uncle, the uncle! Made such a fool of! Ha, ha, ha, ha!"

Chichikov's position was embarrassing: the valet was standing right there with gaping mouth and popping eyes.

"Your Excellency, it was tears that thought up this laughter," he said.

"Excuse me, brother! No, it's killing! But I'd give five hundred thousand just to see your uncle as you present him with the deed for the dead souls. And what, is he so old? What's his age?"

"Eighty, Your Excellency. But this is in the closet, I'd...so that..." Chichikov gave a meaning look into the general's face and at the same time a sidelong glance at the valet.

"Off with you, my lad. Come back later," the general said to the valet. The mustachio withdrew.

"Yes, Your Excellency...This, Your Excellency, is such a matter, that I'd prefer to keep it a secret..."

"Of course, I understand very well. What a foolish old man! To come up with such foolishness at the age of eighty! And what, how does he look? is he hale? still on his feet?"

"Yes, but with difficulty."

"What a fool! And he's got his teeth?"

"Only two, Your Excellency."

"What an ass! Don't be angry, brother . . . he's an ass . . . "

"Correct, Your Excellency. Though he's my relative, and it's hard to admit it, he is indeed an ass."

However, as the reader can guess for himself, it was not hard for Chichikov to admit it, the less so since it is unlikely he ever had any uncle.

"So if you would be so good, Your Excellency, as to . . . "

"As to give you the dead souls? But for such an invention I'll give them to you with land, with lodgings! Take the whole cemetery! Ha, ha, ha, ha! The old man, oh, the old man! Ha, ha, ha, ha! Made such a fool of! Ha, ha, ha, ha!"

And the general's laughter again went echoing all through the general's apartments.[*]

---

* The end of the chapter is missing. In the first edition of the second volume of *Dead Souls* (1855), there was a note: "Here omitted is the reconciliation of Betrishchev and Tentetnikov; the dinner at the general's and their conversation about the year 'twelve; the betrothal of Ulinka and Tentetnikov; her prayer and lament on her mother's grave; the conversation of the betrothed couple in the garden. Chichikov sets out, at General Betrishchev's request, to call on his relatives and to inform them of his daughter's betrothal, and he goes to see one of these relations – Colonel Koshkarev." – TRANS.

CHAPTER THREE

"NO, NOT LIKE that," Chichikov was saying as he found himself again in the midst of the open fields and spaces, "I wouldn't handle it like that. As soon as, God willing, I finish it all happily and indeed become a well-to-do, prosperous man, I'll behave quite differently: I'll have a cook, and a house full of plenty, but the managerial side will also be in order. The ends will meet, and a little sum will be set aside each year for posterity, if only God grants my wife fruitfulness . . .

"Hey, you tomfool!"

Selifan and Petrushka both looked back from the box.

"Where are you going?"

"Just as you were pleased to order, Pavel Ivanovich – to Colonel Koshkarev's," said Selifan.

"And you asked the way?"

"If you please, Pavel Ivanovich, since I was pottering with the carriage, I . . . saw only the general's stableboy . . . But Petrushka asked the coachman."

"What a fool! I told you not to rely on Petrushka: Petrushka's a log."

"It takes no sort of wisdom," said Petrushka, with a sidelong glance, "excepting as you go down the hill you should keep straight on, there's nothing more to it."

"And I suppose you never touched a drop, excepting the home brew? I suppose you got yourself well oiled?"

Seeing what turn the conversation was taking, Petrushka merely set his nose awry. He was about to say that he had not even begun, but then he felt somehow ashamed.

"It's nice riding in a coach, sir," Selifan said, turning around.
"What?"

"I say, Pavel Ivanovich, that it's nice for your honor to be riding in a coach, sir, better than a britzka, sir – less bouncy."

"Drive, drive! No one's asking your opinion."

Selifan gave the horses' steep flanks a light flick of the whip and addressed himself to Petrushka:

"Master Koshkarev, I hear tell, has got his muzhiks dressed up like Germans; you can't figure out from far off – he walks cranelike, same as a German. And the women don't wear kerchiefs on their heads, pie-shaped, like they do sometimes, or headbands either, but this sort of German bonnet, what German women wear, you know, a bonnet – a bonnet, it's called, you know, a bonnet. A German sort of bonnet."

"What if they got you up like a German, and in a bonnet!" Petrushka said, sharpening his wit on Selifan and grinning. But what a mug resulted from this grin! It had no semblance of a grin, but was as if a man with a cold in his nose was trying to sneeze, but did not sneeze, and simply remained in the position of a man about to sneeze.

Chichikov peered into his mug from below, wishing to know what was going on there, and said: "A fine one! and he still fancies he's a handsome fellow!" It must be said that Pavel Ivanovich was seriously convinced that Petrushka was in love with his own beauty, whereas the latter even forgot at times whether he had any mug at all.

"What a nice idea it would be, Pavel Ivanovich," said Selifan, turning around on his box, "to ask Andrei Ivanovich for another horse in exchange for the dapple-gray; he wouldn't refuse, being of friendly disposition towards you, and this horse, sir, is a scoundrel of a horse and a real hindrance."

"Drive, drive, don't babble!" Chichikov said, and thought to himself: "In fact, it's too bad it never occurred to me."

The light-wheeled coach meanwhile went lightly wheeling along. Lightly it went uphill, though the road was occasionally uneven; lightly it also went downhill, though the descents of country roads are worrisome. They descended the hill. The road went through meadows, across the bends of the river, past the mills. Far away flashed sands, aspen groves emerged picturesquely one from behind the other; willow bushes, slender alders, and silvery poplars flew quickly past them, their branches striking Selifan and Petrushka as they sat on their box. The latter had his peaked cap knocked off every moment. The stern servitor would jump down from the box, scold the stupid tree and the owner who had planted it, but never thought of tying the cap on or at least of holding it with his hand, still hoping that maybe it would not happen again. Then the trees became thicker: aspens and alders were joined by birches, and soon a forest thicket formed around them. The light of the sun disappeared. Pines and firs darkled. The impenetrable gloom of the endless forest became denser, and, it seemed, was preparing to turn into night. And suddenly among the trees – light, here and there among the branches and trunks, like a mirror or like quicksilver. The forest began to brighten, trees became sparser, shouts were heard – and suddenly before them was a lake. A watery plain about three miles across, with trees around it, and cottages behind them. Some twenty men, up to their waists, shoulders, or chins in water, were pulling a dragnet towards the opposite shore. In the midst of them, swimming briskly, shouting, fussing enough for all of them, was a man nearly as tall as he was fat, round all around, just like a watermelon. Owing to his fatness he might not possibly drown, and if he wanted to dive, he could flip over all he liked, but the water would keep buoying him up; and if two more men had sat on his back, he would have gone on floating with them like a stubborn bubble on the surface of the water, only groaning slightly under the weight and blowing bubbles from his nose and mouth.

"That one, Pavel Ivanovich," said Selifan, turning around on the box, "must be the master, Colonel Koshkarev."

"Why so?"

"Because his body, if you'll be pleased to notice, is a bit whiter than the others', and he's respectably portly, as a master should be."

The shouts meanwhile were getting more distinct. The squire-watermelon was shouting in a ringing patter:

"Hand it over, Denis, hand it over to Kozma! Kozma, take the tail from Denis! You, Big Foma, push there along with Little Foma! Go around to the right, the right! Stop, stop, devil take you both! You've got me tangled in the net! You've caught me, I tell you, damn it, you've caught me by the navel!"

The draggers on the right flank stopped, seeing that an unforeseen mishap had indeed occurred: the master was caught in the net.

"Just look," Selifan said to Petrushka, "they've dragged in the master like a fish."

The squire floundered and, wishing to disentangle himself, turned over on his back, belly up, getting still more tangled in the net. Fearful of tearing it, he was floating together with the caught fish, only ordering them to tie a rope around him. When they had tied a rope around him, they threw the end to shore. Some twenty fishermen standing on the shore picked it up and began carefully to haul him in. On reaching a shallow spot, the squire stood up, all covered with the meshes of the net, like a lady's hand in a net glove in summer – looked up, and saw the visitor driving onto the dam in his coach. Seeing the visitor, he nodded to him. Chichikov took off his cap and bowed courteously from his coach.

"Had dinner?" shouted the squire, climbing onto the shore with the caught fish, holding one hand over his eyes to shield them from the sun, and the other lower down in the manner of the Medici Venus stepping from her bath.

"No," said Chichikov.

"Well, then you can thank God."

"Why?" Chichikov asked curiously, holding his cap up over his head.

"Here's why!" said the squire, winding up on shore with the carp and bream thrashing around his feet leaping a yard high off the ground. "This is nothing, don't look at this: that's the real thing over there! . . . Show us the sturgeon, Big Foma." Two stalwart muzhiks dragged some sort of monster from a tub. "What a princeling! strayed in from the river!"

"No, that's a full prince!" said Chichikov.

"You said it. Go on ahead now, and I'll follow. You there, coachman, take the lower road, through the kitchen garden. Run, Little Foma, you dolt, and take the barrier down. I'll follow in no time, before you . . . "

"The colonel's an odd bird," thought Chichikov, finally getting across the endless dam and driving up to the cottages, of which some, like a flock of ducks, were scattered over the slope of a hill, while others stood below on pilings, like herons. Nets, sweepnets, dragnets were hanging everywhere. Little Foma took down the barrier, the coach drove through the kitchen garden, and came out on a square near an antiquated wooden church. Behind the church, the roofs of the manor buildings could be seen farther off.

"And here I am!" a voice came from the side. Chichikov looked around. The squire was already driving along next to him, clothed, in a droshky – grass-green nankeen frock coat, yellow trousers, and a neck without a tie, after the manner of a cupid! He was sitting sideways on the droshky, taking up the whole droshky with himself. Chichikov was about to say something to him, but the fat man had already vanished. The droshky appeared on the other side, and all that was heard was a voice: "Take the pike and seven carp to that dolt of a cook, and fetch the sturgeon here: I'll take him myself in the droshky." Again came voices: "Big Foma and Little Foma! Kozma and Denis!" And when he drove up to the porch of the house, to his greatest amazement the fat squire was already standing there and received him into his embrace. How he had managed to fly there was inconceivable. They kissed each other three times crisscross.

"I bring you greetings from His Excellency," said Chichikov.

"Which Excellency?"

"Your relative, General Alexander Dmitrievich."

"Who is Alexander Dmitrievich?"

"General Betrishchev," Chichikov replied in some amazement.

"Don't know him, sir, never met him."

Chichikov was still more amazed.

"How's that? . . . I hope I at least have the pleasure of speaking with Colonel Koshkarev?"

"Pyotr Petrovich Petukh, Petukh Pyotr Petrovich!"[1] the host picked up.

Chichikov was dumbfounded.

"There you have it! How now, you fools," he said, turning to Selifan and Petrushka, who both gaped, goggle-eyed, one sitting on his box, the other standing by the door of the coach, "how now, you fools? Weren't you told – to Colonel Koshkarev's . . . And this is Pyotr Petrovich Petukh . . . "

"The lads did excellently!" said Pyotr Petrovich. "For that you'll each get a noggin of vodka and pie to boot. Unharness the horses and go at once to the servants' quarters."

"I'm embarrassed," Chichikov said with a bow, "such an unexpected mistake . . . "

"Not a mistake," Pyotr Petrovich Petukh said promptly, "not a mistake. You try how the dinner is first, and then say whether it was a mistake or not. Kindly step in," he said, taking Chichikov under the arm and leading him to the inner rooms.

Chichikov decorously passed through the doors sideways, so as to allow the host to enter with him; but this was in vain: the host could not enter, and besides he was no longer there. One could only hear his talk resounding all over the yard: "But where's Big Foma? Why isn't he here yet? Emelyan, you gawk, run and tell that dolt of a cook to gut the sturgeon quickly. Milt, roe, innards, and bream – into the soup; carp – into the sauce. And crayfish, crayfish! Little Foma, you gawk, where are the crayfish? crayfish, I say, crayfish?!" And for a long time there went on echoing "crayfish, crayfish."

"Well, the host's bustling about," said Chichikov, sitting in an armchair and studying the walls and corners.

"And here I am," said the host, entering and bringing in two youths in summer frock coats. Slender as willow wands, they shot up almost two feet taller than Pyotr Petrovich.

"My sons, high-school boys. Home for the holidays. Nikolasha, you stay with our guest, and you, Alexasha, follow me."

And again Pyotr Petrovich Petukh vanished.

Chichikov occupied himself with Nikolasha. Nikolasha was talkative. He said that the teaching in his school was not very good, that more favor was shown those whose mamas sent them costlier presents, that the Inkermanland hussar regiment was stationed in their town, that Captain Vetvitsky had a better horse than the colonel himself, though Lieutenant Vzemtsev was a far better rider.

"And, tell me, what is the condition of your papa's estate?" asked Chichikov.

"Mortgaged," the papa himself replied to that, appearing in the drawing room again, "mortgaged."

It remained for Chichikov to make the sort of movement with his lips that a man makes when a deal comes to nought and ends in nothing.

"Why did you mortgage it?" he asked.

"Just so. Everybody got into mortgaging, why should I lag behind the rest? They say it's profitable. And besides, I've always lived here, so why not try living in Moscow a bit?"

"The fool, the fool!" thought Chichikov, "he'll squander everything, and turn his children into little squanderers, too. He ought to stay in the country, porkpie that he is!"

"And I know just what you're thinking," said Petukh.

"What?" asked Chichikov, embarrassed.

"You're thinking: 'He's a fool, a fool, this Petukh! Got me to stay for dinner, and there's still no dinner.' It'll be ready, most honorable sir. Quicker than a crop-headed wench can braid her hair."

"Papa, Platon Mikhalych is coming!" said Alexasha, looking out the window.

"Riding a bay horse," Nikolasha added, bending down to the window. "Do you think our gray is worse than that, Alexasha?"

"Worse or not, he doesn't have the same gait."

An argument arose between them about the bay horse and the gray. Meanwhile a handsome man entered the room – tall and trim, with glossy light brown curls and dark eyes. A big-muzzled monster of a dog came in after him, its bronze collar clanking.

"Had dinner?" asked Pyotr Petrovich Petukh.

"I have," said the guest.

"What, then, have you come here to laugh at me?" Petukh said crossly. "Who needs you after dinner?"

"Anyhow, Pyotr Petrovich," the guest said, smiling, "I have this comfort for you, that I ate nothing at dinner: I have no appetite at all."

"And what a catch we had, if only you'd seen! What a giant of a sturgeon came to us! We didn't even count the carp."

"I'm envious just listening to you," said the guest. "Teach me to be as merry as you are."

"But why be bored? for pity's sake!" said the host.

"Why be bored? Because it's boring."

"You eat too little, that's all. Try and have a good dinner. Boredom was only invented recently. Before no one was bored."

"Enough boasting! As if you've never been bored?"

"Never! I don't know, I haven't even got time to be bored. In the morning you wake up, you have to have your tea, and the steward is there, and then it's time for fishing, and then there's dinner. After dinner you just barely have time for a snooze, then it's supper, and then the cook comes – you have to order dinner for the next day. When could I be bored?"

All the while this conversation was going on, Chichikov was studying the guest.

Platon Mikhalych Platonov was Achilles and Paris combined: trim build, impressive height, freshness – all met together in him. A pleasant smile, with a slight expression of irony, seemed to make him still more handsome. But in spite of it all, there was something sleepy and inanimate in him. Passions, sorrows, and shocks had brought no wrinkles to his virginal, fresh face, nor at the same time did they animate it.

"I confess," Chichikov spoke, "I, too, cannot understand – if you will allow me the observation – cannot understand how it is possible, with an appearance such as yours, to be bored. Of course, there may be other reasons: lack of money, oppression from some sort of malefactors – for there exist such as are even ready to make an attempt on one's life."

"That's just it, that there's nothing of the sort," said Platonov. "Believe me, I could wish for it on occasion, that there was at least some sort of care and anxiety. Well, at least that someone would simply make me angry. But no! Boring – and that's all."

"I don't understand. But perhaps your estate isn't big enough, there's too few souls?"

"Not in the least. My brother and I have about thirty thousand acres of land and a thousand peasant souls along with it."

"And yet you're bored. Incomprehensible! But perhaps your estate is in disorder? the harvests have been poor, many people have died?"

"On the contrary, everything's in the best possible order, and my brother is an excellent manager."

"I don't understand!" said Chichikov, shrugging.

"But now we're going to drive boredom away," said the host. "Run to the kitchen, Alexasha, tell the cook to hurry up and send us some fish tarts. Where's that gawk Emelyan and the thief Antoshka? Why don't they serve the hors d'oeuvres?"

But the door opened. The gawk Emelyan and the thief Antoshka appeared with napkins, laid the table, set down a tray with six carafes filled with varicolored liqueurs. Soon, around the tray and the carafes lay a necklace of plates – caviar, cheeses, salted mushrooms of various sorts, and from the kitchen a newly brought something on covered dishes, from which came a gurgling of butter. The gawk Emelyan and the thief Antoshka were fine and efficient folk. The master had given them these appellations only because everything came out somehow insipid without nicknames, and he did not like insipid things; he himself had a good heart, yet he loved a spicy phrase. Anyhow, his servants were not angered by it.

The hors d'oeuvres were followed by dinner. Here the good-natured host turned into a real bully. The moment he noticed someone taking one piece, he would immediately give him a second, muttering: "Without a mate neither man nor bird can live in this world." The guest ate the two – he heaped on a third, muttering: "What good is the number two? God loves the trinity." The guest ate the third – then he: "Who ever saw a cart with three wheels? Does anyone build a cottage with three corners?" For four he had yet another saying, and also for five. Chichikov ate about a dozen helpings of something and thought: "Well, the host can't come up with anything more now." Not so: the host, without saying a word, put on his plate a rack of veal roasted on a spit, the best part there is, with the kidneys, and of such a calf!

"Milk-fed for two years," said the host. "I took care of him like my own son!"

"I can't!" said Chichikov.

"Try it, and then say 'I can't.'"

"It won't go in. No room."

"There was no room in the church either. The governor came – they found room. And there was such a crush that an apple had nowhere to fall. Just try it: this piece is the same as the governor."

Chichikov tried it – the piece was indeed something like a governor. Room was found for it, though it seemed impossible to find any.

With the wines there also came a story. Having received his mortgage money, Pyotr Petrovich had stocked up on provisions for ten years to come. He kept pouring and pouring; whatever the guests left was finished by Nikolasha and Alexasha, who tossed off glass after glass, yet when they left the table, it was as if nothing had happened, as if they had just been drinking water. Not so the guests: with great, great effort they dragged themselves over to the balcony and with great effort lowered themselves into their armchairs. The host, the moment he sat down in his, which was something like a four-seater, immediately fell asleep. His corpulent self turned into a blacksmith's bellows. Through his open mouth and the nostrils of his nose it began producing sounds such as do not exist even in the latest music. Everything was there – drum, flute, and some abrupt sound, like a dog's barking.

"What a whistler!" said Platonov.

Chichikov laughed.

"Naturally, once you've had a dinner like that," Platonov said, "how could boredom come to you! What comes is sleep."

"Yes," Chichikov said lazily. His eyes became extraordinarily small. "All the same, however, I can't understand how it's possible to be bored. There are so many remedies for boredom."

"Such as?"

"There are all sorts for a young man! You can dance, play some instrument . . . or else – get married."

"To whom, tell me?"

"As if there were no nice and rich brides in the neighborhood?"

"There aren't."

"Well, then, you could go and look elsewhere." Here a rich thought flashed in Chichikov's head, his eyes got bigger. "But there is a wonderful remedy!" he said, looking into Platonov's eyes.

"Which?"

"Travel."

"Where to?"

"If you're free, then come with me," said Chichikov, thinking to himself as he looked at Platonov: "And it would be nice: we could split the expenses, and the repairs of the carriage could go entirely to his account."

"And where are you going?"

"How shall I say – where? I'm traveling now not so much on my own as on someone else's need. General Betrishchev, a close friend and, one might say, benefactor, asked me to visit his relatives . . . of course, relatives are relatives, but it is partly, so to speak, for my own self as well: for to see the world, the circulation of people – whatever they may say – is like a living book, a second education."

Platonov fell to thinking.

Chichikov meanwhile reflected thus: "Truly, it would be nice! It could even be done so that all the expenses would go to his account. It could even be arranged so that we would take his horses and mine would be fed on his estate. I could also spare my carriage by leaving it on his estate and taking his for the road."

"Well, then, why not take a trip?" Platonov was thinking meanwhile. "It really might cheer me up. I have nothing to do at home, the management is in my brother's hands anyway; so there won't be any trouble. Why, indeed, not take a trip?"

"And would you agree," he said aloud, "to being my brother's guest for a couple of days? Otherwise he won't let me go."

"With great pleasure! Even three."

"Well, in that case – my hand on it! Let's go!" said Platonov, livening up.

"Bravo!" said Chichikov, slapping his hand. "Let's go!"

"Where? where?" the host exclaimed, waking up and goggling his eyes at them. "No, gentlemen, I ordered the wheels taken off your coach, and your stallion, Platon Mikhalych, is now ten miles away from here. No, today you spend the night, and tomorrow, after an early dinner, you'll be free to go."

"Well, now!" thought Chichikov. Platonov made no reply, knowing that Petukh held fast to his customs. They had to stay.

In return, they were rewarded with a remarkable spring evening. The host arranged a party on the river. Twelve rowers, manning twenty-four oars, with singing, swept them across the smooth back of the mirrory lake. From the lake they swept on to the river, boundless, with gently sloping banks on both sides. No current stirred the water. They drank tea with *kalatchi* on the boat, constantly passing under cables stretched across the river for net fishing. Still before tea the host had already managed to undress and jump into the river, where he spent about half an hour with the fishermen, splashing about and making a lot of noise, shouting at Big Foma and Kozma, and, having had his fill of shouting, bustling, freezing in the water, he came back aboard with an appetite and drank his tea in a manner enviable to see. Meanwhile the sun went down. Brightness lingered in the sky. The echoes of shouting grew louder. Instead of fishermen, groups of bathing children appeared on the banks everywhere, splashing in the water, laughter echoed far away. The rowers, setting twenty-four oars in motion, would all at once raise them, and the boat would glide by itself, like a light bird, over the moveless mirror surface. A healthy stalwart, fresh as a young wench, the third from the tiller, led the singing alone, working in a clear, ringing voice; five picked it up, six carried it on – and the song poured forth as boundlessly as all Rus; and, hand on ear, the singers themselves were as if lost in its boundlessness. It felt somehow free, and Chichikov thought: "Eh, really, someday I'm going to get me a little country estate!" "Well, where's the good in it," thought Platonov, "in this mournful song? It makes one still more sick at heart."

It was already dusk as they were coming back. In the darkness the oars struck waters that no longer reflected the sky. Barely visible were the little lights on the shores of the lake. The moon was rising when they pulled in to shore. Everywhere fishermen were cooking fish soup on tripods, all of ruff, the fish still quiveringly alive. Everything was already home. Geese, cows, and goats had been driven home long ago, and the very dust they raised had long settled, and their herdsmen stood by the gates waiting for a crock of milk and an invitation for fish soup. Here and there some human chatter and clatter could be heard, the loud barking of dogs from this village, and distant barking from villages farther away. The moon was rising, the darkness began to brighten, and finally everything became bright – lake and cottages; the lights in the windows paled; one could now see the smoke from the chimneys, silvered by moonbeams. Nikolasha and Alexasha swept past them just then on two dashing steeds, racing each other; they raised as much dust as a flock of sheep. "Eh, really, someday I'm going to get me a little country estate!" Chichikov was thinking. A young wench and little Chichikies again rose in his imagination. Who could help being warmed by such an evening?

And at supper they again ate too much. When Pavel Ivanovich came to the room where he was to sleep, and, getting into bed, felt his tummy: "A drum!" he said, "no governor could possibly get in!" Just imagine such a coincidence: on the other side of the wall was the host's study. The wall was thin and one could hear everything that was being said there. The host was ordering the cook to prepare for the next day, in the guise of an early lunch, a decided dinner. And how he was ordering it! It was enough to make a dead man hungry. He sucked and smacked his lips. One heard only: "And fry it, and then let it stew nice and long!" And the cook kept saying in a thin falsetto: "Yes, sir. It can be done, sir. That can be done, too, sir."

"And make a covered pie, a four-cornered one. In one corner put sturgeon cheeks and cartilage, and stuff another with buckwheat and mushrooms with onions, and sweet milt, and brains, and something else as well, whatever you know . . . "

"Yes, sir. That could be done, sir."

"And so that on one side, you understand, it gets nice and brown, but on the other let it be a bit lighter. From the bottom, from the bottom, you understand, bake it from the bottom, so that it gets all crumbly, so that it gets all juicy through and through, so that you don't feel it in your mouth – it should melt like snow."

"Devil take it!" thought Chichikov, tossing and turning. "He just won't let me sleep."

"And make me a pig haggis. Put a piece of ice in the middle so that it plumps up nicely. And put things around the sturgeon, garnishes, more garnishes! Surround it with crayfish, and little fried fish, and layer it with a stuffing of smelts with some finely minced horseradish, and mushrooms, and turnips, and carrots, and beans, and isn't there some other root?"

"Some kohlrabi or star-cut beets could be put in," said the cook.

"Put in both kohlrabi and beets. And for the roast you'll make me a garnish like this . . . "

"Sleep's gone completely!" said Chichikov, turning on his other side, burying his head in the pillows, and covering himself up with a blanket so as not to hear anything. But through the blanket came unremittingly: "And fry it, and bake it, and let it plump up nicely." He finally fell asleep at some turkey.

The next day the guests overate so much that Platonov was no longer able to ride on horseback; the stallion was sent with Petukh's stableboy. They got into the coach. The big-muzzled dog walked lazily behind the coach. He, too, had overeaten.

"No, it's too much," said Chichikov, as they left the place. "It's even piggish. Are you uncomfortable, Platon Mikhalych? Such a comfortable carriage it was, and suddenly it's become uncomfortable. Petrushka, you must have been fool enough to start repacking? There are boxes sticking out everywhere!"

Platon laughed.

"That I can explain for you," he said. "Pyotr Petrovich put things in for the road."

"Right you are," said Petrushka, turning around from the box, "we were ordered to put everything in the coach – pasterries and pies."

"Right, sir, Pavel Ivanovich," said Selifan, turning around from the box, merrily, "such a respectable master. A regaling landowner! Sent us down a glass of champagne each. Right, sir, and ordered them to give us food from the table – very good food, of a delicate aromer. There's never yet been such a respectful master."

"You see? He's satisfied everyone," said Platon. "Tell me simply, however: do you have time to stop by at a certain estate, some six miles from here? I'd like to say good-bye to my sister and brother-in-law."

"With great pleasure," said Chichikov.

"You won't be any the worse for it: my brother-in-law is quite a remarkable man."

"In what sense?" said Chichikov.

"He's the foremost manager that has ever existed in Russia. In a little over ten years he's made it so that a run-down property that used to bring in barely twenty thousand now brings in two hundred thousand."

"Ah, a respectable man! Such a man's life merits being told for people's instruction! I'll be very, very pleased to make his acquaintance. And what is his name?"

"Kostanzhoglo."[2]

"And his first name and patronymic?"

"Konstantin Fyodorovich."

"Konstantin Fyodorovich Kostanzhoglo. Very pleased to make his acquaintance. It's instructive to get to know such a man." And Chichikov started inquiring about Kostanzhoglo, and everything he learned about him from Platonov was indeed amazing.

"Look here, this is where his land begins," said Platonov, pointing to the fields. "You'll see at once the difference from the others. Coachman, take the road to the left here. Do you see this young forest? It's been planted. With someone else, it wouldn't have grown that much in fifteen years, but his grew in eight. Look, the forest ends here. Now it's a wheat field; and after a hundred and fifty acres there will be a forest again, also planted, and so on. Look at the field, how much thicker the growth is than anywhere else."

"I see that. How does he do it?"

"Well, you can ask him, you'll see that . . . * He's a know-all, such a know-all as you won't find anywhere else. He not only knows which plant likes which kind of soil, he also knows in what sort of surroundings, next to what kind of trees a certain grain should be planted. We all have our land cracking with drought, but he doesn't. He calculates how much humidity is necessary, and grows enough trees; with him everything plays a double or triple role: the forest is a forest, but the fields profit from the leaves and the shade. And he's like that with everything."

---

*Four illegible words in Gogol's manuscript. – TRANS.

"An amazing man!" said Chichikov, gazing curiously at the fields.

Everything was in extraordinarily good order. The woods were fenced off; there were cattle yards everywhere, also arranged not without reason and enviably well tended; the haystacks were of gigantic size. Everywhere was abundance and fatness. One could see at once that a top-notch owner lived here. Having climbed a small rise, they saw on the other side a large estate scattered over three hillsides. Everything here was rich: smooth streets, sturdy cottages; if a cart stood somewhere, the cart was a sturdy one and new as could be; if one came upon a horse, the horse was a fine and well-fed one; or upon horned cattle, then they were of the choicest quality. Even the muzhik's pig had an air of nobility. Precisely here, one could see, lived those muzhiks who, as the song says, shovel silver with their spades. There were no English parks here, no gazebos, whimsical bridges, or various avenues in front of the house. Workshops stretched between the cottages and the master's yard. On the roof there was a big lantern, not for the view, but for seeing where, and in what shop, and how the work was going on.

They drove up to the house. The owner was absent; they were met by his wife, Platonov's sister, fair-haired, fair-skinned, with a real Russian expression, as handsome, but also as half-asleep, as he was. It seemed she did not care much for what others cared about, either because her husband's all-absorbing activity left no share for her, or because she belonged, by her very constitution, to that philosophical order of people who, while having feelings, and thoughts, and intelligence, live somehow only halfway, look at life with half an eye, and seeing its upsetting struggles and anxieties, say: "Let them rage, the fools! So much the worse for them."

"Greetings, sister!" said Platonov. "And where is Konstantin?"

"I don't know. He ought to have been back long ago. He must have gotten busy."

Chichikov paid no attention to the hostess. He was interested in looking over the dwelling of this extraordinary man. He hoped to discover in it the properties of the owner himself, as one can tell by the shell what sort of oyster or snail sits in it. But there was nothing of the sort. The rooms were completely characterless – spacious, and nothing else. No frescoes, no paintings on the walls, no bronzes on the tables, no whatnots with china or cups, no vases of flowers or statuettes – in short, it was somehow bare. Plain, ordinary furniture, and a grand piano standing to one side, and covered with dust at that: apparently the mistress rarely sat down to it. From the drawing room [the door opened to the master's study]*; but there, too, everything was the same – plain and bare. One could see that the owner came home only to rest, not to live there; that for thinking over his plans and ideas he had no need of a study with upholstered armchairs and various comfortable conveniences, and that his life consisted not of charming reveries by the blazing fireplace, but of real business. His thoughts proceeded at once from circumstances, the moment they presented themselves, and turned at once into business, without any need of being written down.

"Ah! here he is! He's coming, he's coming!" said Platonov.

Chichikov also rushed to the window. A man of about forty, lively, with a swarthy appearance, was coming up to the porch. He was wearing a velour peaked cap. On both sides of him, their hats off, walked two persons of lower rank – walked, talking and discussing something with him. One seemed to be a simple muzhik; the other, in a blue *sibirka,*[3] some foxy-looking itinerant dealer.

"Order them to take it, then, my dear!" the muzhik said, bowing.

<hr>

*The bracketed words were supplied by the editor of the 1857 edition of *Dead Souls*. – TRANS.

"No, brother, I've already told you twenty times: don't bring any more. I've got so much material stored up that I don't know what to do with it."

"With you, dear Konstantin Fyodorovich, it will all be put to use. Such a clever man as you is not to be found in the whole world. Your healthfulness will find a place for anything. So give orders to take it."

"I need hands, brother; bring me workers, not materials."

"But you won't lack for workers. Whole villages of ours will come to be hired: the breadlessness was such that no one remembers the like of it. It's a pity you won't just take us, you'd get tried and true service from us, by God you would. With you one gets ever wiser, Konstantin Fyodorovich. So give orders to take it for the last time."

"But you said before that it would be the last time, and now you've brought it again."

"For the last time, Konstantin Fyodorovich. If you don't accept it, no one will. So order them to take it, my dear."

"Well, listen, this time I'll take it, and that only out of pity, so that you won't have brought it in vain. But if you bring it next time, you can whine for three weeks – I won't take it."

"Yes, sir, Konstantin Fyodorovich; rest assured, next time I won't ever bring it. I humbly thank you." The muzhik went away pleased. He was lying, however, he would bring it again: "maybe" is a great little word.

"Now then, Konstantin Fyodorovich, sir, do me a kindness . . . knock off a bit," said the itinerant dealer in the blue *sibirka*, who was walking on the other side of him.

"You see, I told you from the very start. I'm not fond of bargaining. I tell you again: I'm not like some other landowner whom you get at just as his mortgage payment is due. Don't I know you all! You've got the lists and know who has to pay and when. So, what could be simpler? He's pressed, he gives it to you for half the price. But what's your money to me? My things can go on lying there for three years! I have no mortgage to pay..."

"It's real business, Konstantin Fyodorovich. No, sir, it's so that I...it's only so as to have dealings with you in the future, and not for anything mercenary. Kindly accept a little deposit of three thousand."

The dealer took a wad of greasy bills from his breast pocket. Kostanzhoglo took them with great coolness, and put them into the back pocket of his frock coat without counting them.

"Hm," thought Chichikov, "just as if it were a handkerchief!"

A moment later Kostanzhoglo appeared in the doorway of the drawing room.

"Hah, brother, you're here!" he said, seeing Platonov. They embraced and kissed each other. Platonov introduced Chichikov. Chichikov reverently approached the host, planted a kiss on his cheek, and received from him the impression of a kiss.

Kostanzhoglo's face was very remarkable. It betrayed its southern origin. His hair and eyebrows were dark and thick, his eyes eloquent, brightly gleaming. Intelligence shone in every expression of his face, and there was nothing sleepy in it. One could notice, however, an admixture of something bilious and embittered. What, in fact, was his nationality? There are many Russians in Russia who are of non-Russian origin but are nevertheless Russians in their souls. Kostanzhoglo was not interested in his origins, finding the question beside the point and quite useless for the household. Besides, he knew no other language than Russian.

"Do you know what has occurred to me, Konstantin?" said Platonov.

"What?"

"It has occurred to me to take a trip over various provinces; maybe it will cure my spleen."

"Why not? It's quite possible."

"Together with Pavel Ivanovich here."

"Wonderful! And to what parts," Kostanzhoglo asked, addressing Chichikov affably, "do you now purpose to travel?"

"I confess," said Chichikov, inclining his head to one side and grasping the armrest of the chair with his hand, "I am traveling, for the moment, not so much on my own necessity as on another's. General Betrishchev, a close friend and, one might say, benefactor, asked me to visit his relatives. Relatives are relatives, of course, but it is partly, so to speak, for my own self as well; because, indeed, to say nothing of the good that may come from it in the hemorrhoidal respect, the fact alone that one sees the world, the circulation of people . . . whatever they may say, it is, so to speak, a living book, the same as learning."

"Yes, it does no harm to peek into certain corners."

"An excellent observation, if you please," Chichikov adverted, "indeed, it does no harm. You see things you wouldn't see otherwise; you meet people you wouldn't meet otherwise. Conversing with some people is as good as gold. Teach me, my most esteemed Konstantin Fyodorovich, teach me, I appeal to you. I wait for your sweet words as for manna."

Kostanzhoglo was embarrassed.

"What, though? . . . teach you what? I have only a pennyworth of education myself."

"Wisdom, my most esteemed sir, wisdom! the wisdom for managing an estate as you do; for obtaining an assured income as you have; for acquiring property as you do, not dreamlike, but substantial, and thereby fulfilling the duty of a citizen and earning the respect of one's compatriots."

"You know what?" said Kostanzhoglo, "stay with me for a day. I'll show you all my management and tell you about everything. There isn't any wisdom involved, as you'll see."

"Stay for this one day, brother," the hostess said, turning to Platonov.

"Why not, it makes no difference to me," the man said indifferently, "what about Pavel Ivanovich?"

"I, too, with the greatest pleasure . . . But there's this one circumstance – I must visit General Betrishchev's relative. There's a certain Colonel Koshkarev . . . "

"But he's . . . don't you know? He's a fool and quite mad."

"That I've heard already. I have no business with him myself. But since General Betrishchev is my close friend and even, so to speak, benefactor . . . it's somehow awkward."

"In that case, I tell you what," said Kostanzhoglo, "go to him right now. I have a droshky standing ready. It's even less than six miles away, you'll fly there and back in no time. You'll even get back before supper."

Chichikov gladly took advantage of the suggestion. The droshky was brought, and he drove off at once to see the colonel, who amazed him as he had never been amazed before. Everything at his place was extraordinary. The village was scattered all over: construction sites, reconstruction sites, piles of lime, brick, and logs everywhere in the streets. There were some houses built that looked like institutions. On one there was written in gold letters: FARM IMPLEMENT DEPOT, on another: MAIN ACCOUNTING OFFICE, on a third: VILLAGE AFFAIRS COMMITTEE; SCHOOL OF NORMAL EDUCATION OF SETTLERS – in short, devil knows what was not there! He thought he might have entered a provincial capital. The colonel himself was somehow stiff. His face was somehow formal, shaped like a triangle. His side-whiskers stretched in a line down his cheeks; his hair, hairstyling, nose, lips, chin – everything was as if it had just been taken from a press. He began speaking as if he were a sensible man. From the very beginning he began to complain of the lack of learning among the surrounding landowners, of the great labors that lay ahead of him. He received Chichikov with the utmost kindness and cordiality, took him entirely into his confidence, and with self-delight told him what labor, oh, what labor it had cost him to raise his estate to its present prosperity; how hard it was to make a simple muzhik understand the lofty impulses that enlightened luxury and the fine arts give a man; how necessary it was to combat the Russian muzhik's ignorance, so as to get him to dress in German trousers and make him feel, at least to some extent, man's lofty dignity; that, despite all his efforts, he had so far been unable to make the peasant women put on corsets, whereas in Germany, where his regiment had been stationed in the year 'fourteen, a miller's daughter could even play the piano, speak French, and curtsy. Regretfully, he told how great was the lack of learning among the neighboring landowners; how little they thought of their subjects; how they even laughed when he tried to explain how necessary it was for good management to set up a record office, commission offices, and even committees, so as to prevent all theft, so that every object would be known, so that the scrivener, the steward, and the bookkeeper would not be just educated somehow, but finish their studies at the university; how, despite all persuasions, he was unable to convince the landowners of how profitable it would be for their estates if every peasant were so well educated that, while following the plough, he could at the same time read a book about lightning rods.

At this Chichikov thought: "Well, it's unlikely that such a time will ever come. Here I am a literate man, and I've yet to read *The Countess La Vallière*."

"Terrible ignorance!" said Colonel Koshkarev in conclusion. "The darkness of the Middle Ages, and no way to remedy it...Believe me, there is none! And I could remedy it all; I know of one way, the surest way."

"What is it?"

"To dress every last man in Russia the way they go about in Germany. Nothing more than that, and I promise you everything will go swimmingly: learning will rise, trade will develop, a golden age will come to Russia."

Chichikov was looking at him intently, thinking: "Well, it seems there's no point in standing on ceremony with this one." Not leaving matters in the bottom drawer, he straightaway explained to the colonel thus and so: there was a need for such and such souls, with the drawing up of such and such deeds.

"As far as I can see from your words," said the colonel, not embarrassed in the least, "this is a request – is that so?"

"Exactly so."

"In that case, put it in writing. It will go to the commission for divers petitions. The commission for divers petitions, having made note of it, will forward it to me. From me it will go on to the village affairs committee, where all sorts of decisions and revisions will be made concerning the matter. The steward-in-chief together with the whole office will give his resolution in the soon-most time, and the matter will be settled."

Chichikov was dumbstruck.

"Excuse me," he said, "things will take too long that way."

"Ah!" the colonel said with a smile, "there's the benefit of paperwork! It will indeed take longer, but nothing will escape: every little detail will be in view."

"But, excuse me . . . How can one present it in writing? It's the sort of matter that . . . The souls are in a certain sense . . . dead."

"Very well. So you write that the souls are in a certain sense dead."

"But how can I – dead? It's impossible to write that. They're dead, but it must seem as if they're alive."

"Well, then, you write: 'But it must seem or it is required that they seem as if alive.'"

What was to be done with the colonel? Chichikov decided to go and see for himself what these commissions and committees were; and what he found there was not only amazing, but decidedly exceeded all understanding. The commission for divers petitions existed only on a signboard. Its chairman, a former valet, had been transferred to the newly formed village construction committee. He had been replaced by the clerk Timoshka, who had been dispatched on an investigation – to sort things out between the drunken steward and the village headman, a crook and a cheat. No official anywhere.

"But where is . . . but how am I to get any sense?" Chichikov said to his companion, an official for special missions, whom the colonel had given him as a guide.

"You won't get any sense," said the guide, "everything here is senseless. Here, you may be pleased to note, the building commission directs everything, disrupts everybody's work, sends people wherever it likes. The only ones who profit from it are those on the building commission." He was obviously displeased with the building commission. "It's customary here for everybody to lead the master by the nose. He thinks everything's as it ought to be, but it's so in name only."

"He ought, however, to be told that," thought Chichikov, and, having come to the colonel, he announced that his estate was in a muddle, and one could not get any sense, and that the building commission was stealing right and left.

The colonel seethed with noble indignation. Seizing pen and paper he straightaway wrote eight most severe inquiries: on what grounds had the building commission arbitrarily disposed of officials outside its jurisdiction? How could the steward-in-chief have allowed the chairman to go on an investigation without handing over his post? And how could the village affairs committee regard with indifference the fact that the committee for petitions did not even exist?

"Well, here comes mayhem," Chichikov thought, and he began to bow out.

"No, I won't let you go. In two hours, no more, you will be satisfied in everything. I will now put your matter in the charge of a special man who has just finished a course at the university. Sit in my library meanwhile. Here there is everything you might need: books, paper, pens, pencils – everything. Help yourself, help yourself, you are the master."

So spoke Koshkarev as he led him into the library. It was a huge room, with books from floor to ceiling. There were even stuffed animals. Books in all fields – forestry, cattle breeding, pig breeding, gardening, thousands of assorted journals, guide-books, and a multitude of journals presenting the latest devel-opments and improvements in horse breeding and natural science. There were such titles as: *Pig Breeding as a Science*. Seeing that these things were not for the pleasant passing of time, he turned to another bookcase. From the frying pan into the fire. They were all books of philosophy. One bore the title: *Philosophy in a Scientific Sense*. There was a row of six volumes entitled: *A Preparatory Introduction to the Theory of Thinking in Their Entirety, Totality, Essence, and Application to the Comprehen-sion of the Organic Principles of the Mutual Divarication of Social Production*. Whichever book Chichikov opened, there was on every page a manifestation, a development, an abstract, enclos-ures, disclosures, and devil knows what was not there. "No, this is all not for me," Chichikov said, and turned to the third bookcase, which contained everything in the line of the arts. Here he pulled out some huge book with immodest mytho-logical pictures and began studying them. This was to his taste. Middle-aged bachelors like such pictures. They say that re-cently they have begun to be liked even by little old men who have refined their taste at the ballet. What can be done about it, in our age mankind likes spicy roots. Having finished studying this book, Chichikov was already pulling out another of the same sort, when suddenly Colonel Koshkarev appeared with a beaming face and a paper.

"It's all done and done splendidly. This man alone decidedly understands enough for all of them. For that I'll set him over them: I'll establish a special higher board and make him presi-dent. This is what he has written . . . "

"Well, thank God," thought Chichikov, and he got ready to listen. The colonel began to read:

"Setting about the consideration of the assignment I have been charged with by Your Honor, I have the privilege here-with to report on the above: (1) The very request of Mister

Collegiate Councillor Pavel Ivanovich Chichikov, Esquire, contains a certain misunderstanding: in the explanation of the demand for registered souls overtaken by various unexpected-nesses, those who have died were also included. This was most probably meant to indicate those nearing death, and not those who have died; for those who have died are not purchasable. What is there to purchase, if there's nothing? Logic itself tells us as much. And in literary sciences, as is obvious, he never got very far…" Here Koshkarev paused momentarily and said: "At this point, the slyboots…he needles you a little. But consider what a glib pen – the style of a state secretary; and he was at the university only three years, and hasn't even finished the course." Koshkarev went on: "…in literary sciences, as is obvious, he never got very far, for he speaks of the souls as *dead*, while anyone who has taken a course in human knowledge knows for a certainty that the soul is immortal. (2) Of the above-mentioned registered souls, prescribed, or prescinded, or, as he is pleased to put it incorrectly, dead, there are none present who are not mortgaged, for they are not only all mortgaged without exception, in their totality, but they are also re-mortgaged for an additional hundred and fifty roubles per soul, except for the small village of Gurmailovka, which is in dispute on occasion of the lawsuit of the landowner Predishchev, and therefore can be neither purchased nor mortgaged."

"Why, then, did you not declare that to me before? Why have you detained me over nothing?" Chichikov said vexedly.

"But how could I know beforehand? That's the benefit of paperwork, that everything can now be plainly seen in front of our eyes."

"What a fool you are, you stupid brute!" Chichikov thought to himself. "You've rummaged in books, and what have you learned?" Bypassing all courtesy and decency, he grabbed his hat – and left. The coachman stood holding the droshky ready and with the horses still harnessed: to feed them a written request would have been called for, and the decision – to give the horses oats – would have been received only the next day. Rude and discourteous though Chichikov was, Koshkarev, despite all, was remarkably courteous and delicate with him. He squeezed his hand forcibly and pressed it to his heart, and thanked him for giving him an occasion for seeing the course of the paper procedure at work; that a dressing-down and tongue-lashing were undoubtedly needed, because everything was capable of falling asleep, and the springs of estate management would then slacken and rust; that, owing to this event, he had had a happy thought: to set up a new commission which would be called the commission for supervision of the building commission, so that no one would then dare to steal.

"Ass! Fool!" thought Chichikov, angry and displeased all the way back. He was already riding under the stars. Night was in the sky. There were lights in the villages. Driving up to the porch, he saw through the windows that the table was already laid for supper.

"How is it you're so late?" said Kostanzhoglo, when he appeared at the door.

"What were you talking about so long?" said Platonov.

"He's done me in!" said Chichikov. "I've never seen such a fool in all my born days."

"That's still nothing!" said Kostanzhoglo. "Koshkarev is a comforting phenomenon. He's necessary, because the follies of clever people are made more obvious by the caricature of their reflection in him. They've set up offices, and institutions, and managers, and manufactures, and factories, and schools, and commissions, and devil knows what else. As if they had some sort of state of their own! How do you like this, I ask you? A landowner who has arable land and not enough peasants to work it, started a candle factory, invited master candle-makers from London, and became a merchant! There's an even bigger fool: he started a silk factory!"

"But you, too, have factories," Platonov observed.

"And who started them? They started of themselves: wool accumulated, there was nowhere to sell it, so I started weaving broadcloth, simple, heavy broadcloth; I have it all sold for a low price at the markets. Fish scales, for example, have been thrown away on my bank for six years in a row; what was I to do with them? I started boiling them for glue and made forty thousand. With me everything's like that."

"What a devil!" Chichikov thought, staring at him with all his eyes, "he just rakes it in!"

"And I don't build buildings for that; I have no houses with columns and pediments. I don't invite master craftsmen from abroad. And I'll never tear peasants away from tilling the soil. I have people work in my factories only in lean years, and only those from elsewhere, for the sake of bread. There can be many such factories. Just study your management a bit more closely and you'll see – every rag can be of use, every bit of trash can bring income, so much that later you'll just push it away, saying: no need."

"That's amazing! And what's most amazing is that every bit of trash can bring income!" said Chichikov.

"Hm! and not only that! . . . " Kostanzhoglo did not finish what he was saying: the bile rose in him, and he wanted to abuse his neighboring landowners. "There's still another clever fellow – what do you think he set up for himself? An alms-house, a stone building on his estate! A pious enterprise! . . . But if you wish to help, help everyone to do his duty, don't tear them away from their Christian duty. Help the son to care for his sick father, don't give him the chance of getting him off his back. Better give him the means of sheltering his neighbor and brother, give him money for that, help him with all your powers, and don't pull him away, or else he'll give up all Christian obligations entirely. Don Quixotes in every sense! . . . It comes to two hundred roubles a year for a man in an almshouse! . . . On that money I could keep ten people on my estate!" Kostanzhoglo got angry and spat.

Chichikov was not interested in the almshouse: he wanted to talk about how every bit of trash could bring income. But Kostanzhoglo was angry now, his bile was seething, and the words came pouring out.

"And here's another Don Quixote of enlightenment: he's set up schools! Now, what, for instance, is more useful to a man than literacy? And how did he handle it? Muzhiks from his estate come to me. 'What's going on, my dear?' they say. 'Our sons have got completely out of hand, don't want to help us work, they all want to become scriveners, but there's need for only one scrivener.' That's what came of it!"

Chichikov had no use for schools either, but Platonov took up the subject:

"But that should be no hindrance, that there's no need for scriveners now: there will be later. We must work for posterity."

"But you at least be intelligent, brother! What do you care about this posterity? Everyone thinks he's some kind of Peter the Great! Look under your feet, don't gaze into posterity; make it so that the muzhik is well off, even rich, so that he has time to study of his own will, but don't take a stick in your hand and say: 'Study!' Devil knows which end they start from!... Listen, now, I'll let you be the judge now..." Here Kostanzhoglo moved closer to Chichikov and, to give him a better grasp of the matter, boarded him with a grapnel – in other words, put a finger in the buttonhole of his tailcoat. "Now, what could be clearer? You have peasants, so you should foster them in their peasant way of life. What is this way of life? What is the peasant's occupation? Ploughing? Then see to it that he's a good ploughman. Clear? No, clever fellows turn up who say: 'He should be taken out of this condition. The life he leads is too crude and simple: he must be made acquainted with the objects of luxury.' They themselves, owing to this luxury, have become rags instead of people, and got infested with devil knows what diseases, and there's no lad of eighteen left who hasn't already tried everything: he's toothless and bald behind – so now they want to infect these others with it all. Thank God we have at least this one healthy stratum left, as yet unacquainted with such whimsies! We must simply be grateful to God for that. Yes, for me the ploughmen are worthiest of all. God grant that all become ploughmen!"

"So you suppose that ploughing is the most profitable occupation?" asked Chichikov.

"The most rightful, not the most profitable. Till the soil in the sweat of your face.[4] That is said to us all; it is not said in vain. Age-old experience has proven that man in his agricultural quality has the purest morals. Where ploughing lies at the basis of social life, there is abundance and well-being; there is neither poverty nor luxury, but there is well-being. Till the soil, man was told, labor . . . no need to be clever about it! I say to the muzhik: 'Whoever you work for, whether me, or yourself, or a neighbor, just work. If you're active, I'll be your first helper. You have no livestock, here's a horse for you, here's a cow, here's a cart . . . Whatever you need, I'm ready to supply you with, only work. It kills me if your management is not well set up, and I see disorder and poverty there. I won't suffer idleness. I am set over you so that you should work.' Hm! they think to increase their income with institutions and factories! But think first of all to make every one of your muzhiks rich, and then you yourself will be rich without factories, mills, or foolish fancies."

"The more one listens to you, most honored Konstantin Fyodorovich," said Chichikov, "the more one has a wish to listen. Tell me, my esteemed sir: if, for example, I should have the intention of becoming a landowner in, say, this province, what should I pay most attention to? what should I do, how should I act in order to become rich in a short period of time, and thereby, so to speak, fulfill the essential duty of a citizen?"

"What you should do in order to become rich? Here's what..." said Kostanzhoglo.

"Time for supper!" said the mistress, rising from the sofa, and she stepped into the middle of the room, wrapping a shawl around her chilled young limbs.

Chichikov popped up from his chair with the adroitness of an almost military man, flew over to the mistress with the soft expression of a delicate civilian in his smile, offered her the crook of his arm, and led her gala-fashion through two rooms into the dining room, all the while keeping his head agreeably inclined a bit to one side. The servant took the lid off the tureen; they all moved their chairs up to the table, and the slurping of soup began.

Having polished off his soup and washed it down with a glass of liqueur (the liqueur was excellent), Chichikov spoke thus to Kostanzhoglo:

"Allow me, most honored sir, to bring you back to the subject of our interrupted conversation. I was asking you what to do, how to act, how best to go about..." [*]

* * * *

"An estate for which, if he were to ask even forty thousand, I'd count it out to him at once."

"Hm!" Chichikov fell to pondering. "And why is it," he spoke somewhat timidly, "that you don't buy it yourself?"

"But one needs finally to know one's limits. I have plenty to keep me busy around my own properties without that. Besides, our gentry are shouting at me without that, saying I supposedly take advantage of their extremities and their ruined estates to buy up land for next to nothing. I'm sick of it, finally."

"The gentry are quite capable of wicked talk!" said Chichikov.

[*]Two pages are missing from the manuscript. In them the subject of Khlobuev's estate, mentioned in what follows, was introduced. – TRANS.

"And with us, in our own province . . . You can't imagine what they say about me. They don't even call me anything else but a skinflint and a first-degree niggard. They excuse themselves for everything: 'I did squander it all, of course,' they say, 'but it was for the higher necessities of life. I need books, I must live in luxury, so as to encourage industry; but one may, perhaps, live without squandering all, if one lives like that swine Kostanzhoglo.' That's how it is!"

"I wish I were such a swine!" said Chichikov.

"And all that because I don't give dinners and don't lend them money. I don't give dinners because it would be oppressive for me, I'm not used to it. But to come and eat what I eat – you're quite welcome! I don't lend money – that's nonsense. If you're truly in need, come to me and tell me in detail how you'll make use of my money. If I see from your words that you'll dispose of it intelligently, and the money will clearly bring a profit – I won't refuse you, and won't even take interest on it. But I won't throw money to the winds. Let me be excused for that. He's planning some sort of dinner for his ladylove, or furnishing his house on a crazy footing, and I should lend him money! . . . "

Here Kostanzhoglo spat and almost uttered several indecent and abusive words in the presence of his spouse. The stern shadow of gloomy hypochondria darkened his lively face. Down and across his forehead wrinkles gathered, betraying the wrathful movement of stirred bile.

Chichikov drank off a glass of raspberry liqueur and spoke thus:

"Allow me, my esteemed sir, to bring you back to the subject of our interrupted conversation. Supposing I were to acquire that same estate you were pleased to mention, in how much time and how quickly can one get rich to such an extent . . . "

"If what you want," Kostanzhoglo picked up sternly and curtly, still full of ill humor, "is to get rich quickly, then you'll never get rich; but if you want to get rich without asking about time, you'll get rich quickly."

"So that's it!" said Chichikov.

"Yes," Kostanzhoglo said curtly, as if he were angry with Chichikov himself. "One must have a love of work; without it nothing can be done. One must come to love management, yes! And, believe me, there's nothing dull about it. They've invented the idea that country life is boring . . . but I'd die of boredom if I spent even one day in the city the way they do. A proprietor has no time to be bored. There's no emptiness in his life – everything is fullness. One need only consider this whole varied cycle of yearly occupations – and what occupations! occupations that truly elevate the spirit, to say nothing of their diversity. Here man walks side by side with nature, side by side with the seasons, a participant and conversant with everything that is accomplished in creation. Spring has not yet come, but work is already under way: supplies of firewood and everything for the floodtime; preparing seed; sorting and measuring grain in the granaries, and drying it; establishing new rents. The snow and floods are over – work is suddenly at the boil: here boats are being loaded, there forests are being thinned out, trees replanted in gardens, and the soil dug up everywhere. The spade is at work in the kitchen gardens, in the fields the plough and harrow. And the sowing begins. A trifle! They're sowing the future harvest! Summer comes – the mowing, the ploughman's greatest feast. A trifle! Then comes harvest after harvest: rye followed by wheat, barley by oats, and then there's the pulling of the hemp. The piling of hayricks, the stacking of sheaves. August is now half over – everything's being brought to the threshing floors. Autumn comes – the ploughing and sowing of winter crops, repairing of granaries, threshing. Winter comes – here, too, work doesn't sleep: first deliveries to town, threshing on all the threshing floors, transporting the threshed grain from the threshing floors to the barns, cutting and sawing of wood in the forests, deliveries of brick and materials for spring construction. But it's simply impossible for me to embrace it all. Such a diversity of work! You go and have a look here and there: to the mill, to the workshops, to the factories, and to the threshing floors! You also go and have a look at the muzhik working for himself. A trifle! But for me it's a feast if a carpenter has good command of his axe, I'm ready to stand there for two hours: such joy work gives me. And if you also see with what purpose it is all being done, and how everything around you brings increase upon increase, producing fruit and profit. I cannot even tell you what a pleasure it is. And not because the money's growing – money is money – but because all this is – your handiwork; because you see yourself being the cause and creator of it all, how from you, as from some sort of magician, abundance and good pour out on everything. No, where can you find me an equal delight?" said Kostanzhoglo, his face looking up, the wrinkles disappearing. He was as radiant as a king on the day of his solemn coronation. "No, you won't find such a delight in the whole world! Here, precisely here, man imitates God: God granted Himself the work of creation, as the highest delight, and He demands that man, too, be a creator of prosperity and the harmonious course of things. And this they call dull!"

As to the singing of a bird of paradise, Chichikov lost himself in listening to the sweet sounds of the proprietor's talk. His mouth was watering. His eyes became unctuous and acquired a sweet expression; he could have gone on listening forever.

"Konstantin! it's time we got up," said the mistress, rising from her chair. Platonov rose, Kostanzhoglo rose, Chichikov rose, though he wanted to go on sitting and listening. Offering her the crook of his arm, he led the mistress back. But his head was not affably inclined to one side, his maneuvering lacked adroitness, because his thoughts were occupied with essential maneuvers and considerations.

"However you describe it, all the same it's boring," Platonov said, walking behind him.

"Our guest seems far from stupid," the host was thinking, "temperate in his speech, and no whippersnapper." And this thought made him still more cheerful, as if he had warmed himself up with his own conversation and rejoiced to find a man ready to listen to intelligent advice.

Later, when they were all settled in a snug little candle-lit room across from the glass balcony door that served as a window, Chichikov felt cozier than he had felt for a long time. It was as if after long peregrinations he had now been received under his own roof, and to crown it all, had now obtained all that he desired and had dropped his pilgrim's staff, saying: "Enough!" So enchanting was the mood brought upon his soul by the host's reasonable talk. For every man there are certain words that are as if closer and more intimate to him than any others. And often, unexpectedly, in some remote, forsaken backwater, some deserted desert, one meets a man whose warming conversation makes you forget the pathlessness of your paths, the homelessness of your nights, and the contemporary world full of people's stupidity, of deceptions for deceiving man. Forever and always an evening spent in this way will vividly remain with you, and all that was and that took place then will be retained by the faithful memory: who was there, and who stood where, and what he was holding – the walls, the corners, and every trifle.

So, too, did everything remain in Chichikov's memory that evening: this unpretentiously furnished little room, and the good-natured expression that settled on the host's face, and the pipe brought to Platonov, with its amber mouthpiece, and the smoke that he began blowing into Yarb's fat muzzle, and Yarb's snorting, and the comely mistress's laughter, interrupted by the words: "Enough, don't torment him," and the cheery candles, and the cricket in the corner, and the glass door, and the spring night looking in at them through it, leaning its elbow on the treetops, where in the thicket spring nightingales were whistling away.

"Sweet is your talk to me, my esteemed Konstantin Fyodorovich," said Chichikov. "I may say that in the whole of Russia I have never met a man to equal you in intelligence."

He smiled.

"No, Pavel Ivanovich," he said, "if you want to know an intelligent man, then we do indeed have one of whom it may truly be said, 'This is an intelligent man,' and of whom I am not worth the shoe sole."

"Who is he?" Chichikov asked in amazement.

"Our tax farmer, Murazov."

"This is the second time I'm hearing about him!" Chichikov exclaimed.

"He's a man who could manage not just a landowner's estate, but a whole country. If I had a country, I'd make him minister of finance at once."

"I've heard. They say he's a man who surpasses all belief, he's made ten million, they say."

"Ten, nothing! it's way over forty. Soon half of Russia will be in his hands."

"You don't say!" Chichikov exclaimed, dumbfounded.

"Quite certainly. His capital must be growing now at an incredible rate. That's clear. Wealth grows slowly only when you have just a few hundred thousand; a man with millions has a big radius; whatever he gets hold of becomes two or three times more than it was. The field, the range is all too vast. There are no rivals here. No one can vie with him. Whatever price he assigns to a thing, so it stays: there's no one to bid higher."

Pop-eyed and openmouthed, Chichikov gazed into Kostanzhoglo's eyes as if rooted to the spot. There was no breath in him.

"The mind boggles!" he said, recovering himself slightly. "Thought is petrified with fear. People are amazed at the wisdom of Providence as they examine a little bug; for me it is more amazing that such enormous sums can pass through a mortal's hands! Allow me to put a question to you concerning one circumstance; tell me, this, to be sure, was originally acquired not quite sinlessly?"

"In the most irreproachable fashion, and by the most correct means."

"I can't believe it, my esteemed sir, excuse me, but I can't believe it. If it were thousands, very well, but millions . . . excuse me, but I can't believe it."

"Quite the contrary, with thousands it's hard to be quite sinless, but to make millions is easy. A millionaire has no need to resort to crooked ways. Just go on and take the straight road, take all that lies before you! No one else will pick it up."

"The mind boggles! And what's most mind-boggling is that the whole thing started from a kopeck!"

"It never happens otherwise. It's the rightful order of things," said Kostanzhoglo. "He who was born with thousands, who was brought up on thousands, will acquire no more: he already has his whims and whatnot! One ought to begin from the beginning, not from the middle. From below, one ought to begin from below. Only then do you get to know well the people and life amidst which you'll have to make shift afterwards. Once you've suffered this or that on your own hide, and have learned that every kopeck is nailed down with a three-kopeck nail, and have gone through every torment, then you'll grow so wise and well schooled that you won't blunder or go amiss in any undertaking. Believe me, it's the truth. One ought to begin from the beginning, not from the middle. If anyone says to me: 'Give me a hundred thousand and I'll get rich at once' – I won't believe him: he's striking at random, not with certainty. One ought to begin with a kopeck!"

"In that case I'll get rich," said Chichikov, "because I'm beginning, so to speak, from almost nothing."

He had in mind the dead souls.

"Konstantin, it's time we let Pavel Ivanovich rest and get some sleep," said the mistress, "but you keep babbling."

"And you will certainly get rich," said Kostanzhoglo, not listening to the mistress. "Rivers, rivers of gold will flow to you. You won't know what to do with such money."

Pavel Ivanovich sat as one enchanted, and his thoughts were whirling in a golden realm of growing dreams and reveries.

"Really, Konstantin, it's time Pavel Ivanovich slept."

"But what is it to you? Go yourself, if you want to," the host said, and stopped: loudly, through the whole room, came the snoring of Platonov, after whom Yarb began to snore even louder. For a long time already a distant banging on iron rails had been heard. It was getting past midnight. Kostanzhoglo observed that it was indeed time to retire. They all wandered off, having wished each other good night and hastening to make use of the wish.

Only Chichikov was unable to sleep. His thoughts were wakeful. He was pondering how to become a landowner like Kostanzhoglo. After his conversation with the host, everything had become so clear; the possibility of getting rich seemed so obvious. The difficult matter of management had now become so plain and simple, and seemed so suited to his very nature, that he began to have serious thoughts of acquiring not an imaginary but a real estate; he decided then and there that with the money he would get from the bank for mortgaging his fantastic souls, he would acquire a by no means fantastic estate. He already saw himself acting and managing precisely as Kostanzhoglo instructed – efficiently, prudently, not introducing anything new before learning thoroughly everything old, examining everything with his own eyes, getting to know all the muzhiks, spurning all excesses, giving himself only to work and management. He already anticipated beforehand the pleasure he would feel when a harmonious order was established and all the springs of management began working briskly, energetically pushing each other. Work would be at the boil, and just as a well-running mill swiftly produces flour from grain, so all sorts of trash and rubbish would start producing pure gold, pure gold. The wondrous proprietor stood before him every moment. He was the first man in the whole of Russia for whom he felt personal respect. Until now he had respected men either for their high rank or for their great wealth! He had never yet respected any man for his intelligence proper. Kostanzhoglo was the first. Chichikov also understood that there was no point in talking with such a man about dead souls, and that the mere mention of it would be inappropriate. He was now occupied with another project – to buy Khlobuev's estate. He had ten thousand: another ten thousand he meant to borrow from Kostanzhoglo, who had just himself announced his readiness to help anyone who wished to get rich and take up estate management. The remaining ten thousand he could pledge to pay later, once the souls had been mortgaged. He could not yet mortgage all the souls he had bought, because there was still no land for him to resettle them on. Though he averred that he had land in Kherson province, it as yet existed mostly in intent. The intention was still to buy up land in Kherson province because it was sold there for next to nothing and was even given away free, if only people would settle there. He also thought about the need to hurry up and buy whatever runaway and dead souls could be found, because landowners were hastening to mortgage their estates, and it might soon be that in all Russia there was no corner left not mortgaged to the treasury. All these thoughts filled his head one after another and kept him from sleeping. Finally sleep, which for four full hours had held the whole house, as they say, in its embrace, finally took Chichikov into its embrace as well. He fell fast asleep.

CHAPTER FOUR

THE NEXT DAY everything was arranged in the best possible way. Kostanzhoglo gladly gave him the ten thousand without interest, without security – simply with a receipt. So ready he was to assist anyone on the path to acquisition. Not only that: he himself undertook to accompany Chichikov to Khlobuev's, so as to look the estate over. After a substantial breakfast, they all set out, having climbed all three into Pavel Ivanovich's carriage; the host's droshky followed empty behind. Yarb ran ahead, chasing birds off the road. In a little over an hour and a half, they covered ten miles and saw a small estate with two houses. One of them, big and new, was unfinished and had remained in that rough state for several years; the other was small and old. They found the owner disheveled, sleepy, just awakened; there was a patch on his frock coat and a hole in his boot.

He was God knows how glad of the visitors' arrival. As if he were seeing brothers from whom he had been parted for a long time.

"Konstantin Fyodorovich! Platon Mikhailovich!" he cried out. "Dear friends! I'm much obliged! Let me rub my eyes! I really thought no one would ever come to see me. Everyone flees me like the plague: they think I'll ask them to lend me money. Oh, it's hard, hard, Konstantin Fyodorovich! I see that it's all my fault! What can I do? I live like a swinish pig. Excuse me, gentlemen, for receiving you in such attire: my boots, as you see, have holes in them. And what may I offer you, tell me?"

"Please, no beating around the bush. We've come to see you on business," said Kostanzhoglo. "Here's a purchaser for you – Pavel Ivanovich Chichikov."

"I'm heartily pleased to meet you. Let me press your hand." Chichikov gave him both.

"I should very much like, my most esteemed Pavel Ivanovich, to show you an estate worthy of attention . . . But, gentlemen, allow me to ask, have you had dinner?"

"We have, we have," said Kostanzhoglo, wishing to get out of it. "Let's not tarry but go right now."

"In that case, let's go."

Khlobuev picked up his peaked cap. The visitors put their caps on their heads, and they all set out on foot to look over the estate.

"Let's go and look at my disorder and dissipation," Khlobuev said. "Of course, you did well to have your dinner. Would you believe it, Konstantin Fyodorovich, there isn't a chicken in the house – that's what I've come to. I behave like a swine, just like a swine!"

He sighed deeply and, as if sensing there would be little sympathy on Konstantin Fyodorovich's part and that his heart was on the callous side, he took Platonov under the arm and went ahead with him, pressing him close to his breast. Kostanzhoglo and Chichikov remained behind and, taking each other's arm, followed them at a distance.

"It's hard, Platon Mikhalych, hard!" Khlobuev was saying to Platonov. "You can't imagine how hard! Moneylessness, breadlessness, bootlessness! It all wouldn't matter a straw to me if I were young and alone. But when all these adversities start breaking over you as you're approaching old age, and there's a wife at your side, and five children – one feels sad, willy-nilly, one feels sad . . ."

Platonov was moved to pity.

"Well, and if you sell the estate, will that set you to rights?" he asked.

"To rights, hah!" said Khlobuev, waving his hand. "It will all go to pay the most necessary debts, and then I won't have even a thousand left for myself."

"Then what are you going to do?"

"God knows," Khlobuev said, shrugging.

Platonov was surprised.

"How is it you don't undertake anything to extricate yourself from such circumstances?"

"What should I undertake?"

"Are there no ways?"

"None."

"Well, look for a position, take some post?"

"But I'm a provincial secretary. They can't give me any lucrative post. The salary would be tiny, and I have a wife and five children."

"Well, some private position, then. Go and become a steward."

"But who would entrust an estate to me! I've squandered my own."

"Well, if you're threatened with starvation and death, you really must undertake something. I'll ask my brother whether he can solicit some position in town through someone."

"No, Platon Mikhailovich," said Khlobuev, sighing and squeezing his hand hard, "I'm not good for anything now. I became decrepit before my old age, and there's lower-back pain on account of my former sins, and rheumatism in my shoulder. I'm not up to it! Why squander government money! Even without that there are many who serve for the sake of lucrative posts. God forbid that because of me, because my salary must be paid, the taxes on poorer folk should be raised: it's hard for them as it is with this host of bloodsuckers. No, Platon Mikhailovich, forget it."

"What a fix!" thought Platonov. "This is worse than my hibernation."

Meanwhile, Kostanzhoglo and Chichikov, walking a good distance behind them, were speaking thus with each other:

"Look how he's let everything go!" Kostanzhoglo said, pointing a finger. "Drove his muzhiks into such poverty! If there's cattle plague, it's no time to look after your own goods. Go and sell what you have, and supply the muzhiks with cattle, so that they don't go even for one day without the means of doing their work. But now it would take years to set things right: the muzhiks have all grown lazy, drunk, and rowdy."

"So that means it's not at all profitable to buy such an estate now?" asked Chichikov.

Here Kostanzhoglo looked at him as if he wanted to say: "What an ignoramus you are! Must I start you at the primer level?"

"Unprofitable! but in three years I'd be getting twenty thousand a year from this estate. That's how unprofitable it is! Ten miles away. A trifle! And what land! just look at the land! It's all water meadows. No, I'd plant flax and produce some five thousand worth of flax alone; I'd plant turnips, and make some four thousand on turnips. And look over there – rye is growing on the hillside; it all just seeded itself. He didn't sow rye, I know that. No, this estate's worth a hundred and fifty thousand, not forty."

Chichikov began to fear lest Khlobuev overhear them, and so he dropped still farther behind.

"Look how much land he's left waste!" Kostanzhoglo was saying, beginning to get angry. "At least he should have sent word beforehand, some volunteers would have trudged over here. Well, if you've got nothing to plough with, then dig a kitchen garden. You'd have a kitchen garden anyway. He forced his muzhiks to go without working for four years. A trifle! But that alone is enough to corrupt and ruin them forever! They've already grown used to being ragamuffins and vagabonds! It's already become their way of life." And, having said that, Kostanzhoglo spat, a bilious disposition over-shadowed his brow with a dark cloud . . .

"I cannot stay here any longer: it kills me to look at this disorder and desolation! You can finish it with him on your own now. Quickly take the treasure away from this fool. He only dishonors the divine gift!"

And, having said this, Kostanzhoglo bade farewell to Chichikov, and, catching up with the host, began saying good-bye to him, too.

"Good gracious, Konstantin Fyodorovich," the surprised host said, "you've just come – and home!"

"I can't. It's necessary for me to be at home," Kostanzhoglo said, took his leave, got into his droshky, and drove off.

Khlobuev seemed to understand the cause of his departure.

"Konstantin Fyodorovich couldn't stand it," he said. "I feel that it's not very cheery for such a proprietor as he to look at such wayward management. Believe me, I cannot, I cannot, Pavel Ivanovich . . . I sowed almost no grain this year! On my honor. I had no seed, not to mention nothing to plough with. Your brother, Platon Mikhailovich, is said to be an extraordinary man; and of Konstantin Fyodorovich it goes without saying – he's a Napoleon of sorts. I often think, in fact: 'Now, why is so much intelligence given to one head? Now, if only one little drop of it could get into my foolish pate, if only so that I could keep my house! I don't know how to do anything, I can't do anything!' Ah, Pavel Ivanovich, take it into your care! Most of all I pity the poor muzhiks. I feel that I was never able to be . . .* what do you want me to do, I can't be exacting and strict. And how could I get them accustomed to order if I myself am disorderly! I'd set them free right now, but the Russian man is somehow so arranged, he somehow can't do without being prodded . . . He'll just fall asleep, he'll just get moldy."

---

* One word is illegible in the manuscript. – TRANS.

"That is indeed strange," said Platonov. "Why is it that with us, unless you keep a close eye on the simple man, he turns into a drunkard and a scoundrel?"

"Lack of education," observed Chichikov.

"Well, God knows about that. We were educated, and how do we live? I went to the university and listened to lectures in all fields, yet not only did I not learn the art and order of living, but it seems I learned best the art of spending more money on various new refinements and comforts, and became better acquainted with the objects for which one needs money. Is it because there was no sense in my studies? Not really: it's the same with my other comrades. Maybe two or three of them derived something truly useful for themselves from it, and maybe that was because they were intelligent to begin with, but the rest only tried to learn what's bad for one's health and fritters away one's money. By God! We went and studied only so as to applaud the professors, to hand them out awards, and not to receive anything from them. And so we choose from education that which, after all, is on the mean side; we snatch the surface, but the thing itself we don't take. No, Pavel Ivanovich, it's because of something else that we don't know how to live, but what it is, by God, I don't know."

"There must be reasons," said Chichikov.

Poor Khlobuev sighed deeply and spoke thus:

"Sometimes, really, it seems to me that the Russian is somehow a hopeless man. There's no willpower in him, no courage for constancy. You want to do everything – and can do nothing. You keep thinking – starting tomorrow you'll begin a new life, starting tomorrow you'll begin doing everything as you ought to, starting tomorrow you'll go on a diet – not a bit of it: by the evening of that same day you overeat so much that you just blink your eyes and can't move your tongue, you sit like an owl staring at everybody – and it's the same with everything."

"One needs a supply of reasonableness," said Chichikov, "one must consult one's reasonableness every moment, conduct a friendly conversation with it."

"Come, now!" said Khlobuev. "Really, it seems to me that we're not born for reasonableness at all. I don't believe any of us is reasonable. If I see that someone is even living decently, collecting money and putting it aside – I still don't believe it. When he's old, the devil will have his way with him – he'll blow it all at once! We're all the same: noblemen and muzhiks, educated and uneducated. There was one clever muzhik: made a hundred thousand out of nothing, and, once he'd made the hundred thousand, he got the crazy idea of taking a bath in champagne, so he took a bath in champagne. But I think we've looked it all over. There isn't any more. Unless you want to glance at the mill? It has no wheel, however, and the building is good for nothing."

"Then why look at it!" said Chichikov.

"In that case, let's go home." And they all turned their steps towards the house.

The views were all the same on the way back. Untidy disorder kept showing its ugly appearance everywhere. Everything was unmended and untended. Only a new puddle had got itself added to the middle of the street. An angry woman in greasy sackcloth was beating a poor girl half to death and cursing all devils up and down. Two muzhiks stood at a distance, gazing with stoic indifference at the drunken wench's wrath. One was scratching his behind, the other was yawning. Yawning was evident in the buildings as well. The roofs were also yawning. Platonov, looking at them, yawned. "My future property – my muzhiks," thought Chichikov, "hole upon hole, and patch upon patch!" And, indeed, on one of the cottages a whole gate had been put in place of the roof; the fallen-in windows were propped with laths filched from the master's barn. In short, it seemed that the system of Trishka's caftan[5] has been introduced into the management: the cuffs and skirts were cut off to patch the elbows.

They went into the house. Chichikov was rather struck by the mixture of destitution with some glittering knickknacks of the latest luxury. Amid tattered utensils and furnishings – new bronze. Some Shakespeare was sitting on an inkstand; a fashionable ivory hand for scratching one's own back lay on the table. Khlobuev introduced the mistress of the house, his wife. She was topnotch. Even in Moscow she would have shown herself well. She was dressed fashionably, with taste. She preferred talking about the town and the theater that was being started there. Everything made it obvious that she liked the country even less than did her husband, and that she yawned more than Platonov when she was left alone. Soon the room was full of children, girls and boys. There were five of them. A sixth was carried in. They were all beautiful. The boys and girls were a joy to behold. They were dressed prettily and with taste, were cheerful and frisky. And that made it all the sadder to look at them. It would have been better if they had been dressed poorly, in skirts and shorts of simple ticking, running around in the yard, no different in any way from peasant children! A visitor came to call on the mistress. The ladies went to their half of the house. The children ran after them. The men were left by themselves.

Chichikov began the purchase. As is customary with all purchasers, he started by running down the estate he was purchasing. And, having run it down on all sides, he said:

"What, then, will your price be?"

"Do you know?" said Khlobuev. "I'm not going to ask a high price from you, I don't like that: it would also be unscrupulous on my part. Nor will I conceal from you that of the hundred souls registered on the census lists of my estate, not even fifty are actually there: the rest either died of epidemics or absented themselves without passports, so you ought to count them as dead. And therefore I ask you for only thirty thousand in all."

"Come, now – thirty thousand! The estate is neglected, people have died, and you want thirty thousand! Take twenty-five."

"Pavel Ivanovich! I could mortgage it for twenty-five thousand, you see? Then I'd get the twenty-five thousand and the estate would stay mine. I'm selling only because I need money quickly, and mortgaging means red tape, I'd have to pay the clerks, and I have nothing to pay them."

"Well, take the twenty-five thousand anyway."

Platonov felt ashamed for Chichikov.

"Buy it, Pavel Ivanovich," he said. "Any estate is worth that price. If you won't give thirty thousand for it, my brother and I will get together and buy it."

Chichikov got frightened . . .

"All right!" he said. "I'll pay you thirty thousand. Here, I'll give you two thousand now as a deposit, eight thousand in a week, and the remaining twenty thousand in a month."

"No, Pavel Ivanovich, only on condition that I get the money as soon as possible. Give me at least fifteen thousand now, and the rest no later than two weeks from now."

"But I don't have fifteen thousand! I have only ten thousand now. Let me get it together."

In other words, Chichikov was lying: he had twenty thousand.

"No, Pavel Ivanovich, if you please! I tell you that I must have fifteen thousand."

"But, really, I'm short five thousand. I don't know where to get it myself."

"I'll lend it to you," Platonov picked up.

"Perhaps, then!" said Chichikov, and he thought to himself: "Quite opportune, however, that he should lend it to me: in that case I can bring it tomorrow." The chest was brought in from the carriage, and ten thousand were taken from it for

Khlobuev; the remaining five were promised for the next day: promised, yes; but the intention was to bring three; and the rest later, in two or three days, and, if possible, to delay a bit longer still. Pavel Ivanovich somehow especially disliked letting money leave his hands. And if there was an extreme necessity, still it seemed better to him to hand over the money tomorrow and not today. That is, he acted as we all do! We enjoy showing the petitioner the door. Let him cool his heels in the anteroom! As if he couldn't wait! What do we care that every hour, perhaps, is dear to him, and his affairs are suffering for it! "Come tomorrow, brother, today I somehow have no time."

"And where are you going to live afterwards?" Platonov asked Khlobuev. "Have you got another little estate?"

"No little estate, but I'll move to town. That had to be done in any case, not for ourselves but for the children. They'll need teachers of catechism, music, dance. One can't get that in the country."

"Not a crust of bread, and he wants to teach his children to dance!" thought Chichikov.

"Strange!" thought Platonov.

"Well, we must drink to the deal," said Khlobuev. "Hey, Kiryushka, bring us a bottle of champagne, brother."

"Not a crust of bread, yet he's got champagne!" thought Chichikov.

Platonov did not know what to think.

The champagne was brought. They drank three glasses each and got quite merry. Khlobuev relaxed and became intelligent and charming. Witticisms and anecdotes poured ceaselessly from him. There turned out to be much knowledge of life and the world in his talk! He saw many things so well and so correctly, he sketched his neighboring landowners in a few words, so aptly and so cleverly, saw so clearly everyone's defects and mistakes, knew so well the story of the ruined gentry – why, and how, and for what reason they had been ruined – was able to convey so originally and aptly their smallest habits, that the two men were totally enchanted by his talk and were ready to acknowledge him a most intelligent man.

"Listen," said Platonov, seizing his hand, "how is it that with such intelligence, experience, and knowledge of life, you cannot find ways of getting out of your difficult position?"

"Oh, there are ways!" said Khlobuev, and forthwith unloaded on them a whole heap of projects. They were all so absurd, so strange, so little consequent upon a knowledge of people and the world, that it remained only to shrug one's shoulders and say: "Good lord! what an infinite distance there is between *knowledge of the world* and the ability to use that knowledge!" Almost all the projects were based on the need for suddenly procuring a hundred or two hundred thousand somewhere. Then, it seemed to him, everything could be arranged properly, and the management would get under way, and all the holes would be patched, and the income would be quadrupled, and it would be possible for him to repay all his debts. And he would end with the words: "But what do you want me to do? There simply is no such benefactor as would decide to lend me two hundred or at least one hundred thousand! Clearly, God is against it."

"What else," thought Chichikov. "As if God would send such a fool two hundred thousand!"

"There is this aunt of mine who's good for three million," said Khlobuev, "a pious little old lady: she gives to churches and monasteries, but she's a bit tight about helping her neighbor. And she's a very remarkable little old lady. An aunt from olden times, worth having a look at. She has some four hundred canaries alone. Lapdogs, and lady companions, and servants such as don't exist nowadays. The youngest of her servants is about sixty, though she shouts 'Hey, boy!' to him. If a guest behaves improperly somehow, she orders him bypassed one course at dinner. And they actually do it."

Platonov laughed.

"And what is her last name, and where does she live?" asked Chichikov.

"She lives here in town – Alexandra Ivanovna Khanasarova."

"Why don't you turn to her?" Platonov said sympathetically. "It seems to me, if she just entered a little more into the situation of your family, she'd be unable to refuse you, however tight she is."

"Ah, no, quite able! My aunt has a hard character. This little old lady is a rock, Platon Mikhalych! And there are already enough toadies hanging around her without me. There's one there who is after a governorship, foisted himself off as her relative . . . God help him! maybe he'll succeed! God help them, all! I never knew how to fawn, and now less than ever: my back doesn't bend anymore."

"Fool!" thought Chichikov. "I'd look after such an aunt like a nanny looking after a child!"

"Well, now, such talk makes one dry," said Khlobuev. "Hey, Kiryushka! bring us another bottle of champagne."

"No, no, I won't drink any more," said Platonov.

"Nor I," said Chichikov. And they both declined resolutely.

"Then at least give me your word that you'll visit me in town: on the eighth of June I'm giving a dinner for our town dignitaries."

"For pity's sake!" exclaimed Platonov. "In this situation, completely ruined – and still giving dinners?"

"What can I do? I must. It's my duty," said Khlobuev. "They've also invited me."

"What's to be done with him?" thought Platonov. He still did not know that in Russia, in Moscow and other cities, there are such wizards to be found, whose life is an inexplicable riddle. He seems to have spent everything, is up to his ears in debt, has no resources anywhere, and the dinner that is being given promises to be the last; and the diners think that by the next day the host will be dragged off to prison. Ten years pass after that – the wizard is still holding out in the world, is up to his ears in debt more than ever, and still gives a dinner in the same way, and everybody thinks it will be the last, and everybody is sure that the next day the host will be dragged off to prison. Khlobuev was such a wizard. Only in Russia can one exist in such a way. Having nothing, he welcomed visitors, gave parties, and even patronized and encouraged all sorts of actors passing through town, boarded them and lodged them in his house. If someone were to peek into the house he had in town, he would never know who the owner was. One day a priest in vestments served a *molieben*[6] there, the next day French actors were having a rehearsal. Once someone unknown to nearly everyone in the house installed himself in the drawing room with his papers and set up an office there, without embarrassing or troubling anyone in the house, as if it were an ordinary thing. Sometimes there was not a crumb in the house for whole days, and sometimes such dinners were given as would satisfy the taste of the most refined gastronome. The host would appear festive, gay, with the bearing of a wealthy gentleman, with the step of a man whose life is spent amid ease and plenty. At times, on the other hand, there were such hard moments that someone else in his place would have hanged or shot himself. But he was saved by a religious sense, which was strangely combined in him with his wayward life. In these hard, bitter moments he would open a book and read the lives of those toilers and sufferers who trained their spirit to rise above sufferings and misfortunes. His soul softened at such times, his spirit became tender, and his eyes filled with tears. And – strange thing! – at such moments unexpected help would always come to him from somewhere. Either one of his old friends would remember him and send him money; or some unknown lady traveler, chancing to hear his story, would, with the impetuous magnanimity of a woman's heart, send him a generous donation; or some lawsuit, of which he had never heard, would be won in his favor. With reverence, with gratitude, he would then acknowledge the boundless mercy of Providence, have a *molieben* of thanksgiving served, and – again begin his wayward life.

"I'm sorry for him, really, I am!" Platonov said to Chichikov, when, after saying good-bye, they left him.

"A prodigal son!" said Chichikov. "There's no point in being sorry for such people."

And soon they both stopped thinking about him. Platonov, because he looked upon people's situations lazily and half-sleepily, just as upon everything else in the world. His heart commiserated and was wrung at the sight of others' suffering, but the impressions somehow did not get deeply impressed on his soul. He did not think about Khlobuev because he also did not think about himself. Chichikov did not think about Khlobuev because all his thoughts were taken up with the acquired property. He counted, calculated, and figured out all the profits of the purchased estate. And however he considered it, whichever side of the deal he looked at, he saw that the purchase was in any case profitable. He might do it in such a way that the estate got mortgaged. He might do it in such a way that only the dead and the runaways got mortgaged. He could also do it so that all the best parts were sold off first, and only then mortgage it. He could also arrange it so that he himself managed the estate and became a landowner after the fashion of Kostanzhoglo, drawing on his advice as a neighbor and benefactor. He could even do it in such a way that the estate was resold into private hands (if he did not feel like managing it himself, of course), and keep the runaway and dead ones for himself. Then another profit presented itself: he could slip away from those parts altogether without paying this Kostanzhoglo the borrowed money. In short, whichever way he turned the deal, he saw that in any case the purchase was profitable. He felt pleasure – pleasure at having now become a landowner, not a fantastic landowner, but a real one, a landowner who already had land, and forests, and people

– not dream people, who dwell in imagination, but existing ones. And gradually he began hopping up and down, and rubbing his hands, and humming, and mumbling, and he trumpeted out some march on his fist, putting it to his lips like a trumpet, and even uttered several encouraging words and appellations for himself, in the genre of snookums and sweetie pie. But then, remembering that he was not alone, he suddenly quieted down, and tried to stifle somehow this immoderate fit of inspiration, and when Platonov, taking some of these sounds for speech addressed to him, asked him: "What?" – he replied: "Nothing."

Only here, looking around him, did he notice that they were driving through a beautiful grove; a comely fence of birches stretched to right and left of them. Between the trees flashed a white stone church. At the end of the street a gentleman appeared, coming to meet them, in a peaked cap, with a knobby stick in his hand. A sleek English hound was running on long legs in front of him.

"Stop!" Platonov said to the coachman, and jumped out of the carriage.

Chichikov also got out of the carriage behind him. They went on foot to meet the gentleman. Yarb had already managed to exchange kisses with the English hound, with whom he had obviously been long acquainted, because he offered his fat muzzle indifferently to receive a lively kiss from Azor (so the English hound was called). The frisky hound named Azor, having kissed Yarb, ran up to Platonov, licked his hands with his frisky tongue, leaped up at Chichikov's chest intending to lick his lips, did not make it, and, having been pushed away, ran again to Platonov, to try at least to lick him on the ear.

Platon and the gentleman who was coming to meet them came together at that moment and embraced each other.

"For pity's sake, brother Platon! what are you doing to me?" the gentleman asked animatedly.

"What do you mean?" Platon replied indifferently.

"What, indeed! For three days not a word, not a peep from you! The stableboy brought your horse from Petukh. 'He went off with some gentleman,' he said. Well, send word at least: where, why, and how long? For pity's sake, brother, how could you do such a thing? God knows what I've been thinking all these days!"

"Well, what can I do? I forgot," said Platonov. "We stopped at Konstantin Fyodorovich's . . . He sends his respects to you, and sister does, too. Allow me to introduce Pavel Ivanovich Chichikov. Pavel Ivanovich – my brother Vassily. I beg you to love him as you do me."

Brother Vassily and Chichikov took off their caps and kissed each other.

"Who might this Chichikov be?" thought brother Vassily. "Brother Platon isn't fastidious about his acquaintances, he certainly did not find out what sort of man he is." And he looked Chichikov over as far as decency allowed, and saw that he was standing with his head slightly inclined, and had an agreeable look on his face.

For his part, Chichikov also looked brother Vassily over as far as decency allowed. He was shorter than Platon, his hair was darker, and his face far less handsome; but in the features of his face there was much life and animation. One could see that he did not dwell in drowsiness and hibernation.

"You know what I've decided, Vassily?" brother Platon said.

"What?" asked Vassily.

"To take a trip around holy Russia with Pavel Ivanovich here: it may just loosen and limber up my spleen."

"How did you decide so suddenly . . . ?" Vassily started to say, seriously perplexed by such a decision, and he almost added: "And, what's more, think of going with a man you've never seen before, who may be trash or devil knows what!" And, filled with mistrust, he began studying Chichikov out of the corner of his eye, and saw that he behaved with extraordinary decency, keeping his head agreeably inclined a bit to one side, and with the same respectfully cordial expression on his face, so that there was no way of knowing what sort of man Chichikov was.

Silently the three of them walked down the road, to the left of which there was a white stone church flashing among the trees, and to the right the buildings of the master's house, which were also beginning to appear among the trees. At last the gates appeared. They entered the courtyard, where stood the old manor house under its high roof. Two enormous lindens growing in the middle of the courtyard covered almost half of it with their shade. Through their low-hanging, bushy branches the walls of the house barely flickered from behind. Under the lindens stood several long benches. Brother Vassily invited Chichikov to be seated. Chichikov sat down, and Platonov sat down. The whole courtyard was filled with the fragrance of flowering lilacs and bird cherry, which, hanging from the garden into the yard on all sides over the very pretty birch fence that surrounded it, looked like a flowering chain or a bead necklace crowning it.

An adroit and deft lad of about seventeen, in a handsome pink cotton shirt, brought and set down before them carafes of water and a variety of many-colored kvasses that fizzed like lemonade. Having set the carafes down before them, he went over to a tree and, taking the hoe that was leaning against it, went to the garden. All the household serfs of the Platonov brothers worked in the garden, all the servants were gardeners, or, better, there were no servants, but the gardeners sometimes performed their duties. Brother Vassily always maintained that one could do without servants. Anyone can bring anything, and it was not worth having a special class of people for that; the Russian man is good, efficient, handsome, nimble, and hardworking only as long as he goes about in a shirt and homespun jacket, but as soon as he gets into a German frock coat, he becomes awkward, uncomely, inefficient, and lazy. He maintained that he keeps himself clean only so long as he wears a shirt and homespun jacket, but as soon as he gets into a German frock coat, he stops changing his shirt, does not go to the bathhouse, sleeps in the frock coat, and under it breeds bedbugs, fleas, and devil knows what. In this he may even have been right. The people on their estate dressed somehow especially neatly and nattily, and one would have had to go far to find such handsome shirts and jackets.

"Would you care for some refreshment?" brother Vassily said to Chichikov, pointing to the carafes. "These are kvasses of our own making; our house has long been famous for them."

Chichikov poured a glass from the first carafe – just like the linden mead he used to drink in Poland: bubbly as champagne, and it went in a pleasant fizz right up his nose.

"Nectar!" said Chichikov. He drank a glass from another carafe – even better.

"In what direction and to what places are you thinking mainly of going?" brother Vassily asked.

"I'm going," said Chichikov, rubbing his knee with his hand to accompany the slight rocking of his whole body and inclining his head to one side, "not so much on my own necessity as on another man's. General Betrishchev, a close friend and, one might say, benefactor, has asked me to visit his relatives. Relatives, of course, are relatives, but it is partly, so to speak, for my own sake as well, for – to say nothing of the benefit in the hemorrhoidal respect – to see the world and the circulation of people – is already in itself, so to speak, a living book and a second education."

Brother Vassily lapsed into thought. "The man speaks somewhat ornately, but there's truth in his words," he thought. "My brother Platon lacks knowledge of people, the world, and life." After a short silence, he spoke aloud thus:

"I am beginning to think, Platon, that a journey may indeed stir you up. Your mind is hibernating. You've simply fallen asleep, and you've fallen asleep not from satiety or fatigue, but from a lack of living impressions and sensations. I, for instance, am quite the contrary. I'd very much like not to feel so keenly and not to take so closely to heart all that happens."

"Who makes you take it all so closely to heart?" said Platon. "You seek out worries and invent anxieties for yourself."

"Why invent, if there are troubles at every step even without that?" said Vassily. "Have you heard what trick Lenitsyn has played on us? He's appropriated the waste land where our people celebrate Krasnaya Gorka."[7]

"He doesn't know, so he seized it," said Platon. "The man's new here, just come from Petersburg. He must be told, and have it explained to him."

"He knows, he knows very well. I sent to tell him, but he responded with rudeness."

"You must go yourself and explain it. Have a personal talk with him."

"Ah, no. He puts on too many airs. I won't go to him. You can go if you like."

"I'd go, but I don't want to mix in it. He may deceive me and swindle me."

"I'll go, if you like," said Chichikov.

Vassily glanced at him and thought: "He loves going places, this one!"

"Just give me an idea of what sort of man he is," said Chichikov, "and what it's about."

"I'm ashamed to charge you with such an unpleasant mission, because merely to talk with such a man is already an unpleasant mission for me. I must tell you that he is from simple, petty-landowning nobility of our province, got his rank serving in Petersburg, set himself up somehow by marrying someone's illegitimate daughter, and puts on airs. He sets the tone here. But, thank God, in our province people aren't so stupid: for us fashion is no order, and Petersburg is no church."

"Of course," said Chichikov, "and what is it about?"

"It's nonsense, in fact. He hasn't got enough land, so he appropriated our waste land – that is, he reckoned that it wasn't needed and that the owners had forgotten about it, but it so happens that from time immemorial our peasants have gathered there to celebrate Krasnaya Gorka. For that reason, I'm better prepared to sacrifice other, better land than to give up this piece. Custom is sacred to me."

"So you're prepared to let him have other land?"

"I would have been, if he hadn't acted this way with me; but he wants, as I can see, to do it through the courts. Very well, we'll see who wins. Though it's not so clear on the map, there are still witnesses – old people who are living and who remember."

"Hm!" thought Chichikov. "I see they're both a bit off." And he said aloud:

"But it seems to me that the business can be handled peaceably. Everything depends on the mediator. In writ . . . " [*]

* * * *

" . . . that for you yourself it would also be very profitable to transfer, to my name, for instance, all the dead souls registered on your estates in the last census lists, so that I pay the tax on them. And to avoid causing any offense, you can perform the transfer through a deed of purchase, as if the souls were alive."

"Well, now!" Lenitsyn thought. "This is something most strange." And he even pushed his chair back, so entirely puzzled he was.

"I have no doubts that you will agree entirely to this," Chichikov said, "because this is entirely the same sort of thing we've just been talking about. It'll be completed between solid people, in private, and there'll be no offense to anyone."

[*]Two pages are missing from the manuscript. – TRANS.

What to do here? Lenitsyn found himself in a difficult position. He could never have foreseen that an opinion he had just formulated would be so quickly brought to realization. The offer was highly unexpected. Of course, there could be no harm for anyone in this action: the landowners would mortgage these souls anyway, the same as living ones, so there could be no loss for the treasury; the difference was that they would all be in one hand rather than in several. But all the same he was at a loss. He knew the law and was a businessman – a businessman in a good sense: he would not decide a case unjustly for any bribe. But here he hesitated, not knowing what name to give to this action – was it right or wrong? If someone else had addressed him with such an offer, he would have said: "This is nonsense! trifles! I have no wish to fool around or play with dolls." But he liked his guest so much, they agreed on so many things with regard to the success of education and learning – how could he refuse? Lenitsyn found himself in a most difficult position.

But at that moment, just as if to help him in his woe, the young, pug-nosed mistress, Lenitsyn's wife, came into the room, pale, thin, small, and dressed tastefully, like all Petersburg ladies. Following her came a nurse carrying a baby in her arms, the first-born fruit of the tender love of the recently married couple. Chichikov naturally approached the lady at once and, to say nothing of the proper greeting, simply by the agreeable inclining of his head to one side, disposed her greatly in his favor. Then he ran over to the baby. The baby burst into howls; nevertheless, by means of the words: "Goo, goo, darling!" and by flicking his fingers and the carnelian seal on his watch chain, Chichikov managed to lure him into his arms. Taking him into his arms, he started tossing him up, thereby provoking the baby's pleasant smile, which made both parents very happy.

Whether from pleasure or from something else, the baby suddenly misbehaved. Lenitsyn's wife cried out:

"Ah, my God! he's spoiled your whole tailcoat."

Chichikov looked: the sleeve of the brand new tailcoat was all spoiled. "Blast it, the cursed little devil!" he muttered vexedly to himself.

The host, the hostess, and the nurse all ran to fetch some eau de cologne; they began wiping him on all sides.

"It's nothing, nothing at all," Chichikov was saying. "What can an innocent baby do?" At the same time thinking to himself: "And so well aimed, the cursed little canaille!" "A golden age!" he said when he was well wiped off and the agreeable expression had returned to his face again.

"And indeed," the host said, addressing Chichikov, also with an agreeable smile, "what can be more enviable than the age of infancy: no cares, no thoughts of the future . . . "

"A state one would immediately exchange for one's own," said Chichikov.

"At a glance," said Lenitsyn.

But it seems they were both lying: had they been offered such an exchange, they would straightaway have backed out of it. And what fun is it, indeed, sitting in a nurse's arms and spoiling tailcoats!

The young mistress and the firstborn withdrew with the nurse, because something on him had to be put right: having rewarded Chichikov, he had not forgotten himself either.

This apparently insignificant circumstance won the host over completely to satisfying Chichikov. How, indeed, refuse a guest who has been so tender to his little one and paid for it magnanimously with his own tailcoat? Lenitsyn reflected thus: "Why, indeed, not fulfill his request, if such is his wish?"[*]

---

[*]The rest of the chapter is missing from the manuscript. – TRANS.

ONE OF THE LATER CHAPTERS

AT THE VERY moment when Chichikov, in a new Persian dressing gown of gold satin, sprawling on the sofa, was bargaining with an itinerant smuggler-merchant of Jewish extraction and German enunciation, and before them already lay a purchased piece of the foremost Holland shirt linen and two pasteboard boxes with excellent soap of first-rate quality (this was precisely the soap he used to acquire at the Radziwill customs; it indeed had the property of imparting an amazing tenderness and whiteness to the cheeks) – at the moment when he, as a connoisseur, was buying these products necessary for a cultivated man, there came the rumble of a carriage driving up, echoed by a slight reverberation of the windows and walls, and in walked His Excellency Alexei Ivanovich Lenitsyn.

"I lay it before Your Excellency's judgment: what linen, what soap, and how about this little thing I bought yesterday!" At which Chichikov put on his head a skullcap embroidered with gold and beads, and acquired the look of a Persian shah, filled with dignity and majesty.

But His Excellency, without answering the question, said with a worried look:

"I must talk with you about an important matter."

One could see by his face that he was upset. The worthy merchant of German enunciation was sent out at once, and they were left alone.

"Do you know what trouble is brewing? They've found another will of the old woman's, made five years ago. Half of the estate goes to the monastery, and the other half is divided equally between the two wards, and nothing to anyone else."

Chichikov was dumbfounded.

"Well, that will is nonsense. It means nothing, it is annulled by the second one."

"But it's not stated in the second will that it annuls the first."

"It goes without saying: the second annuls the first. The first will is totally worthless. I know the will of the deceased woman very well. I was with her. Who signed it? Who were the witnesses?"

"It was certified in the proper manner, in court. The witnesses were the former probate judge Burmilov and Khavanov."

"That's bad," thought Chichikov, "they say Khavanov's an honest man; Burmilov is an old hypocrite, reads the epistle in church on feast days."

"Nonsense, nonsense," he said aloud, and at once felt himself prepared for any trick. "I know better: I shared the deceased woman's last minutes. I'm informed better than anyone. I'm ready to testify personally under oath."

These words and his resoluteness set Lenitsyn at ease for the moment. He was very worried and had already begun to suspect the possibility of some fabrication on Chichikov's part with regard to the will. Now he reproached himself for his suspicions. The readiness to testify under oath was clear proof that Chichikov was innocent. We do not know whether Pavel Ivanovich would have had the courage to swear on the Bible, but he did have the courage to say it.

"Rest assured, I'll discuss the matter with several lawyers. There's nothing here that needs doing on your part; you must stay out of it entirely. And I can now live in town as long as I like."

Chichikov straightaway ordered the carriage readied and went to see a lawyer. This lawyer was a man of extraordinary experience. For fifteen years he had been on trial himself, but he had managed so that it was quite impossible to remove him from his post. Everyone knew him, and knew that he ought to have been sent into exile six times over for his deeds. There were suspicions of him all around and on every side, yet it was impossible to present any clear and proven evidence. Here there was indeed something mysterious, and he might have been boldly recognized as a sorcerer if the story we are telling belonged to the times of ignorance.

The lawyer struck him with the coldness of his looks and the greasiness of his dressing gown, in complete contrast to the good mahogany furniture, the golden clock under its glass case, the chandelier visible through the muslin cover protecting it, and generally to everything around him, which bore the vivid stamp of brilliant European cultivation.

Not hindered, however, by the lawyer's skeptical appearance, Chichikov explained the difficult points of the matter and depicted in alluring perspective the gratitude necessarily consequent upon good counsel and concern.

To this the lawyer responded by depicting the uncertainty of all earthly things, and artfully alluded to the fact that two birds in the bush meant nothing, and what was needed was one in the hand.

There was no help for it: he had to give him the bird in the hand. The philosopher's skeptical coldness suddenly vanished. He turned out to be a most good-natured man, most talkative, and most agreeable in his talk, not inferior to Chichikov himself in the adroitness of his manners.

"If I may, instead of starting a long case, you probably did not examine the will very well: there's probably some sort of little addition. Take it home for a while. Though, of course, it's prohibited to take such things home, still, if you ask certain officials nicely . . . I, for my part, will exercise my concern."

"I see," thought Chichikov, and he said: "In fact, I really don't remember very well whether there was a little addition or not" – as if he had not written the will himself.

"You'd best look into that. However, in any case," he continued good-naturedly, "always be calm and don't be put out by anything, even if something worse happens. Don't despair of anything ever: there are no incorrigible cases. Look at me: I'm always calm. Whatever mishaps are imputed to me, my calm is imperturbable."

The face of the lawyer-philosopher indeed preserved an extraordinary calm, so that Chichikov was greatly . . . *

"Of course, that's the first thing," he said. "Admit, however, that there may be such cases and matters, such matters and such calumnies on the part of one's enemies, and such difficult situations, that all calm flies away."

"Believe me, that is pusillanimity," the philosopher-jurist replied very calmly and good-naturedly. "Only make sure that the case is all based on documents, that nothing is merely verbal. And as soon as you see that the case is reaching a denouement and can conveniently be resolved, make sure – not really to justify and defend yourself – no, but simply to confuse things by introducing new and even unrelated issues."

"You mean, so as . . . "

"To confuse, to confuse – nothing more," the philosopher replied, "to introduce into the case some other, unrelated circumstances that will entangle other people in it, to make it complicated – nothing more. And then let some Petersburg official come and sort it out. Let him sort it out, just let him!" he repeated, looking into Chichikov's eyes with extraordinary pleasure, the way a teacher looks into his pupil's eyes while explaining some fascinating point in Russian grammar.

"Yes, good, if one picks circumstances capable of blowing smoke in people's eyes," said Chichikov, also looking with pleasure into the philosopher's eyes, like a pupil who has understood the fascinating point explained by his teacher.

"They'll get picked, the circumstances will get picked! Believe me: frequent exercise makes the head resourceful. Above all remember that you're going to be helped. In a

---

*The sentence is unfinished in the manuscript. – TRANS.

complicated case there's gain for many: more officials are needed, and more pay for them...In short, more people must be drawn into the case. Never mind that some of them will get into it for no reason: it's easier for them to justify themselves, they have to respond to the documents, to pay themselves off...So there's bread in it...Believe me, as soon as circumstances get critical, the first thing to do is confuse. One can get it so confused, so entangled, that no one can understand anything. Why am I calm? Because I know: if my affairs get worse, I'll entangle them all in it – the governor, the vice-governor, the police chief, and the magistrate – I'll get them all entangled. I know all their circumstances: who's angry with whom, and who's pouting at whom, and who wants to lock up whom. Let them disentangle themselves later, but while they do, others will have time to make their own gains. The crayfish thrives in troubled waters. Everyone's waiting to entangle everything." Here the jurist-philosopher looked into Chichikov's eyes again with that delight with which the teacher explains to the pupil a still more fascinating point in Russian grammar.

"No, the man is indeed a wizard," Chichikov thought to himself, and he parted from the lawyer in a most excellent and most agreeable state of mind.

Having been completely reassured and reinforced, he threw himself back on the springy cushions of the carriage with careless adroitness, ordered Selifan to take the top down (as he went to the lawyer, he had the top up and even the apron buttoned), and settled exactly like a retired colonel of the hussars, or Vishnepokromov himself – adroitly tucking one leg under the other, turning his face agreeably towards passersby, beaming from under the new silk hat cocked slightly over one ear. Selifan was ordered to proceed in the direction of the shopping arcade. Merchants, both itinerant and aboriginal, standing at the doors of their shops, reverently took their hats off, and Chichikov, not without dignity, raised his own in response. Many of them were already known to him; others, though itinerant, being charmed by the adroit air of this gentleman who knew how to bear himself, greeted him like an acquaintance. The fair in the town of Phooeyslavl was never-ending. After the horse fair and the agricultural fair were over, there came the fair of luxury goods for gentlefolk of high cultivation. The merchants who came on wheels planned to go home not otherwise than on sleds.

"Welcome, sir, welcome!" a German frock coat made in Moscow kept saying, outside a fabric shop, posing courteously, his head uncovered, his hat in his outstretched hand, just barely holding two fingers to his round, glabrous chin and with an expression of cultivated finesse on his face.

Chichikov went into the shop.

"Show me your little fabrics, my most gentle sir."

The propitious merchant at once lifted the removable board in the counter and, having thereby made a passage for himself, wound up inside the shop, his back to his goods, his face to the buyer.

Standing back to his goods and face to the buyer, the merchant of the bare head and the outstretched hat greeted Chichikov once again. Then he put his hat on and, leaning forward agreeably, his two arms resting on the counter, spoke thus:

"What sort of cloth, sir? Of English manufacture, or do you prefer domestic?"

"Domestic," said Chichikov, "only precisely of that best sort known as English cloth."

"What colors would you prefer?" inquired the merchant, still swaying agreeably with his two arms resting on the counter.

"Dark colors, olive or bottle green, with flecks tending, so to speak, towards cranberry," said Chichikov.

"I may say that you will get the foremost sort, of which there is none better in either capital," the merchant said as he hoisted himself to the upper shelf to get the bolt; he flung it down adroitly onto the counter, unrolled it from the other end, and held it to the light. "What play, sir! The most fashionable, the latest taste!"

The cloth gleamed like silk. The merchant could smell that there stood before him a connoisseur of fabrics, and he did not wish to begin with the ten-rouble sort.

"Decent enough," said Chichikov, stroking it lightly. "But I tell you what, my worthy man, show me at once the one you save for last, and there should be more of that color . . . those flecks, those red flecks."

"I understand, sir: you truly want the color that is now becoming fashionable in Petersburg. I have cloth of the most excellent properties. I warn you that the price is high, but so is the quality."

"Let's have it."

Not a word about the price.

The bolt fell from above. The merchant unrolled it with still greater art, grasping the other end and unrolling it like silk, offered it to Chichikov so that he would have the opportunity not only of examining it, but even of smelling it, and merely said:

"Here's the fabric, sir! the colors of the smoke and flame of Navarino!"[8]

The price was agreed upon. The iron yardstick, like a magician's wand, meted out enough for Chichikov's tailcoat and trousers. Having snipped it a little with his scissors, the merchant performed with both hands the deft tearing of the fabric across its whole width, and on finishing bowed to Chichikov with the most seductive agreeableness. The fabric was straightaway folded and deftly wrapped in paper; the package twirled under the light string. Chichikov was just going to his pocket when he felt his waist being pleasantly encircled by someone's very delicate arm, and his ears heard:

"What are you buying here, my most respected friend?"

"Ah, what a pleasantly unexpected meeting!" said Chichikov.

"A pleasant encounter," said the voice of the same man who had encircled his waist. It was Vishnepokromov. "I was prepared to pass by the shop without paying any attention, when suddenly I saw a familiar face – how can one deny oneself an agreeable pleasure! There's no denying the fabrics are incomparably better this year. It's a shame and a disgrace! I simply couldn't find... Thirty roubles, forty roubles I'm prepared to ... ask even fifty, but give me something good. I say either one has something that is really of the most excellent quality, or it's better not to have it at all. Right?"

"Absolutely right!" said Chichikov. "Why work, if it's not so as to have something really good?"

"Show me some moderate-priced fabrics," a voice came from behind that seemed familiar to Chichikov. He turned around: it was Khlobuev. By all tokens he was buying fabric not merely on a whim, for his wretched frock coat was quite worn out.

"Ah, Pavel Ivanovich! allow me to speak with you at last. One can't find you anymore. I came by several times – you're always out."

"My esteemed friend, I've been so busy that, by God, I've had no time." He looked around, hoping to elude explanations, and saw Murazov coming into the shop. "Afanasy Vassilyevich! Ah, my God!" said Chichikov. "What a pleasant encounter!"

And Vishnepokromov repeated after him:

"Afanasy Vassilyevich!"

And Khlobuev repeated:

"Afanasy Vassilyevich!"

And, lastly, the well-bred merchant, having carried his hat as far away from his head as his arm permitted, and, all of him thrust forward, pronounced:

"To Afanasy Vassilyevich – our humblest respects!"

Their faces were stamped with that doglike servility that is rendered unto millionaires by the doglike race of men.

The old man exchanged bows with them all and turned directly to Khlobuev:

"Excuse me: I saw you from far off going into the shop, and decided to trouble you. If you're free afterwards and my house is not out of your way, kindly stop by for a short while. I must have a talk with you."

Khlobuev said:

"Very well, Afanasy Vassilyevich."

"What wonderful weather we're having, Afanasy Vassilyevich," said Chichikov.

"Isn't that so, Afanasy Vassilyevich," Vishnepokromov picked up, "it's extraordinary."

"Yes, sir, thank God, it's not bad. But we need a bit of rain for the crops."

"We do, very much," said Vishnepokromov, "it would even be good for the hunting."

"Yes, a bit of rain wouldn't hurt," said Chichikov, who did not need any rain, but felt it so pleasant to agree with a man who had a million.

And the old man, having bowed to them all again, walked out.

"My head simply spins," said Chichikov, "when I think that this man has ten million. It's simply impossible."

"It's not a rightful thing, though," said Vishnepokromov, "capital shouldn't be in one man's hands. That's even the subject of treatises now all over Europe. You have money – so, share it with others: treat people, give balls, produce beneficent luxury, which gives bread to the artisans, the master craftsmen."

"This I am unable to understand," said Chichikov. "Ten million – and he lives like a simple muzhik! With ten million one could do devil knows what. It could be so arranged that you wouldn't have any other company than generals and princes."

"Yes, sir," the merchant added, "with all his respectable qualities, there's much uncultivatedness in Afanasy Vassilyevich. If a merchant is respectable, he's no longer a merchant, he's already in a certain way a negotiant. I've got to take a box in the theater, then, and I'll never marry my daughter to a mere colonel – no, sir, I won't marry her to anything but a general. What's a colonel to me? My dinner's got to be provided by a confectioner, not just any cook . . . "

"What's there to talk about! for pity's sake," said Vishnepokromov, "what can one not do with ten million? Give me ten million – you'll see what I'll do!"

"No," thought Chichikov, "you won't do much that's sensible with ten million. But if I were to have ten million, I'd really do something."

"No, if I were to have ten million now, after this dreadful experience!" thought Khlobuev. "Eh, it would be different now: one comes to know the value of every kopeck by experience." And then, having thought for a moment, he asked himself inwardly: "Would I really handle it more intelligently?" And, waving his hand, he added: "What the devil! I suppose I'd squander it just as I did before," and he walked out of the shop, burning with desire to know what Murazov would say to him.

"I've been waiting for you, Pyotr Petrovich!" said Murazov, when he saw Khlobuev enter. "Please come to my little room."

And he led Khlobuev into the little room already familiar to the reader, and so unpretentious that an official with a salary of seven hundred roubles a year would not have one more so.

"Tell me, now, I suppose your circumstances have improved? You did get something from your aunt?"

"How shall I tell you, Afanasy Vassilyevich? I don't know whether my circumstances have improved. I got only fifty peasant souls and thirty thousand roubles, which I had to pay out to cover part of my debts – and I again have exactly nothing. And the main thing is that this thing about the will is most shady. Such swindling has been going on here, Afanasy Vassilyevich! I'll tell you right now, and you'll marvel at such goings-on. This Chichikov..."

"Excuse me, Pyotr Petrovich: before we talk about this Chichikov, allow me to talk about you yourself. Tell me: how much, in your estimation, would be satisfactory and sufficient for you to extricate yourself completely from these circumstances?"

"My circumstances are difficult," said Khlobuev. "And in order to extricate myself, pay everything off, and have the possibility of living in the most moderate fashion, I would need at least a hundred thousand, if not more. In short, it's impossible for me."

"Well, and if you had it, how would you lead your life then?"

"Well, I would then rent a little apartment and occupy myself with my children's upbringing, because I'm not going to enter the service: I'm no longer good for anything."

"And why are you no longer good for anything?"

"But where shall I go, judge for yourself! I can't start as an office clerk. You forget that I have a family. I'm forty, I have lower-back pains, I've grown lazy; they won't give me a more important post; I'm not in good repute. I confess to you: I personally would not take a lucrative post. I may be a worthless man, a gambler, anything you like, but I won't take bribes. I wouldn't get along with Krasnonosov and Samosvistov."

"But still, excuse me, sir, I can't understand how one can be without any path; how can you walk if not down a path; how can you drive if there's no ground under you; how can you float if the bark isn't in the water? And life is a journey. Forgive me, Pyotr Petrovich, those gentlemen of whom you are speaking are, after all, on some sort of path, they do work, after all. Well, let's say they turned off somehow, as happens with every sinner; yet there's hope they'll find their way back. Whoever walks can't fail to arrive; there's hope he'll find his way back. But how will one who sits idle get to any path? The path won't come to me."

"Believe me, Afanasy Vassilyevich, I feel you're absolutely right, but I tell you that all activity has decidedly perished and died in me; I don't see that I can be of any use to anyone in the world. I feel that I'm decidedly a useless log. Before, when I was younger, it seemed to me that it was all a matter of money, that if I had hundreds of thousands in my hands, I'd make many people happy: I'd help poor artists, I'd set up libraries, useful institutions, assemble collections. I'm a man not without taste, and I know that in many respects I could manage better than those rich men among us who do it all senselessly. And now I see that this, too, is vanity and there's not much sense in it. No, Afanasy Vassilyevich, I'm good for nothing, precisely nothing, I tell you. I'm not capable of the least thing."

"Listen, Pyotr Petrovich! But you do pray, you go to church, you don't miss any matins or vespers, I know. Though you don't like getting up early, you do get up and go – you go at four o'clock in the morning, when no one's up yet."

"That is a different matter, Afanasy Vassilyevich. I do it for the salvation of my soul, because I'm convinced that I will thereby make up at least somewhat for my idle life, that, bad as I am, prayers still mean something to God. I tell you that I pray, that even without faith, I still pray. One feels only that there is a master on whom everything depends, as a horse or a beast of burden smells the one who harnesses him."

"So you pray in order to please the one you pray to, in order to save your soul, and this gives you strength and makes you get up early from your bed. Believe me, if you were to undertake your work in the same fashion, as if in the certainty that you are serving the one you pray to, you would become active and no man among us would be able to cool you down."

"Afanasy Vassilyevich! I tell you again that this is something different. In the first case I see that anyway I'm doing something. I tell you that I'm ready to go to the monastery, and I'll do whatever labors and deeds they impose on me there, even the heaviest. I'm sure that it's not my business to reason about what will be asked of those who make me do it; there I obey and know that I'm obeying God."

"And why don't you reason that way in worldly matters as well? In the world we must also serve God and no one else. Even if we serve another, we do it only while being convinced that God tells us to do so, and without that we would not serve. What else are all our abilities and gifts, which vary from one person to another? They are tools for our prayer: the one is in words, and the other is in deeds. You cannot go to a monastery: you're tied to the world, you have a family."

Here Murazov fell silent. Khlobuev also fell silent.

"So you suppose that if you had, for instance, two hundred thousand, you would be able to shore up your life and live more economically therafter?"

"That is, at least I would occupy myself with what I would be able to do – my children's upbringing; it would be possible for me to provide them with good teachers."

"And shall I tell you this, Pyotr Petrovich, that in two years you'd again be over your head in debt, as in a net?"

Khlobuev was silent for a while, and then began measuredly:

"Not really, though, after such experience . . . "

"What's experience?" said Murazov. "You see, I know you. You're a man with a good heart: a friend will come to borrow money from you – you'll give it to him; you'll see a poor man and want to help; a nice guest will come – you'll want to receive him better, and you'll obey that first good impulse and forget your accounting. And allow me finally to tell you in all sincerity that you are unable to bring up your own children. Children can be brought up only by a father who has already done his own duty. And your wife . . . she, too, is good-hearted . . . she wasn't brought up at all so as to be able to bring up children. I even think – forgive me, Pyotr Petrovich – mightn't it even be harmful for the children to be with you?"

Khlobuev thought a little: he began to examine himself mentally on all sides and finally felt that Murazov was partly right.

"You know what, Pyotr Petrovich? hand it all over to me – your children, your affairs; leave your family, and the children: I'll take care of them. Your circumstances are such that you are in my hands; you're heading for starvation. Here you must be prepared to do anything. Do you know Ivan Potapych?"

"And respect him greatly, even though he goes around in a *sibirka*."

"Ivan Potapych was a millionaire, got his daughters married to officials, lived like a tsar; but once he was bankrupt – what to do? He went and became a shop clerk. It was no fun for him going from a silver platter to a simple bowl: it seemed he couldn't set a hand to anything. Now Ivan Potapych could gobble from a silver platter, but he no longer wants to. He could save it all up again, but he says: 'No, Afanasy Ivanovich,* now I do not serve myself or for myself, but because God has judged so. I don't wish to do anything of my own will. I listen to you, because I wish to obey God and not people, and because God speaks only through the mouths of the best people. You are more intelligent than I am, and therefore it is not I who answer, but you.' That is what Ivan Potapych says; and he, if the truth be told, is many times more intelligent than I am."

"Afanasy Vassilyevich! I, too, am ready to acknowledge your power over me, I am your servant and whatever you want: I give myself to you. But don't give me work beyond my strength: I'm no Potapych, and I tell you that I'm not fit for anything good."

*Thus in the manuscript; it should be Vassilyevich. – TRANS.

"It is not I, Pyotr Petrovich, who will impose it on you, but since you wish to serve, as you yourself say, sir, here is a God-pleasing deed for you. There is a church being built in a certain place on voluntary donations from pious people. There's not enough money, a collection must be taken. Put on a simple *sibirka*... you see, you're a simple man now, a ruined nobleman, the same as a beggar: why pretend? With ledger in hand, in a simple cart, go around to the towns and villages. You'll get a blessing and a loose-leaf ledger from the bishop, and go with God."

Pyotr Petrovich was amazed by this completely new duty. He, a nobleman, after all, of a once ancient family, was to set out with a ledger in his hand, to beg donations for a church, and go bouncing along in a cart to boot! And yet it was impossible to wriggle out of it or avoid it: it was a God-pleasing thing.

"Thinking it over?" said Murazov. "You'll be performing two services here: one for God, and the other – for me."

"What for you?"

"Here's what. Since you'll be going to places where I've never been, you'll find out everything on the spot, sir: how the muzhiks live there, where the richer ones are, where the needy, and what condition it's all in. I must tell you that I love the muzhiks, perhaps because I myself come from muzhiks. But the thing is that all sorts of vileness is going on among them. Old Believers[9] and various vagabonds confuse them, sir, get them to rebel against the authorities, yes, against the authorities and the regulations, and if a man is oppressed, he rebels easily. Why, as if it's hard to stir up a man who is truly suffering! But the thing is that reprisals ought not to start from below. It's bad when it comes to fists: there'll be no sense to it, only the thieves will gain. You're an intelligent man, you'll examine things, you'll find out where a man indeed suffers from others, and where from his own restless character, and then you'll tell me about it all. I'll give you a small sum of

money just in case, to give to those who truly suffer innocently. For your part, it will also be helpful to comfort them
with your word, and to explain to them as best you can that
God tells us to endure without murmuring, and to pray in
times of misfortune, and not to be violent and take justice into
our own hands. In short, speak to them, not rousing anyone
against anyone else, but reconciling them all. If you see hatred
in anyone against whomever it may be, apply all your efforts."

"Afanasy Vassilyevich! the task you are entrusting to me,"
said Khlobuev, "is a holy task; but remember whom you are
entrusting it to. You might entrust it to a man who is of almost
holy life and already knows how to forgive others."

"But I'm not saying you should accomplish it all, only as
much as possible, whatever you can. The thing is that you will
come back from those parts with some knowledge in any case,
and will have an idea of the situation in that area. An official
will never meet anyone personally, and a muzhik will not be
frank with him. While you, collecting for the church, will call
on all sorts of people – tradesmen, merchants – and will have
the chance to question them all. I'm telling you this, sir,
because the governor-general now has special need of such
people; and you, bypassing all official promotions, will get a
position in which your life will not be useless."

"I'll try, I'll apply my efforts, as far as my strength allows,"
said Khlobuev. And reassurance could be noted in his voice,
his back straightened, and his head lifted, as with a man upon
whom hope shines. "I see that God has granted you understanding, and you know certain things better than we near-
sighted people."

"Now allow me to ask you," said Murazov, "what Chichikov is and what sort of affair it is?"

"I can tell you unheard-of things about Chichikov. He pulls
such deals . . . Do you know, Afanasy Vassilyevich, that the will
is false? The real one has been found, in which the whole estate
goes to the wards."

"What are you saying? But who, then, concocted the false will?"

"That's just the thing, it's a most vile affair! They say it was Chichikov, and that the will was signed after death: they dressed up some woman in place of the deceased, and it was she who signed it. In short, a most tempting affair. They say thousands of petitions have come from all sides. Marya Yeremeevna is now besieged by wooers; two functionaries are already fighting over her. That's what sort of affair it is, Afanasy Vassilyevich!"

"I've heard nothing about it, but the affair is indeed not quite sinless. I confess, I find Pavel Ivanovich Chichikov a most mysterious person," said Murazov.

"I, too, sent in a petition for myself, as a reminder that there exists a nearest heir . . . "

"They can fight it out among themselves for all of me," Khlobuev thought on his way out. "Afanasy Vassilyevich is no fool. He must have given me this charge after thinking it over. Just let me accomplish it – that's all." He began thinking about the road, at the same time as Murazov was still repeating to himself: "A most mysterious man to me, this Pavel Ivanovich Chichikov! If only such will and perseverance were put to good use!"

And meanwhile, indeed, petition after petition kept coming to the courts. Relatives turned up of whom no one had ever heard. As birds come flying to carrion, so everything came flying down upon the incalculable wealth left by the old woman. Denunciations of Chichikov, of the spuriousness of the last will, denunciations of the spuriousness of the first will also, evidence of theft and of the concealment of certain sums. Evidence turned up against Chichikov of his buying dead souls, of smuggling goods while he was still in customs. Everything was unearthed, the whole story of his past was found out. God knows how they got wind of it all and learned it. Yet there was evidence even of such things as Chichikov thought no one knew of except for himself and his four walls. So far it was all still a court secret and had not yet reached his ears, though a trustworthy note he had recently received from his lawyer gave him some idea that trouble was brewing. The content of the note was brief: "I hasten to inform you that there will be some fuss around the case; but remember that you ought by no means to worry. The main thing is to be calm. Everything will be taken care of." This note set him completely at ease. "The man is indeed a genius," said Chichikov.

To crown all blessings, the tailor brought his suit at that moment. Chichikov felt a strong desire to look at himself in the new tailcoat of the flames and smoke of Navarino. He pulled on the trousers, which hugged him marvelously on all sides, an artist's ideal. The hips were so nicely fitted, the calves, too; the cloth hugged all the details, imparting to them a still greater resilience. Once he had tightened the clasp behind him, his stomach became like a drum. He beat on it with a brush, adding: "Such a fool, but, overall, what a picture he makes!" The tailcoat, it seemed, was even better tailored than the trousers: not one wrinkle, tight all around his sides, curving at the overlap, showing his full curvature. It was a little too tight under the right arm, but that made it fit still better at the waist. The tailor, standing there in complete triumph, merely said: "Rest assured, outside Petersburg there's no such tailoring anywhere." The tailor was from Petersburg himself, and had put on his shingle: "A foreigner from London and Paris." He was not given to joking, and wanted with these two cities to stop up the maws of all the other tailors at once, so that in the future no one could come out with such cities, and they would have to content themselves with writing some "Karlsroo" or "Copenhar."

Chichikov magnanimously paid the tailor and, left alone, began to examine himself at leisure in the mirror, like an artist, with aesthetic feeling and *con amore*. It turned out that everything was somehow even better than before: the little cheeks were more interesting, the chin more alluring, the white collar imparted its color to the cheek, the blue satin tie imparted its hue to the collar; the shirtfront, pleated in the latest fashion, imparted its hue to the tie, the rich velvet waistcoat imparted its hue to the shirtfront, and the tailcoat of the flames and smoke of Navarino, gleaming like silk, imparted its hue to everything! He turned to the right – good! He turned to the left – even better! The curve of the waist was like a courtier's or such a gentleman's as jabbers away in French so that next to him a Frenchman himself is nothing, one who, even when angry, does not disgrace himself indecently with a Russian word, who cannot even swear in Russian, but will give you a good scolding in French dialect. Such delicacy! He tried, inclining his head slightly to one side, to assume a pose as if he were addressing a middle-aged lady of the latest cultivation: it was a picture to see. Painter, take up your brush and paint! In his pleasure, he straightaway performed a light leap, like an entrechat. The chest of drawers shook and a flask of eau de cologne fell to the ground; but this caused no hindrance. He quite properly called the stupid flask a fool, and thought: "Whom shall I visit first of all? The best . . . "

When suddenly in the front hall – something like the clank of spurred boots and a gendarme in full armor, as if he were a whole army in one person. "You are ordered to appear at once before the governor-general!" Chichikov was simply stunned. Before him stuck up a fright with a mustache, a horsetail on his head, a baldric over one shoulder, a baldric over the other, an enormous broadsword hanging at his side. He fancied there was also a gun hanging from the other side, and devil knows what else: a whole army just in one man! He tried to protest, but the fright uttered rudely: "To appear at once!" Through the door to the front hall he saw another fright flit by; he looked out the window – there was a carriage as well. What to do? Just as he was, in his tailcoat of the flames and smoke of Navarino, he had to get in and, trembling all over, drive to the governor-general's, the policeman along with him.

In the anteroom he was not even allowed to come to his senses. "Go in! The prince is waiting for you," said the official on duty. Before him as through a mist flashed the anteroom with messengers receiving packages, then a hall through which he passed, thinking only: "He'll just up and seize me, and with no trial, no anything – straight to Siberia!" His heart began to pound harder than the heart of the most jealous lover. The door finally opened: before him was the office, with portfolios, shelves, books, and the prince as wrathful as wrath itself.

"Destroyer, destroyer," said Chichikov. "He'll destroy my soul, slaughter me, like a wolf a lamb!"

"I spared you, I allowed you to remain in town, when you ought to have been put in jail; and again you've besmirched yourself with the most dishonest swindling a man has yet besmirched himself with."

The prince's lips were trembling with wrath.

"What is this most dishonest action and swindling, Your Excellency?" asked Chichikov, trembling all over.

"The woman," said the prince, stepping closer and looking straight into Chichikov's eyes, "the woman who signed the will at your dictation, has been seized and will confront you."

Chichikov turned pale as a sheet.

"Your Excellency! I'll tell you the whole truth of the matter. I am guilty, indeed, guilty; but not so guilty. I've been maligned by my enemies."

"No one can malign you, because there is many times more vileness in you than the worst liar could invent. In all your life, I suppose, you've never done anything that was not dishonest. Every kopeck you earned was earned dishonestly, and is a theft and a dishonest thing deserving of the knout and Siberia. No, it's enough now! This very minute you will be taken to jail, and there, together with the worst scoundrels and robbers, you must wait for your fate to be decided. And this is still merciful, because you are many times worse than they are: they dress in wool jerkins and sheepskins, while you . . . "

He glanced at the tailcoat of the flames and smoke of Navarino and, taking hold of the bellpull, rang.

"Your Excellency," Chichikov cried out, "be merciful! You are the father of a family. Don't spare me – but spare my old mother!"

"You're lying!" the prince cried wrathfully. "You pleaded with me the same way before, by your children and family, which you never had, and now – your mother!"

"Your Excellency, I am a scoundrel and an utter black-guard," said Chichikov, in a voice . . . * "I was indeed lying, I have no children or family; but, as God is my witness, I always wanted to have a wife, to fulfill the duty of a man and a citizen, so as later to earn indeed the respect of citizens and author-ities . . . But what calamitous coincidences! With my blood, Your Excellency, with my blood I had to procure my daily sustenance. Temptations and seductions at every step . . . enemies, and destroyers, and thieves. My whole life has been like a violent storm or a ship amidst the waves at the will of the winds. I am a man, Your Excellency!"

Tears suddenly poured in streams from his eyes. He col-lapsed at the prince's feet just as he was, in his tailcoat of the flames and smoke of Navarino, in his velvet waistcoat and satin tie, new trousers and hairdo exuding the clean scent of eau de cologne.

"Get away from me! Call the guards to take him away!" the prince said to those who came in.

"Your Excellency!" Chichikov cried, seizing the prince's boot with both hands.

A shuddering sensation ran through the prince's every fiber.

"Get away, I tell you!" he said, trying to tear his foot from Chichikov's embrace.

---

*The phrase is unfinished in the manuscript. – TRANS.

"Your Excellency! I will not move from this spot before I obtain mercy!" Chichikov said, not letting go of the prince's boot and sliding, together with his foot, across the floor in his tailcoat of the flames and smoke of Navarino.

"Away, I tell you!" he said, with that inexplicable feeling of disgust that a man feels at the sight of an extremely ugly insect that he does not have the courage to crush underfoot. He gave such a shake that Chichikov felt the boot strike his nose, lips, and nicely rounded chin, but he would not let go of the boot and held the leg still harder in his embrace. Two hefty policemen pulled him away by force, and, holding him under his arms, led him through all the rooms. He was pale, crushed, in the insensibly frightful state of a man who sees black, inescapable death before him, that fright which is contrary to our nature . . .

Just at the doorway to the stairs they ran into Murazov. A ray of hope suddenly flickered. Instantly, with unnatural force, he tore from the grip of the two policemen and threw himself at the feet of the amazed old man.

"Pavel Ivanovich, my dear fellow, what's happened?"

"Save me! they're taking me to jail, to death . . . "

The policemen seized him and led him away without allowing him to be heard.

A dank, chill closet with the smell of the boots and leg wrappings of garrison soldiers, an unpainted table, two vile chairs, a window with an iron grate, a decrepit woodstove, through the cracks of which smoke came without giving any warmth – this was the dwelling in which they placed our hero, who had just begun to taste the sweetness of life and attract the attention of his compatriots in his fine new tailcoat of the flames and smoke of Navarino. He was not even given time to arrange to take the necessary things with him, to take the chest with the money in it. His papers, the deeds of purchase for the dead souls – the officials now had it all! He collapsed on the ground, and the carnivorous worm of terrible, hopeless sorrow wrapped itself around his heart. With increasing speed it began to gnaw at his heart, all unprotected as it was. Another day like that, another day of such sorrow, and there would be no Chichikov in this world at all. But someone's all-saving hand did not slumber even over Chichikov. An hour later the door of the jail opened: old Murazov came in.

If someone tormented by parching thirst were to have a stream of spring water poured down his dry throat, he would not revive as poor Chichikov did.

"My savior!" said Chichikov, and, suddenly seizing his hand, he quickly kissed it and pressed it to his breast. "May God reward you for visiting an unfortunate man!"

He dissolved in tears.

The old man looked at him with mournfully pained eyes and said only:

"Ah, Pavel Ivanovich! Pavel Ivanovich, what have you done?"

"I am a scoundrel ... Guilty ... I transgressed ... But consider, consider, can they treat me like this? I am a nobleman. Without a trial, without an investigation, to throw me into jail, to take away everything – my things, my chest ... there's money in it, all my property, all my property is in it, Afanasy Vassilyevich – property I acquired by sweating blood ... "

And, unable to restrain the impulse of sorrow again overwhelming his heart, he sobbed loudly, in a voice that pierced the thick walls of the jail and echoed dully in the distance, tore off his satin tie, and, clutching at his collar with his hand, tore his tailcoat of the flames and smoke of Navarino.

"Pavel Ivanovich, it makes no difference: you must bid farewell to your property and to all there is in the world. You have fallen under the implacable law, not under the power of some man."

"I have been my own ruin, I know it – I did not know how to stop in time. But why such a terrible punishment, Afanasy Vassilyevich? Am I a robber? Has anyone suffered from me?

Have I made anyone unhappy? By toil and sweat, by sweating blood, I procured my kopeck. Why did I procure this kopeck? In order to live out the rest of my days in comfort, to leave something to my children, whom I intended to acquire for the good, for the service of the fatherland. I erred, I don't deny it, I erred... what to do? But I erred because I saw that I'd get nowhere on the straight path, and that to go crookedly was straighter. But I toiled, I strained. And these scoundrels who sit in the courts taking thousands from the treasury or robbing people who aren't rich, filching the last kopeck from those who have nothing... Afanasy Vassilyevich! I did not fornicate, I did not drink. And so much work, so much iron patience! Yes, it could be said that every kopeck I procured was redeemed with sufferings, sufferings! Let one of them suffer as I did! What has my whole life been: a bitter struggle, a ship amidst the waves. And, Afanasy Vassilyevich, I have lost what was acquired with such struggle..."

He did not finish and sobbed loudly from unendurable heartache, collapsed on the chair, ripped off the torn, hanging skirt of his tailcoat and flung it away from him, and, putting both hands to his hair, which before he had zealously tried to strengthen, he tore it mercilessly, delighting in the pain with which he hoped to stifle his unquenchable heartache.

"Ah, Pavel Ivanovich, Pavel Ivanovich!" Murazov was saying, looking at him mournfully and shaking his head. "I keep thinking what a man you'd be if, in the same way, with energy and patience, you had embarked on good work and for a better purpose! If only any one of those who love the good would apply as much effort to it as you did to procuring your kopeck!... and knew how to sacrifice to that good their own self-love and ambition, without sparing themselves, as you did not spare yourself in procuring your kopeck!..."

"Afanasy Vassilyevich!" said poor Chichikov, seizing both of his hands in his own. "Oh, if I could manage to be set free, to get back my property! I swear to you, I would henceforth lead a completely different life! Save me, benefactor, save me!"

"But what can I do? I would have to fight with the law. Even supposing I ventured to do it, the prince is a just man, he will never back down."

"Benefactor! you can do anything. I'm not afraid of the law – I can find ways to deal with the law – but the fact that I've been thrown into jail innocently, that I will perish here like a dog, and that my property, my papers, my chest . . . save me!"

He embraced the old man's legs and wetted them with his tears.

"Ah, Pavel Ivanovich, Pavel Ivanovich!" old Murazov kept saying, shaking his head. "How blinded you are by this property! Because of it, you don't even hear your own poor soul!"

"I'll think about my soul, too, only save me!"

"Pavel Ivanovich!" old Murazov said and stopped. "To save you is not in my power – you can see that yourself. But I'll try to do all I can to alleviate your lot and set you free. I don't know whether I'll succeed, but I'll try. And if perchance I do succeed, Pavel Ivanovich, then I'll ask a reward from you for my labors: drop all these attempts at these acquisitions. I tell you in all honesty that even if I lost all my property – and I have much more than you do – I wouldn't weep. By God, the point of the thing is not in this property, which can be confiscated, but in that which no one can steal and carry off! You have already lived enough in the world. You yourself call your life a ship amidst the waves. You have enough already to live on for the rest of your days. Settle yourself in some quiet corner, near a church and simple, good people; or, if you're burning with desire to leave posterity behind you, marry a good girl, not rich, accustomed to moderation and simple household life. Forget this noisy world and all its seductive fancies; let it forget you, too. There is no peace in it. You see: everything in it is either an enemy, a tempter, or a traitor."

Chichikov fell to thinking. Something strange, some hitherto unknown feelings, inexplicable to himself, came to him: as if something wanted to awaken in him, something suppressed since childhood by stern, dead precepts, by the inimicalness of a dull childhood, the desolateness of his family home, by familyless solitude, abjectness, and a poverty of first impressions, by the stern glance of fate, which looked dully at him through some clouded window buried under a wintry blizzard.

"Only save me, Afanasy Vassilyevich," he cried out. "I'll lead a different life, I'll follow your advice! Here's my word on it!"

"Watch out now, Pavel Ivanovich, don't go back on your word," Murazov said, holding his hand.

"I might go back on it, if it weren't for such a terrible lesson," poor Chichikov said with a sigh, and added: "But the lesson is a harsh one; a harsh, harsh lesson, Afanasy Vassilyevich!"

"It's good that it's harsh. Thank God for that, pray to Him. I'll go and do what I can for you."

With these words the old man left.

Chichikov no longer wept or tore his tailcoat and his hair: he calmed down.

"No, enough!" he said finally, "a different, different life. It's really time to become a decent man. Oh, if only I could somehow extricate myself and still be left with at least a little capital, I'd settle far away from ... And the deeds? ... " He thought: "What, then? why abandon this business, acquired with such labor? ... I won't buy any more, but I must mortgage those. The acquisition cost me labor! I'll mortgage them, I will, in order to buy an estate. I'll become a landowner, because here one can do much good." And in his mind there awakened those feelings which had come over him when he was at Kostanzhoglo's, listening to his host's nice, intelligent conversation, in the warm evening light, about how fruitful and useful estate management is. The country suddenly appeared so beautiful to him, as if he were able to feel all the charms of country life.

"We're all stupid, chasing after vanity!" he said finally. "Really, it comes from idleness! Everything's near, everything's close at hand, yet we run to some far-off kingdom. Is it not life, if one is occupied, be it even in a remote corner? The pleasure indeed consists in labor. And nothing's sweeter than the fruit of one's own labors . . . No, I'll occupy myself with labor, I'll settle in the country and occupy myself honestly, so as to have a good influence on others as well. What, am I really such a good-for-nothing? I have abilities for management; I possess the qualities of thrift, efficiency, reasonableness, and even constancy. Once I make up my mind, I feel I have them. Only now do I feel truly and clearly that there exists a certain duty that man must fulfill on earth, without tearing himself away from the place and corner he has been put in."

And a life of labor, far removed from the noise of the cities and those seductions invented in his idleness by the man who has forgotten labor, began to picture itself to him so vividly that he almost forgot the whole unpleasantness of his situation, and was, perhaps, even ready to give thanks to Providence for this harsh lesson, if only he were let go and at least part of his money were returned to him. But . . . the single-leafed door of his unclean closet opened and in walked an official person – Samosvistov, an epicure, a daredevil, an excellent friend, a carouser, and a cunning beast, as his own friends called him. In time of war this man might have done wonders: if he had been sent to sneak through some impassable, dangerous places, to steal a cannon right out from under the enemy's nose – it would have been just the thing for him. But, for lack of a military career in which he might have been an honest man, he did dirty and mucked things up. Inconceivably, he was good with his friends, never sold anyone, and, once he gave his word, he kept it; but his own superiors he regarded as something like an enemy battery which one had to make one's way through, taking advantage of every weak spot, breach, or negligence . . .

"We know all about your situation, we've heard everything!" he said, once he saw that the door was tightly shut behind him. "Never mind, never mind! Don't lose heart: it will all be fixed up. Everything will work out for you and – your humble servants! Thirty thousand for us all – and nothing more."

"Really?" Chichikov cried out. "And I'll be completely vindicated?"

"Roundly! and get a nice reward for your losses."

"And for your efforts? . . . "

"Thirty thousand. It goes to everyone – our boys, and the governor-general's, and the secretary."

"But, excuse me, how can I? All my things . . . my chest . . . it's all sealed now, under surveillance . . . "

"You'll have it all within the hour. It's a deal, then?"

Chichikov gave him his hand. His heart was pounding, and he had no trust that it was possible . . .

"Good-bye for now! Our mutual friend asked me to tell you that the main thing is – calm and presence of mind."

"Hm!" thought Chichikov, "I understand: the lawyer!"

Samosvistov disappeared. Chichikov, left alone, still did not trust his words, when, less than an hour after this conversation, the chest was brought: papers, money, and all in the best order. Samosvistov had come as an administrator: reprimanded the guards for lack of vigilance, ordered more soldiers set to strengthen the watch, not only took the chest, but even selected all the papers that could in any way compromise Chichikov; tied it all together, sealed it, and told a soldier to take it immediately to Chichikov himself in the guise of things necessary for the night and for sleeping, so that along with the papers, Chichikov also even received all the warm things needed to cover his mortal body. This speedy delivery delighted him unutterably. He acquired great hope, and again was already imagining all sorts of attractions: theater in the evening, a dancer he was dangling after. The country and its quiet paled; town and noise again grew more vivid, clear . . . Oh, life!

And meanwhile a case of boundless proportions was developing in the courts and chambers. The pens of scriveners worked away and, taking sniffs of tobacco, the quibbling heads labored, admiring, like artists, each scrawly line. The lawyer, like a hidden magician, invisibly controlled the whole mechanism; he entangled decidedly everyone, before anyone had time to look around. The tangle increased. Samosvistov surpassed himself in his unheard-of courage and boldness. Having found out where the seized woman was being kept, he went straight there and entered with the air of such a dashing fellow and superior that the sentinel saluted him and stood at attention.

"Have you been here long?"

"Since morning, sir!"

"How soon will you be relieved?"

"Three hours, sir!"

"I shall need you. I'll tell the officer to detail someone else instead."

"Yes, sir!"

And, going home, without delaying a moment, to avoid mixing with anyone and to have all ends buried, he dressed himself up as a gendarme, tricked out in mustache and sidewhiskers – the devil himself could not have recognized him. Going to the house where Chichikov was, he seized the first wench he found there, handed her over to two daredevil officials, also in the know, and himself went straight to the sentinels, with mustache and rifle all in order:

"Go, the officer sent me to replace you." He exchanged places with the sentinel and stood there with his rifle.

This was just what was needed. Instead of the former woman, another was found there who knew and understood nothing. The former one was tucked away somewhere, so that afterwards nobody knew what had become of her. Meanwhile, as Samosvistov was pursuing his role as warrior, the lawyer was working wonders in the civilian area: he informed the governor indirectly that the prosecutor was writing a denunciation of him; he informed the police official that another official, living under cover, was writing denunciations of him; he assured the official living under cover that there was a still more undercover official who was informing on him – and drove them all into a situation where they had to turn to him for advice. A muddle of the following sort occurred: denunciation rode upon denunciation, and such things began to be discovered as the sun had never looked upon, and such as even did not exist at all. Everything was employed and made use of: who was an illegitimate son, and who had a mistress of what family and origin, and whose wife was dangling after whom. Scandals, temptations, and it all got so mixed up and intertwined with the story of Chichikov and the dead souls that it was quite impossible to grasp which of these affairs was the chief nonsense: both seemed of equal worth. When the documents finally began to reach the governor-general, the poor prince could not understand a thing. The rather intelligent and efficient clerk who was charged with making an abstract almost lost his mind: it was quite impossible to grasp the threads of the affair. The prince was at that time preoccupied with a number of other matters, one more unpleasant than another. In one part of the province there was famine. The officials who were sent to distribute grain managed it somehow improperly. In another part of the province, the Old Believers were astir. Someone had spread it among them that an Antichrist had been born who would not leave even the dead alone and was buying up dead souls. People repented and sinned and, under the pretext of catching the Antichrist, bumped off some non–Antichrists. In another place, the muzhiks had rebelled against the landowners and police captains. Some tramps had spread rumors among them that a time was coming when peasants must be landowners and dress themselves up in tail-coats, and landowners must dress in simple caftans and be muzhiks – and the whole region, without considering that there would then be too many landowners and police captains, had refused to pay any taxes. There was need to resort to strong measures. The poor prince was in a very upset state of mind. At this moment it was announced to him that the tax farmer had come.

"Show him in," said the prince.

The old man came in . . .

"Here's your Chichikov! You stood up for him and defended him. Now he's been caught in such an affair as the worst thief wouldn't venture upon."

"Allow me to tell you, Your Excellency, that I do not quite understand this affair."

"A forged will, and such a one! . . . It's public flogging for a thing like that!"

"Your Excellency, I say this not to defend Chichikov. But the affair has not yet been proved: there has been no investigation."

"There is evidence: the woman who was dressed up in place of the deceased has been seized. I want to question her purposely in your presence." The prince rang and ordered the woman brought.

Murazov fell silent.

"A most dishonest affair! And, to their disgrace, the foremost officials of the town are mixed up in it, the governor himself. He ought not to turn up together with thieves and wastrels!" the prince said hotly.

"But the governor is one of the heirs, he has the right to make a claim; and if others are latching on to it from all sides, well, Your Excellency, that is a human thing. A rich woman died, sir, without making intelligent and just arrangements; so those eager to profit by it flew down from all sides – it's a human thing..."

"But why such abominations?...The scoundrels!" the prince said with a feeling of indignation. "I don't have one good official: they are all scoundrels!"

"Your Excellency! who among us is as good as he ought to be? The officials of our town are all human, they have merits and many are quite knowledgeable, and no one is far removed from sin."

"Listen, Afanasy Vassilyevich, tell me, I know that you alone are an honest man, what is this passion of yours for defending all sorts of scoundrels?"

"Your Excellency," said Murazov, "whoever the man may be whom you call a scoundrel, he is still a human being. How not defend a man if you know that he does half his evil out of coarseness and ignorance? For we do unjust things at every step, and at every moment are the cause of another's misfortune, and not even with any bad intention. You, Your Excellency, have also committed a great injustice."

"What!" the prince exclaimed in amazement, completely struck by such an unexpected turn in the talk.

Murazov paused, fell silent, as if pondering something, and finally said:

"Well, let's say for instance in the Derpennikov[*] case."

"Afanasy Vassilyevich! A crime against the fundamental laws of the state, tantamount to the betrayal of one's country!"

"I am not justifying him. But is it fair when a youth who in his inexperience was seduced and lured by others is judged on a par with someone who was one of the instigators? The same lot fell to Derpennikov as to some Voronoy-Dryannoy;[10] but their crimes are not the same."

---

[*]That is, Tentetnikov, called Derpennikov in Gogol's early drafts. – TRANS.

"For God's sake . . . " the prince said with visible agitation, "tell me, do you know anything about it? I just recently wrote directly to Petersburg about alleviating his lot."

"No, Your Excellency, I'm not saying it because I know something that you don't know. Though there is indeed one circumstance that might serve in his favor, he himself would not consent because another man would suffer by it. But what I think is only that you were perhaps pleased to be in too great a hurry then. Forgive me, Your Excellency, I am judging according to my weak understanding. You have ordered me several times to speak frankly. When I was still a superior, sir, I had many workers, both bad and good . . . One also has to take a man's earlier life into account, because if you don't consider everything with equanimity, but start by yelling at him – you'll merely frighten him, and never obtain a real confession: but if you question him sympathetically, as brother to brother – he himself will speak it all out and won't even ask for leniency, and there won't be any bitterness against anyone, because he will see clearly that it is not I who am punishing him, but the law."

The prince lapsed into thought. At that moment a young official came in and stood deferentially, a portfolio in his hand. Care and travail showed on his young and still fresh face. One could see it was not for nothing that he served as a special agent. He belonged to the number of those few who do their clerical work *con amore*. Burning neither with ambition, nor with the desire for gain, nor with the imitation of others, he worked only because he was convinced that he had to be there and nowhere else, that life had been given him for that. To pursue, to analyze, and, having grasped all the threads of the most complicated case, to explain it – this was the thing for him. The labors, the efforts, the sleepless nights were abundantly rewarded if the case finally began to clarify itself before him, and the hidden causes revealed themselves, so that he felt he could convey the whole of it in a few words, clearly and distinctly, in such fashion that it would be obvious and under-standable to anyone. It could be said that a student does not rejoice so much when some very difficult phrase and the true meaning of a great writer's thought are revealed to him, as he rejoiced when a very tangled case untangled itself before him. And yet... *

" ... by grain in those places where there is famine; I know these things better than the officials do: I'll look personally into who needs what. And, with Your Excellency's permission, I'll also talk a bit with the Old Believers. They'll be more willing to speak with their own kind, with simple folk. So, God knows, maybe I can help settle things peaceably with them. And I won't take any money from you, by God, it's shameful to think of one's own gain at a time like this, when people are dying of hunger. I have supplies of ready grain; I've just sent to Siberia, and by next summer they'll deliver more."

"God alone can reward you for such service, Afanasy Vassi-lyevich. And I will not say a single word, because – as you can feel yourself – no word is adequate here. But let me say one thing about your request. Tell me yourself: do I have the right to overlook this affair, and will it be just, will it be honest on my part to forgive the scoundrels?"

"Your Excellency, by God, you can't call them that, the less so as there are some quite worthy people among them. Man's circumstances are very difficult, Your Excellency, very, very difficult. It may so happen that a man seems thoroughly guilty; but once you go into it – it wasn't him at all."

"But what will they themselves say if I overlook it? Some of them will turn up their noses still more, and even say that they scared me. They'll be the first not to respect..."

"Your Excellency, allow me to give you my opinion: gather them all together, let them know that you are informed of

---

*Part of the manuscript is missing. The text continues on a new page, in midsentence. – TRANS.

everything and present to them your own position exactly as you have just now been pleased to present it to me, and ask their advice: what would each of them do in your place?"

"Do you really think they will understand the noblest impulses better than chicanery and opportunism? Believe me, they'll laugh at me."

"I don't think so, Your Excellency. The Russian man, even one who is worse than others, still has a sense of justice. Unless he's some sort of Jew, and not a Russian. No, Your Excellency, you have nothing to hide. Tell them exactly as you told me. For they denounce you as an ambitious and proud man who won't even listen to anything, so self-confident you are – so let them see it all as it is. What do you care? Your cause is right. Tell it to them as if you were bringing your confession not to them, but to God Himself."

"Afanasy Vassilyevich," the prince said, reflecting, "I'll think about it, and meanwhile I thank you very much for your advice."

"And order Chichikov's release, Your Excellency."

"Tell this Chichikov to take himself away from here as soon as possible, and the further the better. Him I can never forgive."

Murazov bowed and went straight from the prince to Chichikov. He found Chichikov already in good spirits, quite calmly occupied with a rather decent dinner that had been brought to him in covered dishes from some quite decent kitchen. From the first phrases of their conversation, the old man understood at once that Chichikov had already managed to talk with one or two of the pettifogging officials. He even understood that the invisible participation of the expert lawyer had interfered here.

"Listen, Pavel Ivanovich, sir," he said, "I am bringing you freedom, on condition that you leave town at once. Get all your belongings ready – and go with God, don't put it off for a moment, because things are worse than you think. I know, sir, that there's a man here who is inciting you; I tell you in secret that yet another case is developing here, and that no powers will save him. He is glad, of course, to drag others down, so as not to be bored, but things are getting sorted out. I left you in a good state of mind – better than you're in now. My advice is not offered lightly. By God, the point is not in this property, on account of which people argue and stab each other, as if one could have well-being in this life without thinking about the next. Believe me, Pavel Ivanovich, sir, until people abandon all that they wrangle over and eat each other for on earth, and think about the well-being of their spiritual property, there won't be any well-being of earthly property. There will be times of hunger and poverty, as much for all the people as for each one separately . . . That is clear, sir. Whatever you say, the body does depend on the soul. How then can you want things to go properly? Think not about dead souls, but about your living soul, and God help you on a different path! I, too, am leaving tomorrow. Hurry! or without me there will be trouble."

Having said this, the old man left. Chichikov fell to thinking. The meaning of life again seemed of no small importance. "Murazov is right," he said, "it's time for a different path!" Having said this, he left the prison. One sentry lugged the chest, another the suitcase with linen. Selifan and Petrushka were as glad of their master's deliverance as of God knows what.

"Well, my gentles," said Chichikov, addressing them benignly, "we must pack up and go."

"We'll get rolling, Pavel Ivanovich," said Selifan. "The road must have settled: there's been enough snow. It's time, truly, that we quit this town. I'm so sick of it I don't even want to look at it."

"Go to the carriage maker and have the carriage put on runners," said Chichikov, and he himself went to town, though he had no wish to pay farewell calls on anyone. It was awkward after all these happenings – the more so as there

were many highly unfavorable stories about him going around
town. He avoided meeting anyone and only stopped on the
quiet to see that merchant from whom he had bought the cloth
of the color of the flames and smoke of Navarino, bought
another three yards for a tailcoat and trousers, and went to
the same tailor. For double the price, the master undertook to
increase his zeal, and kept the whole sewing populace sitting
up all night working by candlelight with needles, irons, and
teeth, so that the tailcoat was ready the next day, albeit a little
late. The horses were all harnessed. Chichikov did try the
tailcoat on, however. It was fine, the same as the previous
one. But, alas! he noticed some smooth patches showing pale
on his head and remarked ruefully: "Why did I give myself
over to such contrition? And, what's more, tear my hair out!"
Having paid the tailor, he finally drove out of town in some
strange disposition. This was not the old Chichikov. This was
some wreckage of the old Chichikov. The inner state of his
soul might be compared to a demolished building, which has
been demolished so that from it a new one could be built; but
the new one has not been started yet, because the definitive
plan has not yet come from the architect and the workers are
left in perplexity. An hour before him, old Murazov set out in a
burlap kibitka with Potapych, and an hour after Chichikov's
departure an order was issued that the prince, on the occasion
of his departure for Petersburg, wished to see all his officials to
a man.

In the great hall of the governor-general's house, all the
official ranks of the town assembled, from governor down to
titular councillor: the heads of offices and departments, councillors, assessors, Kisloyedov, Krasnonosov, Samosvistov, those
who took bribes, those who did not take bribes, those who
were false, those who were half false, and those who were not
false at all – all waited with a certain not entirely calm expect-
ancy for the governor-general to appear. The prince came out
neither gloomy nor bright: his look was firm, as was his

step . . . The whole official assembly bowed – many quite low. Responding with a slight bow, the prince began:

"As I am leaving for Petersburg, I considered it proper to meet with all of you and even partly to explain the reason to you. A very tempting affair sprang up among us. I suppose that many of those present know to what I am referring. This affair led to the uncovering of other no less dishonest affairs, which finally involved such people as I had hitherto considered honest. I am also informed of a hidden aim to get everything so tangled that it would prove utterly impossible to resolve it with any formal propriety. I even know who is the mainspring and through whose hidden . . . * though he concealed his participation very skillfully. But the point is that I intend to deal with it not through a formal investigation of documents, but through a speedy court-martial, as in time of war, and I hope that the soverign will give me this right, once I have explained the affair to him. On those occasions when it is not possible to conduct a case in civil fashion, when whole shelves of documents get burned, and when, finally, by a superfluity of false and unrelated evidence, and false denunciations, people try to obscure a case that is obscure to begin with – I consider court-martial the sole method, and I should like to know your opinion."

The prince paused, as if awaiting a response. All stood staring at the ground. Many were pale.

"Still another affair is known to me, though those who did it are quite sure that it cannot be known to anyone. Its investigation will not proceed on paper, because I myself shall be plaintiff and petitioner and bring forth self-evident proofs."

Some one among the officials gave a start; certain of the more timorous ones were also disconcerted.

"It goes without saying that the main instigators will be stripped of rank and property; the rest will be removed from

---

*The phrase is unfinished in the manuscript. – TRANS.

435

their posts. Naturally, many innocent people will suffer among this number. It cannot be helped. The affair is too dishonest and cries out for justice. I know that it will not even be a lesson to others, because to replace those who are thrown out, others will come, and the very people who hitherto were honest will become dishonest, and the very ones who are found worthy of trust will deceive and sell out – but in spite of all that, I must deal cruelly, for justice cries out. I know I shall be accused of harsh cruelty, but I know that those will also . . . * the same ones will accuse me . . . * I must now turn myself into a mere instrument of justice, an axe that must fall upon heads."

A shudder involuntarily passed over all faces.

The prince was calm. His face expressed neither wrath nor inner turmoil.

"Now the same man in whose hands the fate of so many lies, and whom no entreaties can sway, this same man now throws himself at your feet, he pleads with you all. Everything will be forgotten, smoothed over, forgiven; I myself will intercede for you, if you fulfill my request. And my request is this. I know that no methods, no fears, no punishments can eradicate falsity: it is too deeply rooted. The dishonest practice of accepting bribes has become a need and a necessity even for people who were not born to dishonesty. I know that for many it is even no longer possible to go against the general current. But now, as at a decisive and sacred moment, when there is need to save the fatherland, when every citizen brings everything and sacrifices everything – I must call out at least to those in whose breast there beats a Russian heart, and to whom the word 'nobility' still means something. Why talk about which of us is more to blame! I am perhaps more to blame than anyone; perhaps I received you too sternly in the beginning; perhaps, by excessive suspiciousness, I repulsed those of you who sincerely wished to be of use to me, though I, for my part,

*The edge of the page is torn in the manuscript. – TRANS.

could also reproach them. If they indeed loved justice and the good of their country, they ought not to have been offended by the haughtiness of my treatment, they ought to have suppressed their own ambition and sacrificed themselves. It cannot be that I would have failed to notice their selflessness and lofty love of the good and not finally have accepted their useful and intelligent advice. After all, the subordinate ought rather to adjust to the character of his superior, than the superior to the character of his subordinate. That is at least more rightful, and easier, since the subordinates have one superior, while the superior has hundreds of subordinates. But let us leave aside who is the more to blame. The point is that it is time for us to save our country; that our country is perishing, not now from an invasion of twenty foreign nations, but from ourselves; that beyond the rightful administration, another administration has been formed, much stronger than the rightful one. They have set their own conditions; everything has been evaluated, and the prices have even become common knowledge. And no ruler, be he wiser even than all other lawgivers and rulers, has enough power to correct the evil, however much he may restrict the actions of bad officials by appointing other officials to watch over them. Nothing will be successful until each one of us feels that, just as in the epoch when people took arms and rose up against the enemy, so he must rise up against falsity. As a Russian, as one bound to you by ties of blood, of one and the same blood, I now address you. I address those of you who have at least some notion of what nobility of mind is. I invite you to remember the duty each man faces in any place. I invite you to consider your duty more closely, and the obligation of your earthly service, because we all have only a dim idea of it now, and we hardly . . . *

---

*Here the manuscript breaks off. – TRANS.

NOTES

1. The city of Tula, some hundred miles south of Moscow, most famous for its gunsmiths – immortalized by Nikolai Leskov (1831–95) in his *Tale of Cross-eyed Lefty from Tula and the Steel Flea* – was also known for samovars and gingerbread.

2. August von Kotzebue (1761–1819) was a German playwright who lived for some years in Russia, where his plays were very successful. Suspected (rightly) of being an agent of the tsar, he was stabbed to death in the theater by a German student named Sand. Cora and Rolla are characters in his plays *The Sun Maiden* and *The Spanish in Peru, or the Death of Rolla.*

3. The Order of St. Anna (i.e., St. Anne, mother of the Virgin) had two degrees, one worn on the neck, the other on the breast. The star was the decoration of the Order of St. Stanislas, a Polish civil order founded in 1792, which began to be awarded in Russia in 1831.

4. A tax farmer was a private person authorized by the government to collect various taxes in exchange for a fixed fee. The practice was obviously open to abuse, and it was abolished by the reforms of the emperor Alexander II in the 1860s.

5. Russians sometimes affected the uvular French *r* when speaking their own language, thinking it a sign of gentility.

6. The *Son of the Fatherland* was a reactionary political and literary review published in Petersburg between 1812 and 1852.

7. Pavel Petrovich is the emperor Paul I (1754–1801), son of Peter III (1728–62), whose life was cut short by the machinations of his wife, who thus became the empress Catherine II, called the Great (1729–96). Paul I also came to an untimely end, at the hands of conspirators headed by Count Pahlen. Marshal Mikhail Illarionovich Kutuzov (1745–1813), prince of Smolensk, after losing to Napoleon at the battle of Austerlitz in 1805, successfully led the defense of Russia against the French invasion of 1812.

8. The six-week Advent fast leading up to Christmas is sometimes called St. Philip's fast, because it begins on the day after the saint's feast day (November 14).

9. Karlsbad (Karlovy Vary), close to the German border in what is now the Czech Republic, is known for its salutary hot springs. The Caucasus also has hot springs, mineral waters, and mountain air.

10. Clicquot is the name of one of the finest champagnes. Nozdryov uses it in lowercase as an adjective, and combines it superlatively but absurdly with *matradura*, the name of an old Russian dance. Plebeian kvass is made from fermented rye bread and malt.

11. A *balyk* is made from a special dorsal section of flesh running the entire length of a salmon or sturgeon, which is removed in one piece and either salted or smoked. It is especially fancied in Russia.

12. Opodeldoc (originally *oppodeltoch*) was the name given by the Swiss alchemist and physician Theophrastus Bombastus von Hohenheim, known as Paracelsus (1493–1541), to various medicinal plasters; it is now applied to soap liniments mixed with alcohol and camphor. Nozdryov applies it to Chichikov in a far-fetched pun on *delo*, the Russian word for "deal." Hence our spelling.

13. Fenardi was an actual street acrobat and conjurer, well known in the 1820s.

14. *Sophron* is a Greek common noun meaning a wise, sensible, intelligent person.

15. The popular French song "Malbrough s'en va-t-en guerre" expressed the pleasure the French took in the misfortunes of John Churchill, duke of Marlborough (1650–1722), who led the English forces in the War of the Spanish Succession in the Low Countries. The duke's name is variously misspelled in French transcriptions as "Malbrough," "Malborough," and even "Malbrouk."

16. Nozdryov probably means *haut sauternes*, a nonexistent variety of the great sweet white wines of Bordeaux.

17. Alexander Suvorov (1729–1800), the greatest Russian general of his time, successfully led Russian forces against the Turks at Izmayil, put down the Polish insurrection in 1794, and led the opposition to the French revolutionary armies until he was stopped by Maréchal Masséna at Zürich in 1799.

18. Colonies of soldier-farmers were first created by the emperor Alexander I (1777–1825), and were placed mainly in Ukraine. The empress Catherine II began the inviting of German settlers to Russia, particularly to the province of Saratov.

19. Mikhailo, or Mikhail – Misha or Mishka in the diminutive – is the common Russian name for a bear.

20. Alexander Mavrocordato (1791–1865), a Greek statesman born in Constantinople, and the admirals Andreas Vokos Miaoulis (1768–1835) and Constantine Canaris (1790–1877) all distinguished themselves in the Greek war of independence (1821–28). Bobelina, an Albanian woman, outfitted three ships at her own expense and fought on the Greek side in the same war. Prince Pyotr Bagration (1765–1812), a Russian general born in Georgia, was a leader of the opposition to Napoleon's invasion and was mortally wounded at the battle of Borodino.

21. In Ezekiel (38:2, 3, 18; 39:11, 15) Gog is named as prince of Meshech and Tubal, in some unclear relation with "the land of Magog." In Revelation (20:8) Gog and Magog are called "the nations which are in the four quarters of the earth." But in the popular mind, the rhyming names suggest two evil monsters.

22. Russians (and others) have a custom of making the sign of the cross over their mouths when they yawn, to keep evil spirits from flying in.

23. Koshchey the Deathless is a wicked character from Russian folktales. The hero of the tales must cross the sea, come to an island, find an oak tree, dig up a chest under the oak tree, find in the chest a hare, in the hare a duck, in the duck an egg, and in the egg a needle. When the hero breaks off the point of the needle, Koshchey dies.

24. Theodoros Colocotronis (1770–1843), a Greek general, was another hero of the Greek war of independence.

25. The line "caw itself away at the top of its crow's voice" flew here from the fable *The*

Crow and the Fox, by Ivan Krylov (1769–1844). It is proverbial in Russia.

26. Napoleon, at the head of a 500,000-man army, invaded Russia in 1812. At the end of the same year, he managed to retreat with only a few thousand troops. Later in *Dead Souls* these events will be referred to simply as "the year 'twelve."

27. *Rus* was the old name for Russia, before *Rossiya* came into use in the sixteenth century. In the nineteenth century, *Rus* began to be used again, especially in romantic apostrophes to the fatherland. It is in this sense, or in an ironic parody of it, that Gogol uses the word.

28. A *kulich* is a rich, sweet yeast bread, generally cylindrical in form, baked especially for Easter.

29. The different denominations of Russian banknotes were given different colors; red was the color of the ten-rouble bill.

30. Johann Friedrich von Schiller (1759–1805), German romantic idealist poet and playwright, profoundly influenced Russian literature and thought in the early nineteenth century.

31. A *zertsalo* was a small three-faced glass pyramid bearing an eagle and certain edicts of the emperor Peter the Great (1682–1725), which stood on the desk in every government office.

32. The "Komarinsky" is a Russian dance song with rather racy words, which Gogol replaces here with the Russian equivalent of "blankety-blank."

33. Werther and Charlotte are characters from *The Sorrows of Young Werther* (1774), a novel by Johann Wolfgang von Goethe (1749–1832). What Chichikov recites, however, is not from that novel (written in prose), but from a poem by the forgotten Russian poet Vassily Tumansky (1800–60) entitled *Werther to Charlotte (an Hour Before His Death)*.

34. The English pedagogue Joseph Lancaster (1778–1838) established a monitorial system of education in which a master taught the best pupils, who then taught others.

35. A play on *Sprechen sie Deutsch?* ("Do you speak German?"), which in Russian pronunciation rhymes with the postmaster's patronymic.

36. Vassily I. Zhukovsky (1783–1852), poet and translator, was a friend of Pushkin and of Gogol; his translation of Homer's *Odyssey* was an inspiration to Gogol in the writing of *Dead Souls*. The poem *Lyudmila*, an adaptation of *Lenore* by the German poet Gottfried August Bürger (1747–94), was published in 1808, and was "a not-yet-faded novelty" only in such places as the town of N.

37. Edward Young (1683–1765) was an English poet who was a precursor of the romantics; his *Night Thoughts* were translated into Russian in 1780. Karl Eckartshausen (1752–1803), a German mystical writer, published his *Key* in 1791.

38. Nikolai Karamzin (1766–1826) was already well-known for his sentimental tales and travel writing when he published his great history of Russia, on which his reputation now stands. The *Moscow Gazette* was a conservative daily newspaper subsidized by the government.

39. A "kiss" in this case is an airy, sweet meringue.

40. *Baiser*, French for "kiss," is russified by Nozdryov, who then makes a diminutive of it, *bezeshka*, our "bitsy *baiser*."

41. A *kalatch* (pl. *kalatchi*) is a very fine white bread shaped like a purse with a looped handle.

42. The naming of the church is an absurd development along the lines of St. Martin's in the Fields or St. Mark's in the Bouwerie: *nedotychki* means "bunglers" or "botchers"; it may, by some stretch of the

imagination, be a topographical name – Bungler's Hill, or Botcher's Lane.

43. A phonetic transcription of mispronounced French, meaning: *ce qu'on appelle histoire* ("what's known as a story, or scandal"). There will be other such transcriptions in what follows: "orerr" for *horreur*, "scandaleusities," and the postmaster's "finzerb" for *fines herbes*, the minced dried herbs used in cooking, which he apparently thinks is the name of some dish.

44. Rinaldo Rinaldini, an Italian brigand, is the eponymous hero of a novel by the German writer Christian August Vulpius (1762–1827), which had a resounding success throughout Europe and created the type of the Italian brigand in literature. Vulpius was Goethe's brother-in-law.

45. *Commérages* is French for the gossip spread by *commères*, inquisitive, chatty women.

46. The original Vauxhall was a seventeenth-century pleasure garden in London. Russian adopted the name as a common noun referring to an outdoor space for concerts and entertainment, with teahouse, tables, and so on.

47. Kopeikin is the name of a robber in folklore; it derives from *kopeika*, the hundredth part of a rouble, anglicized as "kopeck." Gogol offered to change the name if his publisher ran into trouble from the censors.

48. Semiramis, legendary queen of Assyria and Babylonia, is credited with founding the city of Babylon, famous for its hanging gardens, which were one of the seven wonders of the ancient world.

49. Revel, or Reval, now Tallinn, is the capital city of Estonia. A Revel inn – that is, an inn run by Estonians – implies inexpensiveness and simplicity.

50. Moscow and Petersburg are commonly referred to as the "two capitals" of Russia.

51. The number 666, corresponding to the name of the beast in Revelation (13:18), signifies the Antichrist. The vogue of mysticism followed the predilections of the emperor Alexander I in the later years of his reign.

52. The Russian terms for the godmother and godfather of the same person, in relation to each other, are *kum* and *kuma* (pronounced "kooMAH"). The canons of the Orthodox Church forbid them to marry.

53. The reference is in all likelihood to the novel entitled *The Duchess de La Vallière* (referred to in volume 2, chapter 3 of *Dead Souls* as *The Countess La Vallière*), the work of the French writer Stéphanie-Félicité de Genlis (1746–1830), who was teacher of the children of the duke of Orléans. It may also be to a work of the duchess de La Vallière herself, Louise de La Baume Le Blanc (1644–1710), once a favorite of Louis XIV, who ended her life as a Carmelite nun and wrote pious reflections on her sinful past.

54. In the Orthodox marriage service, the best men hold crowns over the heads of the couple, symbolic of martyrdom as a witnessing to the Kingdom of God.

55. Gogol was living in Italy when he wrote *Dead Souls*, and here, from his "beautiful distance," compares the landscapes of Italy and Russia.

56. Solon (630?–560? B.C.), the lawgiver of Athens, was one of the seven sages of Greece. The quotation is from Krylov's fable *The Musicians*.

57. The Orthodox Church does not celebrate marriages during the Great Lent, the forty-day fast preceding Holy Week and Easter.

58. A euphemism for bribes. Prince Alexander N. Khovansky (1771–1857) was director of the state bank from 1818 until his death; his signature was reproduced on all state banknotes. Ironically, the name

Khovansky comes from the Ukrainian word *khovat*, meaning "to hide" or "to secrete away."

59. Cantonists were the children of soldiers, who were assigned to the department of the army from birth and educated at state expense in special schools.

VOLUME TWO

1. *Petukh* is Russian for "rooster"; moreover, Petya, the diminutive of Pyotr, is the common name for a rooster. Pyotr Petrovich Petukh is thus a rooster not only backwards and forwards but three times over.

2. A Greek name, which Gogol finally settled on after using the odd hybrids Skudronzhoglo and Gobrozhoglo in earlier redactions. Although this character represents Gogol's attempt to portray the ideal landowner, uniting the best qualities of two great Orthodox nations, he seems to have been at pains to give him a name that has a particularly ugly sound in Russian.

3. A *sibirka* is a short caftan with a fitted waist and gathered skirts, often trimmed with fur, having a seamless back, small buttons or clasps in front, and a short standing collar.

4. Kostanzhoglo paraphrases Genesis 3:19, which reads: "In the sweat of your face you shall eat bread" (Revised Standard Version).

5. Krylov's fable *Trishka's Caftan*, describing the patching process that Gogol uses metaphorically here, became proverbial in Russia.

6. A *molieben* (pronounced "molYEHben") is an Orthodox prayer service for any occasion, from the blessing of a new beehive to petitioning for a sick person's recovery.

7. There is a Russian custom of commemorating the dead on the Tuesday after St. Thomas's Sunday (the first Sunday after Easter). The celebration is called *Krasnaya Gorka* ("Pretty Hill"), probably because the graves (little hills) are prettily decorated for the occasion. The accompanying festivities required more space than a village cemetery would afford.

8. Navarino, or Pylos, is a Greek port in the southwest Peloponnesus on the Ionian Sea where, in 1827, the joint naval forces of Russia, England, and France destroyed the Turkish fleet.

9. The Old Believers, called *Raskolniki* ("schismatics") in Russian, split off from the Orthodox Church in the mid-seventeenth century, in disagreement with reforms carried out by the patriarch Nikon. Some sects of the Old Believers refused obedience to the civil authorities, claiming that they, like the Church, were under the sway of the Antichrist.

10. Voronoy-Dryannoy is a highly implausible last name combining "raven-black" and "trashy."

ABOUT THE TRANSLATORS

RICHARD PEVEAR has published translations of Alain, Yves Bonnefoy, Alberto Savinio, Pavel Florensky, and Henri Volohonsky, as well as two books of poetry. He has received fellowships or grants for translation from the National Endowment for the Arts, the Ingram Merrill Foundation, the Guggenheim Foundation, the National Endowment for the Humanities, and the French Ministry of Culture.

LARISSA VOLOKHONSKY was born in Leningrad. She has translated works by the prominent Orthodox theologians Alexander Schmemann and John Meyendorff into Russian.

Together, Pevear and Volokhonsky have translated *The Complete Short Novels* of Anton Chekhov, *The Collected Tales* of Nikolai Gogol, and *The Brothers Karamazov, Crime and Punishment, Notes from Underground, Demons, The Idiot* and *The Adolescent* by Fyodor Dostoevsky. They have been twice awarded the PEN Book-of-the-Month Club Translation Prize, for their version of *The Brothers Karamazov* and more recently for *Anna Karenina*. They are married and live in France.

CHINUA ACHEBE
Things Fall Apart

AESCHYLUS
The Oresteia

THE ARABIAN NIGHTS
(2 vols, tr. Husain Haddawy)

AUGUSTINE
The Confessions

JANE AUSTEN
Emma
Mansfield Park
Northanger Abbey
Persuasion
Pride and Prejudice
Sanditon and Other Stories
Sense and Sensibility

HONORÉ DE BALZAC
Cousin Bette
Eugénie Grandet
Old Goriot

SIMONE DE BEAUVOIR
The Second Sex

SAMUEL BECKETT
Molloy, Malone Dies,
The Unnamable
(US only)

SAUL BELLOW
The Adventures of Augie March

HECTOR BERLIOZ
The Memoirs of Hector Berlioz

WILLIAM BLAKE
Poems and Prophecies

JORGE LUIS BORGES
Ficciones

JAMES BOSWELL
The Life of Samuel Johnson
The Journal of a Tour to
the Hebrides

CHARLOTTE BRONTË
Jane Eyre
Villette

EMILY BRONTË
Wuthering Heights

MIKHAIL BULGAKOV
The Master and Margarita

SAMUEL BUTLER
The Way of all Flesh

JAMES M. CAIN
The Postman Always Rings Twice
Double Indemnity
Mildred Pierce
Selected Stories
(1 vol. US only)

ITALO CALVINO
If on a winter's night a traveler

ALBERT CAMUS
The Outsider (UK)
The Stranger (US)
The Plague, The Fall,
Exile and the Kingdom,
and Selected Essays
(in 1 vol.)

WILLA CATHER
Death Comes for the Archbishop
My Ántonia
(US only)

MIGUEL DE CERVANTES
Don Quixote

RAYMOND CHANDLER
The novels (2 vols)
Collected Stories

GEOFFREY CHAUCER
Canterbury Tales

ANTON CHEKHOV
The Complete Short Novels
My Life and Other Stories
The Steppe and Other Stories

KATE CHOPIN
The Awakening

CARL VON CLAUSEWITZ
On War

S. T. COLERIDGE
Poems

WILKIE COLLINS
The Moonstone
The Woman in White